44 Cranberry Point

Dear Reader,

If this is your first visit to Cedar Cove, Washington, welcome! All the people in town are eager to introduce themselves. And if you're here for a repeat visit, welcome back. There's been a lot going on in town. Charlotte, Jack, Olivia, Grace, Cecilia and the others are looking forward to bringing you up-to-date on everything that's happened. You'll also discover surprises along the way…as well as some romance and a few laughs.

I promise a final resolution to the mystery about the man who died in the Beldons' B and B. After all, Peggy and Bob just want their lives to return to normal. But…there's another mystery developing, and this one involves the McAfees.

If you'd like to drop me a note, just log on to my Web site at www.debbiemacomber.com and sign the guest book. If you're interested in regular updates on the Cedar Cove characters, log on and click on the Cedar Cove button. As a bonus, I include the characters' favorite recipes…. If you're not online but don't want to miss out, you can write me at P.O. Box 1458, Port Orchard, Washington 98366.

Speaking of Port Orchard… If you happen to visit, you might notice a resemblance between my hometown and Cedar Cove. Not the characters, mind you, but just about everything else. Towns like this are great to visit in real life—*and* between the pages of a book.

Now, please grab something to drink (Peggy Beldon would make you a cup of tea!), find a comfortable spot and begin your visit to Cedar Cove. I'm *so* glad you're here.

Warmest regards,

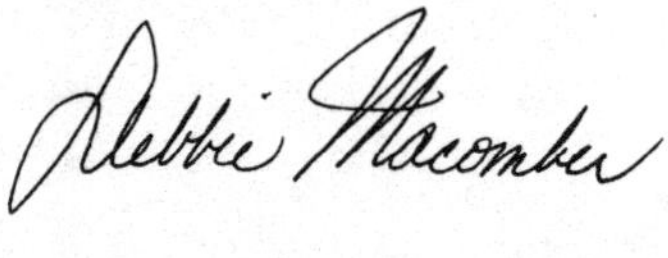

DEBBIE MACOMBER

44 Cranberry Point

MIRA®

MIRA®

ISBN 978-0-7394-4630-0

44 CRANBERRY POINT

Printed in U.S.A.

To Leslee Borger and
her incredible mother, Ruth Koelzer

CAST OF CHARACTERS

Some of the Residents of Cedar Cove, Washington

Olivia Lockhart Griffin: Divorced from Stan Lockhart. Now married to Jack Griffin. Family court judge in Cedar Cove. Mother of Justine and James. Lives at 16 Lighthouse Road.

Charlotte Jefferson: Mother of Olivia, widow, lifelong resident of Cedar Cove.

Justine (Lockhart) Gunderson: Daughter of Olivia, married to Seth, mother of Leif.

Seth Gunderson: Justine's husband. Co-owner, with Justine, of The Lighthouse Restaurant.

James Lockhart: Olivia's son and Justine's younger brother. In the navy. Lives in San Diego with wife, Selina, and daughter, Isabella.

Stanley Lockhart: Olivia's ex-husband and father of James and Justine. Now lives in Seattle and divorced from his second wife.

Will Jefferson: Olivia's brother, Charlotte's son. Married and lives in Atlanta.

Grace Sherman: Olivia's best friend. Librarian. Widow. Mother of Maryellen and Kelly. Lives at 204 Rosewood Lane.

Dan Sherman: Grace's dead husband.

Maryellen Sherman: Oldest daughter of Grace and Dan. Mother of Katie.

Kelly Jordan: Maryellen's sister, married to Paul, mother of Tyler.

Jon Bowman: Photographer, chef and father of Katie. Engaged to Maryellen.

Jack Griffin: Newspaper reporter and editor of *The Cedar Cove Chronicle.* Recovering alcoholic, married to Olivia Lockhart. Father of Eric, who lives in Nevada with his wife, Shelly, and their twin boys.

Zachary Cox: Accountant, remarried to Rosie. Father of Allison and Eddie Cox. Lives at 311 Pelican Court.

Cliff Harding: Retired engineer and now horse breeder living near Cedar Cove. Divorced father of Lisa, who lives in Maryland. He has an on-and-off relationship with Grace Sherman.

Cecilia Randall: Navy wife, living near Cedar Cove. Accountant. Married to Ian Randall, submariner. Lost a baby, Allison.

Bob and Peggy Beldon: Retired. Own the Thyme and Tide Bed and Breakfast at 44 Cranberry Point. Have two adult children.

Roy McAfee: Private detective, retired from Seattle police force. Two adult children. The McAfees live at 5 Harbor Street.

Corrie McAfee: Roy's wife and office manager.

Troy Davis: Cedar Cove sheriff.

Pastor Fleming: Local Methodist minister.

Ben Rhodes: Retired naval officer. Member of the Senior Center. Involved with Charlotte Jefferson.

One

Peggy Beldon walked into her newly planted garden, taking real pleasure in the sights and smells that surrounded her. This was her private place, her one true source of serenity. The fresh briny scent of the water off Puget Sound drifted toward her as she watched the Washington State ferry glide from Bremerton toward Seattle on its sixty-minute journey. This was a typical May afternoon in Cedar Cove—comfortably warm with just a hint of a breeze.

Peggy uncoiled the garden hose and moved carefully between the rows of leaf lettuce, sweet peas and pole beans. She had a strong practical streak, expressed in her vegetable and herb gardens; she satisfied her craving for beauty with the flower gardens in front. Looking back at the house that always had been her dream, Peggy smiled. She'd grown up in Cedar Cove, graduated from the local high school and married Bob Beldon on his return from Vietnam. The early years had been difficult because of Bob's reliance on alcohol. But then, to her eternal gratitude, he'd discovered Alcoholics Anonymous; it had saved their marriage and quite possibly Bob's life. Until AA, Bob had spent most nights drinking, by himself or with friends. When he drank, he became a different person, no longer the man she'd married. She didn't like to think about that time. Thankfully, her husband had remained sober for twenty-one years.

Walking between the rows, Peggy gently watered the seedlings. Several years earlier, Bob had accepted early retirement and with the severance package, they'd purchased the house on Cranberry Point. Peggy had loved it for as long as she could remember. Situated on a point of land overlooking Sinclair Inlet, the two-story structure, built in the late 1930s, had seemed like a mansion to her. Over the years, it had changed owners a number of times and had started to deteriorate, since no one had cared enough to provide the maintenance it needed. By straining their finances, Bob and Peggy had managed to buy it for a price far below its current market value.

Her husband was a talented handyman and within a few months they were able to hang out a sign for their Bed and Breakfast. Peggy hadn't known how much business to expect, how many guests would be attracted to the Thyme and Tide B and B, as they'd called it. She'd hoped, of course, that they'd make enough to supplement their retirement income—and they had. She was proud of the success they'd achieved. Their traditional home, warm hospitality and her cooking had brought them steady customers and a growing reputation. They'd even been reviewed in a national magazine, which had reserved its highest praise for the food, especially her baking. The reviewer had spent two whole sentences describing her blueberry muffins and homemade fruit cobbler. She had twenty blueberry bushes and eight raspberry canes, and she pampered them lovingly. Each summer she was rewarded with an ample supply for her guests and her family. Life had seemed about as perfect as it could get.

Then the unimaginable happened.

More than a year ago, a stranger had knocked on their door in the middle of a dark, stormy night. If it hadn't been so clichéd she might've been amused, but this was no laughing matter. The man had rented a room and then promptly locked himself inside.

A hundred times since, Peggy had regretted not insisting he complete the usual paperwork. It was late, and he'd seemed so tired that they'd simply shown him to his room. They could deal with the necessities in the morning, over breakfast.

But by morning, the stranger was dead.

Ever since, Peggy had felt as if they were caught in some kind of whirlwind, tossed about by forces beyond their control. Bad enough that the man had died in their home, but then they'd learned that he'd carried false identification. Nothing was as it seemed. By the end of that day, after hours with the sheriff and the coroner, there'd been more questions than answers.

She saw Bob pull the riding lawn mower out of the garage. At the sound of the engine, Peggy paused in watering her seedlings, one hand shading her eyes. Even after all these years of marriage, she never grew tired of their life together. They'd survived the bad times with their love intact. And their attraction, too. Bob was tall and had kept his shape, his sandy brown hair neatly trimmed. His arms were already tanned from exposure to the sun. He loved his workshop and she was genuinely impressed by what he could do with a few pieces of oak or pine. She'd fallen in love with Bob Beldon as a teenager and she loved him still.

Now, however, she was worried. She didn't want to think about the dead man, but it was unavoidable, especially after what they'd recently found out. Sheriff Davis had identified their mystery guest as Maxwell Russell. To say Bob was shocked would be putting it mildly. He'd been with Max in Vietnam. Dan Sherman, who was also dead, Bob, Max and another man named Stewart Samuels had belonged to that squadron. They'd gotten lost in a Southeast Asian jungle with tragic results.

Once the identity of the dead man was established, another shocking revelation had come to light. The sheriff, with the help of local private investigator Roy McAfee, had discovered that Max Russell's death was no accident.

He'd been poisoned.

The water bottle he'd carried with him had been laced with odorless, tasteless Rohypnol, commonly known as the "date rape" drug. The dose had been large enough to stop his heart. Maxwell Russell had gone to bed, tired from a long day of travel, and he never woke up.

Bob rode past her on the lawn mower with a quick wave, and Peggy continued to water her garden, but a pang went through her. At this very moment Bob could be in danger, but he seemed content to ignore any risk rather than admit her concerns were legitimate.

As she set aside the hose, Peggy caught sight of Sheriff Davis's patrol car coming down Cranberry Point. She immediately felt the tension between her shoulder blades. She hoped he planned to talk some sense into Bob.

Her husband must have seen the patrol car at the same time Peggy did because he cut the engine and climbed off the lawn mower. Sheriff Troy Davis turned into the driveway, then stepped out of his vehicle. In the beginning, when it looked like Bob might be a suspect in the murder case, Davis wasn't nearly as welcome here as he was now.

The sheriff, who was probably a little heavier than he should be, took a moment to hike up his pants and adjust his gun before heading across the lawn to meet Bob. Unwilling to be left out of the conversation, Peggy shut off the water and hurried across the half-mown grass.

"Peggy." Davis touched the brim of his hat and nodded in her direction. "I was just telling Bob it might be a good idea if the three of us sat down and talked."

Peggy nodded in return, appreciating the fact that he wanted to include her.

Bob led the way to the patio, and Peggy was grateful she'd taken time that morning to sweep it off. The three of them sat at the round pine table Bob had built several years earlier. He'd painted it a deep gray-blue, a color that complemented the white siding. The striped umbrella was up and the patio was awash in sunshine.

"I thought I'd update you on my conversation with Hannah Russell."

A couple of months earlier, after Max's identity had been uncovered, his daughter had asked to meet with Bob and Peggy. It had been an uncomfortable meeting, but Peggy's heart had ached for the young woman. She'd answered Hannah's questions to the best of her ability.

For her part, there was little Hannah could tell them. All she knew was what her father had told her—he was taking a short trip, although he hadn't divulged where. That was the last she'd heard. When he didn't return to California, she'd filed a missing persons report with the police. A year had passed before she learned his fate.

"I feel so bad for her," Peggy said. Hannah had lost her mother some time before and was now an orphan with no other family.

"She was pretty upset," Troy admitted. "You can imagine how painful it was to learn her father was dead. But to discover he'd been murdered…" He shook his head.

"Did she have any idea who might've done this?"

"None," Davis told them. "She asked me to thank you for your kindness. Talking with you helped her resolve in her own mind what happened to her father. Peggy, she mentioned the letter you wrote, and I could tell it meant a great deal to her."

Peggy bit her lip. "How's she getting on with her life?"

The sheriff hesitated. "I can't really say. She said she no longer has any reason to stay in California and implied that she's thinking of moving. I asked her to keep in touch and she promised she would."

Peggy could understand the young woman's feelings. With both of her parents gone, Hannah was rootless. Peggy sympathized with her desire to leave the area where she'd grown up, where she was surrounded by so many memories. Every place she turned, every place she looked, Hannah must be reminded of the parents she'd loved.

"What did you find out about Colonel Samuels?" Bob asked, eyes narrowed as he gazed at Troy Davis.

Stewart Samuels was the fourth man in Vietnam with Bob and Dan and Max. Peggy knew the sheriff had recently been in contact with him. The colonel had been cleared in Max's murder, at least as far as Davis was concerned, but her husband obviously had doubts. While Bob and the other two were eager to be discharged, back in the early seventies, Samuels had stayed in the Army and risen through the ranks.

"At this point I don't consider the colonel a suspect."

"He's some mucky-muck in Army Intelligence from what I hear," Bob muttered, as if that should be motive enough.

"Who lives in the Washington D.C. area," Sheriff Davis stated calmly. "I've had him checked out by a number of people. He's highly respected. He's been cooperative and willing to help in any way he can. Perhaps you should talk to him yourself, Bob."

Her husband declined with a sharp shake of his head. Bob wanted as little to do with the past as possible. Coping with what had happened to Dan, who'd committed suicide, and to Max, had been hard enough. The less he had to think about the past, or its effect on the present, the better.

"Is Bob in danger?" Peggy asked bluntly. Her husband might prefer not to acknowledge the likelihood of a threat, but Peggy wanted a realistic assessment of their situation.

"I think he might be at risk," the sheriff said quietly.

It wasn't what Peggy had hoped to hear, but she was grateful for his frankness. They had to face the truth, however unpleasant, and take appropriate precautions.

"Nonsense," Bob insisted. "If anyone wanted me dead, I'd be six feet under by now."

Maybe, but Peggy wasn't willing to take chances with her husband's life.

"Why don't we arrange an extended vacation?" she suggested. It'd been years since they'd been away from the Bed and Breakfast, and they could use a break.

"For how long?" Bob asked.

"Until the case is solved," Peggy told him, pleading with her eyes. This wasn't the time to put on a brave front—not in her opinion, anyway.

"No way." Bob's quick refusal shouldn't have come as any surprise. He'd been quite content to live in denial. Denial and featherbeds! *Someone* had to point out the very real possibility that he was in danger and because he was, so was she.

"I'm not leaving Cedar Cove."

"Now, Bob..."

"I won't let anyone or anything drive me out of my own home."

A chill shot up Peggy's spine. "But—"

"No, Peg," he said, and his face hardened with resolve. "How long are we supposed to stay away? One month? Two?" He paused. "More than that?"

It wasn't a question Troy could answer.

"Max was found dead over a year ago. I was supposedly in danger then, right?"

Sheriff Davis exchanged a concerned look with Peggy. "I understand what you're saying, but we didn't know then what we know now."

"I'm not running! I spent half my life running, and I won't do it again. If somebody wants me dead, then so be it."

Peggy gasped.

"I'm sorry, honey," her husband said, stretching his arm across the table to clasp her fingers with his. "I refuse to live like that, looking over my shoulder all the time."

"Then perhaps you could compromise," Davis said. "There's no need to invite someone into your home who might want to harm you."

"What do you mean?" Bob leaned closer, his stomach pressed against the rounded edge of the pinewood table. Peggy realized that despite his defiant words he was afraid. His body language revealed what he was unwilling to admit.

"I don't know how many reservations you have for the B and B, but I'd advise you to not take any more."

"We can easily cancel the ones we have," Peggy murmured. Any number of businesses in town would welcome the additional bookings.

Bob directed his gaze at Peggy. "Would that make you more comfortable?"

She swallowed and nodded.

Bob continued to look unsure, as if even this one concession was more than he felt inclined to make.

"I've been worried ever since Jack and Olivia's wedding," she whispered.

A week earlier, Bob had stood up as Jack Griffin's best man. That was just a day or two before they'd learned Max Russell had been murdered.

"All right." Bob's voice was heavy with reluctance. "We'll cancel the reservations."

"No guests," Peggy said.

"No guests," he confirmed, "until this matter is settled once and for all."

This was going to hurt financially, but it didn't matter. What did matter was having the reassurance that her husband was safe.

"I'll do what I can to solve this quickly," Troy promised them.

Peggy could only wonder how long that would take.

Two

Cecilia Randall stood on the navy pier and watched the aircraft carrier *George Washington* sail into Sinclair Inlet. After six months serving in the Persian Gulf, her husband, Ian, was finally home. Cecilia had often heard people talk about hearts swelling and dismissed the expression as exaggerated, sentimental. Now she knew what it meant, how it felt. Her heart swelled with love, pride and patriotism as the massive ship headed toward Bremerton.

The other navy wives and hordes of friends and family crowded the pier. Colorful banners waved in the wind, along with Welcome Home signs. News helicopters from the Seattle television stations circled the area, taping the event for the five-o'clock broadcast. The joy and excitement around her was infectious, despite the dreary, cloudy day. Even the lead-gray skies and the threat of imminent rain didn't dampen Cecilia's mood. A band played in the background, and the American flag rippled in the breeze. It could have been a Norman Rockwell painting.

Cecilia's dearest friends, two other navy wives, Cathy Lackey and Carol Greendale, stood with her, each holding a toddler against her hip while madly waving. Cecilia hoped that before long she'd be a mother again herself.

"I think I see Andrew," Cathy cried. She screeched with happiness and waved one arm wildly above her head. Then she pointed his daddy out to her young son.

Three thousand sailors, dressed in white navy uniforms, stood along the rail, feet apart, hands behind their backs, as they lined the perimeter of the flight deck. At this distance it was impossible for Cecilia to find Ian. The wind whipped at her face and she shouted and waved. Perhaps Ian would see her.

"Take Amanda," Carol said, heaving her three-year-old daughter toward Cecilia.

She gladly held the toddler. There'd been a time when even looking at this little girl brought her pain. Allison, Ian's and her baby daughter, was born the same week as Amanda. Had she lived, Allison, too, would've been three years old. But she'd died after clinging to life for only a few days. Her death had ripped the marriage apart. If not for a wise family court judge who ignored convention and denied their divorce, they might have ended up like so many other sad marriage statistics.

"Ian, over here," Cecilia shouted, as she thrust one arm high above her head. "Do you see your daddy?" she asked Amanda.

The little girl's arms were tight around Cecilia's neck, and she buried her face in Cecilia's shoulder.

"There's Daddy, there's Daddy," Carol said, pointing to the aircraft carrier.

Amanda looked up then, smiling, and Carol reached for her daughter again.

An eternity passed before the gangplank was lowered and the sailors disembarked, carrying their duffel bags. Soon there were reunions everywhere. Cathy spotted Andrew and ran toward her husband, weeping with happiness.

Cecilia searched frantically for Ian. Then she saw him, tall and fit and tan, his dark hair visible beneath his white Navy cap. The breath left her lungs at the sight of him and she burst into tears of joy.

Not a minute later, Cecilia was caught up in her husband's arms. They clung to each other, tears still clouding her eyes as Ian brought his mouth to hers.

Their kiss was slow, sensual and filled with six months of longing and need. By the time they'd finished, Cecilia was weak and breathless. Ian was home; her world was complete once again. The universe could have dissolved around her and she wouldn't have cared.

"I've missed you like crazy," she whispered, holding on to him, her fingers massaging the nape of his neck. There was so much to say, so much that was in her heart. None of it mattered right then, however. All she cared about was the feel of Ian's arms around her and the knowledge that he was home and safe and hers, if only on loan from the United States Navy.

"Oh, sweetheart, this has been the longest six months of my life." He continued to hold her tight against him. Cecilia closed her eyes and savored this moment she'd been waiting for.

Ian had three days of shore leave and Cecilia planned to make full use of every one of them. The days—and the nights. His return couldn't have been better planned. As far as she could tell, these next few days were her fertile period.

With his duffel bag over his shoulder, Ian reached for her hand as they walked toward the parking area. Apparently she still wasn't close enough to suit him because he wrapped his arm around her waist and drew her to his side. He smiled and his love washed over her like…like warm sunshine. That was all she could compare it to, the life-giving warmth so absent today. A light drizzle had begun and they walked a little faster, still gazing at each other.

"I love you," she mouthed.

"I can hardly wait to show you how much I love you." Then, as if the question had only now occurred to him, he asked, "You don't have to go back to work, do you?"

She toyed with the idea of letting him worry, but couldn't make herself do it. "As a matter of fact, Mr. Cox gave me all three days off." She handed Ian the car keys, and he promptly unlocked their vehicle.

"I like your boss more and more."

Cecilia did, too, especially now that Mr. and Mrs. Cox had remarried. The office became a much more relaxed place once the couple reunited. But it wasn't the Coxes on Cecilia's mind as Ian drove to their duplex. They met each other's eyes frequently but didn't speak much. Ten minutes later they were home.

"Did you bring back everything I sent you?" Cecilia asked in a husky voice when Ian parked in their assigned spot. They'd moved into military housing just before his most recent deployment, when a unit became available.

"That was very sadistic of you, wife," Ian said, his eyebrows drawing together.

Had she not known him so well, Cecilia might think he hadn't been amused by her small prank. The gleam in his eyes told her otherwise. For each of the last three weeks before he was due home, Cecilia had sent him one piece of a sheer negligee outfit. With the last piece, she'd included a note that promised she'd wear it for him when he got back. In his last e-mail to her, she could almost hear him panting.

"I hope you realize you've created a monster with that little trick of yours."

"A monster I'm eager to tame," she whispered, leaning over to kiss him.

"Oh, honey..." He broke off the kiss. "Let's get inside—fast."

"Aye, aye," she said dreamily, saluting him.

Ian slid out the driver's side and dashed around the front of the car. He opened the passenger door, helped her out and grabbed his duffel bag from the back. Giggling with excitement, they ran through the light rain toward their duplex. Ian was all thumbs as he struggled to unlock their door.

Cecilia had cleaned the place until it sparkled. The sheets on their bed were fresh and turned down, the bedroom shades drawn. After six months of separation she'd known they wouldn't want to wait to make love.

As soon as they got inside, Ian dropped his duffel and reached out for her. Cecilia came willingly, throwing her arms around his neck. He hoisted her up and headed directly for the bedroom. The second they cleared the door, Ian kissed her again, his mouth open and moist, moving urgently against hers.

He released her and immediately started undressing.

"You want me to put on that black nightie for you?" she asked.

"Next time," Ian said, his breathing shallow as he sat on the bed and quickly removed his shoes.

"One more thing..."

He gave her a questioning glance.

She knelt behind him on the bed and rested her chin on his bare shoulder. "I think there's something you should know."

"It can't wait?"

"Well, it could, but I figure this is something you might *want* to know."

"What?" he growled, turning toward her. He grabbed her around the waist, and his dark eyes bore into hers.

Cecilia smiled at her husband, smoothing her hands down his muscular shoulders, loving the feel of him. "I'm thinking this afternoon would be a wonderful time to make a baby."

Ian's eyes flared briefly. "I thought you were on the pill."

Her smile broadened as she slowly shook her head. "Not anymore. I tossed them into the garbage six months ago."

He frowned.

"With you at sea, there wasn't any need for me to be on birth control. Besides—"

"You didn't start again when you knew I was coming home?"

"Nope."

"But—but you knew when I was due back."

"I did...and I've been greatly anticipating your homecoming," she purred.

"But, sweetheart, you never said a word! I don't have anything to protect you from pregnancy."

"Who says I want protection? What I want, sailor man," she whispered, "is a baby."

Ian went completely still.

"Ian?"

Her husband straightened, sitting on the side of the bed with his back to her. "Don't you think this is something we should've discussed first?"

"We're...we're discussing it now."

"At the last possible moment."

"You don't want a baby?"

Ian stood then and faced her. His shoulders were bare and his pants half unzipped. He rubbed his hand over his eyes as if her question had overwhelmed him. "I do want children, but not yet."

"I thought—"

"It's too soon, sweetheart."

"It's been three years." Her desire for a child had grown progressively stronger in the months Ian had been at sea. It made sense to complete her schooling before getting pregnant again, but she'd done that and found a wonderful job. "I'm ready, Ian."

His shoulders sagged. "I'm not... I can't risk getting you pregnant." He zipped his pants and picked up his shirt, yanking it on and shoving his arms into the sleeves. He fastened the buttons with record speed and scooped the car keys from the dresser.

Cecilia bit her lip. He was right; she should've mentioned it earlier. They'd communicated almost daily via e-mail, and phone calls whenever possible. There'd been ample opportunity to discuss the matter long before his arrival home.

Ian walked out of the bedroom, then turned back at the door. "Stay right there," he said, pointing in her direction.

"Where are you going?"

His laugh was weak with impatience. "To the drugstore. Stay where you are, okay? I'll be back before you know it."

It felt as if the sun had disappeared behind a dark cloud.

Perhaps, deep down, Cecilia had known this would be Ian's reaction. Her husband was afraid of another pregnancy, afraid of what it would do to her physically and what it might do to them as a couple.

Cecilia understood why he felt that way because she'd faced those same fears herself. She'd believed—or *wanted* to believe—that Ian, too, had moved past them. Apparently she'd been wrong.

Three

With a sense of joy and celebration, Maryellen Sherman carried the heavy cardboard box out of her rental house and set it in the trunk of her car. Soon she'd be living with Jon Bowman—married to him.

After all this time it hardly seemed possible. The barriers between them had been lowered. No longer could she disguise her love for him. Nor did she have to; they'd admitted their feelings for each other. The misunderstandings were over, pride and anger put aside.

Jon followed with a second box, which he set next to the first. He took her hand and gave it a gentle squeeze, silently letting her know how pleased he was that they were finally going to be together for good.

Katie, their nine-month-old daughter, slept contentedly in her crib as they brought another load out to the car, then hurried back inside the house. Maryellen realized they only had a few more minutes of peace before their daughter woke. Most of her belongings weren't even packed.

"That's it for now?" Jon asked, hands on hips as he glanced around the living room.

"I'll have more later," she promised. Maryellen had barely started packing. She'd lived in this rental house for almost twelve years and what she'd accumulated in that length of time was staggering. Sorting through clothes and books—what to keep, what to give away or throw out—had already taken weeks.

"How much more?" A note of weariness entered Jon's voice.

"Lots. Do you want to pack up a few boxes now?" She was thinking she should probably fill up the back seat of her car before they caravanned to his home.

"What I want is to get you permanently in my house." He sounded as impatient as she felt.

"I'm just as eager to get there." She stepped into the compact kitchen and tried to figure out what else they should take with them this afternoon. Moving had never seemed so complicated or frustrating.

"Did you talk to your mother about a wedding date?"

"She thinks Memorial Day is perfect." Maryellen held back a smile. She suspected her mother was just plain relieved that she and Jon had actually decided to tie the knot. Since they already had a child together, a ceremony was long past due, in Grace Sherman's opinion.

"You're sure you don't mind not having a big fancy wedding?"

Maryellen shook her head. She opened the refrigerator and took out a tall pitcher of iced tea. She'd had all the glamour and glitter with her first marriage. The wedding had been lovely, the marriage itself anything but. She'd been young and naive; the divorce, a year later, had left her reeling emotionally for a long time.

Twelve years after that, when she'd met Jon, she'd still been frightened of falling in love again. In the beginning, she'd spurned him, insulted him and did everything she could think of to keep him out of her life. She felt mortified now when she thought back on everything she'd said and done.

Jon got two glasses from the cupboard and set them on the counter. "You're not getting any bargain in the husband department, you know?"

The anger that flared in her was too hot to be denied. "If you ever say that to me again, I swear I'll...I'll make you suffer."

A smile briefly softened Jon's sharp features. He wasn't a handsome man. He was tall and long-limbed with dark hair and intense brown eyes. And he was quite possibly the most talented photographer she'd ever encountered. His work hung in one of the best Seattle galleries and his name was fast gaining recognition.

"You know everything now," he said and lowered his head, avoiding eye contact.

"You know everything about me, too," she reminded him.

They both had their secrets, painful bits and pieces from their pasts. Now they had each other and, for the first time since her divorce, Maryellen felt she could heal the unresolved griefs of that marriage. She knew it was their pasts that had kept them apart. Despite everything, they'd been drawn toward each other from the very beginning, but the secrets they'd so desperately wanted to hide had almost torn them apart.

"You're not the one with a prison record," Jon muttered.

Clasping his hand, Maryellen raised it to her lips. "I consider it one of my life's greatest blessings that I'll be your wife. Until I met you I was in prison, too—a prison of my own making." That might sound melodramatic, but she meant every word.

His smile was enough to brighten the kitchen, and she slipped her arms around his waist and buried her face against him. "The truth is, I can't wait to spend the rest of my life with you."

His arms tightened around her as she felt a sigh rumble through his chest. "It's a little silly, don't you think, you living here until after the wedding?"

"Perhaps, but I prefer to wait." Maryellen had made too many mistakes, and with this marriage, she wanted to do everything right. When she came to him on their wedding night, she wanted it to be special.

"We have a child together, so it's not as if..." His voice trailed off.

She tilted her head to look up at him, unsure how to say what was in her heart. "Do you mind terribly much?"

"I mind like hell, but I can wait if it means that much to you."

She nodded and then kissed his jaw to let him know she appreciated his patience. Jon tangled his fingers in her dark hair as he pressed his mouth to hers. She tasted his passion and his desire, and her resolve weakened. This was all so new and exciting. Their physical need for each other had always been explosive, their hunger undeniable.

Suddenly Katie let out a wail from the back bedroom. Jon sighed and broke off the kiss.

By the time Maryellen reached Katie's room, her daughter was standing up in her crib, both arms raised to her mother. Maryellen lifted her out, and after changing Katie's diaper, carried her into the kitchen and placed her in the high chair. Her afternoon snack of juice and an arrowroot cracker was already waiting for her.

Awake now and in a good mood, Katie grabbed her juice cup and eagerly brought it to her mouth. She took a noisy slurp, then banged the cup against the plastic tray.

"Every time I look at her, I feel a sense of wonder," Jon said and squatted down so he was eye-level with his daughter. "You're daddy's little girl, aren't you?"

Katie rewarded him with a broad four-tooth grin.

Jon automatically retrieved his camera from the counter and started snapping pictures.

"Jon." Maryellen laughed, unable to stop herself. He was so predictable. When she'd first begun working with him at the Harbor Street Art Gallery, he'd asked her out a dozen times. Maryellen had refused all his invitations. She hadn't wanted a man in her life. Later she'd succumbed—and soon afterward she'd discovered to her shock that she was pregnant. She'd made every effort to keep Jon out of her child's life. And hers…

Like a lot of other women, she'd chosen to be a single mother. Not until Katie was born had she come to realize how much her daughter needed a father and how much she herself wanted and needed Jon's help in rearing their child. Then it seemed too late. While Jon obviously loved their daughter, he wanted little or nothing to do with her.

When he'd finished taking photographs of Katie, Jon focused the camera on her. Before Maryellen could react he'd snapped several pictures. When he'd first turned his camera on her, early in their relationship, she'd felt both self-conscious and flattered; now she simply trusted him, never protesting when he aimed his Nikon at her, no matter how unexpected the moment might be. In many ways Jon was most comfortable behind the camera's lens. It was through photography that he revealed his personality and emotions.

"I want you and Katie with me as soon as possible," he said when he'd rewound the film and removed the cartridge.

"It won't be long. Two weeks."

He looked as if he wanted to argue, but seemed to change

his mind. "We've waited this long, I don't suppose another two weeks will kill me."

"The anticipation is half the pleasure."

He growled something she couldn't decipher. She could guess, though, and it made her smile.

"I thought we could ask Pastor Flemming to officiate." Maryellen didn't attend church regularly, but her mother's best friend, Olivia Lockhart, had recently married Jack Griffin, and the Methodist minister had performed the ceremony. She'd found it deeply moving.

"What about Judge Lockhart—or Griffin, I guess?"

"She's using both names," Maryellen said.

Jon nodded.

"I—I'd like a religious service." Olivia was a longtime family friend, but Maryellen had already decided against a civil wedding. When she spoke her vows, she was committing herself, before God and the community, to love Jon for the rest of her life.

Jon's eyes narrowed. "You want to be married in a church? You're sure?"

"Either at the Methodist Church or perhaps on your property, if that's all right?" Jon had inherited the land from his grandfather and had built a beautiful two-story house there. The acreage overlooked Puget Sound, with Mount Rainier as a backdrop.

"It's fine," he said. "What about the reception?"

"At the house, too." All at once she wondered if she was asking too much of him. "I don't imagine we'll have many guests, just family and a few friends. All we'd need to serve is wedding cake and champagne. If the weather cooperates, we could be married outside." With the rhododendrons, many of which grew wild on the property, and the azaleas in bloom, the place would be stunning.

He nodded. "Perhaps we should serve a few hors d'oeuvres. I can easily prepare them a day or two before."

"Jon..."

"A friend of mine can do the pictures, but I want to take the ones of you myself."

Maryellen could tell he was warming to the subject of their wedding. "Can we put all this together in two weeks?" she asked.

Jon didn't hesitate. "Of course we can." At her delighted smile, he added, "Any other requests?"

She had one, but wasn't sure how to ask.

"What?" The question was wary, as if he sensed her mood.

"The guest list..."

"How many?"

"It's not the number. Mom and my sister and a few friends, but there are a couple of people I'd like to invite and I don't know if you'd approve."

Katie squealed and dropped the heavy-bottomed cup on her tray.

Jon kissed Maryellen's temple. "You know there's almost nothing I can refuse you. Who do you want to invite?"

She leaned into him, not wanting to see his face when she told him. "Your father and stepmother." Jon had only recently revealed how his parents had chosen to protect his younger brother at his expense. They had lied on the witness stand and, as a result, Jon had been convicted of dealing drugs. He'd served seven years in prison. Not once in all those years or the years since had he spoken to either his father or his stepmother.

Jon tensed and slowly released Maryellen. "No. They are no longer part of my life. They cast me aside and—"

"You're all they have left." His brother had died a tragic

death and Maryellen was convinced that his family regretted what they'd done, both in betraying Jon and in not forcing his brother to face the consequences of his crime.

Jon clasped her shoulders hard, almost hurting her with the fervor of his emotions. "We will never speak of this again, understand? I have no family other than you and Katie." Taking a shuddery breath, he let her go.

She wanted to argue, and longed to help heal the relationship between Jon and his family, but she could see he wasn't ready. His parents had a granddaughter they knew nothing about. Surely that was an opportunity for new beginnings. Still, it wasn't Maryellen's place to step in, especially since Jon's feelings on the subject were this adamant.

"What about a honeymoon?" Jon asked. "Nothing fancy, but someplace we can get away for a night or two."

"You want a honeymoon?" Maryellen had been so involved with plans for her move and for the actual wedding, she hadn't given a honeymoon any thought.

"Damn straight I want a honeymoon."

"What about Thyme and Tide?" Bob and Peggy Beldon's Bed and Breakfast was said to be the best in town.

Jon shook his head. "I already looked into that, but they aren't taking guests until this murder is solved."

"Oh…" That was a disappointment.

"How about a night in Seattle? Just the two of us. Your mother will take Katie, won't she?"

Maryellen laughed softly. "In a heartbeat."

"Seattle, then?"

Maryellen nodded.

"The honeymoon will be the very best part." Jon kissed her nose, and Katie giggled as if she'd never seen anything funnier. "That amuses you, does it?" Jon said, smiling. "I guess I see your point."

"We're going to have a beautiful wedding," Maryellen said with certainty. The prospect of it made this chaos of packing and moving seem worthwhile. Within a couple of weeks she'd be Jon's wife. The three of them would be a family.

Four

Charlotte Jefferson dressed nervously for her court appearance. She'd spent many an afternoon in the Kitsap County Courthouse, proudly watching her only daughter officiate as a family court judge. In Charlotte's opinion, her daughter was one of the wisest judges in the entire state. She got a thrill just watching Olivia mete out decisions, looking so official in her black robe.

This afternoon, however, Charlotte wouldn't be in Olivia's courtroom but in Judge Robson's. She wouldn't be alone, either. Together with several of her dearest friends, she'd be facing the consequences of civil disobedience. Still, serving time in the slammer, if it came to that, would be a small price to pay if her actions got the town council to finally bring a health clinic to Cedar Cove.

Laura, Bess and the others, including Ben Rhodes, were scheduled to meet her in the foyer outside Judge Robson's courtroom at one o'clock.

Charlotte donned her best Sunday dress, complete with the Easter hat she'd purchased back in 1966. It was a broad-brimmed yellow one with a single white plume tucked in the satin band. If Judge Robson decided to incarcerate her and the others, she intended to walk into that jail cell as finely dressed as she would've been for any church service.

Olivia and Jack didn't seem to think a prison term was likely, but Charlotte had heard rumors about Judge Robson. He was supposed to be much more by-the-book than Olivia, more of a hard-liner, and—again according to rumor— fond of making an example of the occasional miscreant.

The doorbell chimed and Harry, her cat, leaped down from the foot of her bed with an uncharacteristic display of energy and trotted into the living room. Since Olivia and Jack were out of town on their honeymoon, Charlotte wondered who it might be. Embarrassment had prevented her from asking Justine, her granddaughter, to accompany her. Olivia, of course, was well aware of the entire situation, unhappily so. But Charlotte refused to let the rest of her family and friends know, although it was impossible to keep such news completely quiet.

The peephole in the front door answered her question. Ben Rhodes stood on the other side, looking as dapper and debonair as ever. Despite her age, her heart did a tiny flip-flop at the sight of him. After all these years as a widow, she'd assumed she was too old and set in her ways to fall in love, but Ben had shown her that even long-held assumptions could be wrong.

"Ben!" She unbolted the four dead bolt locks on her front door. "What are you doing here?" she demanded, although she was more than glad to see him. "We're supposed to meet at the courthouse, remember?"

"I know, but I thought I'd escort my favorite gal into court. Are you ready?"

Charlotte straightened the skirt of her floral dress, feeling, for just a second, like the heroine in a 1950s musical.

Ben made the whole mess seem like an adventure rather than a scandal—or worse. "How do I look?"

A smile lazily crossed Ben's full mouth. At times it was difficult to forget that he wasn't really Cesar Romero, the wonderful Cuban actor. In her opinion, Ben could have been the other man's double. "You look lovely," he told her.

But adventure or not, Charlotte couldn't quite control her nervousness. "Oh, dear...I just don't know what's going to happen to us."

Ben gently patted her hand. "I don't believe the council wants that kind of negative publicity. I can just imagine what the Seattle newspapers would say about a town punishing a handful of senior citizens because we were demonstrating for health care."

"Unlawful assembly," Charlotte muttered under her breath. "I, for one, am willing to serve my time if that's what it takes to wake this town up." Just being with Ben strengthened her resolve. He made her feel brave, helped her stand up for her principles and act on the power of her convictions.

"I completely agree with you. However..." He hesitated and then forcefully expelled his breath. "I don't think we need to worry about serving jail time. We'll probably just be fined."

Charlotte just couldn't be sure. She *was* worried, especially considering Judge Robson's reputation. Would she be viewed as the ringleader? She felt particularly anxious about her friends, who'd stood loyally by her when she defied Sheriff Davis.

"I've hired an attorney," Ben informed her. Earlier Ben had agreed to represent them in court, but apparently he'd changed his mind.

Charlotte hadn't wanted to involve lawyers. For one thing,

they charged an arm and a leg, and for another, whatever lawyer Ben had chosen was bound to say something to Olivia when she returned. Charlotte wanted Olivia to know as little as possible, difficult though that would be. She'd hoped to hold down the gossip.

"Sharon Castor said she'd meet us at the courthouse."

"Not Sharon Castor," Charlotte cried. The attorney was frequently in Olivia's courtroom. In fact, Sharon had recently represented Rosemary Cox in her divorce case. Charlotte had been present when her daughter had handed down one of her most controversial joint-custody decisions—a decision that, Charlotte believed, had led to the couple's reconciliation.

"Oh, dear," she said and sighed. "We might as well go." She went into the bedroom for her overnight case, which contained her medications and night cream, and reached for her jacket. Just in case... The day was cool, and from everything she'd read, jail cells were notoriously drafty. She glanced around her bedroom one last time. Once she'd received her sentence, if the worst happened, she'd contact Justine and ask her to take care of Harry.

"Charlotte," Ben said, shaking his head as she entered the living room. "You aren't going to need a suitcase."

"Don't be so sure," she countered grimly. "Suppose Judge Robson decides to make an example of me. I want to be ready." She'd long been a believer in preparing for the worst—and hoping for the best.

Ben tried to argue with her, but she refused to change her mind. In the end, he placed her suitcase in the trunk of his car.

When they arrived at the courthouse, Helen, Laura and Bess were already gathered in the foyer outside Judge Robson's courtroom. The three women rushed frantically to Charlotte's side.

"I'm telling you right now, no one's going to do a body search on me and live to tell about it," Bess declared. She raised her hands in the familiar karate posture. Their entire Senior Center had taken self-defense lessons a few years back and Bess had faithfully attended every class.

"Have you been watching those *Karate Kid* videos again?" Charlotte muttered.

Bess glared at her. "I'm not joking, Charlotte."

"Do you think the judge will let us bring our knitting needles into jail?" Laura asked. "If you want the truth, I have several Christmas projects I'd like to start and frankly I could make good use of the downtime."

Just as Charlotte began to reply, Sharon Castor strolled up to Ben. "This is everyone?" she asked.

Ben nodded.

"Ben's hired us legal representation," Charlotte whispered to her friends. "He seems to think all the judge will do is fine us."

"That's all?" Laura sounded disappointed. "I was looking forward to prison."

In contrast, Bess folded her hands together and raised her eyes toward heaven. "God bless Ben."

Charlotte had to admit she was grateful not to have this entire matter fall upon her shoulders. She was the one who'd led her friends into trouble, and she felt responsible for whatever befell them as a result.

"We're up next," Sharon Castor announced. "Let's go into the courtroom together."

Charlotte adjusted her hat. Ben took her hand and the small party walked into the courtroom. Sharon was in the lead, with Bess, Helen and Laura marching right behind her, and Charlotte and Ben bringing up the rear.

To Charlotte's astonishment, the courtroom was packed—

standing room only. The first people to catch her attention were Bob and Peggy Beldon from the Thyme and Tide Bed and Breakfast.

"We're with you, Charlotte," Peggy called out.

Justine and her husband, Seth, were there, too. Seth held on to Leif, who was almost two years old. The toddler squirmed in his father's arms, but stilled when he saw Charlotte. Justine waved, and Charlotte's eyes blurred with tears, which she furiously blinked back. It seemed half the town had shown up to offer them support.

Enjoying their celebrity status, Bess and Helen waved as if they were prom queens walking in a Fourth of July parade.

"Did you know about this?" Charlotte asked, glancing up at Ben who stood a full head taller than her five foot three.

"Not at all," he confessed, looking around. "Even Troy Davis is here."

The sheriff who'd arrested them had turned up in court to support their efforts now. Charlotte had always been fond of Troy and was willing to forgive his error in judgment. Then again, the dear boy had no choice but to arrest them when they'd declined to break up their demonstration and disperse. He'd sworn to uphold the law, whether he agreed with it or not. His presence this afternoon made his personal feelings very clear.

"Roy and Corrie McAfee are here, too," Ben whispered.

The McAfees were recent additions to the Cedar Cove community. Roy was a former Seattle police detective who'd retired in Cedar Cove and opened his own agency as a private investigator.

Grace Sherman stepped up to Charlotte and gave her a hug. "Olivia asked me to stop by this afternoon," Grace said close to Charlotte's ear. "I didn't think you'd mind if I invited a few library patrons to give you their support."

Charlotte squeezed Grace's hand. Grace and Olivia had been best friends nearly their entire lives. How like Olivia to ask Grace to fill in for her this afternoon, since she couldn't be in court herself. For a very good reason, mind you, one Charlotte fully approved of. Olivia and Jack were in Hawaii on their honeymoon.

The door at the back of the courtroom opened and in walked Maryellen Sherman, who found a seat next to her mother. Jon Bowman was with her, Katie balanced on his hip. Charlotte had taken a liking to the photographer and was pleased to hear those two would soon be married. High time, in her opinion, not that anyone had asked.

"The court will come to order," the bailiff announced. "Judge Robson presiding."

The judge emerged from his chambers and took his seat at the front of the courtroom.

Despite Ben's reassurances, Charlotte's pulse fluctuated wildly before taking up a steady beat again. This might not be pretty. Until she was asked to stand with her friends while the charges were being read, Charlotte didn't realize how frightened she was. Between Bess practicing her karate moves and Laura looking forward to knitting in jail, Charlotte wasn't sure what to expect.

Sharon Castor handled the situation in a most professional manner, Charlotte thought, her estimation of the attorney rising considerably.

"Your Honor," she said, moving halfway to the bench. "Look at this group of law-breakers and tell me what you see."

"Ms. Castor," Judge Robson said. He continued to scan the charges. "Unlawful assembly, refusing to disband—"

"Yes, Your Honor, but my clients were making a statement—a statement they felt could only be made in this manner. They feel Cedar Cove needs a health clinic and I, for one, agree with them."

"Then they should have approached the council."

"Which I did, Your Honor." Charlotte spoke before she could stop herself. "I beg your pardon, Judge Robson," she said, feeling she couldn't let her nerve fail her now. "Both Mr. Rhodes and I attended several council meetings, but to no avail. Mayor Benson said there are no funds to establish a health clinic, but—"

"This isn't the time to discuss the merits of a medical clinic in Cedar Cove."

"Yes, Your Honor," Charlotte murmured, properly chastised. Ben gave her an encouraging smile.

The prosecutor in the case seemed disinclined to send them to jail, Charlotte noted gratefully. He made a few comments and sat back down. Sharon Castor was on her feet again.

"You can save your breath, Ms. Castor. I've made my decision."

The attorney slowly sat down.

"It appears to me that the five of you were trying to make public your case for a health clinic."

Charlotte nodded and noticed the others did, too.

"Your plan has apparently worked. Half the town is here to support you. If anyone from council is in attendance, I sincerely hope they are taking detailed notes. I don't see that anything useful will be served by fining five senior citizens who were on a mission to make Cedar Cove a better place. If I could have your word of honor that you will not assemble again without the necessary permit, then I'd be willing to dismiss all charges."

Charlotte and the others were quick to comply.

As soon as the charges were dismissed, the courtroom

erupted into applause. As they walked out, Charlotte and her friends were given a heroes' reception. They were free, one and all.

Before they left the courthouse, Charlotte and Ben personally thanked Sharon and every person who'd come to their support. She was astonished their case had generated so much interest in the community. All this time Charlotte hadn't spoken about her court date because she didn't want to bother her family or friends with her problems. It was a strong affirmation of the community's affection and respect that so many people were there today.

Ben drove her back to the house. "I had no idea all those people knew about this," she told him as he held the car door for her.

"I didn't either," Ben said.

"I suspect it was Grace who rallied everyone on our behalf."

"The next time I'm in the library, I'm going to thank her all over again."

"I will, too." Charlotte had every intention of letting Olivia know what a wonderful job Grace had done.

"You are much loved in this community, Charlotte Jefferson," Ben said as they mounted her front-porch steps. He carried her small suitcase, which he'd remembered to remove from the trunk.

"I am honored so many of my friends took time out of their busy days and came to court," she murmured, still a little overwhelmed.

"There's someone else you should include on the list of people who love you," Ben said. He sat down on the porch swing while she rummaged in her large purse, searching for the house keys.

"And who would that be?" she asked, thinking she might have stuck the key chain in her overnight bag.

"That would be me."

Charlotte froze. Ben had just declared his love—or so it seemed—and at the most ridiculous of times. She turned to face him. "Are you saying you're in love with me, Ben Rhodes?"

"I am." He looked at her directly, meeting her eyes. "The fact is, Charlotte, I'm wondering if you share my feelings."

He didn't know? He hadn't guessed? This was indeed news. With her keys clenched in her hands, she triumphantly lifted them from her purse. "As a matter of fact, I'm head over heels in love with you and have been for quite a while," she said bluntly. Having admitted her feelings, she blushed and quickly added, "Would you care for a glass of lemonade to celebrate our victory?" She opened the front door.

"Don't mind if I do." Ben followed her into the house. "I just might steal a kiss while I'm at it."

"And I just might let you," Charlotte said with a smile.

Five

The alarm went off and Grace Sherman glanced at the clock radio on the bedside table. 7:00 a.m. Her one day of the work week to sleep in, and she'd forgotten to turn off the alarm the night before. With the new spring schedule, the library didn't open until eleven on Wednesdays. But staying in bed now that she was awake seemed pointless. Sighing, she tossed aside the covers, then sat up and slipped her feet into slippers. She quickly made the bed.

Dan, her husband of more than thirty years, had been dead for some time, and she had the entire bed to herself, but she continued to sleep on one half, never disarranging the other. Old habits were persistent. Habits like waking early. Her daily routine gave her structure and comfort in a life that was increasingly out of control.

As little as three years ago, everything had seemed so normal. Her marriage wasn't particularly happy, but it wasn't unhappy, either. Her life was comfortable. Predictable. Then Dan had disappeared. For an entire year she'd lived in a state of suspension, not knowing what had happened to him, where he'd gonc or who he was with. When she least expected it, just when she'd adjusted to the fact that he must be with someone else, Dan's body was discovered. He'd died from a self-inflicted gunshot wound.

Grace felt she could deal with Dan's death. At the time, he'd already been gone a year and she'd learned to live on her own and even found a certain solace in it. During those first dark, lonely months following his disappearance, she'd become acquainted with Cliff Harding, a horse rancher who lived in Olalla. Cliff had wanted a relationship, but he'd been patient, willing to wait until it felt right to her. Prior to her relationship with Cliff, the last time Grace had been out on a date was in high school. The one and only man in her life had been her husband. After she'd buried Dan, she'd finally agreed to see Cliff—but then she'd foundered and made a drastic mistake. Grace had gotten involved with another man via the Internet.

Chatting with Will Jefferson, her best friend's older brother, had started out innocently enough. From as early as she could remember, Grace had had a crush on Will. That had never gone anywhere, and after high school Will had left for the East Coast, where he attended college and then stayed. He'd written her a letter after Dan's death, and the correspondence had continued by e-mail. He'd flattered her ego, become her friend, and before she realized what was happening, she'd fallen in love with him, despite the fact that he was married.

She was embarrassed to admit how foolish she'd been. Grace knew from the beginning that Will had a wife. At first she'd pretended they were merely friends and that his marital status didn't matter. But it did. When Will assured her he was divorcing his wife, she'd wanted to believe him, wanted to be part of his life badly enough to swallow his lies. Thankfully she'd learned the truth in time to save her dignity, but at a painful price.

As a result of her liaison with Will, she'd lost Cliff Harding's love, friendship and respect. He no longer wanted anything to do with her and after months of neglect, months of misleading him—no, lying to him—she couldn't blame Cliff at all. He'd said it would be better if they went their separate ways. Twice she'd gone to him. Twice she'd asked for another chance to prove herself. Twice he'd said no.

Grace had wanted to make amends and to recover what she'd lost with Cliff. She now recognized her "love" for Will as the infatuation it was, fueled by the clandestine nature of the relationship. And she recognized the genuineness of her feelings for Cliff.

She was sure Cliff still loved her, too. She saw it, *felt* it, but he sadly shook his head. Cliff's wife had cheated on him for years and he refused to become trapped in another relationship where trust was compromised.

As far as Cliff was concerned, it was over between them.

With both Will and Cliff out of her life, Grace was lonely. Terribly lonely. Other than her work, some valued friends and her two daughters and grandchildren, she had few outside interests.

Dressed in her robe and slippers, she moved slowly into the kitchen, Buttercup, her golden retriever, at her heels. The dog ventured outside through the doggy door, and Grace picked up the local newspaper from the front porch and placed it on the kitchen table. While Buttercup did her business, Grace prepared a pot of coffee.

Her sense of loneliness was accentuated even more now that Olivia had remarried. Grace was happy for her dearest friend and yet she was afraid that Olivia wouldn't have as much time for her anymore. She was ashamed of her Internet lapse with Olivia's brother, and felt somewhat distanced from Olivia as a result.

"Well, Buttercup," Grace murmured as the dog came back inside. "Shall we see what's on the agenda for today?" She poured herself a cup of coffee while Buttercup lapped water from her bowl. A fund-raising committee meeting for the animal shelter was scheduled for that evening. One positive thing Grace had done for herself after the breakups with both Will and Cliff was to become a volunteer at the Cedar Cove Animal Shelter.

Two Saturdays a month she interviewed potential pet owners, walked and fed the animals and did whatever else she could to be useful. Janet Webb, who was in charge of fund-raising, had asked Grace to be on her committee and she'd gladly accepted.

Buttercup finished her drink and sat down at Grace's feet while Grace sipped her coffee. As she mulled over her day, she scanned the headlines, then got dressed—khaki cotton trousers, a white tailored shirt, her favorite black blazer—and drove to the library.

Grace's afternoon passed quickly. Following work, rather than race home before her meeting, Grace strolled along the waterfront. The marina was lovely, especially this time of year. In a couple of months, the Thursday-night Concerts on the Cove would start again. Cliff had often joined her for the concerts. They'd buy dinner and sit on the grass.... Grace shook her head in an effort to dispel her memories of Cliff. He'd insisted it was over and she had no choice but to accept his decision.

Before she left for the meeting, Grace went to the Pot Belly Deli where she bought a sandwich, eating it at a small table by herself. Then she drove out to the shelter.

Janet Webb and the other committee members had already arrived. "I'm so glad you're on our committee," Janet said and introduced Grace to Mary Sanchez and Margaret White, both long-standing volunteers. Janet and Margaret were about the same age as Grace, but Mary was in her mid-thirties.

"We're looking for something that'll bring the entire community together," Janet explained as Grace took a seat at the table in the conference room. "For the last few years we've done the usual bake sales and car washes."

"We had a dog wash that one year," Margaret reminded her.

"Yes, and while those fund-raising events have been successful, they've been fairly small-scale. I'd like something with a little more...punch."

"What about a bachelor auction?" Mary suggested excitedly. It was clear she'd been thinking about the idea for quite some time and was nearly out of her chair with enthusiasm. "I've read about them and I think it's a wonderful idea, don't you?"

Janet hesitated. "Maybe, but I'm married and so are a lot of other women in town."

"Yes, but I'm not and, well, I know I'd certainly be willing to pay for the pleasure of having a handsome man at my disposal for an entire evening." She glanced eagerly toward Grace. "I'll bet other single women would, too."

Grace wasn't so sure, but she hated to squelch Mary's enthusiasm. "Has anyone else noticed that there seem to be more animals that need adoption lately?" she asked. "Especially dogs..." The ideas started to churn in her mind. "What about a dog auction—or perhaps the shelter could do that along with the bachelors?"

"A dog and bachelor auction?"

"Why not?" Grace asked. "We could pair up the dogs with the bachelors."

Janet seemed to be considering the idea. "That sounds promising."

"The dog would be auctioned off first, and then the bachelor. Or the other way around."

"The bachelors would need to be a variety of ages, right?" Mary asked.

"Of course," Janet said, smiling ever so slightly.

Grace could tell that she was warming to the idea.

"Be sure and ask Cliff Harding to participate," Margaret White said, leaning closer to the table. "I think he's the most adorable man I've seen in ages, and he's single, too."

"Who?" Janet asked, frowning.

"Cliff Harding," Margaret repeated. "You obviously haven't noticed him around town, but trust me, I have. He's a hunk."

Mary looked across the table at Grace. "You were going out with him for a while, weren't you?"

It was all Grace could do to nod. Cliff was a natural choice for the bachelor auction. Her enthusiasm for the project did a nosedive, but she didn't dare show her feelings.

"Can you think of anyone else who'd agree to be auctioned off for charity?" Janet asked.

"Bruce Peyton," Grace suggested with a shrug. "He's a widower who brings his daughter into the library once a week."

"Ah, yes," Mary said. "I remember when his wife was killed in an automobile accident. When was that, anyway?"

"It must've been two or three years ago," Margaret replied. "I knew her mother, Sandy. Tragic, tragic accident. I think Stephanie's death was what killed her. Sandy was gone within a year—cancer."

Grace felt terrible for the little girl who'd lost both her mother and grandmother within such a short period. She didn't know Bruce well, but he seemed loving and protective of his daughter. She didn't envy him the task of raising the little girl on his own.

"Ben Rhodes has stirred a few hearts down at the Senior Center," Grace said, wondering how Charlotte would feel about this.

Mary nodded in approval. "Ben's an excellent choice and, seeing that he's retired navy, he just might be able to get us a few young seamen who'd be willing to do a good deed for charity."

"That's a great idea." Janet seemed absolutely delighted now. She quickly wrote down the names on the pad. "Barry Stokes is always good about donating his time and talent to charity auctions."

Barry was the local auctioneer whose big red barn and auction headquarters could be seen from the highway.

"This is going to be just great," Mary burbled.

"It's certainly better than another bake sale."

"Why don't we talk to Seth and Justine Gunderson about letting us use The Lighthouse for the event?" Grace said.

"Perfect," Mary agreed. "We want to make this classy. The restaurant's just the right size, too."

Janet picked up a pen and pad and started writing down suggestions and assignments. "Okay, I'll see what I can do to get The Lighthouse. I'll get in touch with Barry, too." Janet made a second notation for herself. "Mary and Margaret, why don't you two make up a list of potential bachelors?"

The women nodded simultaneously.

Janet pointed her pen in Grace's direction. "How about if you work on publicizing the event—posters, newspaper ads, radio and the like?"

Grace nodded. "Of course."

"I'll ask for volunteers to work the auction at the next board meeting." Janet looked pleased with herself. "I think we're onto something really wonderful this year."

The four women continued to discuss the event and it was

after eight before they ended the meeting. Margaret White walked out to the parking lot with Grace. "I don't know about anyone else but I'd write a blank check to spend an evening with Cliff Harding."

Grace forced a smile.

"I nearly pass out every time he comes to the vet's office." She giggled like a schoolgirl. "See you next week," she said. She climbed into her car and drove off.

Grace slid into her own vehicle and braced her hands against the steering wheel. The thought of Cliff with another woman made her feel a regret so strong that for a moment she was nearly sick to her stomach. She couldn't bear it and at the same time realized she had to.

Worst of all, she was to blame for her own unhappiness.

Six

Peggy put the finishing touches on the dinner table as Bob straightened up the family room. He was pleased Peggy had chosen to serve their guests in the kitchen rather than the formal dining room. Jack and Olivia, who were back from their honeymoon, were coming for dinner, and he considered Jack as much family as friend. Olivia now, too. In some ways, however, Jack was even closer than family.

Although Bob had twenty-one years of sobriety behind him, he knew he was a single drink away from insanity. He still took it one day at a time and routinely attended AA meetings. It was through Alcoholics Anonymous that he'd met Jack Griffin. Bob and Peggy had been living in the Spokane area when Jack approached Bob and asked him to be his AA sponsor. That was the beginning of their strong friendship.

After Bob and Peggy returned to Cedar Cove and purchased this house, they'd invited Jack to visit. He'd fallen in love with the small-town community. When the editor's job opened up at the *Cedar Cove Chronicle,* Jack—a longtime newsman—had applied and been offered the position. Soon after he moved to town, he met Judge Olivia Lockhart. It'd taken some mighty fast talking on Jack's part, but he'd finally convinced her to marry him. Bob was proud to have stood up as Jack's best man.

"Honey, would you fill the water glasses?" Peggy asked as she scurried about the kitchen.

"Sure thing." His wife was a marvel, Bob thought as he dumped ice cubes into the pitcher. Peggy was a master gardener, homemaker and cook extraordinaire. The scent of her chicken cordon bleu wafted through the kitchen and made his mouth water. He knew she'd prepared his favorite broccoli salad and a special mashed-potato casserole as part of their meal. Peggy had made a habit of cooking all his favorite dishes since Sheriff Davis's last visit—as if she was determined to make his last days on earth happy ones. Not that she'd admit it, he realized, but Bob knew she was worried and he humored her.

Much of the success of Thyme and Tide was due to Peggy's skill at making people feel welcome and comfortable. Bob didn't discount his own talents. He was a reasonably adequate handyman, but it was Peggy who held everything together, including his life.

She was busy at the sink—doing what, he could only guess. He finished his assigned duty, set the pitcher aside and came up behind her, sliding his arms around her waist.

"Bob," she protested as he spread kisses down the side of her neck. "We have guests due any minute."

"Hmm."

"*They're* the oncs on the honeymoon, not us."

"Does that mean you're not interested in a little hanky-panky?"

"Bob Beldon!"

"Is that a yes, you are, or a no, you're not?"

"It's a yes, but could you kindly wait until after our guests leave?" She feigned impatience, but Bob knew her far too well. Their marriage had gone through several stages, some good and some difficult, but through it all their love life had remained active. Peggy's talents extended into the bedroom and for that, Bob was most appreciative.

The doorbell chimed and Bob released his wife. Peggy made a show of tucking in her blouse. This was the first week they'd been without overnight guests, and the absence of people in the house had taken some getting used to. Bob enjoyed it for a change, but he knew that before long they'd both grow bored.

"Do you want me to get that?" Peggy asked.

"No, I will."

Peggy sighed, and Bob sensed that she was nervous. She didn't know Olivia well, and he could tell that Peggy sincerely hoped they'd all be friends. She hadn't worked quite this hard to impress someone in a very long while. Dinner in the kitchen would be more intimate, more casual, and definitely suited Jack's personality. Olivia's, too, he hoped....

Jack and Olivia Griffin stood at the front door, looking relaxed and very much in love. Jack had his arm around Olivia's waist as if he couldn't bear to be apart from her.

"Welcome back," Bob said, stepping aside to let them in. "You both look fabulous."

"We *are* fabulous," Jack said, smiling down at Olivia.

Bob had to admit they made an interesting couple. Jack was by far the more easygoing of the two. Olivia held an important position in the community, so perhaps it was only natural that she'd be more formal. Yet they were good together, good for each other in the same way he and Peggy were.

"Welcome," Peggy said as she walked into the living room. "I hope you had a wonderful honeymoon." Jack came forward to kiss her cheek.

"We did," Olivia told her, smiling. "Unfortunately, we have to be back at work first thing in the morning."

"I've got to get out the Friday edition of the paper," Jack said, "and Olivia's due in court."

"I was lucky to get as much time off as I did," she added.

Peggy hung Olivia's jacket in the hall closet. Jack shrugged off his raincoat and threw it over the back of a chair.

"Are we early?" he asked, glancing at his watch.

"Not at all, your timing's perfect." Peggy scooped up his coat and quickly brought it to the closet. "I've got just a few things to do and then dinner will be on the table."

"How can I help?" Olivia asked as she followed Peggy into the kitchen.

"Most everything's finished, but you can keep me company."

Bob was grateful for a few minutes alone with his friend. Rather than lead Jack into the family room, he stayed in the formal living room. The last time he'd sat here had been with Roy McAfee and Sheriff Davis. That was the day he'd met Hannah Russell, the daughter of the man who'd died in his home. The daughter of a long-forgotten friend. Bob didn't want to think about any of it, but he couldn't ignore the dead man, either.

"You're looking well," Bob said. He sat in the wingback chair by the fireplace.

Jack claimed its twin, which was angled on the other side of the fireplace. "I don't know why Olivia waited so long to marry me. The woman's crazy about me, you know." He chuckled at his own remark.

"I suppose you think Peggy and I invited you to dinner because of your charming personality."

"Any other reason I should hear about?"

Bob went very still. He hadn't meant to introduce the subject quite so soon, but Jack had given him the perfect opportunity. "Listen, Jack, you're the best friend I've got. You know that, right?"

The smile faded from Jack's eyes at the seriousness in Bob's tone. "Yeah, I guess."

"I need a favor."

Jack nodded. "Anything."

"Thanks, Jack." Bob spoke quietly and hoped his gratitude was evident.

"Does this have anything to do with Maxwell Russell?"

"Yes."

"Anything new?"

"Not really, but Troy Davis stopped by for a visit last week, and he thinks I might be in…some kind of danger."

Jack uncrossed his legs and leaned forward. "*What* kind of danger?"

"He wasn't entirely sure—no one is—but with two of the four-man squad dead, it's a puzzle. Someone murdered Max. That much has been uncovered. Dan's dead, too, and although he committed suicide, I wonder about the timing. There has to be *some* connection between these two deaths."

"What about the fourth man?"

"I can't say, but when Peggy was out of earshot Troy let me know that he's warned Samuels to be careful. There are too many unanswered questions."

Jack frowned. "What did he suggest you do?"

"He thought it might be a good idea if Peggy and I went on an extended vacation."

Jack's frown grew deeper. "Then what the hell are you doing here?"

Bob sat back in his chair and attempted to look as if he wasn't intimidated by his situation. He was, though, and he hoped his acting skills were up to par. He figured he'd played enough roles in the community theater to make a passable showing. “I refuse to run away and hide. If anyone out there wants me dead, then all I can say is let him come and get me.”

“I don’t suppose Davis mentioned you have a stupid attitude?” Jack’s scowl darkened his face.

“He might’ve suggested something along those lines.”

Jack didn’t say anything for a moment. “What does Peggy think about all this?”

Bob didn’t want to discuss that. “She has her opinion and I have mine. I did agree not to take guests until this is settled. It hurts financially, but we’ll survive.”

“One day at a time?”

“Let go and let God,” Bob said, quoting a well-known AA saying.

“What can I do?” Jack asked.

“For now, nothing, but if something should happen to me…”

“Nothing’s going to happen.”

Bob wasn’t prepared to argue, but for his own peace of mind, he needed reassurance. He held up his hand. “I don’t know what the future holds, Jack. If what Davis thinks is true, I could turn up dead, the same as Max.”

“But—”

“There are a lot of things in this world that can’t be forgotten or forgiven.” Bob lived with plenty of regrets but none greater than his unwitting participation in a massacre during the Vietnam War.

“What do you need me to do?” Jack asked.

“I want you to look after Peggy for me.” He worried about his children, too. Both Hollie and Marc lived in the Spokane area. Peggy kept in close touch with both of them, and he talked to his son and daughter once a week.

"You know I'll do whatever I can," Jack promised.

If he were to die, Bob couldn't see either of his children moving to Cedar Cove. They loved their mother but they had lives of their own.

He reached inside his pocket and pulled out two envelopes. "I've written each of my kids a letter. If the worst happens, I want you to give them these."

Jack accepted the envelopes and nodded. "Consider it done."

Bob glanced up just in time to see Peggy and Olivia walk into the living room. "Why are you two sitting here looking so glum? Dinner's ready."

"Dinner." Bob bolted to his feet. "Why didn't you say so?"

"I'm ready anytime," Jack said.

Bob felt better than he had in days. No matter what happened, he could rest easy now.

Seven

Maryellen felt overwhelmed by everything she needed to do before the wedding. The last two weeks had passed in a whirlwind of activity and joyous craziness.

"Just look at these nails," Rachel, her nail tech, said as she picked up a cotton ball to remove the old polish. "What have you been up to?"

"Moving," Maryellen muttered, knowing that would explain everything. Her rental house was completely empty now and her belongings were all at Jon's place, but almost everything remained in boxes. With the wedding preparations demanding all her extra time, she had yet to unpack.

"So when's the big day?"

"Monday," Maryellen said.

"Memorial Day?"

She nodded.

"That's one way to help your husband keep track of your anniversary," Rachel said with a laugh. Apparently she'd forgotten that the actual date changed from year to year. "In my case, however, the first thing I've got to do is *find* a husband." The exasperation in her sigh said it all. For as long as Maryellen could remember, Rachel had wanted to get married. All the women at Get Nailed were single and, during each appointment, Maryellen could count on the main topic of conversation revolving around the lack of decent husband material in Cedar Cove.

"Did you hear the big news?" Rachel asked, rubbing furiously at the old polish.

Maryellen shook her head.

"The animal shelter's holding a dog and bachelor auction."

"With some men, it's one and the same," Terri shouted from the other side of the room. "The men I've dated have been real dogs." She laughed at her own joke, then returned her attention to her client.

Even before Maryellen's engagement, such an event would never have interested her, but she knew the girls at Get Nailed would leap at the opportunity to meet eligible men.

"I'm surprised you haven't heard about the auction. Everyone in town's talking about it."

"Just as long as everyone knows Jon is out of circulation," Maryellen teased.

"Honey, from the moment Jon Bowman looked at you, he was a goner."

Maryellen grinned. At one point—during her avoidance phase—she'd attempted to match Jon up with one of the nail techs. Her plan had backfired and as a result, Maryellen had come to realize how strong the attraction between them was. Then, a few months ago, she'd managed to convince herself that Jon was involved with someone else. The thought of him with another woman had nearly destroyed her. Only later did she learn that he was completely committed to her and Katie.

"Are you excited about the wedding?"

Right now, Maryellen was too tired to be excited. With their jobs, they'd both been working twenty-hour days in an effort to have the house and yard ready for the ceremony. Jon had spent countless hours doing yardwork and planning the reception. Thankfully the guest list was small, under thirty.

Friday was his last day at The Lighthouse Restaurant, where he worked nights as a chef. He was ready to make the transition and dedicate all his time to photography. Maryellen would continue working at the art gallery until the end of the year—or until she became pregnant again. After that, she'd serve as Jon's agent, marketing his pictures and negotiating with galleries around the country.

The thought of a second baby made her feel weak with longing. They'd managed to avoid physical lovemaking, but it had been a strain on both of them. Still, she felt that waiting until they were married was the right decision—for emotional reasons rather than rational ones—although she'd never guessed it would be this difficult.

As soon as Rachel was finished with her nails, Maryellen drove to her mother's house to pick up Katie.

"Leave her with me," Grace insisted. "You've got enough on your mind."

"You're sure?"

"I love having her."

Maryellen and Katie were staying with Grace for the next two nights. "Then I think I should drive out to Jon's and see what I can do to help him get things ready."

"You go ahead."

Maryellen left, grateful her mother had been so understanding. Just as she suspected, Jon was working in the yard, spreading beauty bark around the base of the rhododendrons and azaleas. Both were in full bloom and shockingly vibrant in color. Jon had counted over a hundred blooming rhododendrons on his property. Of them all, Maryellen's favorites were the bright red ones.

When she pulled in the long gravel driveway, Jon walked over to the car and opened her door. "I came to help," she said and although she was tempted, she resisted wrapping her arms around his waist and kissing him.

"I thought you were getting your nails done?"

"I already did." She held out her hands for his inspection. The pale rose polish sparkled in the sunlight. "What can I do?"

"Nothing out here. I wouldn't want you to risk damaging one of those fingernails." He leaned on the shovel. "Why don't you unpack? I've got boxes shoved in every conceivable corner."

"Out of sight, out of mind?"

"Not exactly," he said with a chuckle.

Maryellen took his advice and decided to start in the master bedroom. The kitchen could wait; besides, that area was Jon's domain. He was the cook in the family, although she was willing to do her share of meal preparation. Marriage to her was a partnership, and Maryellen had every intention of being a good wife. If that meant chopping pounds of onions, well...she'd do it. In fact, she'd do *anything* to make her marriage as strong and healthy as possible.

She climbed the stairs to the bedroom, then paused in the doorway, hands on her hips, as she surveyed the room where she'd soon be sleeping. The photograph Jon had taken of her months earlier hung on the wall by the bed. It showed her in a rocking chair nursing Katie when their daughter was a newborn. He'd managed to capture the wonder and awe and love she felt, holding this tiny being in her arms. She'd hardly been conscious of Jon's presence at the time, so absorbed was she by Katie.

It gave her immeasurable joy to place her clothes in the closet next to Jon's. She carefully pushed his shirts aside and her hand lingered there. In two days' time, she would be Jon Bowman's wife. She felt a renewed sense of anticipation—and a surge of love for the man who'd fathered her child.

She opened the dresser drawers and started rearranging his things and making room for her own. That was when she found the letters. Tucked in with old receipts, maps and loose change were a number of envelopes. Most had been opened but a few remained sealed. Curiosity got the better of her and she pulled out a sheet, but then she paused. She refused to begin her marriage with an act of deception—snooping through letters that were addressed to Jon, not to her. Unsure what to do, she stacked them in a neat pile and set them to one side.

She heard the front door open and Jon calling up the stairs. "I'm ready for a break. How about you?"

She walked out of the bedroom to stand at the railing and looked down. "Be with you in a minute. I'm just finishing up here."

"Okay."

"I found a bunch of letters in a drawer. Is there any place you want me to put them?"

He frowned, hesitated and then shrugged. "Toss 'em."

"In the garbage?"

Nodding, he turned and walked into the kitchen.

"Who are they from?"

"No one important," he shouted back.

"An old girlfriend?" she pressed.

He snickered loudly enough for her to hear him all the way up the stairs. "Hardly. Just get rid of the whole bunch."

Maryellen dumped the letters into the plastic garbage bag, but then she couldn't resist. She plucked out the top one and looked at the return address. It was from the small coastal town of Seal Beach, Oregon. Years ago Maryellen had driven through it along Highway 1. She'd stopped for gas and lunch, and for some reason she'd never forgotten the town.

"Who do you know in Seal Beach?" she called down, reluctant to drop the matter. She began to descend the stairs, still clutching the letters.

Jon stepped out of the kitchen. "You aren't going to let this rest, are you?"

She slid her hand down the smooth oak banister as she walked. "I can't help being curious. You'd feel the same if it was me."

Jon shook his head, scowling. "I should've ditched those a long time ago. They're from my parents."

"Some of them haven't even been opened."

He stared up at her. "My father and stepmother are out of my life, Maryellen. They made their choice and I made mine. I want nothing more to do with either of them. Now, please just get rid of those letters, and don't mention them again."

"But—"

"Maryellen, please."

"If you insist." And this time she buried the letters in the bottom of the bag.

An hour later, her clothes hung next to Jon's in the big closet. The dresser drawers were full. At first glance it seemed as if she'd always lived with Jon, always been part of his home and his life. That gave her a feeling of contentment and somehow made their coming marriage even more real.

They ate dinner together, and sipped wine on the upstairs balcony that overlooked the water. Completely at ease, Maryellen laid her head against his shoulder. Jon's arm was around her, his long legs stretched out in front of him. The moment was so tranquil, she didn't immediately realize Jon had fallen asleep.

It was just as well. She needed to get back to her mother's house, spend some time with Katie. By now her daughter would be cranky, and Maryellen didn't want to take advantage of her mother's generosity.

Kissing Jon on the cheek, she slipped out of his arms and sneaked down the stairs, making as little noise as possible. She hated to leave, but in two days she'd be with Jon forever….

Just as she'd predicted, Katie was difficult and unreasonable that night, and her mother was exhausted. As soon as Maryellen reached for Katie, the baby settled against her shoulder, put her thumb in her mouth and promptly fell asleep. Maryellen rocked her for a few minutes, gently rubbing Katie's back.

"I can't believe one tiny baby could have so much energy." Grace sat down in her favorite chair, head thrown back, eyes closed. Opening them again, she said, "You look at peace."

"I am at peace, and so much in love."

Grace's eyes grew moist. "I hope you'll always be as happy as you are now."

Maryellen lowered her gaze.

Her mother understood her perfectly. "What is it?"

"Jon. I found a stack of letters, several of which he hadn't even bothered to open."

"Letters? From whom?"

"His parents. I badly wanted to read them but I didn't. Jon told me to throw them out." Her mother knew about Jon's situation and the way his parents had betrayed him.

"Did you?"

Maryellen nodded. "I didn't want to start our marriage off by being dishonest."

"It seems to me that if Jon has no feelings for his family, he wouldn't have saved those letters."

"I felt the same thing." Maryellen gnawed on her lower lip. "I didn't need to read them to know what they said. Jon's their only family now and they want his forgiveness. They want their son back."

"They have a granddaughter they don't know anything about."

"Yes..."

"And you, Maryellen. They'll be your in-laws."

It hurt her to think of Jon rejecting his parents' attempts at reconciliation—less for their sake than for his. Jon would never be free of the past until he could find a way to forgive his parents.

Her mother seemed deep in thought. "I couldn't bear the idea of anyone keeping me from my grandchildren," she said softly.

That was another point she should consider. Jon might not want anything to do with his family, but his parents had a right to know about Katie. And Katie had a right to know her grandparents.

That evening, Maryellen wrote Jon's family. The letter was brief. She'd memorized the post office box number and the zip code, and that was all she needed. She included a picture of her and Katie and a short message about how well Jon's career was going. Wanting to be sensitive to her husband's feelings, she stated that it would be best if they didn't contact her. She did promise, however, to send them occasional photographs of their granddaughter.

The next morning as Maryellen drove to the post office, she wondered if she was doing the right thing. On the one hand, she knew Jon would disapprove; on the other, she felt his parents deserved some compassion. And what about Katie? What about her future happiness?

The letter slid into the mailbox slot, and whether she was right or wrong remained undecided. Either way, it was too late.

Eight

The Dog and Bachelor Auction had already generated a lot of interest in Cedar Cove. Grace Sherman displayed a large notice in the library and Janet had asked her to deliver posters to the businesses around town. Thursday afternoon, the first week of June, Grace dedicated her lunch hour to making sure the community had all the relevant details.

The Lighthouse Restaurant was her first stop. She waited at the hostess's desk for the young woman to return from seating a couple. Staring out the large windows she admired the view of the water and the Bremerton shipyard on the other side of the cove. Several people were in line ahead of her, but Grace wasn't really in a rush. She needed to speak to either Seth or Justine to confirm that she could place the large poster in the front window and to finalize some details concerning the special menu being created for the event. For now, she was simply enjoying the vista of sea and vibrant blue sky, with the snow-capped Olympic Mountains in the background. Seth and Justine had done an impressive job of reflecting their surroundings in the architecture and decor of the restaurant.

The door opened behind her, but Grace was so absorbed in the view that she didn't pay attention.

"Hello, Grace."

Her heart leapt into her throat as she turned to greet Cliff Harding. "Hello, Cliff." He was as attractive as ever, with his broad shoulders and dark eyes. He wore jeans and a tan jacket with one button fastened. His cowboy hat rested slightly forward, shading his face.

They stared at each other as if neither knew what else to say. Grace wanted to talk, but her tongue felt as if it had grown twice its normal size and refused to cooperate. It'd been weeks since she'd last seen Cliff. In that time she'd grown accustomed to being alone. Accustomed to filling her days and nights with charity projects and anything that kept her mind off what she'd done to destroy their relationship.

"You're looking well," he said after an awkward moment.

"You, too."

He smiled regretfully. "So Maryellen and Jon were married last weekend."

Moisture found its way into Grace's mouth and she nodded. "Yes. The ceremony was lovely. They held the wedding on Jon's property. My daughter was a beautiful bride." These slightly stilted, staccato sentences were the best she could do.

"I wish them both my very best."

Grace knew he did. "Katie didn't make a sound the entire time."

Cliff slid his gaze past her. "Please thank Maryellen for the invitation."

Grace didn't realize her daughter had sent him one.

He removed his hat and held it with both hands. "I didn't attend for...obvious reasons."

Grace looked away.

"I didn't want to do anything to make you feel ill-at-ease," he explained. "This was a happy day for you, as well as for Maryellen and Jon. I thought it might be uncomfortable for us both if I showed up."

He was right, of course. "That was thoughtful of you," she murmured.

The silence stretched between them. Then, as if she'd suddenly remembered the reason she was at The Lighthouse, she said brightly, perhaps too brightly, "I understand you're going to be part of the Dog and Bachelor Auction."

Cliff shifted his weight. "I was approached but I declined."

"Why?" His name had been the first one mentioned. She wondered how long it would be before she could tolerate the thought of Cliff with another woman. Not anytime soon. The ache in the pit of her stomach told her that.

Was it her imagination or did his color heighten at her question? "I didn't see much point in making a bigger fool of myself than I normally do."

"But Cliff, it's for charity."

He shook his head, and privately Grace was pleased but she recognized that her response was purely selfish.

"I figured the committee would get higher bids on a younger man. I recommended Cal Washburn."

"Your trainer?" Grace had met Cliff's trainer on a couple of occasions and liked him, although he was an intense man who seemed to see straight through her. It was unsettling. As she recalled, he spoke with a slight stutter.

Cliff's mouth moved in the barest hint of a smile. "Cal wasn't exactly keen on the idea."

"But he's willing to volunteer?"

"He didn't say, but he's considering it."

"For someone who loves animals as much as you do…"

The smile that had just begun now appeared full force. "Are you trying to make me feel guilty so I'll agree to this, Grace Sherman?"

Grace smiled, too. "Shamelessly."

He shook his head again. "I'm too old."

"Your name came up right away. Apparently you've stirred up more interest than you realized."

"I suppose you were the one who threw my name in the hat?"

Cliff Harding was the last man she'd recommend, and all because of her own self-interest. "It wasn't me." She didn't like admitting it. "Margaret White was the one who suggested you."

He shrugged as if he didn't know the name.

"She works at the vet's office."

He gestured in a way that implied he might recognize her but he wasn't sure. "I've probably seen her then."

Silence again.

Grace couldn't imagine what was taking the hostess so long. She glanced into the dining areas, but the woman seemed to have disappeared after seating the two parties ahead of her.

"Olivia and Jack are home," she said abruptly, trying to make conversation. The silence was unbearable. She couldn't stand next to this man without being reminded of the high price her Internet indiscretion had cost her.

"So I understand."

Grace hadn't seen Olivia so happy, not in years. At the same time, she seemed to be having a little trouble adjusting to married life. A couple of recent phone calls had left Grace feeling there was some stress between Olivia and Jack, although Olivia hadn't been complaining.

"From what I hear, her ex has been visiting Cedar Cove quite a bit."

Grace froze. When Stan found out that Olivia had decided to marry Jack, he'd come to Grace, maudlin and sorry for himself. In a moment of loneliness, she'd agreed to go to dinner with him. It'd been another instance of bad judgment on her part. The last thing she wanted now was for Cliff to learn about that.

"I think Stan knows he made a mistake," Grace said tentatively. If Cliff knew about her dinner with Stan, he wasn't letting on. "People do that—make mistakes they later regret." Her eyes met his, pleading with him to realize how sorry she was. Silently she implored his forgiveness.

Cliff avoided eye contact. "Stan learned that his regrets came too late, didn't he?"

Cliff was telling Grace hers had, too.

The terrible silence was back.

"Charlotte told me what you did for her and her friends," Cliff said next, as if he couldn't bear the silence either.

Grace was furious every time she thought about Troy Davis arresting Charlotte and her group of elderly protestors. For heaven's sake, Ben Rhodes was a retired admiral! Troy should be ashamed of himself.

"Charlotte was trying to better our community. I felt the least we could do was support her efforts."

Cliff tried to hide his amusement by staring down at the carpet.

"What's so funny?"

"You," he said, raising his eyes. That little smile quivered on his mouth. "Remind me never to get on your bad side."

She *was* on his bad side, though, and the reminder instantly sobered her.

"Charlotte was thrilled with the community support and she credits you with that."

"I didn't do much."

"You spread the word."

Grace gave a careless shrug. "It wasn't much," she said again. She hadn't phoned Cliff, couldn't bring herself to do it, but in retrospect she wished she had.

As if reading her thoughts, he said. "I would've been there had I known."

The hostess reappeared just then. "Sorry to keep you waiting." She automatically reached for two menus.

Cliff looked to Grace and she saw the indecision in his eyes. It would mean the world to her if he asked her to join him for lunch. She held his gaze as long as she dared.

He stiffened, and his resolve had obviously returned. "Table for one," he said and walked away from Grace.

Nine

Roy McAfee hadn't been a private investigator for more than a few years, but he'd been in law enforcement his entire career. He was retired from the Seattle police force; after a few months, however, he'd thought he'd go stir-crazy sitting around the house doing nothing. Soon after his move to Cedar Cove, he'd hung out his shingle.

Retirement wasn't for him. Some men took to it, got involved in hobbies and interests. That kind of life was too predictable for Roy. Nothing lured him faster than a good mystery, and he didn't mean one between the covers of a book, either.

Few mysteries had intrigued him more than what was happening right here in Cedar Cove.

He sat down at his desk and reached for Bob Beldon's file. If he reviewed the facts as they'd unfolded, perhaps he'd pick up on something he'd overlooked before. He didn't think it was likely, but it wouldn't hurt to refresh his memory.

It all started the night a stranger had arrived on the doorstep of the Beldons' Thyme and Tide Bed and Breakfast. By morning he was dead.

Bob Beldon had notified Troy Davis, and the coroner came for the body. Soon afterward, it was discovered that the man had undergone extensive plastic surgery and carried false identification. For a few weeks there'd been a lot of speculation as to who he could be. Then silence—and things had died down for a while.

From the first, something about their guest had disturbed Beldon. Bob had experienced a recurring nightmare ever since his return from Vietnam. On occasion, he'd been known to sleepwalk.

Roy stopped reading and leaned back in his chair, recalling his initial thoughts when Beldon had asked him for help. Davis had questioned Beldon for the second or third time and Bob had considered contacting an attorney, but hadn't. Instead he'd come to Roy. Not too far into the conversation, Roy had realized that the other man was afraid he might have been responsible for the stranger's death.

Roy was quick to assure him otherwise, although he'd wondered the same thing in the beginning. But Maxwell's door had been locked from the inside and there'd been no sign of a struggle. The fact of the matter was that until recently, they couldn't be sure *what* had caused the other man's death. The autopsy had shown that his vital organs were in fine shape.

Not long before Bob's appointment with Roy, Grace Sherman had come to him. A year earlier, her husband, Dan, had gone missing. When Dan didn't return, Grace had sought out Roy to help locate her husband. But every lead had been a dead end.

Unanswered questions didn't sit well with him, although he'd shocked Grace with the few things he'd unearthed. One of them was the matter of thirteen thousand dollars Dan had somehow managed to keep from her. Grace had no idea where Dan could've found that kind of cash, which he'd apparently used to buy a trailer. He'd handed over his paycheck every Friday, regular as clockwork. Like most couples, they'd apparently lived month to month.

Then Dan's body had been discovered and with it a suicide note he'd left for Grace. In his last letter to his wife, Dan had described an incident that had taken place during the Vietnam war. He and three others had been separated from their squadron, and they'd stumbled into a village, which they feared was Viet-Cong controlled. Something had happened, and they'd started firing and before the smoke cleared they'd wiped out the entire village, according to Dan. They'd massacred men, women and children. The event had forever marked him. He couldn't live with himself any longer. Or so the letter had indicated.

Grace had been beside herself, not knowing what to do with the information. Roy was afraid he hadn't been much help. He couldn't really advise her; whatever became of these facts was her decision and hers alone.

Shortly afterward, Beldon had repeated the story Dan had written about in his suicide note. He'd mentioned Dan—they'd been two of the four men wandering through that jungle. He'd told Roy that afterward he and Dan hadn't seen each other for almost thirty years. When Bob had come home to Cedar Cove, they'd completely avoided each other.

It seemed too much of a coincidence that Roy would hear this grisly tale from two different people within such a short period of time. On a hunch, he'd gone to Troy Davis and suggested the sheriff check out the other two men who'd been with Dan and Beldon that day.

Sure enough, one of the men—Maxwell Russell—had been reported missing. The unidentified body had turned out to be his. Why he'd come to Cedar Cove and why he'd carried false identification couldn't be explained, though, any more than his death.

Not until later was it discovered that Max Russell had actually been murdered. Poisoned. There'd been evidence in the water bottle found in Russell's rented vehicle.

Once Russell had been identified, his daughter had visited Cedar Cove to collect her father's ashes. Davis had set up a meeting between Hannah and the Beldons, and as a favor to Bob, Roy had been at the house when she came by with the sheriff. Roy learned then that Hannah's mother had died in a car accident, the same one that had badly burned her father. The burns were the reason for Max's plastic surgery and quite possibly why Bob hadn't recognized his old friend.

The circumstances surrounding the car crash led Roy to believe it hadn't been an accident. He'd probably never be able to prove that. The accident report blamed Russell, but Hannah's father had insisted the steering had disconnected. There was nothing to verify his account.

The door to Roy's office opened and his wife walked in with a tray of coffee and freshly baked cookies. Corrie seemed intent on fattening him up, not that he was making much of a fuss. He certainly wasn't turning down homemade cookies.

"Let me guess what you're reading." That know-it-all glint shone in her eyes. "Could it possibly have something to do with the Beldon case?"

"Smarty pants," he said, grinning up at his wife.

"You're going to solve this if it takes the rest of your life, aren't you?"

Roy was close to the answer; he could feel it. He didn't know what he'd missed, if anything, but eventually his instincts would lead him where he had to go. All he needed was patience but that, unfortunately, seemed to be in short supply.

Corrie poured coffee into the mug, added cream and gave it to him. "I get suspicious when you're this quiet."

Roy leaned back in his chair, the mug in his hand. "I'm sifting all the facts through my brain."

"Do you still think the Beldons might be in some kind of danger?"

Roy didn't know how to answer. He shrugged. "Two of the four men are dead. One was murdered and the other committed suicide."

"What about the fourth man?"

"Apparently Davis has talked to Colonel Stewart Samuels. He told me he didn't think Samuels is involved—but who knows?"

Corrie looked down at the file and picked up the top sheet. "It says here he's up for a Congressional Committee assignment. If news of what happened in Nam got out, it could be disastrous to his career, don't you think?"

"True." Roy was well aware of that, but Samuels's military record was impeccable. And he lived on the East Coast. His whereabouts were accounted for during the time around Maxwell Russell's death. To be on the safe side, Roy had checked into the weeks shortly after Dan Sherman's disappearance, but Samuels had been in Europe, on a NATO assignment.

Corrie poured a second mug of coffee, black, and sat in the chair across from Roy's desk. "Linnette phoned this morning." Their twenty-five-year-old daughter had recently graduated as a physician's assistant.

Roy brightened. He adored Linnette and felt close to her. She was bright, beautiful and a source of pride. Her brother was another story. Roy and Mack were frequently at odds.

Linnette had done well in school and Mack, to put it bluntly, hadn't.

"She's applying for a job in Montana, of all places."

With the majority of physicians choosing to work in big cities, many small towns were left without medical professionals. Although she'd grown up in Seattle, Linnette had always been drawn to rural areas, so Roy wasn't surprised by her decision. She'd be filling a critical need and living in the sort of place she liked.

"Did you hear me, Roy? Montana?"

He wasn't sure what had upset Corrie so much. When Linnette had entered the medical program, they'd both known she wouldn't settle down in Seattle.

"I don't want her moving two states away!"

"Corrie—"

He wasn't allowed to finish.

"Linnette doesn't know a soul in Montana. There's plenty of small towns in Washington State that need physician's assistants."

Roy made an effort to hold back his amusement. "It's time to cut the apron strings, Mother."

Evidently not a successful effort. Corrie cast him an exasperated look. "This is our *daughter* we're talking about."

"Yes, dear."

"Don't use that tone of voice with me, Roy McAfee."

"Yes, dear."

"You're not funny. You know that, don't you?"

Roy resisted answering, although it was a struggle. "Where would you be comfortable having Linnette find a job?"

Corrie bit her bottom lip and didn't answer him.

"I have the feeling you'd like her to move right here to Cedar Cove," he joked.

At that his wife's head snapped up and her eyes widened. She set down her coffee, then leapt out of her chair, raced around the desk and kissed him soundly.

"What was that all about?" Roy asked, pleasantly surprised.

"It's because you, my wonderful husband, are much smarter than I give you credit for."

Bewildered, Roy watched her fly out of his office.

Ten

Grace thrust her hands decisively into her garden gloves, ready to head out to the back garden to plant Martha Washington geraniums. It wasn't the way she wanted to spend Friday evening, but she refused to mope around the house. Buttercup waited for her at the kitchen door, tail wagging.

"We'll plant these now and see what we can find at the Farmers' Market tomorrow morning. That sounds like a plan, doesn't it?" The fact that Grace had begun to carry on whole conversations with her golden retriever had to be a sign of how lonely she was.

The Farmers' Market had started the first Saturday of May, and although there were only a few homegrown vegetables available this early in the season, Grace enjoyed going there each week. She almost always ran into a few friends. One or both of her daughters was likely to show up, as well.

The phone rang, startling Grace. She pulled off her right-hand glove and reached for the wall-mounted receiver.

"Hello." She forced a cheerful note into her voice, hoping with all her heart that it was Cliff. He'd weighed heavily on her mind since their chance encounter at the restaurant earlier in the week. Her hope was that he'd been thinking about her, too.

"It's Stanley Lockhart, Grace. How are you?"

Grace felt an immediate stab of disappointment. "Hello, Stan." She kept her voice cool, not wanting to encourage Olivia's ex-husband. "I'm fine."

"Me, too. Listen, would you like to go to dinner tonight?"

She glanced over at the can of clam chowder that was slated to be her evening meal. Still, she preferred to eat soup alone over a three-course meal with Stan Lockhart.

"Sorry, I already have plans."

"You can't change them?" He didn't bother to hide his displeasure.

"No." How like Stan to expect her to alter her evening because *he* needed a dinner companion.

"What if I stop by later?" His enthusiasm was back. "It's important."

"That won't work, either." She couldn't imagine what he had to tell her that was so urgent. Grace sincerely hoped he got the message, but the subtle approach wasn't always successful with Stan. Inbred politeness prevented her from being rude and telling him outright that she wanted to avoid him.

The line went quiet as he contemplated her refusal. "I see," he said, sounding depressed. "Gracie, listen, I hate to be a pest but I'd like to talk to you if we can manage it."

Gracie. From the time she was in grade school, Grace had detested that nickname. She gritted her teeth. Stan hadn't been in touch since that one dinner. Now this. She couldn't even guess what he wanted.

"Why don't you tell me what you need to see me about?"

He hesitated. "It's better if I do it in person. Is there anyplace we can meet? Drinks? Coffee? You say when and where, and I'll be there." His tone took on a pleading quality. Grace knew that Stan's second marriage had recently failed; he still seemed to be shaken. She sympathized, but she didn't want to get involved with him.

"It won't take much of your time, I promise."

She hesitated, fearing that he'd hound her until she gave in. "I plan to be at the Farmers' Market in the morning."

"Perfect." He leaped on the suggestion. "I'll see you there. What time?"

"It opens at nine."

"Make it later. Nine's a little early for me."

So now he expected her to change her Saturday schedule to suit his? What sympathy she felt for him quickly evaporated. "I'll be there at nine, Stan. If I see you then, that'll be fine and if I don't, I don't."

"All right, all right. I'll get there as close to nine as I can. Just remember I'm coming over from Seattle."

She'd forgotten that, but decided it didn't matter; he was the one who considered it so important that they meet.

Saturday morning, Grace loaded Buttercup into her car and drove to the Farmers' Market. Buttercup was a well-behaved dog who loved being around people. The animal shelter had set up an adoption center in the market. Every Saturday the shelter brought down homeless cats and kittens; once a month, Grace took her turn running their booth, which was popular with children and adults alike.

Buttercup strained against her leash in a hurry to view the kittens, and Grace sharply commanded her to heel. She'd been thinking about adopting a cat herself, since she felt bad about leaving Buttercup alone all day and a cat would be company for her.

"Mom."

Grace turned to find Maryellen pushing Katie in her

stroller. "I wondered if I'd see you here." The back section of the stroller was already full.

Grace bent down and kissed Katie, who gurgled and waved her arms. Maryellen positively glowed with happiness, and Grace was delighted. Maryellen was more confident and relaxed, more carefree somehow, than she'd ever been. And—equally important—Katie would have the benefit of growing up with two parents.

"You're out and about early," she said conversationally.

"Jon's working and won't be home until late afternoon."

That meant her son-in-law was somewhere in western Washington photographing trees or birds. Or something.

"I love married life," Maryellen burst out. "Oh, Mom, how could I have been so foolish? Jon is a *wonderful* husband and father."

"Honey, I'm thrilled for you."

"I'd better get back to the house. I bought three pounds of fresh clams and I need to get them into the refrigerator."

"I didn't think you liked clams."

"I don't, but Jon does."

It seemed to Grace that if Jon indulged Maryellen, as she often claimed, her daughter catered to Jon just as much.

Grace bought a pound of clams herself and a jar of marmalade from Carol, the lady who sold homemade jelly. She glanced around and didn't see Stan and figured that was for the best. After strolling down the other aisles, she made her way toward the parking lot.

"Grace," Stan called, waving vigorously. He stood on the marina walkway. "Over here."

With Buttercup trotting beside her, Grace walked to the marina area.

"Seth suggested I sleep in his boat," Stan explained. He looked like he was ready for a tennis date, wearing white shorts and a white cable-knit sweater with a red-and-blue border.

"How's it going?" he asked, striking a relaxed pose, studying her as if he wasn't quite sure where to start.

"Good." She didn't elaborate, preferring to skip the small talk. "What can I do for you?"

His smile was strained. "You know, since Marge and I split and Olivia married that newsman, I've been at loose ends."

Grace didn't like the sound of this. She wondered if he was leading up to asking her out again, and if that was the case, she simply wasn't interested. She had to tell him before he went any further.

"Stan, I realize you must be lonely—"

"Lonely," he repeated and shook his head, a puzzled expression on his face. "No, no, it isn't that. I heard about the Dog and Bachelor Auction."

It took Grace a moment to put two and two together—and then she upbraided herself for being so dense.

"I'd like to volunteer to be one of the bachelors," Stan said eagerly.

She should've known. Stan had always enjoyed being the center of attention. The idea of women bidding on him... That would be the ultimate. In all fairness, he'd do a good job as someone's date for an evening, provided whoever won him knew what to expect.

"It's for charity, right?"

"To raise funds for the animal shelter," she told him.

"Well, you know how I feel about animals." He nodded sagely and she nodded, too, although she'd never noticed any particular liking for animals. "I'm willing to do my part," he went on, "and since I'm available, well, why not?" He cast her a practiced smile. "I imagine I could bring in a few dollars for a worthy cause."

"You don't live in Cedar Cove, remember?"

"You're right, but I did at one time and people here know me. Really, volunteering is the least I can do to help out, and I understand you're the person to talk to."

"Actually, two other women are gathering bachelors' names, but I'd be happy to suggest yours.

Stan grinned. "Thanks." Gratitude radiated from him. "I knew I could count on you."

Buttercup wagged her tail and looked up, anticipating Stan's attention. However the animal lover didn't so much as glance in the dog's direction.

"Have you already been to the market?" Stan asked.

The bags in her hands should be evidence that she had.

"How about if I buy you a cup of coffee and you can fill me in on the details about the auction? Maybe you could help me come up with a strategy."

"A...strategy?"

"Yeah, you know. How to get the ladies to bid on me. Just how many women are expected?"

"I don't know. The tickets haven't gone on sale yet."

"I just had a thought." He straightened, seeming pleased with himself. "I imagine that if the women in town knew exactly who was up for auction, the Animal Shelter would sell more tickets, right?"

Grace wasn't sure about that. "I suppose."

"What if you printed the names of the bachelors directly on the tickets? That might generate even more interest, don't you think?"

Stan was certainly full of ideas. "I'll make that suggestion, too," she murmured.

"Good." His eyes brightened and Grace could see he was quite taken with this bachelor auction. During their one and only dinner date, Stan had practically been crying in his soup, wallowing in self-pity. He'd regrouped fast enough, she thought wryly.

"I'll do what I can to make sure your name's added to the list," she said, eager to leave for home.

"Thanks, Gracie. I appreciate the fact that you're such a good friend."

Grace didn't consider herself that much of a friend, but she let the comment—and the nickname—slide. She directed Buttercup toward the parking lot behind the library, where she'd left her car.

"Nice seeing you again, Grace."

"You, too, Stan."

"Oh, Grace." He jogged the few steps over to her. "When you mention the idea about printing the names..."

"Yes?"

"Be sure and tell them it came from me."

"Of course." She ordered Buttercup to sit and dropped the leash for a moment so she could shift the heavy bags from one hand to the other.

"And seeing that it was my idea—" he paused and laughed playfully "—I think it's only fair that my name be one of those on the list."

"I'll make sure that's understood."

"Great." He grabbed her by the shoulders and briefly hugged her.

As if the thought had suddenly struck him, he asked, "Is there anything I can do for you?"

"Not a thing," she assured him, surprised he'd asked.

"You're sure." His hands lingered on her shoulders.

"Positive."

Just then, behind Stan, Grace caught sight of a male figure in a cowboy hat. *No, please no,* she prayed silently, *don't let that be Cliff.* Her one fear was that he'd heard about her dinner date with Stan and would think she was foolish enough to get involved in a relationship with Olivia's ex-husband.

Stan muttered something about needing to meet a friend. Before she could stop him, he gave her another quick hug and was gone.

Grace's gaze remained fixed on the man with the Stetson. When Stan freed her and left, he no longer obscured her line of vision. Sure enough, it was Cliff. He stood staring at her and even from this distance, she could see him frowning.

She wanted to tell him it wasn't the way it looked. She wasn't involved with Stan. Nor did she want to be.

After a suspended moment, Cliff acknowledged her by touching the brim of his hat. Almost immediately, he turned away.

She wanted to rush over to him and explain, but feared she'd do more harm than good. With a heavy heart, Grace headed home.

Eleven

The board meeting over, Bob Beldon left the community theater, situated just off Heron Street. He'd been active in theater since his high school days; drama class had been his favorite and he'd starred in a number of school productions. If not for Vietnam and everything that happened afterward, he might have considered a career on the stage.

These days he got what he called his "theater fix" by participating in local productions. Currently he served on the board of directors and the group had discussed a number of potential plays for next year's season.

Bob was still thinking about the merits of *Our Town* vs. *The Matchmaker* as he drove down the winding road that led to Cranberry Point. The name of the road always amused him. As far as he knew, there weren't any cranberries growing in the area. There were cranberry bogs in Washington State, but none in or near Cedar Cove. Whistling "Hello, Dolly," he continued driving, free for the moment of the burdens that oppressed him. This was what he loved about the theater. He could immerse himself in a role—in the whole process of staging a play—and put aside his troubles.

His friends in AA might call it denial, but the theater gave him a ready excuse.

Knowing Peggy, she'd have dinner started. Since it was Monday, he guessed she'd probably prepared either stuffed green peppers or her fabulous meat loaf. Either meal suited him just fine.

Still whistling as he pulled into the driveway, he found his wife watering her herb garden. Any time of year, her gardens were something to behold. The name of their B and B, Thyme and Tide, had come from both their proximity to the sea and Peggy's herbs. And of course the old saying about time and tide waiting for no man…

Speaking of time, without guests, they both had plenty of that on their hands. Money was tight, but Peggy was as skilled at budgeting as she was at every other household task. Bob couldn't imagine how they'd manage their money situation otherwise, but thankfully Peggy had it all figured out.

He drove into the garage and then walked out to greet Peggy. Garden hose in hand, she smiled as he approached. The sun was still high, although it was almost six o'clock. According to the calendar, summer would officially arrive later in the month, but as usual it would take another six weeks to show up in the Pacific Northwest. August and September were almost always spectacular. Bob had to remind himself of that in February and March, when the constant drizzle dragged down his normally good spirits.

"Hi, honey," Bob said. He stood at the edge of her garden. The fennel bulbs were flowering, and the parsley and cilantro were just peeking up from the dark, rich soil. "What's for dinner?"

"Meat loaf. How'd the meeting go?"

"Just great." He couldn't contain his smile.

"What's that grin about? Are you keeping something from me?" She jokingly aimed the hose in his direction.

"Not a thing." He chuckled, raising both hands in a gesture of surrender. "I was just thinking we'd probably have meat loaf tonight, is all."

Peggy walked over to the side of the house and turned off the water. "I'm about finished here."

Bob nodded.

"If you've got a moment, I'd like to talk."

He hesitated. When Peggy asked to speak to him in that formal way, it generally wasn't about anything pleasant.

"Is something wrong?"

"Not really."

She seemed rather closemouthed about it, which wasn't good. Now that he studied her, Bob realized he should have seen the signs earlier. Peggy was a talker, a natural conversationalist. She could—and did—talk to anyone about anything. Many of their guests were repeat customers Peggy now counted as friends.

Bob followed her into the mudroom off the kitchen. Peggy changed out of her rubber shoes and methodically put her gardening supplies on the shelf. The contrast between her highly organized work areas and his—well, sometimes it embarrassed him a little. He could be such a slob, he thought ruefully, and yet Peggy was so tolerant of his carelessness, for which he could only be grateful.

"What's going on?" he asked as they entered the kitchen.

Peggy automatically poured them each a cup of tea and set the mugs on the table. "I got a phone call from Hannah Russell this afternoon."

Bob felt the sudden need to sit down. He yanked out the chair and sat, reaching for his tea.

"I'm so worried," Peggy said, sitting across from him.

That got Bob's attention. "About what?" They'd been caught up in this nightmare for so long that he'd grown accustomed to the tension. It had become part of his reality and there was nothing to do but stand firm in the face of each new shock.

"Hannah," Peggy continued as if it should be obvious. "Her mother and father are both gone. She's like a lost soul. She's foundering, Bob." She paused for a moment. "I talked to Hollie today, and she said that in her opinion, Hannah needs a sense of security. I agree with her."

"I suppose that's only natural when someone loses both parents in such a short time." Bob envied the closeness between his wife and daughter. He knew that during his drinking years, he'd lost an important part of his children's lives.

Peggy's hands tightened around her mug. "Hannah phoned to thank me for my letter."

Bob had forgotten that Peggy had written the girl. It was just the sort of thoughtful thing she'd do.

"She wanted to tell me she's moving."

"Where?"

"That's just it," Peggy said, and her face darkened with concern. "She doesn't know. She's sold everything she can. Hollie says that Hannah's running away from her pain—that she'll carry it with her wherever she goes."

Bob nodded. "Hollie's right. I'm not sure leaving California's a good idea for Hannah. She might regret it later, selling things she'll wish she'd kept."

"That's what I told her, but she said it was too late. What she didn't sell she gave away."

Bob's own concern grew. His unease didn't revolve solely around Hannah, either. She might inadvertently have sold something that would help solve this mystery.

"That's not all," Peggy said. "I got the impression that

she's going to travel aimlessly around the country until she finds a place that…feels comfortable. That's how she put it."

Bob sat back in his chair and mulled this over. The young woman was vulnerable. Wandering from place to place wasn't what he'd want for his own daughter. "What about family? Surely she's got aunts and uncles and cousins?"

"Apparently she doesn't have anyone close."

"I see." Bob sipped his tea.

"I asked her to call us from time to time."

"Good."

"But I don't know if she will. She sounded so confused."

Bob considered what he knew about Hannah for a moment and felt a pang of sympathy. "Did you ask if there's a way for us to keep in touch with her?"

Peggy nodded. "She has a cell phone and she gave me the number. The thing is, Bob, how involved do we want to get in her life?" Her gaze held his and he understood his wife's question. She felt a certain responsibility to Hannah. After all, it was in their home that her father had died. And yet—did they want to take on the young woman's problems? That could be more than he and Peggy were really equipped to handle.

"I don't know," he admitted.

"Me neither."

"So, what do you think we should do?" Bob asked. He trusted Peggy's intuition. Hannah aside, Max Russell's death was an uncomfortable subject. It brought up too many unpleasant memories for him and his wife, memories Bob preferred to leave buried.

"I'm not sure, but I do feel badly for her."

Bob agreed. It was hard enough succeeding in the world *with* parents, and usually much harder without. His own children had faltered, but with love and patience had eventually found their way. No thanks to the example he'd set in their early years, Bob admitted. Perhaps this opportunity to help Hannah was also a chance to make up for his missteps twenty-five years ago.

"We should phone her at least once a week," he said decisively. It didn't mean they had to become parent-substitutes, just friends....

Peggy nodded slowly. "That would help, I think," she concurred. "Then Hannah will know there are two people in the world who care about her."

"Right." Bob felt better having made the decision. This was a positive thing to do and just might help him deal with everything that was happening in his own fragile world.

Twelve

Olivia Lockhart Griffin hurried home from the courthouse. Jack had phoned earlier in the day and said he'd be late for dinner. After an idyllic but all-too-brief Hawaiian honeymoon, they'd both been inundated with work. Jack had put in late hours all week and been at the office nearly nonstop the entire weekend. Olivia hated having him gone such long hours, but when he was home, it was lovely. She hesitated—for the most part, it was lovely. Naturally, there were a few adjustments they each had to make, and some of those were more difficult than she would have expected.

After living for almost twenty years without a husband, Olivia was surprised at how easily she'd slipped back into the habit of sharing her life with a man. For the first time since her youngest son had left the family home, she put real effort into creating meals. She sat at the kitchen table now, leafing through a recently purchased cookbook, intent on luring Jack home with a healthy meal made just for him. One regular argument she had with her husband concerned his poor eating habits. Jack tended to grab whatever was quick and easy. Olivia frequently told him his diet contained far too many carbohydrates and fats to maintain a healthy lifestyle; he just as frequently shrugged off her concern.

She studied the recipes. Tofu stir fry? Probably not, but she'd try it later on. The telephone rang, and thinking it might be Jack, she got up to reach for the receiver.

"Hello," she said cheerfully.

"Howdy, little sister."

"Will!" Her brother lived in Atlanta. It had been a real disappointment to her that he hadn't made it to Cedar Cove for her wedding. When she'd called to tell him she'd decided to marry Jack, she'd hoped he'd be able to share her special day. Apparently she'd caught him off guard, because he'd hesitated and then stuttered a weak excuse. She couldn't recall what it was just now, but at the time she'd thought something was wrong, although she couldn't figure out what it might be. Perhaps he wasn't getting along with Georgia, her sister-in-law, or maybe he had problems at work....

"So how's the happy bride?" Will asked, echoing her cheerful tone.

Olivia leaned against the kitchen wall and sighed. "Wonderful. Oh, Will, I don't know why I waited so long. Jack is so good for me."

She loved her husband's spontaneity. Her idea of a honeymoon was to laze on the beach and catch up on her reading. Jack wouldn't hear of it. Every day he had plans for them to go and see and do. Olivia wouldn't have seen any of what Hawaii had to offer if Jack hadn't coaxed her into visiting the tourist sights and activities. The nights were the best. After dinner, they danced under the stars, swam in the fabulous hotel pool and made love until they were spent.

"You sound happy."

"I am."

"I'm glad." He seemed genuinely pleased for her. "On another subject, have you talked to Mom lately?"

"Of course." Charlotte made routine visits to Olivia's courtroom, and usually brought her knitting, and often a friend or two from the Senior Center so she could brag about her daughter the judge. Her mother had shown up alone on Friday afternoon, and they'd chatted afterward, but now that Olivia thought about it, Charlotte had been mysteriously absent all week.

"What did she have to say?"

"Say? Mom?" Olivia repeated. "Well, not much, really. She did tell me that the seniors triumphed in court while I was away. Which I heard from plenty of other sources—trust me. But she's had such strong community support that she's finally got the ear of the mayor."

"Did she mention Ben Rhodes?"

"Her latest boyfriend?" Olivia teased. Her mother had spoken about Ben a number of times, but she'd never said anything out of the ordinary. Ben was retired navy, a widower, and Olivia had assumed he was simply a new addition to her crowd of friends. Charlotte had a way of collecting lost souls.

"Exactly what do you know about Ben?" her brother pressed.

"Not a lot. Why do you ask?" Olivia mulled over what she'd heard about him and realized she didn't really know all that much. "I understand he moved to the area a couple of years ago. I remember Mom saying that Ben's a great bridge player. He apparently spends most days at the Senior Center."

"What about his claims to be a retired navy admiral?"

Claims? Interesting choice of word. Their mother had brought this up a number of times. "I gather Ben served in the navy."

"So he says. Has anyone checked into that?"

"Of course not." Olivia was astonished by the suspicion in her brother's voice. "Why should we?"

"Because, my naive little sister, I don't think either of us has fully grasped what's happening to our mother."

Olivia frowned. "Why do you say that?"

Will sighed heavily. "I phoned Mom twice while you were in Hawaii and all she could talk about was Ben this and Ben that. She hardly mentioned anything or anyone else. It got me thinking that we need to find out what we can about this man who's taking up so much of our mother's time."

Now that her brother had alerted her, it occurred to Olivia that their mother *had* been seeing a great deal of Ben, especially lately. "I don't think that's a bad thing," she felt obliged to say. Ben and her mother had become good friends. Over the years, Charlotte had grown fond of a number of men, including one retired actor in the local nursing home. Because of a stroke, Tom Harding had been unable to speak, but her mother had managed to carry on long conversations with him. Meeting Tom had led to the advent of Cliff Harding in their lives, and Charlotte was friendly with him, too. And now Ben. He was new to Cedar Cove and obviously feeling a bit lost. Frankly, Olivia couldn't see any harm in the friendship.

"I don't think there's any need for alarm…yet," Will agreed with a certain reluctance, "but as I said, how much do we really know about this man?"

"Well…"

"Just what he tells us, right?"

"Well…yes." The doubts Will raised made Olivia's suspicions begin to mount. Caught up in the events of her own life, she hadn't paid nearly enough attention to their mother.

"No one's heard of Ben until the last year or two, am I right?"

"Yes," she murmured. "He moved into the area and started showing up at the Senior Center."

"No family."

"Not here." Olivia briefly recalled Ben talking about children in other parts of the country, but nowhere in Washington State.

"Don't you find that mildly suspicious?"

Olivia considered the question. "Not really."

"Then maybe you should."

She was feeling worried now but not ready to acknowledge it to Will.

"A strange man, without any connection to Cedar Cove, moves into the area. Then he seeks out our mother and before we know it, the two of them are thick as thieves."

"I've met Ben," Olivia inserted. "He's a perfect gentleman."

"Wasn't it Ben who talked Mom into this ridiculous protest rally? The man's responsible for getting our mother arrested and you think he's a good influence?"

That gave Olivia pause. "I think Mom was as much to blame for what happened as Ben."

"I wouldn't be too sure of that."

"Why not?"

"You've been on your honeymoon, Olivia. You're in love and that's great—I couldn't be more pleased for you—but you're looking at the world through rose-colored glasses."

What he said was true…to a point. "What's that got to do with anything?"

"I'm afraid," her brother said slowly, "that Mom might be at risk. How would you feel if some man swindled her out of her life savings?"

"Ben wouldn't do that!"

"Are you sure, Olivia? Would you stake our mother's financial future on your feelings?"

She hesitated. Sitting on the judge's bench, she'd seen far too much of the pain one person could inflict on another. Her hand tightened around the receiver at the idea of anyone taking advantage of her mother.

"You're confident Ben's a stand-up kind of guy?" her brother said, his voice edged with suspicion. "Enough to risk Mom's future?"

"No," Olivia admitted reluctantly.

Will leaped on her answer. "That's what I thought. It's up to you, little sister."

"What's up to me?"

"To check out this Ben Rhodes. I've heard about men like him who prey on widows. I'm sure you've seen the same TV shows I have. We can't be too careful. I'm not there to protect Mom, but you are—and you must. We wouldn't forgive ourselves if we'd stood by and did nothing while a stranger ripped her off."

Olivia didn't know what to say. Will had read so much more into this relationship than she had. He was correct about one thing, though; she'd been preoccupied with her own life.

"What should I do?" she asked.

"Look into his background," Will answered promptly.

"But..." Olivia's mind whirled. "Mom would find out if I started making inquiries about Ben and she'd be furious."

"Then hire someone."

Going behind her mother's back went against her sense of rightness and propriety. "I'd feel better if we discussed this whole thing with Mom first."

"No way." Her brother was adamant. "She'd accuse us of interfering in her life."

"Aren't we?" Olivia didn't think they should dismiss the obvious.

"Yes, but it's for her own good. Don't do it yourself. This investigation should be handled by a professional."

Olivia was of two minds on the matter. Instinct told her she could trust Ben, but at the same time her brother was right. They knew next to nothing about this man who'd become so important to their mother.

"Do you know a private investigator?" Will asked.

"I do. Roy McAfee is a retired Seattle detective. He's good."

"Hire him and don't put it off, Olivia. This could be important."

She sighed unhappily. "All right. I'll talk to Roy."

"Good." Her brother sounded as if a burden had been lifted from his shoulders. "So how's everyone in good ol' Cedar Cove these days?" he asked, the change in his mood immediate.

"Just fine."

"How's Grace?"

Funny he should ask about her friend. "She's fine, too."

"Do you still get together every week?"

"Wednesdays for aerobics class, but that's about it. I don't see her as much as I'd like."

"How come?"

Again Olivia wondered at his sudden interest in Grace. "She's pretty involved with the Dog and Bachelor Auction, which is happening next month. Why all the questions?"

"No reason. It's just that I know you're such good friends."

Funny he didn't ask about Justine and Seth or James and Selina. She would've savored the opportunity to brag about her grandchildren.

"We e-mailed each other for a while," Will confessed.

Grace had never mentioned that to Olivia. "Really?"

"It was no big deal—we're just friends."

The conversation stopped and started after that, with a few more questions about Grace, until finally he ended it. Olivia returned to her dinner plans. Not until she was putting the finishing touches on the grilled Pacific salmon, wild rice and steamed asparagus did it hit her. Her brother was obviously concerned about their mother's relationship with Ben and perhaps rightly so; that remained to be seen. But he had another agenda. And it had to do with Grace.

He seemed awfully curious about her, Olivia mused. More than once he'd drawn the conversation back to her friend, asking her what Grace was up to and whether she was seeing anyone. If they'd been e-mailing each other, then wouldn't he know how Grace was doing?

Just as she started to put a few ideas together—very tentatively—the back door opened and in walked Jack. "You're looking thoughtful," he observed, standing in the doorway off the kitchen.

"Jack!" Not hesitating, she flew into her husband's arms and spread eager kisses across his face.

Jack locked his hands at the small of her back, smiling down on her. "A husband could get accustomed to this sort of reception." He kissed her soundly in return.

Olivia rested her head against his shoulder and sighed, loving the comfort of Jack's arms around her. "I just had the most…disconcerting conversation with my brother."

"What about?"

Olivia told him but excluded the portion about Will's repeated questions regarding Grace.

"Are you going to contact Roy?" Jack asked when she'd finished.

"I suppose I should. Will was concerned and although I think he's overreacting, it can't hurt to know for sure. I guess there's always a chance that Ben's a con man. The clever ones usually have the most convincing aliases. But the truth of it is, I hate the thought of Mom finding out what we've done."

Jack didn't say anything for a long moment. "You can trust Roy not to let any of this out," he finally said.

"I realize that."

Jack shrugged. "Personally, I don't think having Ben investigated is all that necessary."

"Me neither," she concurred, but she'd decided to do it—if only to reassure her brother.

After dinner Olivia and Jack cuddled in front of the television for a repeat episode of *Law & Order.* Olivia had seen this particular show earlier in the year, although Jack hadn't. She didn't object to watching a rerun, but she found herself returning to the conversation with her brother.

Will had talked about e-mailing Grace. Then there was all his interest in what she was doing, whom she was seeing. Although he hadn't actually said anything, she'd sensed Will's disapproval of Grace's participation in the Dog and Bachelor Auction.

A few months ago, Grace had gotten involved in an Internet relationship with a married man. Her friend had been duped, lied to and strung along. Now, with a growing sense of horror, Olivia wondered if that man could have been her brother. Grace's heart was broken after the end of her romance with Cliff Harding, and that was when she'd told Olivia about the other relationship, accepting the blame for her role in this fiasco. Grace had never revealed the name of the married man. At the time Olivia had assumed it didn't matter, that she wouldn't have known who it was, anyway.

Now she wondered. Could it possibly have been Will?

She tried to dismiss the thought. No, of course not! Her

brother would never do anything so underhanded. And if he had, surely Grace would have told her. But if what Olivia suspected was true, it explained Will's weak excuse about not being able to attend her wedding.

"Something on your mind?" Jack asked during a commercial break. His mouth was close to her ear and he took advantage of her closeness to kiss the side of her neck.

"Hmm." Olivia closed her eyes and reveled in his attention.

"This whole thing with your mother and Ben is worrying you, isn't it?"

"Not really," she muttered. She debated mentioning her suspicions about Grace and her brother, but changed her mind. If she said anything, it would be to Grace—but only after she'd had time to sort through the facts as she knew them. Until then, it would be better to say nothing, not to Jack and not to anyone else.

"Good," Jack whispered, tucking his arms more securely around her. "I'd hate to have anything disrupt our television viewing."

Smiling to herself, Olivia poked him in the ribs with her elbow. She'd been doing a lot of smiling since she'd married Jack Griffin, and she didn't think that would change anytime soon.

Thirteen

Cecilia pushed the grocery cart lethargically through the commissary's aisles. She'd been so excited about having her husband home after six months' deployment, counting the days until Ian would be with her again. She'd made elaborate plans for his homecoming and wanted their reunion to be like a second honeymoon. She'd prayed her husband would be as eager to start their family as she was. Only he hadn't been, and now it seemed nothing had gone the way she'd hoped.

"Hey, Cecilia."

At the sound of her name, Cecilia turned to find Cathy Lackey wheeling her grocery cart down the aisle toward her. "I thought that was you," Cathy said.

Cecilia managed a token smile. "How's it going?"

"Great. I left father and son to bond. I'm taking my own sweet time shopping because, frankly, I could use the break. Where's Ian?"

"Home." Cecilia couldn't disguise her misery. "Oh, Cathy, things just aren't working out between us."

"What do you mean?"

Cecilia reached inside her purse for a tissue, humiliated about breaking down in the cereal aisle where anyone might see her.

Cathy glanced over her shoulder. "Listen, let's meet in half an hour at Starbucks. Does that work for you?"

Cecilia nodded. Cathy was the one person in the world she could talk to about her most private concerns. Cathy would understand better than most people, and Cecilia realized she needed her friends more than ever.

Sure enough, Cathy was waiting for her at Starbucks. She was on the patio and had already bought them each a cup of coffee. Because the day was warm and sunny, most of the customers were sitting outside.

"All right, tell me what's happening," Cathy said when Cecilia slid into the chair across from her.

Cecilia picked up her coffee and hung her head, staring at the tabletop. "This homecoming is a complete disaster."

"How do you mean?"

"In the four weeks Ian's been home, we've barely made love." She was embarrassed to be talking about the intimate details of her marriage, even to Cathy, but she could no longer hide her unhappiness. Ian made excuses to stay away from her and it was killing her.

Cecilia looked up to see her friend frowning.

"What's wrong?"

Cecilia bit her lip to keep from crying. "I assumed Ian would want to start our family, but he doesn't. He wants me back on birth control before we make love on a regular basis."

"Are you?"

"Not yet, but my period's due soon. We've used protection, but Ian is adamant—I'm supposed to go back on the pill. Until then it's like I'm his sister. He won't even look at me and I hate it."

"He doesn't want a baby?"

Cecilia shook her head. "Every time I try to mention it, he changes the subject."

Cathy nodded sympathetically.

"Last week, when I refused to let him sidetrack me, he blew up and said he wasn't ready to be a father yet. I asked him when he would be ready and do you know what he said?" She didn't wait for her friend to respond. "Ian said he didn't think he'd ever be ready." Cecilia covered her face with both hands, distraught and weepy.

Cathy placed her hand on Cecilia's forearm. "Do you remember when I told you that I miscarried twice before Andy?"

Cecilia lowered her hands and nodded. She hated being so emotional, but she couldn't help it. She'd created a million romantic fantasies centered on their reunion and everything had gone wrong. Nothing she said or did seemed to work.

"After I miscarried the second time, I was afraid it was the end of my love life. It was as if Andrew had completely lost interest in me as his wife."

Cecilia had trouble believing it. "Andrew?"

Cathy's eyes filled with tears. "The miscarriages affected my husband in ways I didn't understand. I was so wrapped up in me that I didn't see what losing the pregnancies had done to Andrew. He was afraid to make love to me, afraid I'd get pregnant again—afraid I'd suffer again. I was convinced he didn't want me because I couldn't carry his child. And that wasn't it at all." Cathy paused and swallowed visibly. "Our minds play crazy games with us, don't they?"

Cecilia wasn't sure that applied to her situation. Ian was far more vocal about his feelings than Andrew had been, from the sound of it. Ian and Cecilia had worked hard on their communication skills and had learned to be more straightforward in expressing their needs and feelings.

Now this.

"What about that little outfit you bought from the Victoria's Secret catalog?" Cathy asked, lowering her voice to a whisper. "The one you sent him..."

Cecilia shrugged uncomfortably. "I haven't even put it on. Ian was in too much of a hurry the first night and then, well...he just hasn't been all that interested since."

Cathy laughed. "Oh, he's interested, all right, but he's also afraid. If he's in a bad temper..."

"He is," Cecilia confirmed. She couldn't remember her husband ever being as moody as he'd been this last month.

"You know why, don't you," Cathy said, smiling now. "He's frustrated."

"There's no reason for him to be frustrated. I'm ready, willing and able," Cecilia muttered irritably.

"Then let him know that."

"You think?" She hated to feel this hopeful after being disappointed again and again.

Cathy smiled. "Why don't you give that sexy little outfit a try and find out for yourself?"

The question stayed with Cecilia as she drove home, the truck filled with groceries. Her husband was working in the garage attached to their duplex when she returned. He was messing around with an old motorcycle a friend had given him, the engine disassembled and various parts laid out on a tarp. Cecilia had forgotten they even had the thing. Wordlessly he helped her unload the groceries and then went back to whatever he was doing that involved so much of his concentration. She didn't disturb him.

At six, she called Ian inside for dinner. She'd made lasagna, one of his favorite dishes, and he praised her efforts. Cecilia glowed at his approval and waited until Ian was in bed reading before she took a long, hot shower. Heart pounding, she donned the sexy black outfit.

As well as she could, she checked her reflection in the bathroom mirror. With steam from her shower fogging up the view, it was hard to tell if she looked sexy. To be on the safe side, she liberally doused perfume on her wrists and behind both ears.

If her heart was beating hard earlier, it didn't compare with the frantic explosion going on inside her chest when she opened the bathroom door and posed there, one arm raised and resting against the doorframe.

Ian sat in bed reading. His bedside lamp cast a warm glow about the room. He seemed to be deeply involved in his novel and for a moment didn't pay her any heed. When he did happen to glance up to see her standing in the doorway, his mouth fell open.

Her husband stared at her long and hard. Seconds later the book fell out of his hands and toppled onto the carpet. He didn't bother to pick it up. "Cecilia?"

"Yes?" she whispered.

"What exactly are you doing?"

"What do you think?"

"This isn't amusing." He sat up straighter, sliding as far against the headboard as possible, as if he wanted to escape her. Yet at the same time, his gaze didn't waver from hers. His eyes seemed twice their normal size and that encouraged her.

Taking two steps toward her husband, she slowly removed the sheer black dressing gown. It took her a bit of time and she loved the way her husband swallowed convulsively as he watched.

"You like it?" She kept her voice low and sexy.

Ian didn't answer.

"I think you do," she purred seductively, unfastening the bra-style top—which revealed more than it concealed.

Ian groaned and closed his eyes. Knowing she was about to succeed she leaned over him and turned off the light. The instant she was close, he reached for her and pulled her down onto the bed.

Cecilia slipped her arms around his neck and their mouths joined in an urgent kiss. They were twisting against each other, unable to give enough or take enough. It was as though Ian had held back every bit of passion he felt for her until that moment. Their kisses grew even wilder, even fiercer. Cecilia relished his passion, which fed her own.

Moaning, she showed him in every way she knew how that she loved him and needed him and had desperately missed his touch. Ian lowered himself onto her and after the necessary adjustments to his clothing, entered her quickly. Cecilia was ready, more than ready. At their joining, they both cried out at the pure sensation, the overwhelming pleasure.

They fell asleep in each other's arms, sated and content. Once in the night, Ian woke her again and she turned willingly into his embrace. His need was as intense as it had been earlier. With their fingers locked together, he kissed Cecilia, then held her arms above her head as he sank into her. She whimpered at the beauty of their lovemaking, exulted in her husband and cried out when she reached her own fulfillment.

In the morning it was a different story. Cecilia woke to find Ian sitting on the edge of the bed with his back to her. "You did that on purpose," he said gruffly when he realized she was awake.

Cecilia sat up, clutching the sheet to her bare breasts. "Yes." She wasn't going to lie to him.

"You seduced me."

"If you want to look at it like that. I wanted my husband to make love to me." She leaned over and caressed his back with her fingertips. "I've missed you, Ian."

He stood rather than endure her touch. "You want a baby and because I don't, you took matters into your own hands."

On that point he was wrong. "I didn't stop you from using protection, Ian."

"You didn't remind me, either."

"Is that my job or yours?" she asked, keeping her voice as level as she could make it.

Her husband whirled around and glared at her. "You made sure I forgot all about it!"

Despite the seriousness of their conversation, Cecilia smiled. "You're right, I didn't remind you. But at the time I had other things on my mind."

"A baby," he said angrily, accusing her with his eyes.

"Well, yes," she admitted. "But you know that."

Ian's eyes narrowed. "I just hope to God you don't get pregnant, Cecilia."

"That's n-not fair," she stammered, shocked by his vehemence.

"Fair or not, I don't know how I'm going to feel about any child conceived out of your deception."

With that, he stormed out of the bedroom.

Fourteen

Roy McAfee waited until late afternoon to call Hannah Russell. He'd tried earlier and learned the young woman's phone had been disconnected. When he mentioned that to Beldon, Bob had supplied him with Hannah's cell number. Apparently, for whatever reason, she'd kept in touch with the Beldons.

He dialed, leaning back in his office chair.

"Hello?" a tentative voice answered.

"Hannah?"

"Yes, this is Hannah Russell." Her response was a bit more confident now. "Who's this?"

"Roy McAfee from Cedar Cove. We met at the Beldons' Bed and Breakfast when you came to collect your father's ashes."

She hesitated again as if she was having trouble placing him. "I'm sorry, I don't recall meeting you."

Roy could understand her lapse in memory. It had been a traumatic visit for the young woman. He didn't envy her the task of dealing with her father's death and, more than that, the mystery surrounding it.

"I'm a private detective. I was at the house during your visit," he said.

"Oh, yes, I remember now. The Beldons hired you to find out what you could about my father's murder."

"That's correct."

Roy felt her warm up a bit. "What can I do for you?" she asked.

He straightened and glanced down at his list of questions. "Is this a convenient time to talk?"

"Yes, I'm not doing much of anything at the moment."

"Where are you?"

"In Oregon. I suppose the Beldons told you I've sold everything. I decided to move. The problem is, I'm not sure where I'm moving. I suppose that sounds odd. I loaded my car with everything that was important to me and took off. I'm hoping to make a fresh start somewhere."

"Bob did say something along those lines." Roy sympathized with the girl's need to escape the horrors of the past year or two. Briefly he wondered about friends and acquaintances but didn't want to distract her with personal questions when there were other, more pressing ones.

"I'd like to ask you about your father."

A short silence followed. "All right. I'm not sure what I can tell you, though."

"You can help me verify some facts."

"I'll try, but I'm as much in the dark about this as everyone else. I didn't even know he was going to Cedar Cove, let alone why. Then when he died like that…" She choked up for a moment. "That was a shock but learning he was murdered—that was so much worse. I don't know anyone who'd want my father dead."

"I appreciate your willingness to help. I promise I'll do everything in my power to find out who did this."

"Thank you," she said, her voice quavering with emotion.

While doing investigative work, Roy had discovered that family members often held crucial answers but were unaware of it. The key to solving a mystery was asking the right questions.

"What would you like to know?" Hannah murmured, recovering quickly.

"First, tell me about your father's relationship with Stewart Samuels."

Again there was a pause, as though she required time to formulate her thoughts. "Really, there's not much to tell. I never heard my father mention his name until after the car accident. Dad was badly burned and was in the hospital for quite a while. His medical insurance was limited. When it became obvious that he was going to require extensive plastic surgery, he asked me to get in touch with Colonel Samuels. Dad said Colonel Samuels owed him, but he didn't say why."

Roy made a notation indicating when Russell had contacted Samuels. He'd assumed the two men had been in communication since Vietnam, but apparently not.

"What were you supposed to ask the colonel?"

"Dad seemed to think Colonel Samuels would be able to help him get into a veterans' hospital. Which he did."

"How responsive was Colonel Samuels to your call?"

"He was…helpful." It seemed she was about to add something, but changed her mind. He'd question her later about her impression of Samuels; he had more important matters to discuss first.

"Was there anyone else your father asked you to contact?"

"No one. My father was a private person. I don't think he would've gone to Colonel Samuels if there'd been any other way."

"Did your father ever explain why he felt Colonel Samuels owed him?"

"No. He never said."

Roy made another note.

"Did you ever personally meet Samuels?" Roy asked.

"No, but I spoke to him by telephone a number of times. He was able to get my father into the local veterans' hospital. The sad part is that it was all for nothing...." She let the rest fade.

Roy was afraid she was about to dissolve into tears, but she managed to keep her composure.

"The thing is..."

"Yes," Roy encouraged when she paused.

"I don't think Colonel Samuels helped willingly. I probably shouldn't even be saying this, but whenever Dad talked to the colonel, he was upset afterward. I remember once the nurse had to give him a sedative. I was just grateful Dad would receive the necessary medical treatment."

This was interesting. Perhaps Samuels wasn't everything Roy had been led to believe. Sheriff Davis felt that Samuels wasn't involved in the murder, and Roy had confidence in his instincts, but things weren't adding up the way they should.

"Anything else you can remember about Samuels and your father?" he asked.

"Not really... They only spoke a few times, which was probably for the best, seeing the effect he had on my father. I think—no, wait." She stopped abruptly. "I do remember something. It was several months after Dad was released from the hospital. Colonel Samuels phoned the house late one afternoon. Dad took the call and immediately lowered his voice. I realized he didn't want me listening in, so I made an excuse to leave the room." She seemed to be reviewing her memories. "I went into the kitchen, but I could still hear part of the conversation."

"What do you remember?"

"I found it all rather odd. I don't know if this is any help, but as I remember it, Dad said to Colonel Samuels that he'd never told anyone. I'm not sure *what* he never told, but my father was very firm about this secret being safe with him." She finished in a rush. "I'm just wondering if I heard him correctly," she murmured. "I tried to forget it because it wasn't for my ears, if you know what I mean."

"I do." And Roy also had a very good idea what Russell had been talking about. Apparently he hadn't discussed the incident in Vietnam with his daughter. It wasn't Roy's job to enlighten her about her father's past.

"Describe the last time you saw your father."

"Alive, you mean?" Her voice rocked with emotion. "This is all so strange. Dad and I talked every day, and I was sure he'd tell me about any trips. He didn't go out a lot after the accident, and when he did he always wore a hat. He said he didn't want people staring at him, but really, it wasn't necessary. The surgery was extremely successful. Anyway, for Dad just to leave and not mention his plans was unusual.

"I happened to stop by the house to check on him and was surprised to see he had a suitcase packed. I asked him where he was going, but all he said was that he'd made arrangements to be away for a few days. I asked again, but..."

"He still wouldn't tell you?"

"No. Anytime I had a question he didn't want to answer, he pretended not to hear me."

"Can you remember what he took with him?"

"I...I didn't see him drive off, so I don't. He had the one suitcase. That much I know. And his coat and hat, of course. Like I said, he was self-conscious about his scars."

"I'm sure he must have been," Roy concurred, although as she'd said, the plastic surgeon had done a masterful job.

At first glance, one would hardly have known that Russell had undergone extensive surgery.

"That's about it."

Roy jotted down a few more notes.

"Is there anything else?" she asked.

He did have other questions, but Roy wanted to mull over what he'd learned. "Not now. Would it be all right if I called you again sometime?"

"Of course." There was a silence. "I find it hard to accept that anyone would want my father dead. Even now, it's difficult to believe he isn't here."

"I'm sorry, Hannah, for your loss," he said, meaning it. "Thank you for your help."

"If you need any further information, please call."

"I will."

The conversation over, Roy hung up the phone and tilted back in his chair, closing his eyes.

Something was still missing here.

Fifteen

"I swear this class is going to kill me one day," Grace muttered breathlessly as Olivia led the way into the dressing room. Grace used the towel draped around her neck to wipe the sweat off her face. "I'm thinking," she continued, slumping down on the locker-room bench, "that we could just meet for dinner on Wednesday nights and give up this whole aerobics nightmare."

"Come on, Grace, you love our class."

"Wrong, I love to have finished our aerobics class. It's the jumping up and down part that's a drag."

Olivia laughed out loud. It'd been the same whiny song for the last four years. Grace complained constantly about the class but Olivia was convinced that her friend actually enjoyed it. Grace just didn't know she enjoyed it. However, she was the first to arrive each week and while she might moan through the entire routine, she always admitted she felt better afterward. Not immediately, but as soon as she managed to catch her breath.

"What's that goofy grin about?" Grace's narrowed eyes focused suspiciously on Olivia.

"You." Hands on her hips, Olivia laughed again. "You crack me up."

"I'm glad you find me so amusing." Groaning, she raised her bent knee to the bench and untied her tennis shoe. "You'll be sorry one day when I'm taken away in an Aid Car."

Olivia rolled her eyes. "Would it make you feel better if I bought you a piece of coconut cream pie?"

Grace looked up. "It might. Any reason in particular?"

Olivia nodded. "I want to ask you something."

"Sure." Grace nodded as she untied the second shoe and kicked it off.

Her immediate willingness to listen and to help if she could was what made Grace such a good friend. There wasn't a single thing Olivia couldn't share with her. That was the reason this conversation would be so difficult and painful. She was afraid her oldest and dearest friend hadn't been completely honest with her—and she was afraid she knew why.

A half hour later, they sat in the Pancake Palace with large slices of coconut cream pie and coffee.

"I hope you realize this defeats the entire purpose of going to aerobics class." Grace lifted the fork to her mouth and savored the first bite.

"In certain circumstances, only pie will do," Olivia said.

"Is this one of those times?"

Olivia didn't answer her. Instead, she launched the topic that had been on her mind all week. "I got a phone call from Will a little while ago." She studied Grace, hoping to read her reaction to Will's name.

Sure enough, Grace instantly dropped her gaze. So it *was* Will she'd been involved with earlier in the year. A flash of anger, first at Will and then Grace, nearly made her lose her train of thought. Olivia squelched the urge to shake them both.

"Don't you want to know what he wanted?" she asked, trying hard to disguise her feelings.

"Sure."

Olivia sighed. "He wants me to have Ben Rhodes investigated."

Shocked, Grace raised her eyes. "Ben? Whatever for?"

"He thinks Ben's planning to swindle our mother out of her life savings."

Grace's frown revealed her disapproval. "Are you going to do it?"

Olivia hated to admit she'd caved in, but she couldn't see any way around it. "I am. I spoke to Roy earlier in the week, although I think it's a waste of good money."

"Olivia!" Grace seemed horrified, which only made Olivia feel worse. "I can't believe you actually did that."

She regretted it now, but she'd told Will she'd hire someone to look into Ben's background and so she had. "My brother made a good case. Ben doesn't have any family in the area and we really don't know much about him." It sounded ridiculous when she said it out loud. "Will convinced me we should do this. He can be persuasive when he wants to be." Again she watched Grace, studying her reaction.

All Grace did was shake her head as if she couldn't believe Olivia would agree to anything so foolish. In retrospect Olivia agreed with her. She wished she'd sat on it a day or two before calling Roy, but it was too late.

"If Mom ever hears about this, she'll be outraged," Olivia said.

"Yes, she will," Grace muttered.

"I told Will how much I like and trust Ben. I can't imagine him doing anything underhanded."

Grace lowered her eyes and sliced energetically into her

pie with the side of her fork. Olivia had the impression that her friend was concentrating on the pie in an effort to conceal her reluctance to discuss Will.

Olivia looked at her carefully. "Seems to me you haven't asked about Will in a long time," she said in a deceptively casual voice. "Any reason?"

"Not really." Grace's response was devoid of emotion.

"He certainly had questions about you."

Grace reached for her coffee, still avoiding eye contact.

"Aren't you curious about what they were?"

"Not really."

Olivia was tired of waiting for Grace to admit the truth. "It was my brother, wasn't it?" She was unable to keep the anger out of her voice. She was furious with Will and sick at heart that he'd taken advantage of her best friend—not that Grace was completely innocent in any of this.

Grace didn't answer.

"The least you can do is be honest about it, Grace. You were emotionally involved with my brother."

Tears filled Grace's eyes and she slowly nodded.

"Why didn't you tell me?" Olivia asked. Yet she realized that much of the hurt she felt was due to the fact that Grace hadn't confided in her. "We've always shared everything."

"I couldn't tell you. I should have in the beginning, but I didn't. I don't know why—no, that's not true. I do know. You would've disapproved and rightly so."

"How did it get started?" Will had visited Cedar Cove when their mother had cancer surgery, but to the best of Olivia's knowledge, Grace and her brother had barely spoken.

"It was all so innocent in the beginning." Grace stared down at the table and her voice fell to a whisper. "He wrote me after Dan's body was discovered to tell me how sorry he was. It was a lovely letter and at the bottom he put his e-mail address. I e-mailed him back to thank him. Then he e-mailed me back, and before I knew it, we were sending each other messages every day."

"My brother is married."

"Yes, I know that."

Clearly, Grace had entered into this relationship with her eyes open. Olivia was well aware that Internet "relationships" were becoming increasingly common, but she was so disappointed that someone she considered sensible and honorable would get caught up in this kind of mess. She felt the same way about Will. He was her brother and she'd always assumed he was a faithful husband, but apparently that had been a false assumption. Well, he'd hear about this.

"We managed to keep our feelings for each other under control until I spent Thanksgiving with Cliff and his daughter. I couldn't contact Will and he couldn't reach me."

"Will knew you were with Cliff?"

"Oh, yes. And when I returned from the East Coast, everything changed. He said he'd missed me and I'd certainly missed talking to him. Once I admitted that, Will started phoning me and before long he'd...declared his love." She swallowed, and fresh tears glistened in her eyes. "He kept telling me his marriage was miserable and he was getting out."

"You believed it because that was what you wanted to hear."

Grace nodded, then inhaled sharply. "Will suggested we meet in New Orleans. He sent me the plane ticket and booked us a hotel room. I nearly did it." She cupped her hand over her mouth as if to hold back a sob. "I nearly slept with a married man."

Not since Dan's disappearance had Olivia seen her friend

this broken. "What happened?" she asked in a coaxing whisper.

"One night after aerobics, you casually mentioned that Will and his wife had booked a cruise. I refused to believe it. Will told me he and Georgia had split up and that he'd filed for divorce."

This was even worse than Olivia had guessed, but she bit her tongue to keep from saying so. "Don't you think I would've told you that Will was getting a divorce?"

"Yes—no, I wasn't thinking. I was sure you didn't want anyone to know."

"I'd tell you." This was a subtle reminder that Olivia held nothing back and that she'd been hurt by Grace's silence—by her lie of omission.

"Afterward, I was so embarrassed.... I wanted to tell you, but I couldn't do it. The worst of it is that I lied to Cliff. He knew right away. He asked me if there was someone else and I told him no and feigned anger that he'd even think such a thing."

"How did he figure it out?" Grace had lied to both of them, and Olivia wondered how Cliff had been able to see through it and she hadn't.

Grace kept her eyes trained on the tabletop. "His ex-wife had cheated on him for years. He realized what was happening.... I finally admitted I'd met someone on the Internet. I said it had been innocent—to that point—but he wouldn't believe me. Cliff said he refused to be involved with a woman he couldn't trust. That's why he won't have anything to do with me now—and the truth of it is, I don't blame him."

"How did you find out Will and Georgia were still together?"

"I called the house. She answered the phone."

That must have been a shocking revelation but Olivia didn't comment. The injured party in all of this was her sister-in-law.

Grace tried to smile. The effort was futile. "I told Will I never wanted to hear from him again and blocked his e-mail address from my computer. He tried to contact me a number of times, but I immediately deleted any and all messages. I want nothing more to do with him."

Grace had paid a high price for her indiscretion. "I'm sorry it was my brother who did this."

"I am, too." Her voice was strangled and filled with self-incrimination. "But I blame myself. Even when we were in high school, I had the biggest crush on Will. Then, when he actually claimed to love me, it was like a fantasy coming true—and I let it happen. If anyone had told me I'd willingly begin a relationship with a married man, I would've denied it. And yet that's exactly what I did."

"It could have been worse."

"Much worse," Grace said. "If you hadn't mentioned Georgia when you did, I would've met Will in New Orleans. I would've slept with him, too, despite everything I believe. I was head over heels in love with him. Thank God I learned the truth when I did."

"Does Cliff know everything?"

"Not who I was involved with, just that I was."

"You went to him, apologized?"

She nodded. "Twice. But I committed the one sin he can't forgive. It's over."

Olivia wasn't so sure. "He could change his mind, you know. Be patient. Give him time."

"I don't think time's going to make any difference," Grace confessed with heartfelt regret. "If I needed proof of that, I got it a couple of weeks ago."

"How do you mean?"

"I ran into Cliff at The Lighthouse. We talked for a few minutes and then the hostess came to seat us, assuming we were together. He made it abundantly clear that he'd rather dine alone than share a meal with me. I got the message. If he ever felt anything for me, it's dead." Tears trailed down her cheeks as she struggled with her composure.

Olivia reached across the table to clasp her friend's hand. She had some thinking to do—and the person to discuss her thoughts with was her husband.

Later that same night, dressed in her pajamas, Olivia sat on the queen-size bed, arms folded around her knees as she relayed the story to Jack.

"I can't get over the fact that all along it was my own brother." It was still a shock.

Jack frowned as if he too had trouble believing what she'd told him. "How's Grace doing?"

"She's brokenhearted. Cliff doesn't want to see her anymore."

Jack tossed his jacket onto the chair beside the bed.

Olivia pointed at it, silently reminding him to hang it in the closet. For a moment, Jack glanced at the jacket and then at her. Sighing, he grabbed it and found a hanger.

"What do you think?" he asked, turning from the closet.

"About Cliff?" She had to consider that for a moment. "I don't know, but I'm sure he sincerely loved Grace at one time. He doesn't seem like the kind of man who voluntarily turns his feelings on and off."

"Then there's hope."

Jack sat down on the bed as he pulled off his shoes. With a proud grin, he lined them up neatly. Shoes were actually supposed to go in the downstairs hall closet, but Olivia didn't comment. "Remember that Grace played a big role in getting the two of us back together," he said.

"I know."

Jack slid his arms around her and tugged her closer to the edge of the bed. "Do you also remember how we met up the same day at the same movie? Accidentally on purpose?"

"Oh, yeah, that." She laughed at the memory. Their problem, in Grace's opinion, was that they were both too stubborn for their own good.

"I think we owe Grace Sherman a favor."

This perked Olivia up. "Exactly what are you suggesting?"

He was quiet a minute or so. "That benefit for the animal shelter is coming up in July, isn't it?"

"The Dog and Bachelor Auction?"

Jack nodded thoughtfully. "Just remember where there's a will, there's a way."

"Oh, Jack! What a terrible pun." She rolled her eyes. "The fact that there's a Will is exactly what got in the way." Giggling, she nudged him in the shoulder. Only Jack could make her laugh about something so distressing.

He nudged her in return and they smiled at each other.

Then she shook her head. "Cliff isn't one of the bachelors. Grace said he turned them down."

"Did he really? Maybe he needs encouragement. The right kind of encouragement."

"Jack? What are you thinking?"

Eyebrows raised, her husband stayed quiet.

"Jack?"

With a move so fast he left her breathless, Jack swept her into his arms and Olivia fell against him. "Have I mentioned lately that you ask far too many questions?"

"Not lately," she said and giggled again.

He kissed her, and soon neither one of them had a single question to ask.

Sixteen

With the television on in the family room, Peggy sat working the counted cross-stitch pattern. Bob was out for the evening; he had his regular AA meeting at six and following that, he was off to the community theater to read for a part in the latest musical production. The theater had decided to put on *Chicago.*

Peggy spent almost every Thursday night alone and had grown accustomed to having this time to herself. Two of her favorite television shows aired on Thursdays and she could count on not being interrupted.

She yawned and covered her mouth with one hand. It'd been one of those days. The rain had started early that morning and hadn't let up all day. Not a rarity for mid-June, but Peggy had hoped to work in her garden. The rain had been a mixed blessing, though, because she'd been inside when the phone rang that afternoon. It was Hannah Russell.

Apparently Roy McAfee had called her with a number of questions and she hadn't heard back from him. Hannah wondered if there was any news. Peggy hadn't known what to tell her. Unfortunately she didn't have any information for her, either, but it was unlikely that she would. The investigation into Maxwell Russell's death was out of her hands.

Hannah had sounded anxious, and Peggy had tried to reassure her. She wanted to help the young woman, but wasn't sure how. The motherly part of her longed to gather Hannah in her arms and tell her everything would be all right. The girl was hurting, wandering aimlessly to escape her pain. That wouldn't help, because wherever Hannah settled, the anguish would follow. Clichéd though it was, Peggy knew from experience that time really was the great healer.

Determined to finish the cross-stitch pattern of hummingbirds in flight so she could complete another one before Christmas, Peggy glanced down at the page and paused to rub her eyes. Either the manufacturers were making smaller patterns every year or she needed new glasses. She preferred to blame the people who printed the patterns. This cross-stitch was for her daughter and she wanted to complete one for her son, Marc, as well. Although maybe she'd better choose another pattern for Marc's… The oceanscape she'd bought might be a little too complicated.

The back door opened and she looked up. It was early for Bob to be home. "Is that you, sweetheart?"

"Are you expecting some other man?" he teased.

"Not tonight. The naked dancing men are scheduled to arrive on Friday."

"Very funny." He stayed in the kitchen. "Any of that fried chicken left?"

"I thought you'd decided not to eat at night anymore."

"I did."

"Then why are you asking about the chicken?"

"Because I'm a weak man and I'm hungry."

She smiled. "Third shelf down on the left-hand side."

"You're gonna have to do something about this refrigerator," Bob complained. "I can't find a thing to eat in here."

This was a routine complaint. The refrigerator was stuffed with food, but her husband continually claimed there was nothing to eat. Peggy didn't bother to respond.

Munching on a chicken leg, he joined her in the family room off the kitchen.

"It's getting nasty out there."

Peggy could hear the rain pounding against the bay windows in the breakfast nook. "My garden could use it."

"The grass is going to grow and then I'll have to cut it again," he muttered. "I swear it's a vicious cycle."

Concentrating on her needlepoint, Peggy smiled. This, too, was one of his regular lamentations.

A branch struck the window and the wind howled. It reminded her of the night Maxwell Russell had appeared at the door, asking for a room. A chill slithered down her arms. That night was one she'd prefer to forget.

"How about a cup of coffee?" Bob asked.

"Yes, thanks."

The wind howled again and Peggy's eyes met Bob's. He didn't need to say anything; she knew he was thinking the same thing she was. That rainy night…

"Decaf?" Bob called from the kitchen.

"Please." She set her cross-stitch aside and stood, raising her arms in a stretch. "How was the meeting?"

"Good. Jack was there."

Her husband wasn't supposed to tell her who was or wasn't at his AA meetings, but there was little in life they didn't share.

"Olivia and Jack are still in the honeymoon phase," he said, sounding like a serious student of the stages of marriage. "All he could talk about was Olivia."

"It's refreshing to find a man who's madly in love with his wife, don't you think?"

Bob laughed. "That's a loaded question if I ever heard one."

"I like Olivia."

"So do I, but those two are about as different as two people can be."

"Yes, but they're well-suited, too. Jack makes her laugh. And Olivia brings balance into his life."

"He cleaned out his car for her."

"Jack?" This was a noteworthy event. Jack's car was notoriously cluttered with fast-food cartons, old newspapers and what-have-you. For years Peggy had made a joke of it.

"Apparently Olivia's something of a neat freak. Everything in its place and a place for everything."

Peggy frowned. Jack was a born slob. The only thing he'd ever organized in his life was the front page of the newspaper.

"It won't be long before Jack starts complaining," Bob said knowledgeably.

"About what?"

Bob sighed as if the answer should be obvious. "Olivia, of course. Mark my words, Peggy. Jack will give this marriage his best shot, but I don't think he'll be able to maintain Olivia's high standards."

Peggy was not amused. "That's the most negative thing I've heard you say in months."

"Don't get me wrong. I think the world of Jack—and of Olivia—but I can see the writing on the wall with those two."

Peggy was annoyed by his attitude. But before she could chastise Bob, he continued his discussion of the differences between Jack and Olivia.

"She's even got him eating healthy meals. She actually made grilled tofu and eggplant—*eggplant*—last week. I burst out laughing when Jack told me. Can you imagine a meat-and-potatoes man like Jack eating tofu and eggplant?"

"I'll bet it was fabulous." Peggy was a big fan of both and had cooked tofu a number of times. Bob had eaten it, not realizing what it was, and complimented her on dinner. She'd pass along a couple of her recipes to Olivia and explain that the secret was not to say a word.

"He made some excuse as soon as he could and drove to Burger King for a Double Whopper with cheese."

"Shame on him," Peggy murmured, although she smiled at the thought of Jack rushing out the back door, desperate for a fast-food fix.

Bob brought her the coffee in a mug. No sooner had he handed it to her than the lights flickered. "This is turning into some storm. What did the weatherman have to say?"

"I switched channels before the weather came on."

Bob scowled up at the light fixtures. "I'd better find a flashlight before we lose electricity altogether."

Peggy sipped her coffee and set the mug on the counter. "That's not a bad idea."

She followed her husband into the mudroom, where he opened a cupboard door and peered inside. "Have you heard anything on the Russell investigation?" she asked.

Bob glanced over his shoulder as if her question had startled him. "No. What makes you ask?"

"No reason. I was just thinking about everything this afternoon. Doesn't it seem mighty convenient that Dan Sherman killed himself when he did?"

Her husband didn't answer.

"I can't help wondering about that."

The lights flickered again, and this time went out. The

room was pitch-black and silent without the background noise of the TV and the hum of the fridge.

"Bob?"

"I'm here."

He reached for her, his hand clasping her elbow.

There was a pounding in the distance. "What's that?" Peggy asked, jolted by the unexpectedness of it.

"I don't hear anything."

"I do."

Her husband switched on the flashlight and led the way back into the kitchen. The pounding was unmistakable now. Someone was at their front door.

"I hear it," Bob said in a husky whisper.

Panic swelled in Peggy's throat. This was like history repeating itself. "Don't answer it," she whispered fearfully.

Bob ignored her. With the flashlight guiding him, he left her and walked into the other room.

Peggy wanted to cry out, to remind him that it'd been a night like this when Maxwell Russell had come to their door. Their lives hadn't been the same since.

"Bob! No!"

"Don't be ridiculous, Peggy."

She moved behind him, trembling as he released the dead bolt. Her breath seemed to catch in her lungs as he opened the door and flashed the light on their unforeseen guest.

Hannah Russell stood drenched and shivering on the other side of the screen door.

"Hannah," Peggy cried and stepped around her husband to open the screen and let the woman in. "Are you all right?"

"I got lost," she whispered. "I thought I could find your place again on my own, but I was lost, and the rain was coming down so hard and I was sure I was going to drive off the road."

Peggy couldn't imagine why she hadn't phoned. "Come in," she urged. Bob took Hannah's coat and hung it on the hall tree to dry.

It was all Peggy could do to hide her distress when she saw how thin and pale the young woman was. "Come inside where it's warm," she insisted, taking Hannah's arm. "When was the last time you had anything to eat?"

"This morning—I think. I haven't had much of an appetite lately."

The lights flickered and came back on, and Peggy sighed with relief.

Bob clicked off the flashlight.

"I shouldn't have come," Hannah mumbled. "I told myself I wouldn't, but I didn't have anywhere else to go."

"You made the right decision. Bob, bring in her suitcase. I'll put on some soup. Hannah, you go take a hot shower and get out of those wet clothes before you catch a cold."

"I can stay?"

"Of course you can stay with us."

Tears spilled from the young woman's eyes. "Thank you. Thank you so much."

"There's no need to thank us," Peggy said, escorting Hannah to the bathroom down the hall, where there were plenty of thick, fresh towels.

When she returned it was to find her husband studying her. He didn't look nearly as certain about this as Peggy did.

"We'll settle everything in the morning," she promised.

Bob's eyes burned into hers. "That's what you said the night Max Russell arrived."

Seventeen

Rachel Pendergast checked her afternoon appointment schedule at Get Nailed as she ate her Weight Watchers frozen entrée. Jolene Peyton was down for a haircut. Rachel remembered the young girl from previous appointments. She recalled Jolene's father, too, and his uneasiness about being in an establishment frequented by females. She found his attitude fairly typical of single fathers.

Jolene was a motherless child and she'd made it clear that she was eager to have her father remarry. Bruce Peyton's wife had been killed in a car accident two years ago while driving to pick up Jolene from her kindergarten class. From what Rachel had heard, several hours had passed before anyone remembered that Jolene was still at the school. Not surprisingly, the seven-year-old was terrified of being left behind.

Despite Jolene's effort to push Rachel and her father together, Bruce Peyton amused Rachel more than he attracted her. While she enjoyed the child's company, Rachel felt that getting involved with a man so obviously in love with his dead wife had virtually no chance of developing into a healthy relationship.

Just after four, Jolene skipped into the salon, as relaxed in Get Nailed as her own bedroom. “Hi, Rachel,” she said, pigtails bouncing.

The child must be going into third grade this year; to Rachel, she seemed younger than her age—again, not surprising. “Are you ready to get your hair cut?” she asked, taking out a miniature version of the plastic cape.

Bruce followed his daughter into the salon but didn’t show any of her enthusiasm. He nodded briefly in Rachel’s direction, then glanced nervously around as if he suspected someone would wrestle him to the ground and dye his hair blue.

“Here you go,” Rachel said, turning the chair for Jolene to climb into. She adjusted the cape and secured the clasp.

With practiced ease Jolene flipped her pigtails over her shoulder. “I want you to cut it just like you did before.”

“Ah, a woman who knows her own mind,” Rachel murmured. She released the bands holding Jolene’s hair and carefully ran a brush through it. To her surprise Bruce didn’t take a seat or wander into the mall the way he had on previous visits. Instead he stood about two feet behind Rachel, watching every move.

“Do you want to sit down, Bruce?” she asked. He was making her uncomfortable, standing there like that. After cutting Jolene’s hair for the last few months, she would’ve thought he’d trust her with his daughter.

“Dad’s afraid I’m going to talk,” Jolene piped up.

“Jolene!” Bruce growled out a warning.

“He told me I’m not supposed to say anything about you marrying him.”

Rachel jerked around in time to see Bruce throw back his head and groan aloud.

“I don’t think we need to concern ourselves with that,” Rachel said, hoping to reassure him.

"You already met someone?" Jolene sounded horrified. Her big dark eyes widened with dismay.

"No, but—"

"She's going to the auction, though," Terri called out from the nail station on the far side of the salon. "We all are."

"What auction?"

"The Dog and Bachelor Auction being put on by the animal shelter." Terri pointed to the poster on the wall near the front door. "Everyone in town is talking about it."

"I'm saving every penny of my tip money," Jeannie, another nail tech, chimed in. "This could be my last chance."

"I'm more interested in the dogs myself," Rachel said for Bruce's benefit. She could just imagine what he thought of all this chatter about men.

As if the conversation had suddenly made Bruce feel awkward, he walked over to the waiting area and claimed a chair. From the corner of her eye, Rachel saw him reach for a magazine and pretend to read.

"What's a Dog and Bachelor Auction?" Jolene asked, cocking her head to one side. Her gaze met Rachel's in the big mirror.

"It's a fun event where women make bids to adopt a special pet and a date with a bachelor."

"What's a bachelor?"

"A man who isn't married," Rachel explained.

"My dad's not married anymore."

"Hey, Bruce," Terri shouted. "Have you signed up for the auction?"

Bruce lowered the magazine and shook his head. "Not on your life."

"Why not?" Terri pressed. "It's for charity, you know."

"I'm not interested in dating again, thank you very much." His steely-eyed look dared his daughter to comment.

"You said I could have a new mommy," Jolene reminded him, yelling it across the salon.

"Someday," he muttered.

"But that's what you say when you really mean no." Jolene's face fell. "You *promised*." The child seemed about to break into tears. "I'm the only girl in my class without a mommy and you said, you *promised*..."

Every eye in the salon turned to glare at Bruce Peyton.

Feeling sorry for him, Rachel helped the girl out of the chair and led her to the shampoo sink. She hoped that with a bit of distraction, Jolene would forget about her father's promises, as well as the Dog and Bachelor Auction.

When Rachel finished shampooing Jolene's hair, she noticed that Bruce had left the salon. She guessed he'd decided to wander around the shopping center, after all. That was probably for the best, considering the grilling he'd gotten earlier.

"Who else is going to be in the Back-lor auction?" Jolene asked once Rachel had her back in the chair.

"Navy men," Terri supplied gleefully. "An entire aircraft carrier full of sailors arrived last month and I hear several of the crew have volunteered."

"For the sake of charity," Rachel reminded her friends.

"I don't care why they signed up," Jeannie said, filing her customer's nails. "They're fair game."

Her friends' enthusiasm for this auction astonished Rachel. Frankly, she didn't hold out much hope of meeting anyone through a charity function. Yes, it was a clever way to raise funds, but as for meeting men, she'd been disappointed so many times she'd given up hope. Her thirtieth birthday had come and gone with barely a ripple of the calendar page. Her desire to settle into a comfortable married life was still unfulfilled, and Rachel had given up looking.

If she was meant to find a husband, then it would happen. In the meantime she was content.

"Would you pay money to go out with my dad if he was in the auction?" Jolene asked as Rachel sectioned the youngster's hair.

She considered the question and shrugged. She didn't want to disappoint the little girl, but she didn't think Bruce was ready for another relationship. "I don't know."

Jolene frowned as though puzzled by Rachel's answer. "Don't you like my dad?"

"I don't know your father well enough to say if I do or not," she said honestly, hoping to ward off Jolene's persistence.

"But if you bought my dad at the auction, you'd know him."

Rachel finished sectioning Jolene's hair and reached for her scissors. She decided it was time to have a short heart-to-heart with the little girl. "Sweetheart, it embarrasses your father when you talk about him remarrying."

Jolene blinked. "That's what he said, too—that it embarrasses him. But he wouldn't say why."

"I don't think your father's ready to get involved with anyone. He loved your mother very much and I think maybe he doesn't want to fall in love again."

"I loved her, too, but I want a mommy," the girl said plaintively.

"Maybe it's just a friend you need."

"I have friends but they're my age and—" She paused and seemed to contemplate Rachel's words. "Could *you* be my friend?"

Rachel smiled. She thought it was a good idea for them both. Jolene was a motherless child and she was a woman without family. "I'd like that a lot."

"I would, too."

Rachel needed to talk to Bruce, make sure he sanctioned this. She wanted it understood, however, that she wasn't pressuring him into any kind of relationship. This was between her and Jolene. She would enjoy playing a role in the little girl's life, but only if he had no objections.

Just as she was finishing up Jolene's haircut, Bruce returned. He walked over to Valerie, who ran the reception desk, and pulled his wallet out of his rear pocket.

"Hi, Daddy," Jolene called out.

His expression softened as he turned to face his daughter. "All right, all right, ladies," he said and shook his head, looking chagrined. "You talked me into it. I signed up for the Dog and Bachelor Auction."

"You did?" Terri was so excited she nearly leaped up from her table.

"Great," Jeannie cried, equally thrilled.

Bruce glanced at Rachel, obviously anticipating her reaction. She nodded, letting him know she approved, but she hoped he wouldn't be disappointed when she didn't bid on him.

Eighteen

During the summer months, Charlotte's favorite night of the week was Thursday. For a number of years now, the Chamber of Commerce had sponsored Concerts on the Cove, bringing in a variety of free entertainment, from pop groups to jazz quartets. Tonight was an Irish band, with fiddles and one of those Celtic drums—Charlotte couldn't remember what they were called. The concerts brought almost the entire town together once a week, as young and old alike crowded the small waterfront park, enjoying the festive atmosphere.

Before he came by to collect her, Ben had bought their dinner, teriyaki chicken and rice from her favorite take-out restaurant. Walking hand in hand, he carried their folding chairs, while she held on to their food.

"Oh, good. We have our spot," she said, looking at the place under the mountain ash where they usually sat. Some couples shared a song or a favorite movie; Charlotte and Ben had their own patch of lawn in Waterfront Park.

Ben was so thoughtful and considerate toward her, Charlotte mused as he set up the chairs and insisted she sit down.

And she loved his old-fashioned manners—the way he held doors and stood when she entered a room. The world didn't have much time or interest in those niceties anymore, but Charlotte was of a generation that still appreciated them.

They settled in their spot. It was still early, but they always arrived a good hour before the concert began in order to secure their special place.

"Oh, look," she said with the take-out container balanced on her lap. "There's Corrie McAfee. I don't think I've seen her at any of the concerts before."

Corrie glanced around as if she wasn't sure where to go.

"Corrie," Charlotte said, waving her arm. "Over here."

Corrie headed eagerly in Charlotte's direction. "Hello, Mrs. Jefferson."

"Call me Charlotte. You know my friend Ben Rhodes, don't you?"

Although he had his meal in his lap, Ben stood. Charlotte wouldn't have expected anything less.

"This is your first time here, isn't it?" Charlotte asked. "I'm sure you'll enjoy it." She wanted Corrie to know she was welcome. She hadn't had much opportunity to meet the McAfees. They were still considered new to the community, although they'd lived in Cedar Cove for several years. As a private investigator, Roy had probably learned more about this town and its people than he'd ever cared to know. It was important, Charlotte felt, to bring the couple into the fold.

Corrie gestured toward the parking lot. "I finally managed to talk Roy into coming down. He's parking the car."

"Sit here with us." Charlotte invited. "I always bring an extra blanket. It sometimes gets a bit cool in the evenings, but you and Roy would be welcome to sit on it."

"Oh, Roy's bringing a couple of chairs."

"Look, there's Grace Sherman," Charlotte said, waving

enthusiastically at the local librarian. "She has Buttercup with her. That is *such* a well-behaved dog,"

Grace waved back and continued down the waterfront at a brisk pace, the golden retriever trotting dutifully beside her.

Charlotte was proud of having brought Buttercup into Grace's life. Three years ago, a good friend had moved into a retirement center and consequently needed a new home for her pet. Grace had immediately popped into Charlotte's mind. That was shortly after Dan Sherman had turned up missing, and Charlotte understood how lost and lonely her daughter's friend felt.

Roy appeared, walking along the waterfront with two folding chairs, one under each arm. He nodded when he saw Corrie.

"I don't think he's a happy camper about all this," Corrie said under her breath. "I'm the one who's fond of Irish music."

Roy walked across the soft green grass toward them. "Hello, Charlotte, Ben," Roy muttered as he set up the chairs.

Charlotte was surprised to see what a big man Roy was. She'd seen him around town any number of times, but always at a distance and hadn't noticed how tall he was.

Ben stood again and the two men exchanged handshakes. "I don't think we've met," Ben said. "Ben Rhodes."

After they chatted for a few moments, Roy settled next to his wife. They put their heads together, whispering for a moment, and then Roy excused himself.

"We were going to eat after the concert," Corrie explained, "but that chicken looks so good, Roy decided to walk across the street and pick up dinner now."

"The teriyaki is our favorite," Charlotte told her. "This is way more than I can eat. Ben and I should probably share an order but the leftovers are always so delicious the next day."

"Our daughter Linnette's favorite meal is teriyaki chicken," Corrie added conversationally. "Speaking of Linnette," she began. She fumbled nervously with her hands, and then laughed. "That wasn't a very good transition, was it?"

"I didn't realize you had a daughter," Charlotte said. She didn't know the McAfees well enough to know about their children.

"Actually, I've been looking for a chance to talk to both of you about Linnette," Corrie confessed. "She recently graduated as a physician's assistant. It was an arduous program, but Linnette feels strongly about bringing medical professionals to small towns."

Charlotte sat up straighter at this bit of news. "I suppose you've heard how hard Ben and I have worked to get a medical facility built in Cedar Cove."

Corrie nodded. "That's what I wanted to discuss. Do you have any news about what's happening with that?"

For the last two months, Charlotte and Ben had shown up for every single council meeting. They sat in the front row, as if to say they weren't going silently into that long, dark night. For her part, Charlotte had decided she'd keel over dead before she gave up her efforts to get a medical clinic in Cedar Cove.

"I don't know what to tell you," she murmured. "So far, there's been no real progress. Just a lot of talk."

Ben leaned forward. "The argument is that even if the council were to fund a clinic, the town can't afford personnel."

"Linnette applied for a job in Montana, and I hate the thought of our daughter living so far from home." Corrie waved to someone in the distance; the park was fast filling up. "I'd hoped something might turn up here in Cedar Cove.

I miss my daughter and she's only a ferry ride away now. I can't imagine what it'll be like when she's hundreds of miles from home."

"A physician's assistant," Charlotte repeated. "Maybe there *is* something we can do."

"What?" Ben asked, turning to Charlotte.

Charlotte gently patted his knee. "Leave that to me."

Olivia and Jack arrived just then, and Charlotte stood and waved them over. Seeing their friends, family and neighbors was what made these summertime concerts so much fun. Her daughter waved back, but Charlotte noticed that Olivia and Jack seemed to be having a discussion before they made their way through the crowd to join her.

"There's plenty of room here with Ben and me," Charlotte told them. She moved her chair closer to Ben's. Although she'd only taken a few bites of her dinner, she'd much rather visit than eat. Closing the container, she returned it to the plastic bag.

"Hello, Corrie," Olivia said.

To Charlotte's ears, her daughter sounded stressed, although she had no idea why that would be. This was a night for relaxing, for laughter and singing and catching up with friends.

Olivia glanced at Ben and greeted him, but her tone was remote, as if she hadn't decided what to think of her mother's friend.

Her daughter's attitude troubled Charlotte, and she decided to talk to Olivia about it later, when they had a private moment.

"Sit down, sit down," she instructed Olivia. "Jack, you're looking fit these days."

He patted his stomach. "I could lose a few pounds, according to Olivia."

Charlotte smiled. So that was the reason her daughter had asked her to recommend a healthy-eating cookbook. Charlotte had bought them shortly after her cancer treatments and tried some of the recipes. They weren't bad, but over time she'd gradually reverted to eating the way she always had. Old habits were difficult to break.

"You know Corrie McAfee, don't you?" Charlotte said, wanting to make sure Olivia made Corrie feel welcome. "This is the McAfees' first time at Concerts on the Cove."

Olivia nodded to Corrie. "Good to see you again."

"You too," Corrie said.

The two women exchanged long looks. Charlotte didn't know what that was about, either. Surely her daughter and the wife of the local P.I. couldn't possibly be colluding about anything.

"Corrie and I were just talking about a health clinic here in Cedar Cove," Charlotte continued, hoping to include Olivia in the conversation. "The McAfees' daughter is a physician's assistant, and Corrie was just saying how nice it would be if she worked in this area."

Olivia nodded absently.

"A health clinic is important, Olivia," Charlotte said, her voice a little sharper than usual.

"I agree," she muttered, frowning.

"I suppose you think a bigger jail is more of a priority."

"We could use a larger jail, but—"

"You can't be serious!" Charlotte was aghast that her daughter would think additional jail cells should take precedence over the health concerns of their community.

"We do need a bigger jail," Jack concurred. "In fact I just wrote an article this afternoon about the problems with transporting local offenders to jails in Yakima County. But, to my way of thinking, we need a medical facility more."

Olivia nodded once again, silently agreeing with her husband.

Her daughter's lack of verbal support for her cause hurt Charlotte. Olivia was in a position to do much more and she hadn't, because it wasn't important enough to her.

As if he understood her disappointment in Olivia, Ben reached for her hand and gave her fingers a gentle squeeze. She swallowed hard and managed a smile as she turned to this man she'd come to love so late in life.

Nineteen

It was a perfect day for gardening, Peggy thought—sunny but not hot, with a comfortable breeze and an almost cloudless sky.

She'd decided to visit the local nursery, inviting Hannah to join her. Now Peggy loaded a thirty-pound bag of fertilizer into the large garden cart, while Hannah wandered through the aisles of perennials.

"Let me do that," the young woman insisted, hurrying to her side. "I came with you because I wanted to help."

Peggy always enjoyed her trips to the nursery, although she rarely left without filling up the minivan. Her raspberries and blueberries could do with fertilizer. She was out of slug bait, too. Her yard was lovely, with the rhododendrons and azaleas in bloom. The lilacs were coming out, too, and she had both the purple and white varieties along the side of the house. Her small rose garden was prospering, and so was her expanding herb garden.

"We probably should talk about me staying at the house," Hannah said, staring down at the ground as if reluctant to address the subject. Peggy guessed she'd needed several days to work up her courage to discuss the matter of her staying.

"Let's do that later," Peggy suggested. "I was thinking we might go out to lunch when we're finished here." She found the best "girl talks" with Hollie always took place over lunch.

Hannah smiled. "That would be nice."

Hannah had been with them for more than a week. She'd planned to leave once, about three days after her arrival, but Peggy had asked her to stay. As she'd expected, Hannah had accepted the invitation without further argument.

An hour later, they sat on the patio at The Lighthouse eating Caesar salad with grilled shrimp and sipping iced tea.

"You and Bob have been so kind to me," Hannah said.

She still seemed frail, Peggy noted, physically as well as emotionally. "We like having you around."

Hannah looked grateful. "I don't think anyone's ever been so good to me." She reached for her iced tea and took a quick sip. "I should never have stayed this long. Originally I only intended to visit Cedar Cove for one night. But you were so welcoming, and now it's been over a week. I can't continue to take advantage of your friendship like this." She met Peggy's eyes and said earnestly, "I do think of you as my friends, you know."

"We feel the same way," Peggy murmured.

Hannah was nibbling her lower lip again. Peggy considered it a personal challenge to improve not only this girl's health but her emotional outlook. She didn't seem to have much self-esteem. Generally, Peggy thought parents worried excessively about self-esteem these days. Spend enough time with your kids, give them lots of love and reasonable amounts of responsibility, and self-esteem would naturally follow—that was Peggy's theory of child-raising. But in Hannah Russell's case... She was far too thin—to the point of being anorexic. Her clothes hung on her. Peggy had taken a lot of pleasure in tempting Hannah with her prize recipes. Ever since Troy Davis's last visit, she'd been cooking many of her old favorites. She found comfort in that and in providing Hannah with some old-fashioned mothering. Hannah seemed to blossom under Peggy's encouragement and affection.

"Bob and I want you to stay," Peggy said, wondering how many times she'd have to make this point. "We love having you."

Hannah shook her head reluctantly. "I can't do that. I'm not even sure why I came to Cedar Cove. In the beginning I told myself it was because I wanted to learn what I could about how—and why—my father died. I don't like to think about him suffering." There was a stricken look in her eyes. "You don't think he suffered much, do you?"

Peggy didn't know, but she felt a need to reassure Hannah, even if it wasn't the truth. "No, I don't think so. When Bob and I broke into the room, there wasn't any evidence of restlessness." It was as if Maxwell Russell had laid his head on the pillow, closed his eyes and never stirred again. All in all, it wasn't a bad way to exit this life.

Hannah picked at her salad. "I thought I had some questions, but I don't. I probably should. I know that Mr. McAfee seemed to have a lot—but I don't. I'm not sure I even want to know what happened. All I really want is for this nightmare to go away."

Peggy wasn't surprised by her feelings. Sometimes, for some people, uncertainty was easier to live with than a difficult truth. Hannah was obviously one of those people, preferring to simply avoid reality. Peggy had felt that temptation herself, but knew she was strong enough to cope with the truth, whatever it might be.

"I felt drawn to Cedar Cove," Hannah went on. "I was driving and driving, looking for a fresh start, and all I could think about was my first visit here."

"That's understandable."

"Why?" Hannah sounded genuinely curious.

"Well, for one thing, your father died in Cedar Cove. It's here that the mystery will be solved and although you may not want to know what happened or why, you *need* to know. That's what your mind is telling you."

"Do you really think so?" Hannah asked.

Peggy nodded.

"I…think I was drawn back here because of you and Bob." She smiled fleetingly. "When Sheriff Davis brought me to your house, you were so helpful and so nice to me. I felt…oh, I don't know, that you were just the kind of family I wish I'd had."

The young woman's words gladdened Peggy's heart, and saddened her at the same time. Obviously Hannah's childhood had been lacking in some crucial ways. Peggy felt a stab of longing for her own children. She saw her daughter so rarely that Hannah's warmth and gratitude made up for some of what she was missing with Hollie.

"I'll stay," Hannah said decisively, "but only on one condition."

"You're welcome without any conditions," Peggy assured her.

"I want to pay you rent, just as if I was any other guest. I'll need to find a job first, of course, but that shouldn't be too hard. I have lots of experience."

Peggy thought it was important for Hannah to pay rent; it would allow her to feel a sense of pride and self-sufficiency. "I understand Grace is planning to hire someone at the library for the summer," she said. "Why not apply there?"

Hannah considered that for a moment, then shook her head. "I'm not much of a reader, unfortunately. I don't know how good I'd be at helping people find books, you know?"

Peggy wasn't easily discouraged. "What jobs have you held in the past?"

"I worked all through high school at a fast-food place. I didn't really like it, but it gave me a little bit of money. My dad..." She paused and let whatever she'd started to say fade.

"What about working in a day care center? Little Lambs recently advertised for help."

Again Hannah shook her head. "I don't have a lot of patience around little kids. I worked at a Laundromat once, too, but only briefly. I think I'd be good as a store clerk, though."

"I think you would, too," Peggy agreed and Hannah brightened immediately.

"I'll check the Help Wanted listings as soon as we get back to the house," Hannah said eagerly.

"Good idea. We'll pick up a *Chronicle* right now."

Peggy paid for their lunch, and when they arrived back at the house, Bob was there to help her unload the minivan.

"Hannah's decided to live with us for a while," she told her husband, making a point of expressing her pleasure at the girl's decision.

"I plan to pay my own way," Hannah insisted. Clutching her newspaper, she followed Bob into the garage, where he set down the thirty-pound bag of fertilizer. "First thing Monday morning, I'm going to apply for a job."

Bob nodded, but he didn't reveal nearly the enthusiasm Peggy had. She wanted to kick him for his obvious lack of interest. Peggy watched as Hannah's face fell, annoyed that her husband was so blind to how badly the girl needed their approval. Hannah was fragile and needy, and it wasn't that difficult to give her some of the attention she craved.

"I don't want to be any bother." Hannah nervously stepped back.

"You're no bother, Hannah." Bob returned to the minivan. Well, at least he'd said that much and his voice wasn't unfriendly.

"Would you like to help with dinner, Hannah?" Peggy called as she headed into the kitchen.

"Yes...of course." Hannah scurried after her. "I want to do whatever I can."

She was so eager to please and so eager to fit in. She agreed to prepare the potatoes with every sign of happiness.

While Hannah stood at the kitchen sink and peeled potatoes, working carefully and methodically, Bob walked in through the back door.

"We have a visitor," he announced.

Peggy automatically dried her hands on the kitchen towel as Pastor Dave Flemming entered the kitchen.

"Hello, Peggy," he said, smiling broadly.

Pastor Flemming and Bob had become friends over the past year or so. Max Russell's death had shaken Bob and Peggy badly, and they'd started going to church again, something they hadn't done in years. They still attended regularly. Peggy felt it had been a good decision; the services brought her a sense of peace and calm, and she was thankful for that.

"This is Hannah Russell," Bob said, gesturing toward Hannah.

"Hello, Hannah."

"Hello," she said softly, her gaze lowered.

The girl had trouble making eye contact, Peggy noticed, and hoped that with time and lots of attention she'd get over being so timid and self-conscious.

"Bob tells me you're staying here for a while."

Hannah nodded. "Mr. and Mrs. Beldon have been very kind."

"I'd like to invite you to join us on Sunday for worship service. The Beldons attend. You could go with them."

Her eyes flew up. "I don't think I'd be comfortable with that."

"Any particular reason?" Pastor Flemming asked. "It's our goal to make every visitor welcome."

Hannah just shook her head. "No, thanks."

Peggy hoped she'd eventually change her mind. It would do Hannah good, the same way it had them, but she wouldn't pressure her. When and if she attended services, it would be her own decision.

Twenty

Cliff Harding walked out to the barn to take a look at his new filly, Funny Face, born just two weeks ago. Cal, his trainer, was working with the sire in the paddock.

This ranch had been Cliff's lifelong dream. He wasn't a rich man, but he'd invested wisely through the years and cashed in his Internet stocks at precisely the right time. The profits had afforded him the luxury of buying property in the Olalla area and starting his own small horse ranch.

Cliff had known Cal Washburn for a number of years. He'd first met him when the young man worked at Emerald Downs with Thoroughbreds. Cal, who seemed more comfortable around horses than people, was far and away the most gifted trainer he'd ever known. Cliff felt fortunate to have him on a profit-sharing basis. His ability to communicate with animals was uncanny; if Cliff believed in psychic phenomena, which he didn't, he'd almost think Cal could speak to horses in their own language. Unfortunately those communication skills didn't extend to people. Cal wasn't a particularly shy man, but his stutter had been a detriment in relationships, especially with women.

"S-some…l-l-lady ph-ph—called for you." Cal said when he saw him.

Cliff frowned.

Rather than explain, Cal reached inside his pocket for a slip of paper and passed it to him. Cliff didn't recognize the name and for half a second, he experienced a sense of disappointment. A part of him had wanted, had *hoped,* the call would be from Grace.

Things had ended between them several months ago, but he hadn't been able to stop thinking about her. At one time, their relationship had held great promise. After his divorce, he'd rarely dated. He'd spent twenty years married to Susan and for the last ten, the only reason he'd stayed in the marriage had been his daughter, Lisa.

Susan had been unfaithful, not once, but more times than Cliff could count. It was a sickness with her. Cliff had left the marriage with his self-confidence in tatters, and it was years before he'd had any interest in seeking out another relationship.

When he'd met Grace, she'd immediately had a strong effect on him, one of attraction, of liking and respect. Her husband had disappeared and for financial reasons, she'd filed for divorce. He admired the way she'd dealt with the situation. Once Dan Sherman's body was found, he watched her mourn her dead husband, and he grew to love her as she slowly emerged from her grief and pain. He'd looked forward to the day he would ask her to marry him.

It came as a shock when Grace lied to him. The thing was, Grace wasn't a natural liar. She was too easy to see through. That was when he'd decided to call it quits. He'd done so, but not without regret.

After he'd checked on Funny Face and her dam, Cliff went back to the house to return the phone call. He studied the name—Janet Webb—and didn't recognize it or the number. He was mildly curious when the voice on the other end announced that he'd reached the local animal shelter. He asked for Janet and was placed on hold.

"This is Janet Webb." The woman's clipped, professional voice caught him off guard. It sounded as if he'd interrupted some important project and she resented the intrusion.

"Cliff Harding, returning your call," he said in like tones.

"Mr. Harding." Her voice softened into cordiality. "I appreciate your calling me back. I know you've heard about our Dog and Bachelor Auction next week."

"I did hear mention of it." Cliff could hardly ignore the upcoming event; there were posters all over town, frequent articles in the paper—and even in the Seattle news. Cliff would be happy to make a contribution, but he wasn't interested in participating.

"We were disappointed to learn you haven't volunteered to be one of our bachelors." Her tone grew even friendlier.

"Yes, well—"

She didn't allow him to finish. "Your name's come up more than once and from several different people."

"I'm honored, but—"

"I'm sure you won't mind if I add you to the list, then." Her voice was triumphant—as though she'd successfully outwitted him.

The woman was nothing if not persistent. "I don't think so."

His adamant refusal gave her pause. "Is there any particular reason, Mr. Harding, that you don't want to support the animal shelter?"

He opened his mouth to remind her that he did support the shelter, but, again, wasn't allowed to respond.

"One would assume that all animals would hold a place in a horseman's heart. One would assume that a horseman—"

He broke in. "I believe my trainer, Cal Washburn, is one of the bachelors—on my recommendation." Cal wasn't likely to forgive him for that anytime soon. Volunteering Cal was supposed to serve a double purpose: to get Cliff off the hook and to give Cal some exposure to local society, specifically female society. He was a young man, after all. To Cliff's surprise, he'd eventually agreed to participate, as long as he wasn't expected to do any public speaking. Cliff assured him all he'd have to do was to stand up on stage and listen to the women fight over him.

"Yes, I see Mr. Washburn on the list," Janet said. "But what about you?"

"I'm flattered you'd ask me personally, but I'm sorry—no." Even for charity, he had his limits.

"I see," Janet said in a severe voice. "What if I told you that your participation could have a very big impact on the shelter?"

"How do you mean?"

"Someone who prefers to remain anonymous has offered to make a large donation if I can convince you to volunteer for the auction."

"What?" Cliff was sure he'd misunderstood.

"It's true. As I said, someone's offered a substantial donation to the shelter if you'll be one of our bachelors."

Cliff was both amused and chagrinned. "Who?"

"I'm afraid I'm not at liberty to say."

It could only be Grace, Cliff reasoned, but she didn't have the money to make that kind of offer. "Male or female?" he pressed.

Janet Webb laughed nervously. "As I said, I'm not at liberty to reveal the source, Mr. Harding."

"How substantial a donation?"

"Nor am I at liberty to reveal the amount."

He chuckled, completely perplexed by the situation.

"Mr. Harding, I sincerely hope you'll have a change of heart."

Cliff thought about it and sighed. "I suppose I can volunteer." He wasn't happy about it, nor did he appreciate being coerced, but he didn't want to take money away from the shelter. In any case, there was no help for it now; he'd given his word.

After a while, he wandered outside to talk to Cal. "I don't suppose you know anything about that phone call?"

The trainer shook his head.

"Someone offered a donation to the shelter if I agreed to be part of the auction."

Cal's eyes widened. "Y-you g-gonna d-do it?"

Cliff nodded, shrugging his shoulders. "Hey—you didn't have anything to do with this, did you?"

Cal shook his head again. "G-grace?"

Grace's involvement had been his first assumption, too, but it didn't make sense, and not just because of the money. Cliff had recently seen her at the Saturday Farmers' Market, talking to Stan Lockhart, Olivia's ex-husband. The instant she'd seen him she looked guilty. Cliff suspected she'd started dating the other man. The idea of her with Stan bothered him, but Cliff had to put the matter out of his mind. If Grace wanted to see her best friend's ex-husband—well, it wasn't any of his business.

Still, he didn't know how he could have misjudged Grace this badly. She wasn't the woman he'd first believed, not nearly the honest, straightforward person he'd thought, and the realization troubled and saddened him.

He glanced up to find Cal struggling to hide a grin. "Wipe that off your face," he growled.

Cal laughed outright.

"This isn't funny."

Cal laughed again.

Soon Cliff was chuckling, too. He couldn't imagine who'd pay for him to be one of the bachelors, but it might be interesting to find out.

Twenty-One

Jon walked Maryellen and Katie out to the car and buckled their daughter into her protective carrier in the back seat. Maryellen found it harder and harder to head off to work each morning when she longed to spend the day with her husband and child. Jon and Maryellen had agreed she'd quit her job by the end of the year, sooner if they could manage it financially. Maryellen was hoping to get pregnant again, too. She wanted no more than two or three years between Katie and this new baby.

She opened the driver's side door and Jon came over to take her in his arms. "I hate seeing you and Katie leave me every morning," he murmured, echoing her own regrets.

Maryellen slipped her arms around her husband, resting her head on his chest. "I hate leaving you, too."

"It won't be much longer," he promised.

Maryellen nodded. They kissed goodbye and then she climbed into the car and drove into Cedar Cove. Kelly, her younger sister, provided day care for Katie and had done so since Maryellen's return to work the year before. The arrangement worked well for both of them. The extra income helped her sister, and Maryellen felt relieved that her daughter was with family. Kelly's son, Tyler, was wonderful with his cousin and looked after Katie as if she were his little sister. Kelly and her husband, Paul, wanted a second child; although she'd only mentioned it to Maryellen once, Kelly seemed to be having trouble getting pregnant again. Maryellen sympathized but didn't feel she could discuss the subject unless Kelly brought it up first.

There was no time to think about her family once she arrived at the Harbor Street Art Gallery. Summers were their busy season, with plenty of tourist activity and consequently lots of drop-in traffic. Maryellen preferred it that way.

A couple of years earlier she'd broken off her relationship with Jon in an effort to hide the fact that she was pregnant with his child. In order to avoid seeing her—at least before he knew about the pregnancy—he'd moved his work from the local gallery to a well-known Seattle one. His career had grown ever since. His work was back in the Harbor Street gallery now, but it sold out almost as quickly as he could bring it in.

Maryellen knew that Jon had outgrown their gallery, although he was willing to provide a few pieces because of Maryellen and out of loyalty to the owners, who'd given him his start. The demands on his time and talent kept him increasingly busy. Maryellen was looking forward to managing his career and getting his work displayed in galleries all across North America. She had plenty of ideas, including reproductions in both poster-size and as cards.

At noon, Jon called and they chatted briefly. They couldn't be apart for more than a few hours without missing each other and craving contact, even if that was only five minutes on the phone.

"I'm working in my darkroom this afternoon," he told her.

In other words, she shouldn't call him unless absolutely necessary.

"Okay."

"What time will you be home?"

She smiled at the question because she got there within the same ten-minute period every afternoon. "Five-thirty-one," she teased.

"Cute, Maryellen."

"I can be even cuter if you want."

"What I want is you. All of you, all the time."

"That's good to know because I'm more than willing to give you all of me."

Jon laughed. "I'll be waiting for my two favorite women at five-thirty-one."

"Aye, aye, captain." Maryellen smiled as she replaced the receiver, warmed by their brief conversation.

A short while later, while her assistant was on her lunch break, an older couple came into the gallery. The building itself, more than a century old, was a historic site in Cedar Cove. As always, the wide wooden floorboards creaked as she moved out of her small office to greet the customers. The walls of the gallery displayed a variety of artwork—paintings and photographs—by several local artists, but the three pieces Jon had brought in earlier that week had already been sold.

Maryellen watched as the man and woman, arms linked, glanced about the room. They didn't seem typical of the normal tourist traffic. The man wore slacks and a short-sleeved plaid shirt, while the woman had on a rather old-fashioned shirtwaist dress. It looked as if they were on a church outing rather than visiting a small town.

"Hello," Maryellen said warmly. "Welcome to the Harbor Street Art Gallery. Is there anything I can help you find?"

"Hello." The woman smiled and turned to her husband, apparently waiting for him to speak. When he didn't, she said, "We've heard there's a very talented nature photographer from this area whose work is displayed here."

"That would be Jon Bowman." It never failed to thrill Maryellen when a customer inquired about him. "I'm afraid the gallery has sold out of Mr. Bowman's photographs. I'll have more in later in the month."

"Oh." The woman was clearly disappointed.

"His photographs are also available in a gallery in Seattle. I'd be more than happy to give you their name and phone number if you'd like."

She nodded eagerly. "Yes, by all means."

Maryellen walked over to her desk and retrieved a business card from the gallery that displayed Jon's photographs. The man, who was quite tall and formal in his manner, accepted the card. He bowed his head in thanks and stared at it intently.

Something about him caught Maryellen's attention, but she couldn't figure out exactly what it was.

The woman moved closer to her husband. "We heard correctly then? Jon—Mr. Bowman does live in the area?"

"Yes, he does. As it happens, I'm his wife." Maryellen said this with a great deal of pride.

"I thought you might be," the man said, speaking for the first time. His tone was low, a bit gruff, as if he didn't speak often.

Again the woman turned to her husband.

"If you're interested in seeing any of his work—"

"We'd like that very much," the woman said, cutting Maryellen off. "That would mean a great deal to both of us."

Maryellen walked over to the window. "If you stop at The Lighthouse Restaurant, which is just down the street, you'll see several of Jon's photographs on display." She pointed out the window. "Until recently, Jon supplemented his income by working at the restaurant."

"Doing what?" the man asked, sounding shocked.

"He was the chef."

"Jon?" The woman's tone was equally puzzled. "I… didn't realize."

This couple seemed to know Jon. "My husband is a man of many talents." Maryellen hesitated, almost afraid to ask if they were Jon's parents, uncertain what would happen if her suspicions proved to be correct.

"I—" The woman stopped abruptly and clamped her mouth shut.

Maryellen noticed how the man's arm tightened around his wife's; he seemed to be warning her that she was saying too much.

"Jon's an innovative chef. He could've made a name for himself in that field if he'd chosen to do so." Maryellen knew she was chattering, but it was the result of nerves.

"That's wonderful."

"Is there anything else I can show you?" Maryellen asked. "There are several talented local artists whose work we have in the gallery."

"We were only here about Jon's," the man said, starting toward the door. "Thank you for your help."

"You said Jon's your husband?" The woman lingered as if she wasn't ready to leave.

"We need to go," her husband insisted.

"In a minute, dear."

Maryellen studied them, wondering about the silent tug-of-war going on between the older couple. It was clear the woman had more questions, no less clear that the man was eager to be on his way.

"Do you have children?" the woman asked.

Maryellen nodded. "A daughter named Katie."

The woman placed her hand over her heart. "I'm sure she's a delightful child."

"Oh, yes. In looks she resembles my side of the family more, but she has Jon's temperament and his personality." Maryellen gently tested the waters. The woman certainly was curious. "I suspect Katie possesses her father's artistic eye, as well, but only time will tell about that."

"Marion."

The woman nodded. "We do need to go. Thank you so much…"

Maryellen nodded and returned to her desk once the couple had left. It occurred to her a moment later that she recognized the woman's name—Marion. That, combined with the pointed questions about Jon, convinced her they had to be Jon's parents. The ones she'd written shortly before her wedding. Marion and Joseph Bowman. She'd asked that they not answer her letter and they'd abided by her wishes.

Instead they'd come to Cedar Cove. Maryellen's heart leapt into her throat. She could only imagine what Jon would say if he ever found out what she'd done.

Twenty-Two

Roy McAfee was intensely curious about the news that Hannah Russell was living with the Beldons. He wasn't a man who paid attention to idle gossip, but in this instance, he knew and trusted the source—his wife.

The last time Roy had talked to Hannah, she'd been on the road in search of a fresh start. Apparently she'd found what she was looking for right here in Cedar Cove.

Deciding to look into the matter himself, Roy drove out to the Thyme and Tide. Roy didn't have many close friends—a few cops and former cops, all still in Seattle—but over the last couple of years he'd taken a liking to Bob Beldon. Corrie got along well with Peggy, too. It was rare that they found a couple whose company they both enjoyed.

Peggy had the front door open by the time Roy climbed out of the car. She was waiting for him, her smile wide.

"This is a pleasant surprise," she said as she held the screen door. "Bob's golfing with Pastor Dave this afternoon." Checking her watch, she added, "He won't be much longer, though, if you can wait."

"I should have phoned."

"Can I help you?" Peggy asked, leading the way into the kitchen. Without asking, she opened the refrigerator and brought out a big pitcher of lemonade, lemon slices floating on top.

"You might be able to do just that." Roy pulled out a chair and sat down at the round oak table. He wasn't opposed to a glass of Peggy's lemonade, especially since she made it fresh every day.

"What do you need to know?" Peggy filled two glasses and sat across from him.

Roy stretched out his arms, folding his hands on the table. "Corrie told me Hannah Russell's living with you these days."

Peggy nodded. "She came in the middle of that lightning storm we had a couple of weeks back." She shook her head. "Nearly frightened us out of ten years, arriving half-drowned on our front porch. You should've seen her when she first showed up, Roy. She was exactly like a lost kitten in search of a home."

"Where is she now?"

"At work."

Apparently Hannah was more than a visitor. Roy reached inside his shirt pocket for a pad and pen. "She has a job?"

Peggy nodded again. "This is her first day, and she was really worried about it. She's washing dishes at the Pancake Palace." Peggy frowned slightly. "I'd hoped for something better, but she was quite certain this job suited her. Unfortunately, she doesn't have much self-confidence."

Roy recalled his phone conversation with Hannah and remembered how timid her voice had been.

"She's due back any time. I'm curious as to how her first day went."

"I'd like to ask her a couple more questions if you don't mind?"

"Not at all, although Bob's going to be disappointed if he misses you." Peggy picked up her glass of lemonade and took a drink. "Did he mention he got the lead in *Chicago?* He's pretty pleased with himself, so if he has a swelled head when you see him, that's why." She smiled as she said it.

"Good for him," he murmured. Peggy looked proud of her husband, Roy thought, as well she should. "I saw him in *A Christmas Carol* last December and I was really impressed."

"He played four roles in that, including Marley with the clanking chains. The costumes were so good I didn't recognize him at first."

Roy chuckled and noticed a battered blue Honda pulling into the driveway.

"That's Hannah now," Peggy told him. She stood and walked over to the door off the kitchen.

When the girl came into the house, her eyes immediately went to Roy. She offered him a brief smile.

"How was work?" Peggy asked her. She gently placed one arm around Hannah's shoulders.

Hannah shrugged. "All right, I guess."

"Do you remember Mr. McAfee?" she asked.

Hannah's brow furrowed slightly. "You're the private investigator who called me, aren't you?"

"I am, and I have a few more questions for you. Is that all right?"

She shrugged a second time. "I suppose so, although I'm pretty tired at the moment."

Peggy got a fresh glass, filled it with lemonade and set it on the table. "I'll leave you two alone to talk. If you need anything, just give a holler. I'll be out in my garden."

It looked as if Hannah was about to ask Peggy to stay, but she seemed to find sufficient resolve in herself to face Roy on her own. She sat at the table, resting her clasped hands on the place mat. With her lank hair drawn into a ponytail and her eyes lowered, she resembled a shy schoolgirl.

"What would you like to ask me?" she mumbled.

Roy's question had to do with Samuels. Some of the facts didn't fit together in his mind. "I was wondering if you know anything about Colonel Samuels visiting California."

"To see my father, you mean?" she asked, glancing up.

Roy nodded encouragingly. "To the best of your knowledge, do you remember ever seeing him with your father?"

She hesitated. "Yes, now that you mention it, he did come to see my dad once."

Roy frowned as he scanned his notes. "I see I asked this question earlier and you claimed you'd never met Colonel Samuels."

"I didn't personally meet him," Hannah rushed to explain. "But I did see him with my father."

"When was that?"

She narrowed her eyes. "It must've been shortly before Dad left for Cedar Cove—yes, it was only a few days beforehand."

"Was your father agitated?"

"Not really. Why do you ask?"

"No reason," Roy said lightly.

"Is there anything else I can help you with?" she asked and he had the feeling she was eager for the questioning to be over.

"Not right now. I need to sort out a few things first. Will I be able to reach you here?"

"I should be around for a while. The Beldons said I could live with them for the time being. I…I probably shouldn't, but they make it so easy." She lowered her eyes again. "They really are wonderful people."

Roy agreed with her there. "Thank you for your time, Hannah."

"You're welcome."

Roy stood, ready to go, when he saw that Bob's car was turning into the driveway. Walking out of the kitchen, Roy waited until he'd parked in the garage. Bob had opened the trunk, removed his golf clubs and put them away before he noticed Roy.

"Good to see you, Roy," he said as he emerged from the garage. "Actually I'm glad you're here. I need to ask a favor."

"Ask away."

"I mentioned that my car's being worked on next week, didn't I?"

Roy nodded.

"Peggy's got a meeting with her garden club Tuesday night. Is there any chance I can take you up on your offer and borrow your car while mine's in the shop? I'll have it back first thing in the morning."

"No problem." Because Corrie and Roy worked together, her car sat at home most days.

"I appreciate it."

"I can drop it off Monday evening, if you'd like."

"Perfect," Bob said happily. "Why don't you and Corrie come for dinner that night?"

"Sounds good, but I'd better check with the boss." Corrie was the one who kept their social calendar and there'd be hell to pay if he agreed to dinner without clearing it with her beforehand.

"You do that, and get back to me."

Roy left for his office a few minutes later. He collected the mail on his way in and dumped it on his desk.

Corrie generally dealt with the mail before he saw it, but she was gone for the afternoon. It was a lazy day following the Fourth of July weekend, and they weren't completely back on schedule yet.

As he sorted through the bills, flyers and letters, Roy placed the bills in one basket and the personal stuff on Corrie's desk. A postcard caught his attention. It was a plain white one, the kind available at the post office for the price of the stamp.

He turned it over and read the message twice. EVERYONE HAS REGRETS. IS THERE ANYTHING YOU'VE DONE YOU WISH YOU COULD DO OVER? THINK ABOUT IT. There was no signature.

Roy set the card on his desk, staring at it for a long moment. Living the life he had, there were always regrets and misgivings. If someone was asking for a list, he wouldn't know where to start.

Twenty-Three

Ian Randall was in no hurry to get home. For six months at sea, he'd counted every second he was away from Cecilia. He'd crossed off each day on the calendar until they could be together again, eagerly anticipating their reunion. Being apart from her was agony. But now that he was home, he could hardly stand to be around her because it was an even deeper agony to have her there and not make love to her.

As he neared the highway exit that would take him home, Ian slowed the vehicle to a near-crawl. He dreaded what would happen once he walked into the duplex. The tension between them had begun the instant she announced she wanted another baby, and it seemed to increase day by day.

Cecilia tried to pretend everything was as it should be, tried to ignore his bad mood. Every night it was the same: she arrived home from work and immediately set about preparing dinner. While he buried his face in the newspaper, she talked about her day in the office. She was employed by a large accounting firm in Cedar Cove and liked her job, as much as Ian liked his. Above all, they did love each other; there was no question of that. They should be happy.

Nights were the worst. He made excuses not to go to bed at the same time as his wife. He saw the hurt in her eyes, but not once did she confront him.

If Cecilia had brought the situation out into the open, it might have helped. She wanted a baby and the fact was, he didn't. Cecilia had let him know that if they were going to use birth control, it was up to him. After that one disastrous night when she'd seduced him, he decided making love to Cecilia was just too dangerous.

She made him forget. As soon as she was in his arms, he lost all thought except his need for her. The risk of getting her pregnant was just too high.

There'd been a few nights when he'd given in—and been furious with himself afterward. He'd crawled into bed, assuming she was asleep. She wasn't, and he'd surrendered every time without even token resistance. Before he knew how he'd allowed it to happen, they'd made love, and on at least two of those occasions, it was without protection.... He tried to sleep on the sofa, but Cecilia wouldn't let him, insisting she'd sleep there with him.

The only way to be safe was to avoid her. Unfortunately, his self-imposed abstinence didn't always work. Ian had never viewed himself as an undisciplined man; the navy had drilled self-discipline into him from the minute he set foot in boot camp. But when it came to his wife, he had little resistance.

Those times he hadn't used protection—Cecilia was bound to get caught if she hadn't been already.

Ian couldn't bear the thought of another pregnancy going wrong. Losing Allison had nearly destroyed them both. Healing would come in time; he was sure of it. If only Cecilia wouldn't press the issue.

As he approached the stop sign off the freeway, Ian took

a left instead of a right, going in the opposite direction from home. He drove through unfamiliar streets, dread building in him. The second he walked in the door, it would be the same thing all over again—the same desire, the same frustration. He could feel it.

By sheer force of will, he hadn't touched Cecilia in three nights. It had been torture, and Ian just knew he wouldn't be able to resist her tonight.

When he discovered that he was driving down the road to the cemetery where his daughter was buried, Ian slowed and turned in. His baby girl had died after living only a few days. She'd been born with a defective heart and there was nothing the doctors could do. As a submariner he'd been under the polar ice cap at the time and unable to be with Cecilia. In fact, he hadn't even known about his daughter's birth until he learned of her death. Upon his return, he'd requested reassignment aboard an aircraft carrier, and that request had been granted.

Parking the car, Ian climbed out. Hands in his pockets, he walked over to Allison's grave, where he stood on the grass staring down at the small marker that recorded the dates of her birth and death. Amazing, really, that so little information could involve so much pain.

He gazed down at the marker for several minutes. "Hello, Allison," he whispered. He talked to his daughter whenever he visited her grave. He'd never even seen her, never had a chance to hold her or kiss her and he felt cheated to have been denied this one small consolation. The only photo of Allison had been taken in the hospital shortly after her birth. She'd been so tiny. Her life, so short and traumatic, had been filled with pain. Each breath was a struggle.

"I see your mother's been by," Ian said. He noticed the single pink rose, a sure sign that Cecilia had visited recently.

He didn't know how often his wife came to the cemetery, but he suspected it was every three or four days. "Did she tell you she wants another baby?"

Ian took a deep breath. "I don't think it's a good idea." He smiled as he said it. "The thing is, I wasn't ready when your mother told me she was pregnant with you. You took me by surprise, you know? I didn't realize a girl could get pregnant that easily." He hadn't been unhappy at the news, however; he'd been excited because it'd given him a good excuse to do what he wanted to do anyway—marry Cecilia.

His smile faded. Even when she got pregnant, Cecilia wasn't that keen on marriage. She had all kinds of stipulations. Apparently her mother had been pregnant with her when she married Cecilia's father, and the marriage had been a disaster from the beginning. Cecilia had no intention of repeating her mother's mistakes, so she'd insisted on a prenuptial agreement. It was lunacy, but he would've signed anything. The prenuptial had saved him in the end because Judge Lockhart had denied the divorce based primarily on that agreement.

"Your mother doesn't know this yet, but we might be heading back to sea." Although he hadn't told Cecilia, once orders came through, the word would be out soon enough. Under current circumstances, the navy wasn't likely to allow him the luxury of a long shore duty. That was the bad news as well as the good. He didn't want to leave Cecilia again, especially so soon, but he knew that if he was in port much longer, she'd get pregnant for sure.

"Look after your mother while I'm away, will you, sweetheart?" he asked. "Let her know how much I love her."

He waited a moment, nearly overwhelmed by sadness. What astonished him was how much love he felt for his little girl. This was a child he'd never had the privilege of kissing good-night or cradling in his arms, and yet she was as much a part of him as his own heart.

Ten minutes later, Ian left the cemetery and drove home. He half-expected Cecilia to comment that he was later than usual or ask where he'd been. She didn't. She was busy in the kitchen and barely looked up when he walked in the door.

"Did you have a good day?" she asked.

After glancing at the mail, he picked up the evening newspaper and settled into his favorite chair. "All right, I guess."

He opened the front section of the paper to block her from his sight. He found it incredibly sexy to watch his wife, walking barefoot in the kitchen in shorts and a cropped T-shirt. She dressed like that on purpose; Ian was convinced of it. The minute she got home from the office, she changed out of her business clothes and into something seductive. Half the time he couldn't keep his eyes off her.

"I had an all-right day, too," she said conversationally as she carried a large bowl to the table. "I made us a taco salad."

He nodded. "Thanks."

"Are you hungry?"

"Sort of." His appetite hadn't been good since he'd returned home. That was just another sign of the tension he'd been under lately.

"Dinner's ready," Cecilia said, sitting down at the table.

With little enthusiasm, Ian set the newspaper aside and joined her. Most nights he didn't contribute much to the conversation; Cecilia did practically all the talking. Every now and then, he'd ask her something because the silences troubled him more than the sound of her chatter.

This evening, however, she didn't seem to feel like talking, either. He was relieved when she finished dinner and brought her plate to the sink. Apparently her appetite wasn't good, either.

"Are you feeling okay?" he asked.

"I'm fine."

Ian frowned, unsure if he should believe that. But then she smiled so sweetly he couldn't doubt her.

They spent the evening in silence, each of them reading—Cecilia a magazine and he a thriller someone at work had lent him. By nine, she was yawning. "I'm going to bed."

He nodded. "I feel like staying up and reading for a while longer."

She didn't argue with him, but accepted his excuse. Then she wandered into the bedroom and closed the door. So far so good, he thought as he relaxed in his chair.

Ian made a genuine effort to read, but his mind was on everything except the words on the page in front of him. Nine o'clock was damned early for Cecilia to go to bed, he realized all of a sudden. He couldn't figure out why she'd done that. She almost always stayed up until at least ten.

At nine-thirty, he turned out the lights and walked into the darkened bedroom. It took his eyes a moment to adjust to the lack of light. Cecilia was curled up on her side of the bed, and he knew instantly that she was awake.

"Cecilia?"

"What?"

"You awake?"

"Yeah."

"Something's wrong, isn't it?"

She didn't answer him.

The mattress dipped when he sat on the edge of the bed. "You'd better tell me." His heart was starting to pound.

She pretended not to hear him. "Cecilia?"

"Are you coming to bed?"

He supposed the only way he could get her to talk was to join her in bed, so he undressed and slipped beneath the covers. Cecilia moved closer but didn't touch him. "Will you hold me?" she whispered.

"Okay." He lay on his back and Cecilia pressed her head against his shoulder. He wrapped his arm around her. She felt small in his embrace, smaller than usual.

He waited but she didn't say anything. In his heart he knew. He should've guessed right away, he supposed, but denial could be downright comfortable. "You're pregnant, aren't you?"

"Yes." She sobbed once. "Are you angry?"

He snorted softly. "No. I don't have anyone to blame but me."

"I wanted everything to be different than with Allison. I thought you'd be angry then, too, and instead you were so nice about it."

He didn't have anything to say to that.

"The news of a baby should make us happy."

"Are *you* happy?" he asked.

Cecilia didn't answer right away. "I'd be leaping up and down for joy if you were pleased."

His fears wouldn't let him feel good about this. "I'm afraid, Cecilia," he finally said.

"I am, too, but I want our baby so much. I love you, Ian. You got home almost two months ago, and this whole time's been awful. It's…it's like you hate me."

"Cecilia, no…"

"What else am I to think? You hardly talk to me and you won't even go to bed when I do. You think I don't know why? You don't want to make love to me and whenever you do, you hate yourself for it."

She certainly had him pegged. "I got you pregnant, didn't I?"

He could feel her nod.

"Yeah, well, you knew how I felt."

"You knew how I felt, too!" She sniffled, apparently trying not to cry. "I want this baby and I want my husband to love me and be excited and happy and you're not. It's tearing me up inside."

Ian expelled his breath. "I'm trying. Give me a chance to adjust to it, okay?"

Her tears moistened his shoulder.

"Cecilia, please, don't cry."

"I can't help it."

He kissed the tears from her face. Soft kisses, gentle kisses that eventually brought his lips to her mouth. "It'll be all right," he said and hoping to reassure her, kissed her again and again.

"This is our baby," she whispered, and hiccupped on a sob. "I want you to be happy.... I want you to love our baby."

"I will." He closed his eyes and struggled with his conflicting emotions.

"But you don't now?"

He dragged in a deep breath. "I'm trying. That's all I can do."

Cecilia broke free and rolled onto her side, turning away from him.

"Honey, please, do you want me to lie?"

"No."

"Then give me time." He cuddled her spoon fashion and slipped his arm around her middle. From pure habit, his palm cupped her breast. Many a night aboard ship, he'd dreamed of doing exactly this, cuddling his wife, loving her and enjoying the feel of her body so close to his own.

A sigh shuddered through Cecilia and she shifted her little butt closer to his growing arousal. She seemed to take delight in moving seductively against him. "Ian?" she whispered.

He squeezed his eyes shut and didn't respond.

"There's a nice thing about me being pregnant."

He wanted to know what it was, but at the moment the blood flow in his body wasn't headed in the direction of his brain.

"You don't have to wait until I'm asleep to come to bed anymore."

He smiled to himself. With a soft growl, he urged her onto her back. Sighing in surrender and welcome, she slid her arms around his neck and guided his mouth to hers.

"We're going to be all right," she promised him. "We really are."

Ian so badly wanted to believe her. "I know." But anything else he might have said was lost as he buried his fears in his wife's embrace.

Twenty-Four

Charlotte Jefferson couldn't stop smiling. She placed a cherry pie in the oven and set the timer, then turned to her knitting.

"Wipe that silly grin off your face," she chided Harry, her black cat, who sat on the arm of the sofa and studied her with a bemused look. "I know, I know, but this is just so wonderful I can't believe it's really happening."

When the doorbell chimed, Charlotte carefully put her knitting aside and hurried to answer it. She checked the peephole—one could never be too cautious—and saw that it was her daughter. After unbolting the locks, she opened the front door.

"What took you so long?" Olivia sputtered as she barreled past Charlotte. She was halfway into the kitchen before she stopped. Whirling around, she marched back into the living room and then sank abruptly onto the sofa, as though all her energy had drained away.

"Olivia, what's gotten into you?" Charlotte asked, concerned by her daughter's odd behavior.

Olivia bolted to her feet and almost immediately sat down

again. She covered her face with both her hands. "I think I've made a terrible mistake."

"What mistake?"

Olivia dropped her hands and stared forlornly out the living-room window, her shoulders sagging. She looked close to tears. "It's Jack and me."

Charlotte gasped. "My goodness, you've been married less than three months!"

"You think I don't know that? Lately…lately it's like we can't even talk."

"You and Jack? Why? What's wrong?"

"Oh, Mom, I feel so awful. We're just so different and we irritate one another and…and…"

"There, there now," Charlotte cooed softly. Things must be bad for her daughter to show up on her doorstep in this condition. In all the years Olivia had been married to Stan, never once had she run home after an argument or sought her parents' advice.

"I love Jack so much."

"Of course you do." Olivia's feelings for him were apparent months before she admitted she was in love.

Olivia's face crumpled as she struggled to hold back tears. "I love him, but he…he's a slob. And I can't stand it."

"You have to compromise, sweetie."

"You think I haven't tried?" Olivia shook her head. "I hate myself for nagging him to pick up his dirty clothes, but really, why should I follow him around and clean up after him?"

"Wait here," Charlotte murmured. "I'm making a pot of tea." The most serious discussions required tea. For some reason, everything made more sense over a shared cup of strong tea. And whatever had happened between Olivia and Jack appeared to be serious, indeed.

Less than ten minutes later, Charlotte was back. She carried in the tray, complete with a large ceramic pot, two china cups and a plate of homemade cookies. Olivia sat on the edge of the sofa with a wadded tissue in her hands.

"Start at the beginning," Charlotte said as she poured. She handed the first cup and saucer to Olivia, then poured her own. Olivia set the cup on the coffee table, her composure shaky.

"I'm...I'm not sure how this whole thing began, but tonight when I came home and saw the mess in the bathroom, I lost it. I realize Jack doesn't care about tidiness and order the way I do, but that's no excuse for leaving wet towels on the floor. He didn't so much as pick up his dirty underwear."

Charlotte sighed.

"Maybe I shouldn't have said anything but I did, and then Jack yelled at me and..." Her lower lip trembled. "We both said things we shouldn't have. He left and then I left, and now I feel so bad."

"Of course you do," Charlotte said with warm sympathy.

"When we returned from Hawaii, he made an effort to keep the house neat, but it didn't take him long to slip back into his old habits."

"That's a man for you," Charlotte said. "With your father and me, what we quarreled about was his tendency never to throw anything out. I'd get annoyed and put ten-year-old bills in the trash and then he'd get annoyed...." She sighed again, remembering. It seemed such a small thing now.

"I know I have irritating habits, too," Olivia said. "Mother, do you think I'm compulsive?"

Charlotte wasn't about to answer but it didn't matter; Olivia barreled on.

"Just because I insist the cap be on the toothpaste and the towels hung evenly on the rack—that doesn't make me a neat freak, does it?"

"Everyone has a certain, uh, comfort level," Charlotte said, hoping to sidestep the issue. She'd come across that useful term in a magazine article a while ago.

"I can't believe I'm running to my mother with this," Olivia cried. "It's just that I never thought Jack and I would argue so...so horribly."

"Olivia, every couple argues. It's healthy to clear the air."

Olivia nodded. "I know.... But we were both so adamant in what we said and now I think Jack's sorry he ever married me."

"I'm sure that's not true."

"He told me he'd had it with this diet I'd put him on and that if he saw another chunk of tofu he was dumping it in the garbage. But Mom, his diet is atrocious! He thinks I'm picking on him because I want him to lose a few pounds. All I want is for him to make healthier food choices."

"Of course you want him to eat properly, but—"

"He said we got along a lot better when we lived apart."

Charlotte was stunned. "He didn't mean it."

Olivia covered her face again. "I think he did, because right after that he left. I wasn't letting him walk out on me, so I left, too. Can you believe I'd do anything so childish?"

Charlotte had to admit she was somewhat amused. This must have been a humdinger of an argument.

Olivia had hated fighting when she was a little girl, too. It used to upset her to the point that she'd make herself sick.

"What should I do now?" Olivia pleaded. "Should I just go back to the house and pretend nothing happened?"

"Well," Charlotte said, gently patting her daughter's shoulder. "First of all, I'm sure Jack is feeling just as bad as you are. You both need to remember that you were single for a lot of years. Marriage is a major adjustment. Perhaps it would be best if you bought two tubes of toothpaste."

"I *did,*" she said indignantly. "But Jack can't remember which one is his. Half the time he can't find it, and mine's handy, so he uses it." She reached for her cup of tea and took a sip. "Then he gets upset when I say something. According to Jack, it shouldn't make any difference."

"I know."

"You can't possibly know. The other night I found an open jar of peanut butter on the kitchen counter. The knife was still in it."

Charlotte dropped her jaw as though shocked.

"Apparently Jack got up in the middle of the night and made himself a sandwich."

"I take it peanut butter isn't on his diet?" Charlotte tried hard not to smile.

"No, and Jack knows that. It's for his own good."

"Oh, dear."

Olivia raised her head at the sound of a car and she vaulted to her feet, dashing to the window. "Jack just pulled up out front." She squared her shoulders and looked back at Charlotte. Then, as if she were making a court decree, she declared, "Tell him I'm not here."

"Olivia, you're being ridiculous. Your car's parked in my driveway. I'm not going to lie to your husband."

"Look at me, Mother! Just look at me. I'm a sensible adult, or at least I was until I married Jack Griffin. Overnight I'm back to being a teenager. I've never come running to my mother in my life and now—now just look at me. I'm a mess! I'll talk to Jack once I've had a chance to compose myself."

The doorbell chimed. Olivia heaved in a breath. "I need to freshen my makeup...and I don't want him to know... Oh, just tell him whatever you want."

Charlotte frowned.

Olivia disappeared and Charlotte went to the front door. Jack didn't seem surprised when she answered before he'd even knocked. He had on his light raincoat, rumpled as usual, hands deep in his pockets.

"Hello, Jack."

A scowl darkened his face. He nodded. "Hello, Charlotte."

"What can I do for you?"

"Do you have a minute?"

Charlotte hesitated, then gestured him in. "Of course. Come inside."

He stepped into the house and glanced around. Charlotte noticed that his gaze lingered on the two teacups, but he didn't comment on the fact that Olivia was obviously at the house.

"I heard a rumor this afternoon and wanted to see if it was true."

"Sit down," Charlotte invited soberly, trying to hide her amusement at both Olivia and Jack. They were acting like kids—and as Olivia had said, even when she *was* a kid, she hadn't acted like this. Still, amused or not, Charlotte was worried; immature behavior could escalate and end in drastic consequences. This was a good marriage in the ways that counted. She hoped they'd give it the chance it deserved.

He chose the wing chair and stroked Harry's head as he walked past the cat. Harry remained unruffled by all these dramatics. She envied him a little.

"What did you hear?" Charlotte asked as she sat down again. She picked up her knitting, hoping it would calm her.

As if to prove this was an official visit, Jack pulled out his pen and pad. "Rumor has it Ben Rhodes met with the people of Puget Sound Medical and Dental this afternoon."

"You heard?" Charlotte was beside herself with excitement. "He went with Louie Benson."

Jack noted this information on his pad.

"I'm sure Mayor Benson will fill you in on the details."

"I don't suppose this has anything to do with that parcel of land off Heron Street recently bequeathed to the city by the Duncan family?"

Charlotte beamed him a smile. Very little got past Jack Griffin. "It could," she murmured and continued to concentrate on her knitting for fear he'd read the absolute delight in her eyes.

"My guess—"

"I'm not at liberty to say another word, Jack. An announcement will be made by the mayor tomorrow morning."

"So Cedar Cove is going to get its health clinic, after all?"

Charlotte kept her head lowered. "That's a distinct possibility, but you didn't hear it from me, understand?"

Jack chuckled. "Sure enough."

"Is that the only reason you're here?" Charlotte asked. She wondered who'd mentioned the news about the clinic. Bess had come over earlier and Charlotte had shared it with her dear friend. Bess had been thrilled, but she never could keep a secret, no matter how much she promised.

Jack got up and stared into the kitchen. "I didn't actually stop by because of the clinic. That was a convenient excuse. Where's Olivia hiding?"

"I most certainly am not hiding," her daughter announced, moving to the kitchen doorway where she stood with her arms crossed. "I—I was taking Mother's pie out of the oven."

"Oh, dear, I'd forgotten all about it. I didn't hear the timer." Charlotte was so flustered that the cherry pie had completely slipped her mind.

"I think I should give you two a moment alone," Charlotte said, walking past Olivia to check on the pie. Never in all her life had it taken her longer to complete a single row of knitting. She couldn't quite stifle a sigh. In the last thirty minutes, she'd been up and down more times than an elevator.

Olivia remained in the kitchen doorway and it was all Charlotte could do not to push her forward. Jack wasn't standing in the living room because he liked the view. He'd come for his wife and if Olivia had a lick of sense she'd realize it.

They stared at each other and finally Jack spoke. "I promise I won't leave the peanut butter out again," he muttered.

Charlotte resisted the urge not to giggle.

Olivia sniffled. "Oh, Jack, I didn't mean any of those terrible things I said."

"I didn't either."

"It's just that I—I guess I really am a neat freak..."

Jack shook his head. "I'm a slob. I'll try harder, I promise."

"I will, too."

Olivia flew out of the kitchen then. Charlotte peered into the living room and discovered that Jack had his arms around his wife. They hugged each other for a long moment.

Everything was going to be all right, she thought with relief. They'd have their difficulties but their commitment and love for each other was strong enough to keep them together.

"Are you ready to go home?" Olivia asked her husband.

Jack nodded and kissed the top of her head. "Do you really think I'm a sex fiend?"

"Jack!" Olivia glanced over her shoulder and Charlotte pretended not to have heard.

"Best compliment I've had in years."

"Oh, honestly." The laughter was back in Olivia's voice. Arm in arm, they walked out the door.

Sex fiend. Her daughter didn't know how lucky she was.

Twenty-Five

Bob caught sight of the other car as he rounded the corner. He'd spent the last three hours with the theater group, rehearsing his role as the attorney Billy Flynn in the musical *Chicago*. It was now after ten and this late at night, Harbor Street was nearly deserted. He noticed that the blue SUV took each turn he made, the bumper dangerously close to his own. Bob felt his heart leap into his throat just as the vehicle eased back.

He was being followed.

Bob took a left at Heron and the SUV turned left, as well. Knowing he tended to jump to conclusions, he wanted to be sure and made an immediate right. Again the vehicle behind him turned in the same direction. At least it maintained a safe distance.

Now he was convinced; he was indeed being followed. His heart racing, Bob reached for his cell phone. This wasn't an emergency and the car stayed well behind him but it was obvious the driver was tailing him. His first thought was to call Peggy, but he didn't want to needlessly alarm his wife.

Nor could he phone the sheriff's office. No crime had been committed—yet.

He'd ignored the warnings he'd gotten from Sheriff Davis and Roy. After all this time, Bob had refused to believe he was in any real danger. He'd thought everyone was overreacting, and the only reason he'd agreed not to accept guests was to appease Peggy. All at once, he wasn't so sure about anything.

"Roy," he mumbled aloud with relief. He'd call his friend. Roy would know what to do. But try as he might, Bob couldn't remember his home number. He might be able to dig it up from the recesses of his memory, but the only number he could recall was for the office. At this time of night, Roy would almost certainly be at home.

"Great," he muttered under his breath. "Just great. Think. You can figure this out."

Then Bob remembered reading one of those "what to do in case of an emergency" articles in some long-ago publication. If you're being followed, he recalled, the advice was to drive to a police station.

With that in mind, Bob drove directly to the Cedar Cove Sheriff's Office, where he pulled into the half-circle driveway. He stayed in his vehicle as the blue SUV drove past. It slowed briefly, and then sped away.

Tension caused him to tighten his hold on the steering wheel. He sat in the driver's seat and forced his pulse to return to normal by taking deep, even breaths. When he was certain his legs would support him, he opened the car door and climbed out.

"You can't leave your car there," a uniformed officer informed him as he walked into the station.

He began to explain, then changed his mind. He might be making more of this than necessary. "I'll move it in just a moment. I need a phone book."

"You'll move it now."

Bob wanted to argue, to explain, but decided against both. It was easy enough to pull his vehicle around. He parked in the street, then walked back to the station and located a public telephone near the restrooms.

He looked up Roy McAfee's home number and used his cell phone to place the call.

"McAfee," Roy snapped, sounding like the police detective he'd once been.

"Someone was following me," Bob said without introduction.

"When?" Roy's voice was hard as steel.

"Just now."

"Where are you?"

Bob leaned his shoulder against the wall. "At the sheriff's office."

"Good. Did you get the license plate number?"

Bob closed his eyes and shook his head. "No. I was so rattled I didn't even think to look."

"What make was the car?"

That he remembered. "A blue SUV. Ford, I think. Or maybe a Chevy."

"Doesn't narrow it down much. Are you sure you didn't get any of the plate number?"

Bob wanted to kick himself. "No, sorry."

"You okay?"

"Of course I'm all right." He hoped his voice didn't betray how badly this had unsettled him. "What should I do now?"

"Drive over to my house. I'll meet you and follow you home. We can talk there."

"Okay." He climbed back in the car and started the engine. His hand trembled as he turned the ignition key.

He checked the rearview mirror every few seconds during the drive to Roy and Corrie's. He thought he saw the SUV once, but if so it kept a respectable distance that didn't allow him an opportunity to read the license plate. But by then he was so jumpy he would've suspected any car that came within two blocks of him.

When he arrived at the McAfees' home, Roy was already in the car. He pulled in directly behind Bob and followed him down Heron to Cranberry Point.

Peggy was standing at the back door waiting for him as if she knew something was wrong. He was only a few minutes later than he'd told her he'd be.

"What is it?" she asked as he walked from the garage to the house, Roy directly behind him.

Sometimes Bob swore his wife had a sixth sense. "I was followed."

Her eyes widened with alarm. "Just now?"

He nodded. "I called Roy from the sheriff's office. To be on the safe side he decided to follow me home."

"What's happening?" Hannah stepped into the kitchen, her expression curious—and more than a little wary.

"I think we should all sit down," Peggy suggested. Roy came into the house with Bob, and the four of them sat in the family room. Hannah, who was dressed for bed, resembled a lost waif with her long hair falling about her face and huge, frightened eyes.

"Tell us the whole story, from the beginning," Roy said.

There wasn't all that much to tell. Bob explained how the car had come right up on his bumper when he first drove down Harbor Street and then pulled back. How the driver had maintained a reasonable distance as Bob took a number of twists and turns to establish whether or not he was being followed.

"Whoever it was didn't want to be identified," Roy said.

"Did you recognize the person in the car?" Peggy asked.

Bob shook his head. "No—I didn't really look. I mean, when the car first came up behind me the only thought that went through my mind was how close on my tail it was."

"Did you notice if the driver was a male or female?" Roy asked. "One person or two?"

Bob felt like an utter failure. He should be able to answer at least that question, but in all honesty he couldn't. "One, I think. Male...but I'm not sure." Disgusted with himself, he shook his head. "I don't know. I couldn't tell."

Peggy reached for his hand and her fingers curled around his. He was sure she didn't realize how tightly she squeezed.

"Anything else you can remember?" Roy prodded.

"Nothing. But if it happens again, I'll know what to look for."

"Again?" Peggy gasped.

Bob could tell she was badly shaken, but he couldn't come up with a single reassurance. Not even one.

"Who do you think it might be?" Bob asked his friend.

"Whoever it is wanted you to know you were being followed." Roy said, "otherwise he wouldn't have made it this obvious."

"Why?"

"Why else?" Peggy cried. "He's trying to frighten us."

Bob had news for her; the attempt had worked.

"But...who would do such a thing?" Hannah asked. "What sort of person?"

"It might have nothing to do with the murder," Roy told them.

"What else could it mean?"

Roy shrugged. "That I don't know."

If Roy thought he was providing comfort, his tactic hadn't

worked. Not in Bob's opinion, anyway. He was nervous and unable to hide it.

"I'm going to bed," Hannah said into the silence. "Unless you need me for anything?"

"No, no, go to bed," Peggy insisted. "Do you want me to wake you up?"

Hannah nodded. "Please. I didn't mean to sleep in this morning."

"I know. But you don't want it to happen again."

"No, I don't," Hannah agreed. "I need this job."

Their houseguest had been two hours late for work, and the Pancake Palace had phoned looking for her. Peggy had managed to get the girl up and moving, but it had been no easy task. By the time Hannah got into town, the restaurant was practically out of clean dishes. To her credit, Hannah had stayed two hours past her shift in an effort to make up for her tardiness.

"If you're all right, I should probably leave," Roy said, getting to his feet.

"We're fine," Bob lied. "You go on home. Thanks for everything." He deeply appreciated Roy's friendship and concern, which went far beyond their professional relationship.

Bob walked him to the kitchen door, then watched as Roy drove off.

"Are you tired?" he asked Peggy. She stood in the middle of the kitchen, completely still, as if she was afraid to move a single step in any direction.

"You can't be serious about going upstairs and sleeping," she said. When he didn't answer, she added, "You honestly think you'll sleep?"

"No, but that's not the point."

Peggy smiled. "I don't think I can, either. Want to watch some TV?"

They both knew they were in for a long, restless night.

Twenty-Six

Grace Sherman had been looking forward to the Dog and Bachelor Auction with equal measures of anticipation and dread. The fund-raising event had initially been her idea and Mary's, and Grace wanted it to be successful. At the same time, she was aware that she'd be sitting by while the man she loved was on the auction block. She couldn't join in the bidding herself, both because she couldn't afford it and because she knew how he felt about her now. Other women would bid on Cliff and he'd walk away with someone else on his arm.

On the evening of July tenth, the parking lot of The Lighthouse Restaurant was fast filling to capacity. Women lined up outside the door, and it wasn't for dinner and drinks, Grace suspected, although the food, as always, would be exceptional. No, all those women were eager to get the best seats in the house for a close-up view of the dogs and—especially—the bachelors. Even before the auction had begun, everyone could tell it was going to be an unqualified success.

"This is just fabulous," Mary Sanchez said. She stood with Margaret White at the entrance of the restaurant. As soon as the doors opened, they'd collect the tickets that had already been sold. The women waiting to place their bids jostled outside, peeking through the windows, chatting and laughing. The mood was jovial and high-spirited.

"The natives are getting restless," Margaret shouted to Janet Webb over the noise and laughter from outside. Janet was getting everything organized for the cashiers, who were situated at the rear of the restaurant near the bar area.

"Is there anything I can do?" Grace asked. She'd come to offer an extra pair of hands before the auction started. Her official duties, however, had been completed weeks earlier.

"Yes, Grace, there is," Janet said, her tone serious. "I want you to enjoy this event. You've worked hard and the shelter deeply appreciates all your effort."

"It was my pleasure." Grace figured that enjoying this evening wasn't remotely possible, but she was determined to try. All she could hope was that the woman who won Cliff would appreciate what a wonderful man he was.

Janet, the director of the animal shelter, walked over to the restaurant foyer, and gave the signal for the doors to open. As the crowd began to enter, Grace observed with surprise the number of young single women in Cedar Cove. She'd thought most of the people here would be familiar to her but quite a few of the women weren't. Like a crashing tide against the shoreline, people—young women, older ones and even men who were clearly there as spectators—flooded into the restaurant, tipping over chairs and scooting around tables as they jockeyed for seats.

Thankfully Grace had been able to reserve a table for friends. Olivia and Jack showed up a few minutes after the doors opened, and Charlotte and Ben followed. Grace had encouraged her daughters to attend for the entertainment value of the event, but both Maryellen and Kelly had decided to spend the night at home with their husbands and families. Grace didn't blame them.

"Can you believe this crowd," Grace commented to Olivia, looking around. It was difficult to hear over the high-decibel chatter all around them. The atmosphere of fun and excitement was as strong as the pervasive scent of perfume.

Grace could only imagine what it was like in the waiting area where the bachelors and dogs were congregated. Silently she read over the list of the bachelors, fifteen in all. Pairing them up with dogs had been a complicated task, taken on by Janet Webb. Grace wondered what breed—or mixed breed—she'd choose to accompany Cliff. A shepherd of some kind was her guess. Large, gentle and handsome…

The temporary stage, with an extended walking platform, reached halfway into the restaurant, with tables and chairs arranged on both sides. The idea was that the bachelor would walk out with the dog on a leash.

Whoever won could take the dog or the bachelor or both. If the winner only wanted one, then the auction would start over with the remaining entrant, whether man or dog. As Grace read over the rules described in the program, she hoped this novel idea would raise the funds the shelter needed, and more.

"If I'd been one of the bachelors, I bet I would've brought in top dollar," Jack boasted with a cocky grin. "Unfortunately Olivia got me first."

Olivia glanced up from her program and arched one brow. "Unfortunately? Is that a complaint, Mr. Griffin?"

The teasing left his eyes and was replaced with a slow, easy smile. "Not at all. I meant unfortunately for these other ladies." At her smirk, he shook his head. "In all seriousness, though, I think I got the better half of this deal."

"I'm not so sure I agree." Olivia rested her head against him, and Jack's arm came around her shoulders. The gesture was so romantic that Grace had to look away. Rarely had she felt lonelier or more alone, but she was finished with self-recrimination. Life goes on, as the old saying had it, and so would she.

"I see Stanley's one of the bachelors," Charlotte said disapprovingly. She pointed out her ex-son-in-law's name to Ben Rhodes. "Stanley doesn't even live in Cedar Cove."

"I know," Grace murmured, "but Stan wanted to do his part for charity."

"Did you tell him charity begins at home?"

"Mother!" Olivia mildly chastised her.

Charlotte frowned. "I only hope his ego doesn't get the better of him—for once."

In Grace's opinion, it was too late for that. Stan had volunteered under the assumption that any number of women would battle to outbid each other for the opportunity to date him.

"I can't wait to see which dog Janet paired him up with," she said, leaning close to Olivia as the waiters started to circulate with salads.

"You mean you don't know?"

She shook her head. "Janet's not deciding until she's had a chance to mingle with the bachelors and meet them."

"This could be intriguing."

Soon everyone was seated and the main course had been quickly and efficiently served, with Justine directing the waiters from the kitchen. Janet stepped up to the podium set off to one side of the platform and reviewed the rules. Next she introduced the auctioneer and Barry Stokes stepped forward.

Barry greeted everyone with a smile and a few good-natured jokes about bachelors. He managed to work the audience to an even higher level of excitement, periodically reminding everyone of the important role the Animal Shelter played in the community. He pointed out that the final bidding price would be separate for the dog and the man. If the bidder wanted the dog and the bachelor, the bid was actually doubled. So if the bidder wanted either the dog *or* the bachelor, the bidding would begin again. Dogs made wonderful pets, he said at the end of his introduction. And so did bachelors—which brought a roar from the crowd.

The first bachelor presented was Bruce Peyton. Grace knew Bruce through the library; the widower often came in with his young daughter. Grace recalled his wife Stephanie, too, and was well aware that the young father continued to grieve.

Bruce was matched up with a bassett hound. Grace could tell how nervous he was by the way his gaze darted around the room. The order of the bachelors' appearances had been chosen by lottery, and she felt sorry for Bruce, whose name had obviously been pulled first.

The whispers rose as Bruce walked down the runway, the bassett hound trudging beside him. It was clear that Bruce would've preferred to hurry, but that was impossible with the slow-moving dog.

The first bid came from one of the women who worked at Get Nailed. She was immediately outbid by a woman from the local pharmacy. The bidding went back and forth between them until the last moment. Bruce—and the dog—were about to be won for the bargain price of two hundred and thirty-five dollars each when Lois Habbersmith, who worked with Maryellen at the gallery, shocked everyone.

"Three hundred and fifty dollars!"

The two women who'd been bidding stared at each other, shook their heads and sat down.

"Three hundred and fifty dollars, going once, going twice." Barry paused and pointed his gavel at the woman from the salon. "Are you sure you want to quit so soon? The bassett hound alone is a bargain at that price."

The two previous bidders shook their heads again.

"Sold," Barry announced and slammed down the gavel. "Now, which do you want? Bruce or the bassett?"

"Both!"

"Three hundred and fifty dollars each," Barry reminded her.

"Yes." Lois gleefully pulled out her checkbook and maneuvered around several chairs as she made her way to the back of the room.

Barry chuckled. "You're married, Lois. What's Don going to think when you bring home a dog and a bachelor?"

"Don approves."

Several laughs followed, along with good-natured teasing.

Lois dismissed Barry's comment with a wave of her hand. "Don and I already decided we'd get a dog. And I promised him whoever I bid on would be tall enough to reach the second-story windows on the ladder. They need a good washing, and Bruce looks tall enough to do it and young enough not to complain."

"In other words, you purchased your bachelor to relieve Don of washing the outside windows?"

"I did. Those windows haven't been cleaned in three years. Don said to go for it and I did."

"You want me to wash your windows?" Bruce Peyton asked, visibly disappointed. "Hey, is that legal?"

"Sure it is." Barry laughed, nodding his head. "You volunteered for this, and she paid good money for you."

Bruce didn't seem too happy with this turn of events. Giving Barry a disgruntled look, he walked off the stage.

The chatter diminished as the second bachelor was announced—Cal Washburn, the horse trainer Grace had met at Cliff's ranch. He was matched with a spotted gray-and-black Australian Shepherd. Again Grace thought it was a good pairing. Cal was a quiet man, gifted with horses.

Judging by the hushed whispers that rippled across the room, it was evident that Cal was a bachelor of interest. From her vantage point, Grace could see that the dog was trembling and seemed even more nervous than Cal, until Cal crouched down and whispered something in the animal's ear, which instantly quieted him. Grace watched in amazement as the pair proceeded down the runway. The bidding was fast and furious, with cutthroat competition between the girls at Get Nailed and—of all people—Corrie McAfee. In the end, Corrie won.

"Do you want the dog or the bachelor?" Barry asked.

Corrie stood while Roy remained seated with the Beldons. "I want both."

"Isn't that your husband you're sitting with?" Barry pretended to sound shocked. "What's happening to our society when married women walk off with all the eligible bachelors because they need their windows washed?"

Corrie grinned. "You've got it all wrong. The dog's for my son, Mack, and the bachelor's for my daughter."

A loud cheer of approval followed as Corrie walked over to the cashier with her checkbook in hand.

The third bachelor was Stan Lockhart, who was paired with a high-strung white poodle. Stan seemed in his element on the runway, unlike the two previous bachelors. He'd apparently been practicing and he played to the crowd, doing a fairly good impression of a model, complete with one hand in his pocket. He was obviously expecting the high bids garnered by the other bachelors. When the winner, a younger blond woman, opted for the dog and not him, his disappointment was noticeable. The bidding started over, and Stan commanded less money than the poodle.

Grace elbowed Olivia, who didn't seem to know exactly how to react; her expression was a mixture of shock, embarrassment and laughter. To everyone's surprise, Charlotte's good friend Bess Ferryman won Stan. The older woman stood up to proudly claim her prize.

"Don't tell me you're married, too?" the auctioneer demanded.

"Nope, and I'm not buying him to wash any windows, either. I've got a hot date in mind."

"Good for you," Barry said approvingly.

"Dinner, and he's buying, followed by ballroom dancing." Bess marched purposefully toward the cashier. For just a moment, it looked as if Stan might balk, but then he dutifully left the stage.

"Couldn't happen to a nicer guy," Jack whispered to the others. "I'll bet he doesn't offer his services again anytime soon."

Grace was chatting with Olivia and Charlotte when the next bachelor's name was announced.

Cliff Harding.

This was the moment Grace had been dreading all night. In an effort to prove that she was unaffected, she fixed a smile on her face and stared straight ahead, hoping no one could guess at the turmoil inside her.

Cliff was paired with a lovely female golden retriever. When he stepped onto the stage, he was greeted by loud cheers. Grace had long suspected he'd be one of the key figures at this event, and she was right.

Almost immediately, Margaret White leaped into the bidding. Seconds later, the woman who worked for John L.

Scott Realty topped Margaret's two-hundred-dollar bid by another fifty.

"What about you?" Olivia asked, nudging Grace.

"I can't."

"Why not?" Olivia asked, her voice rising with agitation.

It was too complicated to explain. Now wasn't the time to try, so she simply shook her head.

"Grace, you can't just sit there and let some other woman walk away with Cliff. You have to bid."

She felt the same way, but she couldn't do it. While Margaret and the other woman continued to raise each other in fifty-dollar increments, Grace bit her tongue. Her heart pounded like crazy and her mouth went dry as she dealt with two years' worth of confused emotions. Finally she couldn't stand it any longer. Damn it, she was going to bid!

"Five hundred dollars, going one, going twice—"

"Seven hundred dollars," Grace shouted suddenly, leaping to her feet. She just hoped the animal shelter would agree to accept payments, because she didn't have that kind of money in her checking account. Seven hundred dollars would put her over the maximum on her credit card, too. She couldn't go a penny higher.

There was a moment of stunned silence. "Seven hundred dollars. Do we have seven hundred and fifty dollars?"

Grace didn't dare look in Cliff's direction.

"Seven hundred and fifty dollars," Margaret White said, and her voice trembled as if to say this was far higher than she'd intended.

"Go for eight hundred," Olivia encouraged, tugging at Grace's sleeve.

Grace sat back down. "No… I shouldn't have bid when I did. I don't have seven hundred dollars, let alone eight."

"Seven hundred and fifty dollars, going once, going twice, going—"

"Eight hundred dollars," Olivia shouted, startling Grace.

Barry pointed the gavel at Margaret White, who shook her head.

"Sold for eight hundred dollars." He punctuated the sale with a bang of the gavel.

Barry Stokes's eyes narrowed as he peered into the audience. He placed both hands on the sides of the podium and leaned forward. "Is that you, Judge Lockhart?" He didn't wait for an answer. "Last I heard, you and Jack Griffin were married. Now, don't tell me there's trouble between you newlyweds already?"

"Nope," Olivia called back. "And I want Cliff *and* the dog. The dog's for my daughter, Justine, and the bachelor is an early birthday gift for my best friend, Grace Sherman."

"I can't let you do that," Grace insisted in a harsh whisper.

"You can and you will," Olivia said out of the side of her mouth. "Besides, Maryellen and Kelly went in with me." She smiled. "My orders were to bid on Cliff if you didn't—or if you dropped out. I had to bid on the dog, anyway. Justine met her backstage and fell in love with her."

"Maryellen and Kelly?"

"Me, too," Charlotte whispered, leaning across the table. "I did it for Cliff as much as you. As far as I'm concerned, you two belong together."

Grace did look in Cliff's direction then. Although he was relatively close, she couldn't gauge his reaction. All she could hope was that he agreed with Charlotte.

Twenty-Seven

Rachel Pendergast was sweeping up her station at Get Nailed. Her appointments were finished for the day, and she was ready to head back to her house. When the phone rang, she looked up to make sure Valerie, the receptionist, was around to answer it. She wasn't, but Tracey grabbed it and then held up the receiver for Rachel.

"It's that little girl," Tracey said. "You cut her hair not too long ago."

"Jolene?"

Tracey shrugged. "She says she has to talk to you."

"All right." Rachel walked over to the desk, where Tracey handed her the phone. She'd been meaning to call Jolene, anyway. "This is Rachel," she said cheerfully.

"You didn't bid on my dad." Jolene sounded as though she was on the verge of tears. "I thought you were going to bid on him at the Dog and Bachelor Auction."

"Hello, Jolene," Rachel said.

"Hi." Her voice was small and sad.

"I think your dad's very nice, but I don't think he's ready for another relationship. Remember how we talked about that? You said you need another mommy and I asked if I could be your friend instead."

"I remember."

"Is your dad there?"

"Yes, but he's in the other room and he doesn't know I'm calling you."

"Let me talk to him, okay?"

"Okay—only I want to know if you bought a dog and a bachelor at the auction."

"I did, but my friend Karen took the dog. And I'm not meeting my bachelor until Friday night."

"Who is he?"

"Well, I don't know much about him except that his name is Nathan Olsen and he's in the navy."

"Is he in love with you?"

She wished! "No, I barely had a chance to talk to him." After the auction, the restaurant had been chaos. Rachel had only a few minutes to speak to Nate before it was time to leave.

"Oh."

"How about if you and I get together next week?"

"Will you paint my fingernails again?" Jolene asked eagerly.

"If you like."

"Can we talk about girl things?"

"Sure."

Jolene sounded happier now. "I'll get my dad."

A moment later, Bruce got on the line. "Jolene phoned you?" he said in a curt voice.

"Yes, but I was planning to get in touch anyway. She saved me the phone call. I'd enjoy spending another afternoon with Jolene. It seemed to do her good—and me, too, for that matter."

He hesitated. "I thought you might bid for me."

Now Bruce was going to harass her about that, too? "You told me you weren't interested in dating," she said as calmly as she could.

"I'm not—just forget it, all right?"

Gladly! Talk about mixed messages. Bruce couldn't have made his feelings any more obvious; he didn't want to get involved—and that was fine with Rachel. "Can I see Jolene?"

"Yeah, sure, that would be great."

They set up a day and time, and Rachel hung up the phone, more confused than ever. She must have had a puzzled expression on her face because Terri came over to stare at her.

"What's with you?" she asked, one hand on her ample hip. "You look like a feather would bowl you over."

"Bruce Peyton wants to know why I didn't bid on him." Even as she spoke, she was astounded that he'd brought it up.

"Don't worry about it," Terri advised. "You choose your own dates."

Rachel made an effort to put Bruce out of her mind. As far as she could tell, he was a lost cause, and she was through with throwing her life away on dead-end relationships.

That Friday night, Rachel arrived at The Lighthouse ten minutes before she was meeting Nate. She sat on the bench in the foyer, waiting nervously.

She wasn't quite sure why she'd plunked down her hard-earned tip money on him. She suspected it was because the auction was almost over and she hadn't made a single bid. Terri and Jane had both bid on men, but had lost out each time. Rachel felt that at least one of the girls from the salon should "score a bachelor," as Terri put it.

But by the end of the evening, Terri was more interested in drinking Fuzzy Navels than bidding on dogs and bachelors. Jane figured she might as well save her money. And Karen Redfern, a married friend from high school, just wanted a dog.

Then Nate Olsen had stepped onto the platform, walking a lovely and self-assured little spaniel who was destined to become Karen's dog. Bruce was navy and apparently a warrant officer, whatever that was. Although Cedar Cove was basically a navy town, being so close to the Bremerton shipyard, Rachel wasn't too familiar with military life.

She tried to remember what she could of their brief conversation that night. He was a nice-looking man. Trim, tall with dark hair and pleasant features. She'd especially noticed his piercing blue eyes.

Rachel glanced up, and those very eyes were looking at her. He was dressed casually in slacks and a short-sleeve shirt and nothing like she remembered. Tall, yes, but blond, not dark-haired. The eyes she had right—a brilliant blue. The nice-looking part was accurate, too, as far as it went. Only she didn't recall him being *this* attractive. And so young. He must be just out of high school. Good grief, she'd robbed the cradle!

Swallowing her disappointment, she stood, came forward and held out her hand. "Rachel Pendergast, in case you'd forgotten." Her surname was easy to mispronounce.

"Hello, Rachel." His smile dazzled her.

On second glance, he might still be *in* high school. She had to restrain herself not to ask if he was over eighteen. Oh, no, what had she gotten herself into now?

"I can seat you immediately," the hostess said, carrying two menus. "If you'll follow me."

Rachel was convinced every eye in the room was on Nate

and her. He was so young. How could she have missed that at the auction? It must've been awfully dark in there—or those margaritas had impaired her vision. Well, thirty wasn't that old, but at the moment she felt like she could be his mother.

They were shown to a table by the window with a lovely view. Early-evening sunlight played on the sparkling water and the lighthouse in the distance looked downright romantic. Rachel studied the menu and tried hard to think of a conversation-starter. Working with the public she'd never found that a problem. Now she felt distracted, as if she'd become a spectacle for the entire restaurant, sitting there with her date. Her young date. The guy she'd had to buy at an auction.

Finally she couldn't bear not knowing. Lowering the menu she gazed across the table at Nate. "I'm sorry if this is rude, but I need to ask you something. Just how old are you?"

Nate gave her a charming grin. "Twenty-five."

Instantly she felt worlds better. Five years—that wasn't so bad.

"How old are you?" he asked in return.

"Thirty. I've never been married, no kids and I'm a nail tech—which used to be called a manicurist—and hair stylist."

"Never been married either. No kids." He added hesitantly, "In fairness, I should tell you I'm seeing someone else."

Okay, so she'd blown three hundred bucks on another woman's boyfriend, but that didn't mean she couldn't enjoy the evening. Still, she wondered why he'd agreed to be part of the auction if he was seriously involved with someone.

"What about you?"

Rachel shook her head. She hadn't gone to the Dog and Bachelor Auction because she had a burning desire to donate to charity. Well, she did have a soft spot in her heart for animals. But that hadn't been the driving force that had led her to the auction.

"I didn't mean to mislead you."

"You didn't." He was certainly straightforward enough. Almost the first words out of his mouth had been to inform her that there was someone in his life. They talked briefly about this woman, who was from his hometown of Fresno.

They both had the night's special, grilled Pacific salmon, which was as delicious as she'd expected it to be. Although she was technically supposed to pick up the bill, Nate insisted on paying. He escorted her back to her car and then surprised her by asking, "Would you like to walk along the waterfront?"

She agreed, and they strolled side by side toward the marina. He walked with his hands clasped behind his back.

"What's going on over there?" he asked, nodding toward the Waterfront Park.

"I don't know. Want to check it out?"

He shrugged. "Sure."

It didn't take Rachel long to realize it was a wedding party. From a distance they watched the bride and groom exchange their vows. The sun had begun to set, sinking in the glorious blue sky, casting shreds of sunlight across the surface of the water.

For reasons she didn't understand, tears filled Rachel's eyes. If Nate saw, she'd be mortified. She barely knew this man and she'd probably never see him again. Really, there was no reason for them to continue dating. He was involved. She was older. This was it, the beginning and the end of their relationship.

"Rachel?"

He turned her to face him, hands on her shoulders. His frown told her he was both confused and concerned. "What's wrong?"

"I always cry at weddings," she said apologetically, making light of her tears. They fell unrestrained down her face. And yet she wasn't actually a woman prone to tears. Not until that moment, at any rate. Lowering her head, she wiped them from her cheeks, furious with herself. "Sorry."

Without a word, Nate took her in his arms. He didn't say anything, didn't make soothing sounds. All he did was hold her. It'd been so long since a man had touched her with such gentleness, such kindness, that she wasn't sure how to respond.

Looking up at him was a mistake because she discovered that he was staring at her. Then they were kissing. Rachel had no idea who kissed whom first. One thing quickly became evident: What Nate lacked in years he made up for in experience. The man knew how to kiss. His mouth moved seductively over hers in a way that sent goose bumps shooting down her arms. He kissed her as if she were the sweetest thing he'd ever known; he savored her, relished her.

When he lifted his mouth from hers, Rachel's knees were so weak she felt she might collapse in a puddle at his feet. Caught in the sheer wonder of their kiss, she kept her eyes closed.

Thankfully he didn't apologize or make excuses, nor did he seem inclined to explain.

When she felt her composure returning, Rachel opened her eyes. "That was...very nice."

"Yes, it was," Nate whispered, then cleared his throat. "I'll walk you to your car now."

She nodded. One again she'd been wrong; she hadn't

wasted her money. His kiss was worth every penny of the three hundred dollars she'd paid for this evening's date.

All the way back to the restaurant, Nate remained speechless. So did she. The truth was, Rachel didn't know what to say.

She led him to her car and got out her keys. "I had a lovely evening, Nate. Thank you."

He placed his palm against her cheek. "I did, too. But I don't think it's a good idea to see each other again."

"I understand."

"The thing is, I want to."

Rachel was careful not to meet his eyes, otherwise he'd be able to tell how badly she wanted to see him, too. "Life is like that sometimes."

"I know." His words were filled with regret.

She climbed into her car and backed out of her parking spot, hands a little shaky on the steering wheel. Driving off, she saw Nate in her rearview mirror. He stood in the lot, just stood there, watching her. Rachel felt a sense of melancholy as she pulled onto the street and headed home.

Apparently romance just wasn't for her. Damn, damn, damn!

Twenty-Eight

Maryellen's assistant, Lois Habbersmith, arrived at the Harbor Street Gallery shortly before noon. Grateful for the opportunity to escape, Maryellen grabbed the unopened letter and stuffed it in her skirt pocket.

"Lois, I'm going for a walk."

The other woman glanced at her in surprise. Maryellen almost always ate at her desk, grabbing a bite here and there between customers. With the summer half over, tourist traffic was at its peak and the gallery staff was often swamped.

"I won't be long," Maryellen promised. All she needed was a few uninterrupted minutes to read the letter. The moment she'd seen the return address, she'd known. The older couple who'd visited two weeks earlier and asked so many questions about Jon were his father and stepmother. Maryellen had suspected it then. Now she was sure.

As soon as she could, Maryellen left the gallery and walked down to the waterfront park. She slipped onto a picnic bench at the gazebo, removing the envelope from her pocket. For a long moment she stared at it, deciding that the sharply slanted handwriting was more likely a man's than a woman's.

Maryellen's hand trembled as she ripped open the envelope and pulled out a single typed sheet. Glancing at the first paragraph, she could see she'd been correct; his father *was* the one who'd written.

Dear Maryellen,

I imagine it must be a shock to receive this letter. When Marion and I got your very welcome note regarding Jon and your marriage, we were thrilled to have some way of reaching our son. You see, Jon is all we have left in the world that matters. My wife and I made a mistake, a terrible mistake, but we've paid for our sins many times over. Your letter, informing us of your marriage to Jon and the birth of our granddaughter, gave us hope. In all these years, Jon hasn't once acknowledged our letters. He's made it very clear that he desires no contact with his family.

Once we learned that he'd moved onto the piece of land inherited from his grandfather, I drove to Cedar Cove, hoping to talk to him. Marion doesn't know this, but my son threw me off the property. He refused to speak to me. Seeing the hate in him unnerved me, and I decided then that I would bide my time. I prayed that somehow, some way, he'd find his way to forgiveness. Until your letter, I'd almost given up hope.

As you probably guessed, Marion and I were the people who stopped by the art gallery a couple of weeks back. We couldn't get over our good fortune when we met you. In your previous letter, you'd failed to mention that you worked at the gallery.

Your love for Jon is unmistakable. We thank God

he found you and thank God you cared enough to contact us.

Marion and I have often talked about this and are at our wits' end. We have tried every way we know to reach our son, to beg his forgiveness and to bridge this gap of pain and bitterness. You are our only hope. Would you act as a mediator? It would mean the world to us if you'd talk to Jon on our behalf. He won't listen to us but I know he'll listen to you.

Thank you.

Joseph Bowman

P.S. Marion and I did visit the restaurant you mentioned and were impressed by Jon's work. I never realized how gifted my son is. Again I have you to thank for that discovery.

Maryellen read the letter a second time. Jon's father was asking the impossible of her. Her husband was adamant that he wanted nothing to do with his parents. As far as he was concerned, they were no longer part of his life.

As she drove home with Katie at the end of the day, Maryellen was still thinking about what his parents had asked her to do. Although she knew how Jon felt about his family, she'd gone behind his back. In fact, she'd done so against his express wishes. She hated that she'd started her marriage with an act of deception. If Jon ever learned she'd contacted his parents and mailed them photos of Katie, he might never forgive her. She'd taken a terrible risk already and now they were asking her to take another—a risk that was potentially even more disastrous. Maryellen longed to help, but she was afraid of what that would do to her marriage.

When she pulled into the yard, Jon walked out to the car to meet her and Katie. He smiled as he opened the back passenger door and released their daughter from her baby seat. Eager to escape the confines of the restrictive carrier, Katie gleefully flung out her arms and cooed at her father.

"Hi, honey," he said, kissing Maryellen briefly.

"Hi."

Despite her efforts to appear normal, her voice must have betrayed her, because Jon looked back over his shoulder. "Something wrong?"

Maryellen smiled at her husband and shook her head. He continued into the house, carrying Katie, while she followed with the diaper bag. In that instant she knew she couldn't jeopardize their secure world. They were happy. She couldn't afford to compromise their happiness, not Jon's or Katie's—or her own.

They ate on the deck that evening. Jon had poached halibut in wine and lemon, and topped it with a fresh tomato-and-basil salsa. The advantages of having a husband who was a marvelous chef were too numerous to count.

"All right," Jon said, leaning against the wooden slats of his deck chair. "That does it."

"What?" His determined words startled her.

"Turn in your two-week notice."

"Jon…"

"You clearly want to be at home."

"Jon, I can't, not yet." While it was true she wanted to be home with Katie and begin working as Jon's manager, she couldn't leave the gallery in the lurch. The owners had always been wonderful to her; not only that, she couldn't abandon Lois during the busiest time of the year.

"You're miserable," Jon said. Holding his wineglass, he frowned at her, and Maryellen tried to reassure him with a warm, loving smile.

"We were jammed this afternoon," she said, "and I hardly

had a moment to myself, but that's how this business goes. Anyway, Lois isn't ready to assume management responsibilities yet. She's learning, though."

"You aren't getting enough sleep."

"Would you stop trying to fix everything?" Although she meant to use a teasing tone, the remark came out sounding sharp and impatient.

Jon frowned more heavily. "That's what I thought a husband did."

"I'm sorry...." Maryellen didn't dare mention the reason for her mood. Standing, she collected the dirty dishes. "I guess I'm just out of sorts."

Jon brightened suddenly. "Could that mean what I think it means?"

Maryellen shook her head. She certainly hadn't had any problem getting pregnant with Katie and although they weren't using birth control, she wasn't pregnant with their second child yet.

Jon took her news with a light shrug. "I guess we'll just have to try harder. I want to experience this next pregnancy from the beginning."

Maryellen was heartened by the prospect. "That sounds good to me."

While Jon dealt with bills and paperwork downstairs, Maryellen bathed Katie and gently rocked her to sleep. She brushed the soft curls from her daughter's forehead, holding her securely as Katie sucked energetically at her bottle. Maryellen had gradually stopped breastfeeding the month before and now gave Katie a bottle early in the morning and at bedtime.

Maryellen glanced around the nursery, which always brought her a fresh surge of pleasure. Jon had drawn and painted a series of wild animals along the walls, creating for each a background that reflected its natural habitat.

Jon's parents would never see this. Maryellen closed her eyes, discouraged by the hopelessness of the situation.

"The object is to put Katie to sleep, not you," Jon whispered.

She opened her eyes to see him standing in the doorway, arms crossed. He wasn't a handsome man by conventional standards, but the sight of him stirred her emotions and her senses.

"It's been a long day," she said.

"Then take a hot bath, relax, go to bed," Jon advised. "I've got the dishes."

"I already took care of that."

"But Jon..." she protested. Their agreement was that when he cooked, she'd do the cleanup afterward. "You spoil me."

He grinned at that. "I want to spoil you. I love you, Maryellen. You and Katie are my family. You're everything to me."

Instead of bringing joy, his words fell on her like stones. It was her own fault, her own guilt; she'd interfered where she had no right to and cruelly raised his parents' hopes.

"I think I will go to bed early tonight," Maryellen said and placed Katie in her crib. She covered her with a light blanket, waiting to be sure their little girl was truly asleep before she silently left the room.

Jon took the empty bottle downstairs while Maryellen ran hot water into the tub. She scented it with lavender salts, then got in and sank into the soothing bath.

Her decision was made. She had no choice. She'd answer Joseph Bowman's letter the next day and tell him he was asking the impossible of her. She'd mail photos of Katie from time to time and keep his parents updated, but that was all she could promise. She'd also ask them not to contact her again.

The water had cooled by the time Maryellen stepped out of the tub. She dressed in a cotton nightie and a short robe. Jon was watching television and she sat on the sofa beside him, nestling gratefully in his arms.

"Feel better?" he asked, kissing the top of her head.

"Yes."

"Good."

"Remember what you were saying earlier?" she murmured, tilting her head and kissing the side of his jaw.

"About what?"

"Me getting pregnant."

She felt his mouth relax into a smile. "I remember that quite distinctly."

Maryellen glanced toward the television. "How interested are you in that program?"

"I can catch a rerun." He used the remote to turn off the TV, then kissed her as if he'd been waiting all day for just this moment.

Maryellen entwined her arms around his neck and opened her mouth to his exploration. Jon moaned softly, sliding his hand inside the folds of her robe, and sought her breast. Between soft kisses intermingled with lengthier ones, Maryellen reached over to snap off the lamp. They stood and began to walk toward the stairs, but didn't make it to the first step before he gathered her close and kissed her once more.

"I don't think I'll ever get tired of making love to you." He kissed the vulnerable hollow of her throat.

"I should hope not." Maryellen laughed and, walking backward, advanced one step up from him, circling his ear with her tongue. Jon groaned and she moved up an additional step. He followed, his hand again seeking her breasts. This time it was Maryellen who released a soft sigh of pleasure. If they didn't hurry up these stairs, they'd never make it to the bedroom.

As they kissed, Maryellen tore at his shirt while he removed her robe.

"Jon," she whispered, her voice thick with passion. They were halfway up the stairs, both partially undressed.

Still one step below her, he hugged her waist and buried his face between the fullness of her breasts.

Maryellen could feel her knees weakening. Framing his face with both hands, she gazed directly into his eyes. "Come on. I think there's a more comfortable way of doing this. It's called a bed."

Jon grinned up at her and then, in one sweeping motion, he swung her into his arms and carried her up the remaining stairs. Giggling like teenagers, they fell onto the bed and into each other's embrace.

Twenty-Nine

"Who left the milk out overnight?" Bob demanded as Peggy walked into the kitchen early Tuesday morning.

Peggy poured coffee into her favorite mug. "Good morning to you too, sweetheart."

Bob scowled. "I ended up dumping the entire half gallon."

They both realized it could only have been Hannah. Peggy wished she knew what it was about the young woman that irritated her husband so much. Bob took offense at the slightest thing; the milk incident was a good example. Hannah had worked the late shift at the Pancake Palace and returned to the house some time after Bob and Peggy were asleep. Apparently she'd decided to drink a glass of milk before going to bed and forgotten to put the carton back in the refrigerator. Yes, it was a thoughtless act, but it wasn't catastrophic. Bob had leaped at the opportunity to shriek and howl with indignation. Enough was enough.

"Stop it this minute, Bob Beldon," Peggy said calmly after her first sip of coffee. "I'll mention it to Hannah, but she doesn't need you berating her." The girl was timid as it was, and one harsh word from Bob would destroy her.

"Does she think—"

"Bob." Peggy cut him off before he could wake Hannah with his ranting. "Aren't you meeting Pastor Dave this morning?" They had a standing golf date every Tuesday. Whether they played in the morning or the afternoon depended on the pastor's schedule.

Her husband looked at his watch, frowning. He nodded abruptly. "I'll be back before noon."

"Yes, dear," Peggy murmured as she headed for her chair in the living room. Each morning she took a few moments to meditate before beginning her day. In those moments, she organized her thoughts and made mental plans of what she hoped to accomplish. Bob was often reading from the AA Big Book, and she'd gotten into the habit of claiming a little peace and quiet for herself. It allowed her to start the day in a tranquil frame of mind.

Bob paused at the door that led to the patio. "You'll say something to Hannah, right?"

"Yes, dear."

He expelled his breath loudly enough for her to hear. "Don't patronize me, Peggy."

She didn't know what had set off her husband's foul mood, but assumed that whatever was bothering him would work its way out of his system before he finished his golf game. More than likely he'd come home at lunchtime apologetic and contrite.

A few minutes later, just after Peggy had settled into her morning routine, Hannah stepped quietly into the family room. Her hair fell in thin brown tendrils about her face, which was ashen. She bit her lower lip, hesitating as if she wasn't sure she should interrupt Peggy.

"You heard?" Peggy asked softly.

The young woman nodded. "I'm so sorry.... I didn't mean to leave out the milk."

Peggy tried to reassure her with a smile. "I know you didn't."

"I'll pick up another half gallon before I leave for work this afternoon."

"Don't worry about it." Peggy gestured for Hannah to sit across from her. The girl looked shaken and Peggy hoped to comfort her.

"Did you sleep well?" Peggy asked.

Hannah's nod was tentative. "My dad used to yell, too."

The last thing Hannah needed was for Bob to do the same. "Bob didn't mean anything by it."

"I...know. It's just that when I hear a man yell, especially one who's around my dad's age, it...affects me, you know?"

"Of course it does." Peggy's irritation with her husband rose.

"My father was an unhappy person most of my life."

Hannah rarely mentioned her father. Peggy didn't know whether that was because of her grief at his death or because her memories of his accident were too painful to talk about.

"Sometimes at night, when I was a little girl, I'd wake up to the sound of my father shouting."

Peggy felt a moment's shock—and a rush of pity for Hannah. Having lived with an alcoholic for years, she wondered if Max Russell drank, too. "Did your father have a drinking problem?"

Hannah shook her head. "Sometimes he drank too much, but it wasn't a problem. Not a bad one, anyway. Some days he was mean for no reason. He used to shout at Mom and me for the littlest things."

"I'm sorry."

"He wasn't a bad person, you know. I really loved my dad."

"Of course you did." Peggy wondered if Hannah fully understood what her father had experienced during the war.

"My mom stood by him through all the times we had to move and all the fights." Tears filled her eyes. "It's so wrong that she died, so wrong."

"You moved around a lot?"

Hannah needed a minute to compose herself. She swallowed visibly. "Dad was never able to hold down a job for long. He'd be fine for a while, and then he'd drift into this...dark place."

"Dark place?"

"That's what Mom called it. He'd be happy, and suddenly it would be like someone had turned off the lights. I could always tell when it happened. So could Mom. She'd ask me to go to my room and I would, because I knew what was going to follow."

"What was that?" Peggy asked.

Hannah was silent for several minutes. "Nothing pleased him. The napkins had to be put on the table just so or he'd throw them on the floor. Dinners were a nightmare. Mom always did something wrong. The meat was tough, the vegetables were overcooked, the milk was too cold. Either the silverware wasn't properly lined up or the saltshaker wasn't full enough. Everything had to be perfect for Dad. Hard as she tried to please him, it was impossible. Dad found fault with the smallest thing."

This was much worse than Peggy had realized.

"We moved at least once a year. Dad would sometimes use other names, and I had to remember what my name was because he'd change it."

"Your dad used other names?"

Hannah's head snapped up. Her eyes widened. "I never told the sheriff that. Please don't mention it, all right? Dad hadn't done it in a long time and I was afraid that if Sheriff Davis found out, he'd think my dad was a criminal or something."

Peggy sighed, but she managed to swallow the exasperated response that sprang to her lips. It would've helped had the girl revealed this earlier. Apparently, there was still a great deal they didn't know about Maxwell Russell—including why he'd come to Cedar Cove. A chill raced down her spine. They'd been on edge ever since the night someone had followed Bob home, although nothing had happened since.

"My mother was a saint," Hannah whispered.

"She put up with your father's moods all those years?"

Hannah nodded. "Sometimes I'd find her sitting on her bed reading his letters. She said it helped her remember what he was like before the war."

Peggy understood why Tammy Russell had done that. Why she'd kept on hoping, and supporting her husband and—worst of all—putting up with his verbal abuse. She'd still loved him and wanted him to become, once again, the person he used to be. No matter how hopeless that desire.

Peggy understood because she'd done something very similar. She, too, had held on to memories of the past, letting them form her hopes for the future. Before joining Al-Anon, Peggy had tried to manipulate Bob into not drinking. She'd used pressure, guilt, punishment, anger and every other behavior she could think of. None of it had worked until she'd stepped aside, forcing Bob to deal with the consequences of his drinking. But through it all, Peggy had stood by her husband, just like Hannah's mother.

"Dad was in one of his dark moods when the car accident happened," Hannah whispered. "I wanted Mom to leave him, but she wouldn't. I had a job.... I could have supported the two of us, but she wouldn't do it."

"Oh, Hannah, I'm so sorry."

"I am, too.... Mom wasn't supposed to be in the car with him that day. But he was so angry and unreasonable and he demanded that she go with him and then he had the accident—and Mom was killed." Weeping openly now, she covered her face with both hands.

Peggy came out of her chair and wrapped her arms around Hannah's shoulders, murmuring soft, meaningless words of comfort.

"If only Mom hadn't gone that day, she'd be alive now."

"I know, I know," Peggy said.

"Dad was hurt so badly in the fire and Mom...didn't have a chance. I wanted to die then, too...but the accident changed Dad."

"In what way?"

Hannah lifted her head and rubbed the sleeve of her robe over her eyes. "He was calmer, less angry afterward."

"So he was easier to deal with?"

Hannah nodded. "I think Mom's death was what did it. He was lost without her. He went through so much pain, you know, and all the surgery, and...and for the first time in my life, I felt I had a father. He talked to me and called me his little girl and said he loved me. And then...and then he was murdered." She sniffled once.

Peggy could imagine what life had been like for Hannah. Until his accident, Maxwell Russell was a harsh, bitter man who often took his anger out on his wife and daughter. It was little wonder that Hannah vacillated between grief and guilt over the death of her father.

Thirty

Grace checked her watch for the third time in two minutes and used a deep-breathing method to calm her pounding heart. Cliff would be joining her at The Lighthouse any moment now and she was as nervous as if she were fifteen again, going out with a boy for the first time.

Tonight was their dinner date, the one Jack and Olivia, Charlotte, Maryellen, Jon, Kelly and Paul had bought at the Dog and Bachelor Auction. Her friends and family had forked out a whopping eight hundred dollars to arrange this, and Grace was determined to enjoy it. If only she could calm her nerves.

She smiled as she thought of Justine's equally expensive new dog, a golden retriever like her own Buttercup. According to Olivia, the whole family adored Sadie.

And speaking of Olivia… Grace had arrived at the restaurant fifteen minutes early in order to escape her best friend.

Olivia had spent half the afternoon with her, discussing every detail of Grace's outfit, hair and makeup. Anyone might think Grace was entering a beauty pageant or attending the Academy Awards! Olivia's interest was well-intentioned, but Grace had reached her limit, so she'd left the house early and gone straight to the restaurant.

When Cliff did appear, it was all Grace could do not to jump up from her chair. Swallowing suddenly became difficult. Cliff saw her then and walked across the room, his steps slow and measured, as if he felt resigned to this evening but not pleased.

With a stiff smile, she extended her hand to him in a rather formal greeting. "Thank you for being my dinner date," she said, hoping her words were intelligible.

"I should be the one thanking you," he said as he pulled out his chair. "It's good for my ego." He paused, apparently reconsidering his comment. "Now that I think about it, wasn't it Olivia who placed the bid?"

Grace nodded. No one had paid more for a bachelor; Cliff should feel flattered by that. "Justine and Seth love the dog, and apparently Leif's quite taken with her, too."

Cliff smiled at the mention of the dog. She smiled back, more naturally this time. Cliff couldn't seem to take his eyes off her, which made her heart beat faster. Cliff looked more attractive than ever, and she gazed at him avidly. She saw him so seldom these days and when she did, it was a painful reminder of what might have been.

"How are you?" he asked, his voice low.

This wasn't a casual question; she sensed that the moment the words left his lips. He wanted the truth.

"Lonely."

Cliff lowered his eyes, although she'd noticed the worried expression he tried to hide.

His silence unsettled her, so she hurried to fill it. "I have a kitten now." She offered this information eagerly, not just to appease his concern about her loneliness but because she knew he'd be interested. "I got him at the Farmers' Market a month ago. I was doing one of my volunteer stints, and he was the last one left. I named him Sherlock because he's constantly digging into things."

Cliff grinned boyishly and his worried look fled. "What does Buttercup think of him?"

"Actually she's happy to have the company. The two of them sleep together. I have pictures." She reached for her purse and pulled out several photos of her animals, as well as her grandchildren.

"Sherlock," Cliff murmured as he studied the first photograph. "The name suits him."

"I thought so, too," Grace said. "The others are of Tyler and Katie. I refuse to let you escape without updating you on my grandchildren."

His grin deepened. "I just happened to bring a picture of April." He slid one hand into his inside pocket and brought out a photograph.

The waitress came for their drink order, and Cliff suggested a bottle of Washington State Chardonnay. Grace nodded at his choice.

She stared at the picture of Cliff's daughter and granddaughter. She'd met Lisa last Thanksgiving, when they'd flown to Maryland to be with his family. Cliff and his daughter were especially close.

After exchanging photographs, Grace looked at him. "And you?" she asked. "How are you, Cliff?"

"Busy." He didn't respond seriously the way she had; his reply was flippant.

She dropped her eyes in an effort to recover. In one word, he'd let her know she wasn't allowed access to his world anymore. Despite his earlier sincerity, that brief glimpse of caring and concern, this dinner wasn't going to change anything. Olivia and her daughters might as well have saved their money.

Grace's spirits plummeted.

The waitress returned with their wine, uncorked it and poured a sample for Cliff to approve. After the tasting ritual and the pouring, she took their dinner order.

"I'm off to Texas to buy a horse next week," Cliff said as if it was now his turn to fill the ensuing silence. "I hope so, anyway. I've had my eye on a particular quarter horse stud for quite some time." He continued talking about the qualities that made this horse important to him. Most of what he said was beyond Grace's slim knowledge of breeding and horses, but she listened attentively.

"Well, I hope your trip is successful," she said when he'd finished.

Silence again. Their whole evening seemed destined to crawl from one awkward silence to another.

"I feel I can leave the ranch now that I have Cal," he added.

"How is Cal?" she asked. Their conversations never used to be stilted like this. They always had a million things to say to each other, sharing pieces of their lives. Except for what she hadn't shared—her Internet romance with Will Jefferson. Would she never be forgiven for that?

Cliff started to chuckle, and she glanced up.

"What?" Grace smiled, too, although she didn't know why.

"The Dog and Bachelor Auction," he said. "Do you remember that Corrie McAfee bid on him for her daughter?"

"Oh—yes." She'd found it difficult to keep track of which bachelor had gone to whom, although she'd received personal satisfaction from Stan Lockhart's fate. She noticed he hadn't been around town as much lately and in Grace's opinion, that was a good thing.

"Did you read in the paper that thanks to Charlotte and

Ben, the town's worked out a deal with Puget Sound Medical and Dental to set up a clinic?"

"Speaking of Ben..." Grace closed her mouth.

"What about him?"

She shook her head, angry with herself. "Nothing... It's just that Olivia is worried about her mother and Ben."

"Why?"

"Well, no one ever heard of him until recently."

"No one had ever heard of me, either," Cliff reminded her.

"But you aren't dating a judge's mother. In her line of work, Olivia has reason to be suspicious—but I'm sure nothing will turn up."

Cliff picked up his water glass. "Nothing will turn up where?"

In her uneasiness, Grace had already said more than she'd intended. "Forget I said that." She hoped he'd simply put this conversation out of his mind.

No such luck. "Olivia's having a background check done on Ben?" he asked bluntly.

Grace felt dreadful, but she couldn't lie to Cliff again. "Yes. Please don't say anything."

"You think I'd tell *Charlotte* this?"

That made her feel even worse, since Charlotte and Cliff were friends. "No...Cliff, please, I should never have said anything."

He hesitated, then agreed with a shrug. "All right."

"I heard Linnette McAfee's been hired to work at the clinic." It was an obvious change of topic, but he accepted it readily enough and she sighed with relief.

"That's what I understand."

"Since Linnette's moving to town, maybe she'll have a chance to get to know Cal." She gestured vaguely. "More than she could on just a dinner date."

"Cal's a good man," Cliff said casually. "I think getting out more will do him a world of good."

"I like him," Grace said although her contact with Cliff's trainer had been limited to a few short conversations. His shyness and stuttering made communication difficult. Instinctively, she wanted to finish his sentences, to spare him the embarrassment of stammering. But on honest reflection, she supposed her impulse to help had as much to do with her own discomfort as with any perceptions of his.

"He likes you, too."

Instantly Grace's heart lightened.

The waitress approached the table with their first course, shrimp bisque for Grace and Caesar salad for Cliff.

"How are Maryellen and Jon?" he asked as he set down his wineglass.

"Happy and deeply in love." In that instant, Grace wished she could withdraw the words. Talking about love was painful; under different circumstances, those words could have referred to them. "They hope to have another child," she said after a pause.

"What about Kelly and Paul?"

Grace sighed. "Kelly still isn't pregnant and she's starting to get worried."

"I'm sure there's no cause for concern."

Grace agreed, and they lapsed into silence again.

The waitress returned to collect their first-course dishes and bring their entrées. She also refilled their wine. Grace took her first taste of sole topped with a creamy shrimp sauce, and Cliff cut into his prime rib. They both made enthusiastic noises about the excellence of the food.

By the time they'd finished their meals, Grace accepted that nothing she said or did had the power to reach Cliff. So she stopped trying. There seemed little point in more small talk about the town or doings at the library or plans for his ranch; that left them with nothing much to say.

After dinner, Grace drove home, even more lonely and depressed. It was hard not to weep and to berate herself—and humbling to admit she'd failed yet again. Olivia and the girls had paid that money for one reason and one reason only. They'd hoped, as Grace had, that Cliff would have a change of heart. He hadn't.

The phone rang at eight o'clock on Saturday morning. Grace was feeding her animals. Automatically she scooped up the receiver and held it to her ear while she doled out the dog and cat food.

"Well?" Olivia demanded. "How'd it go?"

Grace resisted the urge to break into tears. "We had a very nice dinner, but that's it."

"Don't be so sure."

"Olivia," Grace said with an exaggerated sigh. "I was there. I might as well have had dinner with a statue." She switched the phone to her other ear. "The closest I got to seeing the old Cliff was when he showed me a picture of Lisa and her little girl."

"Give him time."

"No." Grace was surprised by the strength of her conviction. "I'm not going to grovel. I made a mistake. I'm sorry. If Cliff Harding can't get past that, then it's his problem, not mine."

Olivia was silent for a long moment. "Grace is that really you?" she finally asked.

"Of course it's me."

"You sound so…emotionally healthy."

"I'm glad you approve."

"I do," Olivia assured her.

Obviously Cliff had chosen to get on with his life—

minus Grace. She would let him and at the same time get on with hers.

With a renewed sense of vigor, she weeded and watered her small garden.

At noon, a florist's delivery van parked outside her house. Pulling off her garden gloves, Grace walked around front, wondering if the driver had mistaken the address.

"Ms. Grace Sherman?" The deliveryman held a beautiful bouquet of roses, carnations and irises in a variety of pastel shades.

"Yes." Grace vaguely recognized the young man but couldn't remember his name.

"These are for you." He handed her the vase, turned and left.

Grace carried the arrangement into the house and removed the card. As she read the message, tears clouded her eyes. *Life has a funny way of hitting you between the eyes, doesn't it? Thank you for dinner. Cliff.*

She didn't know what he meant but she felt this must be a good sign.

Thirty-One

Ben pushed the grocery cart down the produce aisle while Charlotte sorted through the celery. The grocer tended to put the older bunches in front.

"Do you want me to pick up a few bananas?" Ben asked.

"Please." Bananas were the perfect fruit for people their age, in Charlotte's view.

Ben added a small bunch to their cart. He was so helpful in so many ways. Clyde hadn't been the kind of husband who enjoyed shopping, but Ben was more than patient about doing errands. He seemed to enjoy spending time with her. If she had a hair appointment, he drove her there and either waited in the salon or strolled through the mall. After all these years on her own, such open affection—such romantic gestures—were foreign to her. When she was with Ben she felt...treasured. True, his attention had taken a bit of adjustment on her part, since she was so used to her own company. Charlotte slowly pushed the cart ahead, watching as Ben struck up a conversation with the produce manager.

"Charlotte!"

Hearing her name, Charlotte turned to find her son-in-law strolling toward her, wearing a big grin.

"Don't tell me Olivia's got you doing the shopping," Charlotte said.

Jack chuckled and shook his head. "I came to pick up a few things she refuses to buy. Whoever heard of a house without potato chips and pretzels? Olivia said if I was going to eat fat-laden carbohydrates, I'd have to buy them myself. So here I am." He looked over his shoulder, as if he half expected his wife to follow him inside and criticize his food choices. "I don't suppose you know where they keep the microwave popcorn, do you?"

"Aisle five," Charlotte said. "I like the extra-butter kind myself."

"I'm with you," Jack muttered. "I don't know what it is with Olivia these days."

"How do you mean?"

"First she's on this low-fat kick. Okay, I admit I could lose a few pounds, but I looked like this when she married me and it was good enough for her then."

Charlotte knew her daughter's fitness plan had caused arguments between them, but she'd assumed things were better now. Olivia hadn't complained in weeks.

"Then there's this thing with Ben," he added, scowling. "It's ridiculous."

Charlotte stared at him, certain she'd misunderstood. "What thing with Ben?" she demanded. Thankfully Ben was still busy talking.

Jack looked like a man who'd inadvertently stumbled into a swampful of alligators. "Ah…that was a slip of the tongue. Forget it."

"I most certainly will not forget it," Charlotte slammed a bunch of celery into her cart. "You'd better tell me *everything*."

"Ah..." Jack faltered. "I, uh..." Finally he gave a resigned sigh. "Olivia's having Roy do a background check on him," he said grimly.

"What?" Charlotte felt her blood pressure rise.

"Charlotte?" Ben asked, joining her. He looked at Jack. "Is there a problem?"

"None whatsoever," Charlotte snapped. She smiled at Ben, who'd been nothing but a gentleman from the moment they met. Now her own daughter had gone behind her back and was having the man she loved investigated. Evidently Olivia had no faith in her intelligence or her judgment. Anyone who spent time with Ben would know he was the gentlest, sweetest, most wonderful man on earth. Olivia had met him many times. How could she *do* this? Why? The outrage turned to pain and her eyes filled with tears.

"I...I can't believe Olivia would do something like this," she said, trying to hide the hurt her daughter had caused her. Sniffling, she turned away.

Ben was at her side immediately. He slid his arm around her protectively. "What's going on here, Charlotte?"

Charlotte shouldn't have done it, but she told him. "Olivia's having you investigated. I don't know why she'd do such a thing, but apparently she has. Jack just let it slip...."

Ben's mouth thinned with irritation. "Rest assured there's nothing to find."

"Damn my big mouth," Jack muttered. "It isn't all Olivia, you know."

"What do you mean by that?" Charlotte was rigid with anger now.

"Maybe I should just pay for these potato chips and be on my way," Jack suggested, obviously uncomfortable.

"Like hell!"

Ben's eyes widened. Charlotte was not a woman who used

that kind of language. In fact, she was shocked herself. But there were times when nothing less than a swearword would do. "You tell me the whole story and I mean *now,* Jack Griffin."

Jack shifted his weight from one foot to the other. "Olivia's going to kill me for this."

"Why? She's guiltier than you are."

Jack shrugged. "You don't know Olivia the way I do."

"She's my daughter—if I don't end up disowning her over this." Charlotte had trouble accepting what her daughter had done. "Who put her up to it?" She leaned forward and glared fiercely at her son-in-law. "You, Jack? Was it you?"

He shook his head, raising his hand in a gesture of surrender. "Not me. Will."

This was even worse than she could've imagined. "You've got to be kidding."

Jack cast Ben an apologetic look.

That just made Charlotte angrier. "How dare he?" she sputtered.

"Now, Charlotte," Ben said in a soothing voice. "Let's talk about this calmly."

But Charlotte was in no mood to be mollified. "You tell my daughter that I'm in love with Ben Rhodes and I have every intention of marrying him."

Head down, Jack nodded like a repentant child.

"On second thought, I'll tell her myself."

Jack raised his index finger. "When you do speak to Olivia, I'd appreciate if you gave me a few minutes' notice first."

Ben chuckled, but Charlotte found nothing humorous in the situation. "Then consider yourself warned."

Jack clearly felt terrible, but she didn't blame him for her daughter's actions. No, she knew exactly who was responsible for this…this *insult.*

Despite his protest, Charlotte left Ben to deal with the groceries while she marched over to the courthouse. It was a good three-block walk and uphill at that, but Charlotte's indignation drove her all three of those blocks without a single pause. By the time she got there, however, she was winded. Charlotte leaned against one of the courthouse pillars and placed her hand over her pounding heart, taking slow, deep breaths.

Her expression must have conveyed her mood because no one stopped her or delayed her with conversation. After clearing security, she plowed through the crowded hallway to her daughter's courtroom. She shoved open the door decisively and…

Wouldn't you know it, the room was empty. All the better. Charlotte didn't need any witnesses to this confrontation. She went directly to Olivia's chambers. The mahogany door was closed; she knocked once and opened it without waiting for permission.

Olivia sat at her desk and glanced up, a look of curiosity on her face. "Mother?"

"How dare you, Olivia Lockhart Griffin! How dare you!" Fresh tears welled in her eyes.

Olivia set down her pen and gestured for her mother to take a seat. Charlotte hesitated, then collapsed into the visitor's chair. She reached for her lace handkerchief, tucked in the sleeve of her blouse, and dabbed at the corners of her eyes. "I'm utterly ashamed that my own children would do anything so underhanded and deceitful. How could you do this to me—and to Ben? What's he ever done to you?"

Olivia sighed heavily. "Mom, I can tell you're upset."

"Upset? You don't know the half of it!"

Olivia raised her hand. "I don't blame you. I'm sorry, but Will and I felt that in this day and age one can't be too careful."

"You don't think I'm capable of judging a man's character? Ben is decent and kind and…and honorable."

"I wanted to believe that too, but he has no family in the area."

"No family in the area?" Charlotte repeated. "What's that supposed to mean?"

"Well, what brought him to Cedar Cove?" Olivia briefly closed her eyes, as if she were embarrassed and ashamed, as well she should be. "Will felt, and I agree, that we needed some verification of the things Ben told you."

"Like what?"

"That he's who he says he is, for one thing."

"He is!" Charlotte insisted.

"I know that now, but until I asked Roy to check into Ben's background, we only had his word for it that he's a retired admiral. He just seemed…too good to be true."

Charlotte continued to dab at her eyes and sniffle as the anger was replaced by tears. "I'm so embarrassed. I love Ben."

"Oh, Mother…"

"Don't you *Oh, Mother* me! I'm old enough to know my own feelings and I refuse to listen to a lecture from you." Using the edge of the desk to support herself, she rose to her feet. "Save those condescending little speeches for the courtroom." Having delivered her own insult—though minor in comparison—Charlotte started out of the room.

"Mom, please."

Charlotte stopped in front of the closed door, her back to her daughter.

"I'm sorry," Olivia whispered. "You're right. I should never have done this."

"It's a bit late for sorry, don't you think?"

"Yes." Again Olivia sighed. "I know how you feel about Ben."

"I sincerely doubt that, but go on." She turned to face Olivia now, her expression blank. "His sons aren't having *me* investigated."

Olivia let the comment slide.

"Ben's a companion and a friend and—"

Charlotte didn't know why she bothered. She shook her head, astonished by her own daughter's insensitivity. "I can't believe I'm hearing this from someone who was so recently married. Look at me, Olivia," she commanded, "and listen well. I'm in love. For the first time since your father died, I feel truly alive again. I wake up every morning with a sense of joy because I know that at some point during the day I'll be with Ben."

Olivia closed her eyes again, as if gathering her thoughts. "Mom, I understand what you're saying. It's the same with Jack and me." She opened her eyes, gazing straight at Charlotte.

"How would you feel if I'd had *him* investigated?"

Olivia leaned forward and braced her hands on her desk. "It wouldn't have mattered. I love Jack, and he's got nothing to hide from me."

"And you think Ben has?"

"That's just it—I didn't know."

"And now you do?"

Olivia nodded. "Roy mailed me the report last week. I sent off a copy to Will, telling him we can both rest assured that Ben Rhodes is everything he said he was."

There was a knock at the door. Olivia checked her watch and frowned. "Come in."

To Charlotte's complete shock, Ben opened the door and stepped into the chamber. Both women stared at him, although neither seemed to know what to say. For her part, Charlotte was mortified. She wanted to apologize, to ask his forgiveness on her children's behalf, but her throat closed up at the sight of him.

Olivia recovered first. "Please come in, Ben," she said. "I believe there's been a slight misunderstanding."

"That's what you're calling this?" Charlotte cried.

Olivia threw her mother a silencing look. "Would you care to sit down?"

"Unfortunately," Charlotte said, standing up and entwining her arm with Ben's, "we have to be going."

"Now, Charlotte," Ben countered. "I think it would be best if we talked this out."

"I agree," Olivia said quickly. She focused her attention on Ben. "If I've offended you, Ben, I apologize."

"If?" Charlotte shook her head. She'd always been so proud of Olivia, her daughter the judge. For the first time in longer than she could remember, she had the urge to send Olivia to her room without dinner.

"I love your mother, Olivia," Ben said boldly. "I know you do, too. We have more in common than you realize."

Olivia offered him a tentative smile. "I can see that you're good company for each other."

"Olivia, you're not listening. Ben and I are in *love*."

Her daughter stared at her.

"What I think your mother is trying to tell you," Ben said, "is that I've asked Charlotte to be my wife and she's agreed."

Olivia's gaze veered from Charlotte to Ben. "You're asking my permission to marry my mother?"

"No," Charlotte said, looking up at Ben. "We're getting married with or without your approval."

"I see," Olivia managed. She sank back into her fancy leather chair and apparently had nothing more to say.

Thirty-Two

The alarm buzzed and Cecilia opened one eye, peering at the clock radio on her nightstand. The digital readout told her it was six o'clock and time to get up. She groaned inwardly. It couldn't be six already. She felt as if she'd just gotten to sleep.

It'd been like this when she was pregnant with Allison, too. She'd felt as if she could've slept for days at a time. What made it worse now was that Ian didn't go on duty until the afternoon, so she was the only one who had to get up this early.

The minute she lifted her head from the pillow waves of nausea battered her. Moaning, she laid her head down again and closed her eyes, praying this would pass. Bolting up, covering her mouth, she raced into the bathroom just in time to empty her stomach into the toilet bowl. Still gagging, she closed her eyes again, hoping the worst of it was over.

Blindly she reached for a washcloth draped over the edge of the sink.

"I'll get that for you." Ian rinsed the cloth, wrung it out then handed it to Cecilia.

She patted the cool cloth against her face, straightened and tried to smile.

"Good morning," her husband said softly.

"Hi," she managed to respond as she wiped her mouth.

"Were you sick like this with Allison, too?"

Cecilia nodded. It was the first time he'd asked. They hadn't been married during the initial months of her pregnancy, and she'd never mentioned her problems with morning sickness. By the time they were married, the nausea had passed.

"Was it this bad?"

She nodded again. "Every morning. Until my third month."

Ian sank onto the edge of the bathtub. "Is there anything I can do?" He sounded almost guilty, as if he were personally responsible for her discomfort.

Cecilia moved to his side. "Love me," she whispered. Their relationship had been so strained since he'd learned about the pregnancy, and even before, when he knew she wanted to get pregnant. He was trying to accept this baby, but he treated her with a kind of wariness, as though he was afraid to touch her.

"I do love you," Ian said.

She turned away, and Ian put his arms around her and touched his forehead against her back. "You never told me, you know?" he protested.

"Never told you I was so sick every morning with Allison?" Cecilia asked. "Is that what you mean?" She pressed her hand over his and moved his palm to her flat stomach and held it there. "Would it have made any difference if you'd known?"

"I hear you every morning," he whispered. "You run in here and heave your guts out."

"The doctor says I should eat a soda cracker when I first wake up."

He kissed her neck, his lips lingering for a moment. "Then why don't you?"

"No time. I open my eyes and it's all I can do to make it to the bathroom."

"They can't give you a drug?"

"I won't take anything." She had with Allison, and although the physicians had repeatedly assured her that Allison's heart defect had nothing to do with the pills she'd taken for morning sickness, Cecilia couldn't completely believe it. True or not, she wasn't taking any chances with this pregnancy.

Ian sighed as if he'd give anything for her not to be pregnant. It broke her heart, but she refused to show her pain. She knew that when the baby came, Ian would love his son or daughter with the same intensity that he already loved Allison. He wouldn't be able to stop himself. Until then she'd be patient.

"Stay home today," he urged.

"And waste a sick day?" She couldn't do that. In the months to come she might need them. Besides, with Ian leaving for work in a few hours, it didn't make sense.

"Take a vacation day then."

"Why?" She turned to face him.

"Because I can't stand the thought of you going to work sick."

Little did he know that she had to pull off the road nearly every morning to vomit. "I go to work sick most days." Today wouldn't be any different. "Mr. Cox relies on me, and besides, Allison is coming by this afternoon."

Ian stiffened.

"Mr. Cox's teenage daughter," Cecilia reminded him.

"I know who you meant."

"She's a good kid, and now that her parents are back together, she's doing really well in school."

Ian's shoulders rose as he expelled a breath. "I wonder if the Coxes knew the hell their daughter would put them through when they decided to have a baby."

Despite her upset stomach, Cecilia laughed and stroked her husband's thick hair. "Babies don't come with guarantees. They grow up and turn into teenagers. When the time comes, we'll deal with it." Bending forward she kissed him on the lips. "I'm sorry, honey, but I have to get ready for work."

He grumbled for form's sake, then went back to bed while she dressed.

Cecilia put on her makeup and packed a lunch, although the sight of food made her stomach lurch. But by noon she'd be fine and her appetite would return and she'd need that lunch.

Ian appeared to be sound asleep when she left the duplex. Munching on soda crackers as she drove, Cecilia made it all the way to the office without a single emergency stop. This was progress.

According to the navy doctor, her due date was the first week of May. May fifth. Allison had been born in June. Cecilia had gone into labor on a beautiful summer afternoon, but the perfection of the day hadn't augured a happy event. Being alone had been terrifying, even more so after her baby's birth.

Forcefully Cecilia turned her thoughts away from her first pregnancy. This time everything would be different. This time Ian would be with her and their baby would be born healthy.

Mr. Cox was already in the office when Cecilia arrived. After a few minutes of their usual easy chat, she settled at her desk and immediately began her work. The nausea almost always abated by nine. The first hour of the morning was the worst and odd though it seemed, she felt sick some afternoons once she got home. The second bout was always less intense than the first.

At noon Mary Lou, the receptionist, came into her office. "You have a visitor," she announced.

"I do?" This was unexpected. "Who is it?"

Mary Lou grinned. "Why don't you come and see?"

Cecilia walked to the front of the office and there stood Ian with a small bouquet of flowers. "Ian!" she cried. "What are you doing here?"

"I thought we'd go to lunch, if that's okay?"

"Of course it's okay. Don't you have to work this afternoon?"

"I do, but I've got time to take my wife to lunch."

She was so pleased to see him, it didn't matter one little bit that she'd brought her lunch.

They got sandwiches and drinks at the Pot Belly Deli and walked to the Waterfront Park, where they chose a relatively secluded picnic table.

"I have something for you," he said as she unpacked their lunch.

Ian reached inside his pocket and brought out a plain gold cross on a chain. "I want you to wear this, all right?"

Cecilia was stunned. "Ian, it's beautiful. Thank you."

He walked over to where she was sitting and placed it around her neck and secured the clasp.

"I haven't forgotten our anniversary or anything, have I?" she teased.

"Nope."

"Any special reason you're giving me a gift?"

He shrugged and tried unsuccessfully to hide a smile. He sat back on the picnic bench and unwrapped his veggie-and-cream-cheese croissant. "You're having my baby. Isn't that reason enough?"

Tears rose in Cecilia's eyes. Because of the pregnancy, all her hormones were out of control; the smallest thing set her off. Not that this was small. No, his gift, his acknowledgement of her pregnancy, was the most moving and important moment they'd shared in months. She waved her hand in front of her face, blinking rapidly.

"You're crying?" Ian sounded surprised. "I thought this would make you happy."

"I *am* happy."

"So why are you crying?"

Then she was laughing, almost hysterically—weeping and laughing at the same time. "Because I'm having a baby, silly."

"Oh." Ian took a bite of his sandwich.

"And I love my husband."

He grinned. "Who loves his wife and his baby."

Cecilia cried all the harder then.

"Honey, don't cry. Please."

"It's just that I was so afraid you didn't. Love us, I mean." She sobbed, hiccupped and curled her fingers around the small cross. "Everything's going to be just fine this time, Ian."

His smile slowly disappeared. "I'm trying to believe that."

"I know you are. I'll do everything I can—and I *feel* it *will* be fine, but there are no guarantees."

That was one thing Cecilia understood.

Thirty-Three

Bob Beldon glanced at the menu in the bowling alley's small restaurant, although it wasn't necessary. He knew what he wanted. Two eggs over easy, bacon, cooked crisp, and two pieces of sourdough toast with strawberry jam if they had it. For two-fifty it was the best buy in town.

The waitress strolled past and without asking, filled his coffee cup. "You waiting on someone, hon?"

Bob nodded. The instant he did, Roy McAfee stepped into the crowded restaurant.

"Right on time," Bob commented as Roy slid into the booth across from him.

"Have you ordered?"

"Not yet."

Pad in hand, the waitress returned, filled Roy's mug and stood waiting for their order. Bob went first. Roy asked for a short stack of pancakes. The woman sauntered off and barked the order to the cook.

"What's up?" Roy asked. Bob had called him last night to arrange this meeting.

"Peggy told me something interesting the other day.

I've spoken to Troy Davis, but I wanted to get your opinion, too."

"Sure. What is it?"

"Seems Peggy and Hannah had a little heart-to-heart."

"Did you learn anything?"

"Yes." Bob added sugar and cream, then stirred his coffee. "Hannah let it slip that her father sometimes used false names. Peggy asked her about it, and I gather that through the years Max had amassed a whole slew of names and identifications."

Roy's eyebrows lifted. "It didn't occur to her to bring this up earlier?"

"Apparently not."

Bob reviewed what had led up to this confession. "She left the milk out all night and I got a little upset because it spoiled. After I went to play golf, Hannah came out of her bedroom and started talking to Peggy. From the way she described it, life with her father was no bed of roses, for her or her mother."

"She's never said anything negative about him before, has she?"

Bob needed to think about that. He shrugged. "Not that I can remember. It's like she's been living in a fantasy world. In the beginning she painted a picture of the three of them skipping through the years as happy as can be. Turns out life wasn't quite as blissful as she let us believe."

"Makes sense, I guess," Roy said, cupping his mug with both hands. "She lost both parents within a short period. In tragic circumstances people tend to recall the good times instead of the bad."

Bob supposed his friend was right. "Didn't Troy ask her if she knew anything about her dad using fictitious names?"

"I'm sure he did. Did she explain why she lied?"

"Peggy asked her the same thing. Hannah claimed she was afraid that if anyone found out, there'd be trouble and she couldn't deal with it. From what she said—and didn't say—trouble seemed to follow Max wherever he went."

Frowning, Roy sipped his coffee. "Did she happen to mention any of the names he used? Or where he got the various pieces of ID?"

"No, but if Peggy asks, Hannah will probably tell her." Bob didn't think Hannah trusted him enough to confide that information, but she had a close relationship with his wife.

"Have Peggy ask her and I'll find out what I can. It might give us a lead."

Bob nodded. He'd hoped Roy would volunteer to do exactly that.

"Did Hannah know anything about the fake ID her father carried when he died?"

"She says she didn't."

Roy studied him. "Do you believe her?"

Bob had considered that question carefully and the fact was, he couldn't be sure. He wasn't especially fond of the girl and couldn't account for it, even though he had no real reason to dislike her. Peggy had taken to her fast enough, and heaven knew the young woman needed his wife's affection. Hannah's nervousness and her jittery manner made him uncomfortable. If Bob raised his voice even slightly, she cowered as if she expected him to pounce. Of course, what she'd told Peggy explained a great deal.

"Anyone following you these days?" Roy asked just as the waitress delivered their breakfasts.

"Not that I can tell. Nothing since that night, anyway. I'm beginning to wonder if I imagined it. But I know I didn't. Maybe it's not even connected to Max. Maybe it was some random wacko."

Roy poured hot maple syrup over his pancakes. "You sound disappointed."

"I am. It's ridiculous to live the way Peggy and I are living. I want this resolved, one way or another. I'm also thinking it's time we started taking guests again. This whole mess has cost us thousands of dollars." He took a gulp of coffee. "If someone was really after me, wouldn't he have done something by now?"

Roy nodded. "I tend to agree with you. If someone was going to make a move, it probably would've happened already."

Bob grunted agreement through a mouthful of toast and jam.

"On second thought—"

"Come on, Roy," Bob protested, not giving the other man a chance to finish.

"You want my advice? Then I'll give it to you, and seeing that it's free, you should appreciate my generosity."

"All right, all right." He broke the egg yolk with a corner of his toast. "Share your wisdom."

Roy grinned. "Only accept reservations from people who've stayed at the B and B before. People you know."

"In other words, turn down strangers who arrive in the middle of a dark and stormy night."

His friend chuckled. "You got that figured out."

Bob finished his breakfast and reached for his recently refilled mug. "I have a theory I want to bounce off you."

Roy relaxed, leaning against the back of the booth. "Shoot."

"You know everything—what happened in Nam, right?"

Roy nodded, his expression serious.

"You remember that I didn't have an easy time after the war. I did everything I could to bury the memories. I sought oblivion. It was bad for everyone, especially Peggy and the kids." He paused. "Outwardly Dan Sherman seemed to adjust to civilian life. That's what I assumed, anyway. I didn't see him for decades. And even when I moved back to Cedar Cove, we tended to avoid each other. So I didn't know he struggled with demons, too."

Roy waited while Bob sorted through his thoughts. "From what Hannah told Peggy, Max didn't cope with life after the war any better than I did."

"He drank?"

"Some, I gather, but I don't think that was his only problem. He pretty much became an obsessive-compulsive, although that wasn't the term Hannah used."

"Remember how neatly everything was packed inside his suitcase?"

Bob nodded. They'd all been struck by it.

"What are you thinking?" Roy pressed.

"When I came back from Nam, I realized that someday, some way, I'd have to pay for what happened in that village. If I've learned anything about life these fifty-odd years, it's that there's a symmetry to things." He lowered his voice. "I...took lives, and now it seems someone wants to take mine."

With the words out in the open, Bob felt better. He'd been thinking about this ever since Max's death, but hadn't found the courage to verbalize it.

"Go on," Roy urged.

"I think Dan realized this, too. He preferred to take his own life, choose his own time."

"I—"

"Hear me out," Bob insisted. "I wonder if it's possible that a family member of one of our...victims has hunted the four of us down. He might have confronted Dan, forced him to take matters into his own hands. For that matter, what else would send Max rushing to Cedar Cove? I think whoever's responsible is looking for revenge."

Roy considered his theory. "I don't know. It could be, but I doubt it."

"Why? Plenty of Vietnamese have immigrated to the United States since the war."

"I think it's a bit far-fetched to believe one of them has a vendetta against four American soldiers after all these years. Why wait until now?"

Bob shrugged. "I don't know." Roy could be right; this scenario was probably a fantasy, something he'd invented in his own desperation.

But nothing else made sense, either.

Thirty-Four

Walking into the mall parking lot on Friday evening, Rachel hummed an old Eagles song, trying to get her mind off her pathetic love life. Her one date with bachelor Nate Olsen had been exactly that. One date. One expensive date. It depressed her that she hadn't heard from him in the two weeks since.

Well, so be it; he'd told her he was involved with a girl back home. She could have accepted that, would have without a qualm, but then he had to go and ruin everything by kissing her. Damn, he was one good kisser. As far as Rachel was concerned, he should be arrested for possessing a lethal weapon—his lips. The way he'd kissed her had been so spectacular he'd left her in agony. That single kiss had made her ache even more for a romantic relationship.

Not that she was desperate. Not like some of the women who came into the shop. Only that morning she'd had a client, a working wife and mother, and listened to a litany of woes. The husband drank, was unemployed, hung around the house and was seeing another woman. The really crazy thing was that Rachel's client was mad at this jerk's girlfriend! In

Rachel's opinion, this client was so worried about the trees, she didn't see the forest. Yeah, it was a cliché, but clichés were useful sometimes. Anyway, if her client did toss the bum out on the street where he belonged, he'd soon find some other woman to support him. Rachel had seen it happen again and again.

She was so involved in her thoughts that she almost didn't hear someone call her name.

"Rachel."

She turned around and discovered Bruce Peyton walking rapidly toward her. "Oh, hi," she said, her hands tightening around her car keys. Jolene had spent the previous Sunday at her place. She'd picked up the little girl and dropped her off four hours later, with only a minimal exchange of words with Bruce.

"Hi." He grinned. "Jolene had a really good time last Sunday."

"I did, too." They'd shopped, eaten pizza, watched videos, painted their toenails and chatted.

"She hasn't stopped talking about it."

"I'll give her a call soon and we'll bake those chocolate chip cookies I mentioned."

"She said something about that. I hope you'll send a few of them home with her."

"Of course." Rachel moved toward her car. It'd been a long week, and although she didn't have any special plans, she was eager to get home.

"Are you doing anything tonight?" Bruce asked.

"Not really. Did you want to drop Jolene off?"

"No, no," he said hurriedly and shook his head. "She's spending the night with a friend. It's a slumber party."

"What about this Sunday afternoon?"

"Sure, she'd like that."

"I'll see you then."

"Rachel." He stopped her again, looking decidedly uncomfortable. "Listen. Are you doing anything right now?"

"Now?" she repeated in a puzzled voice.

"I mean, do you have a dinner date or something like that?"

"No."

"Do you want to have dinner with me?"

Bruce was asking her out for dinner? "You and me? Like a date?"

He nodded. "Not an actual date, just dinner with a friend. If you want to. If you've got other plans, that's fine. No big deal. I was thinking of the Taco Shack."

Rachel hesitated.

"You've got plans." A defensive edge sharpened his words.

"No, it's just that I'm not sure this is a good idea."

"How come?"

She had a few questions of her own. "Why are you asking me? Why now?"

His head reared back as if her questions were unexpected. "Why not now? Jolene's with her friends for the night, and the truth is I'm not all that interested in my own company."

It certainly wasn't any fun to sit in a restaurant alone. Rachel knew that because she'd done it herself. And really, what would she do tonight other than watch TV and eat a microwave dinner? "All right."

A smile smoothed out the frown lines on his face. "That's great. Do you want to go with me or just meet there?"

Rachel looked at her car and decided to meet Bruce at the restaurant. With anyone else, she would've suggested she go home, shower and change clothes. But Bruce seemed to be in a rush. It was already nearly seven. Rachel had done a perm late in the afternoon, which had taken longer than she'd expected.

By the time she arrived at the Taco Shack, Bruce had found a place at one of the picnic tables. The menu was posted on the wall above the counter. Rachel knew everything listed on it, since she stopped in at least once a week for takeout.

"What would you like?" Bruce asked when she joined him. He gazed up at the menu.

"I'd like the enchilada platter," she said. "One chicken and one cheese with extra salsa."

Bruce smiled, nodding. "That's my favorite, too, but I prefer two beef enchiladas." He removed his wallet from his back pocket as he approached the counter. The line wasn't too long for a Friday night, although Rachel suspected that in another ten or fifteen minutes, there'd be a wait for a table.

Bruce placed their order and carried a tray with sodas to their table. He unloaded their drinks and pulled out the chair across from her.

Rachel suddenly realized that Bruce had come to the mall just to see her, since he'd been walking in as she was walking out. Still, she found it hard to fathom that after all this time, after their numerous conversations, he actually wanted to take her to dinner.

"Jolene told me you went out on your date with the bachelor," he commented, then sipped his cola.

"I did."

"How'd it go?"

She shrugged and reached for her diet drink. "All right, I guess."

"Are you going to see him again?"

He was mighty curious about her time with Nate Olsen. "Probably not."

He studied her, frowning slightly. "You sound disappointed."

"I am. I like Nate. He's a little young for me, but—"

"He's younger than you are?"

Rachel burst out laughing, attracting the attention of those sitting close by. "You sound like my father."

"Sorry." He lowered his head as though embarrassed. "Forget I said anything."

Bruce seemed jealous, which shocked her. "Bruce?"

He looked up.

"What's all this about?"

"What do you mean?"

Rachel narrowed her eyes. "You know what I mean. Let's not play games, all right? When you came to the mall this evening, it wasn't because you had some errand. It was to seek me out, wasn't it?"

"Anything wrong with that?"

His defenses were up again, but so were hers. "Well, no, but why pretend otherwise? Just be honest, would you?"

He raised his hands, palms up. "I am being honest."

"To yourself, I mean," she elaborated.

The waitress, a high-school kid judging by her appearance, brought their enchilada platters. Rachel glanced down at hers and Bruce looked at his and in a perfectly synchronized movement, they switched plates.

"Do you mind if we eat before we continue this inquisition?"

She gave him a quick grin. Sliding her fork over the cheese enchilada, Rachel cut off her first bite. "I didn't intend to give you the third degree."

"The thing is," Bruce admitted between bites, "I'm not exactly sure why I asked you to dinner. I dropped Jolene off at her friend's house and here it was Friday night, and I didn't feel like spending the evening alone. I got a hankering for enchiladas, but I didn't want to take up an entire table just for myself."

"I usually order mine to go."

"I tried to think of someone who might be interested in coming with me, and you were the first person who popped into my head. So I figured I'd see if you were available."

Rachel wasn't sure she should be flattered. At the moment she was too perplexed to figure it out.

"Jolene likes you a lot," Bruce said halfway through their meal.

Rachel was fond of the little girl, too, but her feelings about the child's father weren't quite as straightforward. Might as well find out what was going on here. "Do you like me, Brucc?" shc asked bluntly.

"Obviously. I didn't stop to analyze it. I thought you might be available and I was right. I'm glad."

"I am, too," she said. "I was headed home for reruns of *NYPD Blue*."

"You don't go bar-hopping with your friends?"

She shook her head. "I learned a long time ago that a bar isn't a good place to meet men." Not decent men, anyway, she amended to herself. Problem was, she didn't know *where* to meet men. She was wary of the Internet and not a club-joiner. She enjoyed crafts but she had yet to meet a single guy hanging out at a quilting bee.

"Have you had many serious relationships?"

She shrugged. "A few." She'd dated a guy back in her early twenties, discovered he was already married and dropped him instantly. That kind of grief she could live without. Ever since then, she'd been careful. Perhaps too careful… "What about you?"

His gaze fell to the table. "There's never been anyone but Stephanie."

The way he said his dead wife's name led Rachel to believe there never would be anyone else.

"I'd like to give this a shot," he said unexpectedly.

"This?"

"Us."

She opened her eyes wide. "Are you saying you'd like to go out with me?"

"Is that so surprising?"

Rachel needed a sip of her soda to ease the sudden dryness in her throat. "Frankly, yes."

"Would you be willing to see me now and again?"

"To what purpose?"

Bruce's mouth narrowed. "You're the kind of person who reads the last page of the book before you buy it, aren't you?"

That was precisely what she did. She laughed. "As a matter of fact, I do."

"I thought so. I don't know to what end. We can agree to play this by ear. Is that okay with you?"

"I guess." She considered it for a moment. "Tell me something first."

"All right."

"Asking me out tonight—did it have anything to do with Nate Olsen?"

The question seemed to trouble him, because he didn't answer immediately.

"Probably," he said at last.

At least he was honest about it.

"If he asks you out again, would you go?"

Now it was her turn to think matters over. "He won't. He's involved with someone else." She was gathering up her pursc as she spoke.

"You're sidestepping the question," he said. He held the restaurant door for her and they walked into the parking lot.

"I know."

"Either you don't want to answer it or you're afraid to."

"I'd rather not discuss Nate, okay? You know," she said confidentially, leaning toward him, "it would've been a perfectly wonderful night if he hadn't kissed me."

"Excuse me?"

"Never mind." She waved her hand dismissively. "It's too hard to explain."

"I guess I shouldn't try to kiss you, then."

"Don't be too hasty," Rachel said with a mischievous smile.

He smiled back.

But he didn't kiss her. Standing in the well-lit parking area outside the restaurant, it would have been awkward to do anything more than exchange pleasantries.

"Do you still want Jolene to come over on Sunday?" Rachel asked.

"Sure. Can I see you then, too?"

Rachel nodded. Bruce opened her car door and she slid into the driver's seat. "Thank you for dinner."

"I'll give you a call sometime tomorrow afternoon."

"Okay."

Rachel pulled onto the highway and drove toward her own neighborhood, feeling more than a little confused. As soon as she got home, she saw that she had a telephone message.

Setting down her purse, she began to slip off her shoes and pushed the Play button on her machine.

Nate Olsen's voice stopped her cold, one shoe off, one foot raised.

"Rachel, hi… I'm sorry I missed you." His words were

followed by a short pause. "I'm still thinking about our dinner and was just wondering if you were, too. I'll talk to you later, okay?"

Thirty-Five

On the first Monday of August, Grace Sherman opened the library and posted the sign for the free movie that would be shown Saturday night. This was a new feature the library had begun in June. It'd been Grace's idea, and the popularity of the event had surprised and delighted her. She believed the library should be part of the community, that it should be responsive to people's needs and interests and attract patrons of all ages. She always chose a movie families could watch together. That often meant a classic; this week's was *The African Queen.*

Mondays were always busy and the morning passed quickly. Loretta Bailey returned to her desk and Grace realized her assistant was already back from lunch. It seemed she'd left only a few minutes ago. If Grace was going to have lunch, she had to take her turn now.

She reached into the bottom drawer for her purse and when she straightened she came face-to-face with Lisa Shore, Cliff Harding's daughter.

"Lisa," she said, recovering quickly. "What a pleasant surprise!"

"Hello, Grace."

She was a lovely young woman who reminded Grace of Cliff in a dozen different ways, although she didn't resemble him physically.

"I can't tell you how happy I am to find you. I took a chance coming into town like this, since I wasn't sure you'd be here. I felt we should talk." The look in her eyes implored Grace.

"What are you doing in Washington?" That was a silly question; she was visiting her father, of course. Grace had no idea how much Lisa knew about what had happened between her and Cliff.

"Rich and I are here to see Dad. I don't suppose you could squeeze in a quick lunch, could you?"

Grace struggled with her composure but managed to respond graciously. "Of course I can. Why don't we sit down for a few minutes first? How's April?"

"Growing by leaps and bounds," Lisa said, obviously proud of her daughter. "Dad and Rich took her into Seattle." She glanced away guiltily. "I told them I had a bad case of cramps, which is actually true, so they suggested I stay home. I wanted to come into town to see you—but that part I *didn't* share with my dad."

Grace understood how difficult it must've been for Lisa to mislead her father. What she had to say must be important.

Grace slung her purse over her shoulder, waved goodbye to Loretta and walked out of the library with Cliff's daughter.

They were barely out the door when Lisa spoke with a quiet intensity. "I just had to find out what went wrong between you and my dad."

Grace sighed, unsure whether or not she should be grateful that Cliff hadn't said anything to his daughter. Then again, maybe he had. It was clear that Lisa knew something, or that she sensed it, anyway.

They bought crab salad sandwiches—the Pot Belly's special of the day—and sat down on a park bench near the marina. Tourists and locals alike strolled past.

"Dad won't tell me a thing," Lisa said as soon as they'd unwrapped their sandwiches. "All I know is that you're not seeing each other anymore."

Grace focused her attention on the boats gently bobbing in the marina. She simply couldn't look Lisa in the eye and explain what she'd done.

"Everything's my fault," Grace said, her voice trembling.

Her confession was followed by a short silence. "That's not what my dad said."

"He's wrong," Grace insisted. "I misled him—no, it's more than that, I deceived him." She refused to minimize her role in their separation. If not for her Internet relationship with Will, she suspected she'd be engaged or even married to Cliff by this time.

"How?"

Grace realized there was no help for it. Lisa had a right to know the truth. "I was seeing Cliff and at the same time involved with another man." There it was—the plain and horrible truth.

Lisa gasped. "But that's what my mother did. Now I understand…"

"I know, I know," Grace whispered. Her betrayal had been unforgivable in Cliff's eyes, a repeat of the betrayals he'd endured during his twenty-year marriage. Grace understood that she'd committed the one unpardonable sin and she accepted responsibility for it.

"Are you still involved with this other man?"

Grace shook her head. "It was quite a while ago."

"Then why aren't you seeing Dad?" Lisa finished the first half of her sandwich. Grace hadn't started hers; she put it in her bag to eat later.

She clasped her hands together. "Cliff won't have anything to do with me. I can deal with that now but it's taken me a long time to reach this point. You have a wonderful father, Lisa. Although we aren't part of each other's lives any more, I'll always love him."

Lisa wrapped up the remaining half of her lunch, then crossed her arms and leaned back on the park bench. "I find that interesting, because Dad said almost those identical words to me. That he isn't part of your life anymore but he loves you."

"He loves me? He said that?"

"He was crazy about you when he brought you out to meet me last year—and he still is."

"But..."

"You have to understand my father. He's a complex man. He doesn't give his heart easily, nor does he stop loving someone just like that." She snapped her fingers for emphasis. "Look at all the chances he gave my mother."

Grace rejoiced at Lisa's words, but that joy was virtually shattered by Cliff's adamant response. He loved her, despite what she'd done, and yet he refused to forgive her.

"I've tried to reach him," Grace said in a low voice. "I was such a fool and when I discovered the other man intended to stay in his marriage..."

"He was married?"

Grace felt her face heat with humiliation. How easy it had been to rationalize her behavior at the time. Now, it mortified her even more. She had no excuse, no justification to offer, other than her own schoolgirl fantasies.

Lisa took her hand and squeezed it gently. "That explains why Dad's acting this way."

Grace hung her head. "You don't know how much I regret everything."

"I'm sure you do," Lisa said gently. "Still, you bid on my dad in the Dog and Bachelor Auction."

"How did you hear about that?" she asked, surprised that Lisa knew about the charity event.

"From Cal. How much did Dad cost you?"

"Your father was my birthday gift from my friends and my daughters, and they paid a whopping eight hundred dollars."

Lisa let out a low whistle.

"No one paid more for any bachelor."

Lisa grinned and gave her a thumbs-up. "Have you gone on your date already?"

Grace nodded and decided she didn't want to discuss their evening out. There really wasn't much to say, which was depressing in itself. "He sent me flowers afterward," she added sadly

"That sounds like my dad. You're probably the only woman other than my mom and me he ever sent flowers to."

If Lisa was hoping to encourage her, she'd failed miserably.

"How long are you in town?" Grace asked, changing the subject.

"Only until tomorrow—that's why I had to speak to you this afternoon. It was now or never."

"I'm so glad you did."

Lisa sighed. "Dad has your picture in his bedroom. Did you know that?"

Grace shook her head.

"It's on his bedside table. He doesn't know I saw it, but I did. It's one of you and Midnight."

"He probably just forgot to take it down." Grace didn't want to get her hopes up, not after the disappointment of their dinner together, and the fact that she hadn't heard from him after receiving the flowers. "Or," she said dejectedly, "he's just very fond of that horse."

"Well, he is, but that's not why he kept the photo in his room."

Grace remembered the day Cliff had taken the picture. It'd been October and her first trip to his ranch. This was before he'd torn down the old barn and replaced it with the bigger, more modern stable. Cliff had given her the "grand tour," and as they walked around his property, he'd shared his vision of the ranch. He spoke of the improvements he hoped to make, the breeding programs he'd planned to institute. She hadn't understood a lot of it, but she'd felt his passion and his love for horses. That same day, he'd shown her his stallion and then stepped back to take her picture as she stood by the corral fence. At that very moment, Midnight had trotted toward her and poked his head over the top rung, curious about this stranger. Grace had turned to admire him and to stroke his sleek black neck. It was that image Cliff had captured on film. He'd shown her the snapshot, but he must have enlarged and framed it.

"I'm worried about my dad," Lisa confided.

"Why? How do you mean?"

"He's working too hard and he doesn't seem nearly as happy as he was the last time I saw him. I didn't notice it until this summer. He's been trying to hide it, but I know my father."

Grace wasn't nearly as happy, either. "I wish I could help, but there's nothing I can do."

"But there is, don't you see?" Lisa said with such fervor that tears sprang to her eyes. "Win him back, Grace. He loves you and you say you love him."

"I do!" Her love for him was real; she wanted Lisa to believe that. "But he doesn't want to see me."

"That's not true. Even Cal said my father's a different person since you two broke up."

"What should I do?" Grace couldn't think of a single thing she'd left unsaid or undone. Despite Cliff's repeated rejections, she'd tried again and again, until it became obvious nothing would change his mind about her.

"Fight for him," Lisa pleaded.

"Who do I fight? Cliff himself? How?"

"Wear him down," Lisa said. "Send him cards and letters."

"E-mails?" she suggested, eyebrows raised.

"Yes," Lisa cried. "Do something—anything—and don't give up until you've broken through his defenses." She twisted sideways on the bench, sitting so she could face Grace. "But only if you sincerely love my father."

"I do," Grace assured her again. "I truly do."

"I felt you must—but I had to find out. I had to know for sure."

The two women hugged. Grace was so moved by the honesty and hopefulness of Lisa's words, she felt like weeping. "Oh, Lisa, I can't thank you enough."

"Don't let me down."

"I won't," she promised.

That very night, Grace wrote Cliff a long e-mail. She began by thanking him for the flowers and then told him how much their dinner date had meant to her. She said, in simple, straightforward sentences, that she missed him and thought of him often.

When she finished she reread the e-mail. In it, she shared her concern for Kelly and Paul and their struggles to have a second child. She wrote humorously about her trials with Sherlock, and how the kitten refused to be ignored, describing the inventive ways he pestered her until Grace lavished attention on him. This was Grace's own less-than-subtle way of telling Cliff she wouldn't go away, either. Not this time.

The next afternoon, during lunch, Grace walked down to the corner drugstore and purchased a handful of cards, some clever, a couple that had dramatic photos of horses, and a few romantic ones.

As soon as she got home from work, she hurried to her computer, animals in tow, and logged on to the Internet, hoping for a response from Cliff. Her heart fell when she found none.

"Did you think this would be easy?" she said to Buttercup. Sherlock scratched at her leg until Grace lifted him onto her lap. She petted him with one hand and typed with the other while she considered the possibilities. It could be that Cliff had deleted the e-mail without even opening it. Or decided to ignore it. Or perhaps he hadn't checked his messages lately.

She e-mailed him a second time and mailed off a card the following morning. Eventually she'd wear him down, as Lisa had said. Eventually he'd see she wasn't going away. She loved Cliff. He was the best thing in her life and she refused to give him up.

Thirty-Six

"Bob!" Peggy shouted from the foot of the stairs. "Phone!"

Bob laid down the script of *Chicago*—he'd been memorizing his lines—and walked to the top of the stairs. He'd been so intent on the scene, he hadn't even heard the phone ring.

"Who is it?" he called.

Wearing her "Kiss the Cook" apron, Peggy stood there looking up at him. "He didn't say."

Mumbling under his breath, Bob hurried to the master bedroom and picked up the phone. "Hello," he muttered impatiently.

"Robert Beldon? This is Colonel Stewart Samuels."

The crisp military tones went through Bob like an electrical charge. It was the voice of a man he'd hoped never to hear from again. The voice of the man who'd led him into battle. A soldier who'd stood with him in a Southeast Asian jungle. Who'd saved his life and then, at the same moment, robbed him of it.

"Yes." With difficulty he managed to respond.

"I'm going to be in the Seattle area in the next few weeks. We need to talk."

It'd been more than thirty years since Bob had last spoken with his commanding officer. He could go another thirty years and it would suit him just fine. So far, the only person in contact with Samuels had been Troy Davis. Bob would've preferred to keep it that way.

The colonel continued, giving the details of his trip to the Pacific Northwest. Bob stood rigid until the other man announced he intended to visit Cedar Cove.

"Is that necessary?" Bob demanded. Seattle was too close for comfort, but having him in Cedar Cove for any length of time was downright intimidating.

"I believe it is. There's a matter between us that requires resolution."

How formal he sounded. So cold-blooded and hard.

"Two of our comrades are dead, one a suicide and one murdered," he said. "I'm hoping we can figure this out, once and for all. Agreed?"

"Yes, I—" Bob wasn't given a chance to finish his sentence.

"Good. I'll have my assistant make the arrangements."

Before Bob could comment further, the phone went dead. Bob stood there unseeing, his hand still on the receiver. After a moment, he replaced the phone and slowly, almost as if he were in a trance, walked down the stairs.

Peggy was in the kitchen with Hannah preparing dinner. When she saw him she abruptly stopped mashing the potatoes.

"Who was that on the phone?" she asked, walking toward him.

He stared at her, still numb inside. "Colonel Samuels."

"Stewart Samuels?" Hannah repeated, moving closer to Peggy.

Peggy glanced at Bob and then at Hannah. "What did he want?"

"He's coming to Cedar Cove."

Hannah let out a small cry of alarm and quickly covered her mouth. "What's he coming for, did he say?"

Peggy wrapped her arm around the young woman's shoulders. "Why are you so afraid?"

Bob wasn't sure if the question was directed at him or Hannah, but their guest was the one who answered.

"He's just so…military."

"I thought you were grateful to him for all his help with your father," Peggy said, looking at Hannah.

"I was…I am. Dad never would've gotten the medical care he needed if it hadn't been for Colonel Samuels. But…he frightens me." She trembled as if a chill had overtaken her.

"Bob?" His wife turned to him for answers he couldn't give. "What's going on?"

"I don't know. He said he had business in the area and felt we should talk. He asked that I set up a meeting with Roy and the sheriff, too."

Peggy frowned. "Does he think Dan Sherman's death and Hannah's father's are linked?"

"I don't know." But it was more than that. Samuels had indicated that he had business with him, too. Bob didn't want to see Stewart Samuels, didn't want to be reminded of the past, and yet it was there, confronting him, and had been every day since his return from Vietnam.

That night, unable to sleep, Bob lay in bed and stared at the ceiling. The digital clock by the telephone told him it was after two, but he was wide awake. Peggy slept peacefully beside him, oblivious to his anguish.

A full moon cast shadows on the walls. With the window open, the scent of the cove, of seawater, wafted toward him. He usually found it relaxing, but tonight his mind refused to let him rest. Every time he closed his eyes, all Bob could see, hear, taste and smell was Vietnam. Tension filled him. He didn't want to go back to those memories, didn't want to think about them, didn't want to feel.

Suddenly he heard the glass door off the kitchen sliding open. Bob's eyes widened with fear. He lay perfectly still as the noise drifted up the stairwell—a noise so slight Bob was sure he must be mistaken. As he strained to hear, the sound of muffled footsteps sent fear shooting through his veins. His adrenaline kicked in and he folded back the sheet and sat on the edge of the bed. Sweat broke out across his forehead. Leaning forward, he closed his eyes to listen more closely, hoping this was his imagination, after all. But the warnings Roy had given him rushed through his mind and he remembered the car that had followed him.

Bob looked around for something he could use to defend himself.

He found nothing. His golf clubs were in the garage, and the sturdiest thing he could take with him was a work boot.

Peggy stirred. Even in her slumber she must have sensed his fear. "What's wrong?" she whispered.

He brought his finger to his lips. "Someone's downstairs."

Bob felt his wife stiffen. She grabbed his arm and scrambled to a sitting position.

"How did they get in?"

"The patio door."

"Did you lock it?"

He nodded.

"Should we phone 911?" Peggy whispered.

A board creaked at the bottom of the stairs. Whoever was in the house was coming after them. It was too late to call the sheriff's office. Both Bob and Peggy froze in horror.

Nothing.

In that one beat of his heart, Bob acted. He refused to sit and wait. If someone had come to kill him, he wasn't going to die without putting up a hell of a fight. Roaring off the bed, he stormed out of the room.

Peggy cried out in an effort to stop him. Fumbling with the light, she lunged for the phone as Bob flew out of the bedroom and into the hallway. He smacked the light switch with his palm.

There, standing at the foot of the stairs, was Hannah. She gasped at the sight of him.

"Hannah!" he cried, furious with her for the scare she'd given him. "It's Hannah," he shouted back at his wife.

"What the hell are you doing sneaking around the house at this time of night?" he demanded.

She cowered before him, quaking, with her head bowed. Her long hair spilled over her shoulders and hid her face.

"Hannah, for heaven's sake, what are you doing?" Peggy ran down the stairs, tying her robe as she did.

"I…I—"

Bob found a folded sheet of paper on the downstairs hall carpet and leaned down to pick it up. A glance told him it was a farewell note from Hannah.

"I…I thought it was time for me to go," the young woman said, her voice so low it was hard to distinguish the words.

"But why would you sneak away in the middle of the night?" Peggy asked.

Hannah shrugged one shoulder.

Apparently the I-don't-know shrug was supposed to explain everything.

"I'm afraid!" she wailed. Seconds later, she broke into sobs.

Peggy immediately slipped an arm around Hannah and guided her into the kitchen. Hannah's suitcase sat in front of the patio door. Apparently she'd opened it and then decided to leave a note at the foot of the stairs.

Bob collapsed at the kitchen table, so badly shaken he couldn't stop trembling. He wanted to scream at Hannah, frighten her the way she'd frightened him, but he knew he dare not.

"Why are you afraid?" Peggy asked gently once she'd sat Hannah down. She filled the kettle and put it on the stove for tea.

"I don't know… I lost both my parents. I can't bear the thought of losing you, too."

"Why do you think you would?" Peggy asked quietly.

"Because…"

"Does this have to do with Colonel Samuels's visit?" Peggy asked next.

Hannah didn't answer, but Bob suspected Peggy was right. For her own reasons, their guest was as worried about the man's visit as he was himself.

Thirty-Seven

Olivia hung her robe in her chamber closet and collected her purse, preparing to leave the courthouse at the end of another long day. Couple after couple stood before her with their lives in shambles, eager to tear apart their homes, willing to destroy their children's security. Each partner seemed intent on proving that he or she was perfectly capable of surviving without the other. There was so much anger and bitterness, so much false pride. Some days she found her task of deciding the fate of these families overwhelming.

She glanced at her watch as she headed toward the parking lot. She was meeting Grace for dinner that evening. It was the first time since Olivia's marriage that Grace had asked to see her outside of their aerobics class on Wednesday night. They phoned each other fairly regularly and occasionally met at the Farmers' Market on Saturday mornings, but her marriage had changed their relationship. They were each discovering how to proceed under these new terms.

Olivia welcomed the opportunity to talk to her lifelong friend. There were things she wanted to discuss—things she couldn't really talk about with anyone else. And something in Grace's voice told her she had concerns of her own.

Once in her car, she drove the short distance between the courthouse and The Lighthouse Restaurant. Her daughter and son-in-law had done a marvelous job and she was proud of their success. Still, as a mother, Olivia worried. Justine was working too hard; she was a young wife and mother, in addition to managing the restaurant's books and occasionally filling in as hostess.

As luck would have it, Justine was working that night. Her face brightened when she saw Olivia. "Hey, Mom," she said with a quick hug. "It's good to see you."

There'd been a time in the not-so-distant past when their relationship had been strained. Justine had been seeing a much older man, and she'd felt defensive and angry at the world. Olivia had wanted so much more for her. She knew that, in some ways, Justine was still grieving over the death of her twin—Jordan had died in a tragic accident at the age of 13. But Justine had finally come to a more peaceful acceptance. Olivia felt that was because of Seth. In fact, everything had changed when Justine fell in love with Seth Gunderson.

"Where's Jack?" Justine asked, looking past Olivia.

"The office, where else?" Jack worked far too many hours, but nothing Olivia said convinced him to delegate some of his tasks. He was involved in every aspect of the newspaper and loved his job. Now that the *Chronicle* had gone to five editions a week, his hours were even worse than they'd been before their marriage. They'd argued about it repeatedly, but Olivia supposed she might as well get used to having a part-time husband. Jack had promised this wouldn't last much longer, but she suspected nothing was going to change until he retired. *If* then…

Justine seated her at a window table, then returned to the

front of the restaurant and talked to one of the waitresses. It was still early in the evening and the restaurant was only about a third full. As soon as she had someone to cover for her, she walked back to Olivia's table.

"Got a moment?" she asked.

"Of course." Grace wouldn't arrive for at least ten minutes.

Her daughter pulled out the chair across from her. "How are things with Grandma?" she asked.

Olivia sighed and wondered how much of the story her daughter knew. Probably all of it. "We're talking again."

Justine smiled, obviously relieved. "Grandma's going to marry Ben, you know?"

Olivia was well aware of that. "She sent me a letter." It hurt that her own mother had written instead of telling her face-to-face. "I didn't mean to hurt her," she admitted. "Will and I had Ben investigated for her own protection, but our concern backfired."

"I know." At least Justine sounded sympathetic.

"Mom was upset about our lack of faith in her," Olivia said. She must have known instinctively how her mother would feel, because she'd found it necessary to hide their inquiries from Charlotte.

"What else did she say in her letter?"

"She said everyone deserves to be happy, regardless of age, and reminded me how pleased she was when I married Jack."

"She's right, you know," Justine murmured.

"Of course she is." Olivia had no disagreement with that. "She wants Will and me to treat Ben fairly and with respect. The same goes for his sons, of course." She frowned. "I don't think she's met them, though, at least not yet." With a quick shrug, she added, "Naturally I intend to respect Mom's wishes. It's been a bit difficult, thinking of my mother with another man, but it's her life and I want her to be happy."

Justine agreed. "I never said anything when you decided to marry Jack," her daughter said softly. "But deep down, I wanted you and Dad to get back together. I knew it would never work, but the little-girl part of me wanted my parents to love each other again."

Olivia was shocked to see tears in her daughter's eyes. Justine blinked furiously, as though embarrassed. "I still think about Jordan," she whispered.

"So do I."

Justine nodded. "Do you remember what day it is?"

Olivia realized with a jolt that she'd been so preoccupied with what was happening in her own life she'd let the date slip. On this day, August tenth, eighteen years ago, her son had drowned. Her entire life and those of her two surviving children had been divided by that date. The time before Jordan's death and the time after.

Wiping the tears from her face, Justine forced a smile. "I didn't mean to get all maudlin. Let's get back to Grandma, before we both dissolve."

Olivia agreed and swallowed past the lump in her throat. "I stopped at Mom's house earlier in the week and we hugged for the first time since she found out, and she forgave me. I'm sure she'll tell you herself, but they've set the date for their wedding."

Justine grinned sheepishly. "I know all about that. Grandma came in earlier today and booked the restaurant for the reception. She talked to Uncle Will, and he said he's coming out for the wedding."

Olivia was glad to know that, because she wanted to give Grace ample warning. When Will arrived, Olivia planned to have a long talk with her brother about his Internet relationship with her best friend. He'd taken advantage of Grace and betrayed his wife, Georgia. Olivia was furious whenever she thought about it.

"Hi, you two," Grace said, coming toward them. "Am I interrupting anything?"

"No, no," Justine said, rising gracefully from the chair. "I was keeping Mom company until you got here." She looked at Olivia, winked and was on her way.

Funny how just a few minutes with her daughter could mean so much. Olivia felt close to Justine and to her son James, too, and considered herself fortunate to have such wonderful children.

"Sorry I'm late," Grace said as she sat down across from Olivia. "It took forever to finish up at the library."

"Don't worry about it. Justine and I had a chance to talk and we don't get to do that nearly often enough."

"I know how she feels," Grace muttered. "You and I have barely any time together these days."

"I'm sorry," Olivia told her friend, and she was sincere. She *had* been neglecting their friendship, but was determined not to let that continue. "How's your week been?"

Grace shrugged noncommitally. "It was the best of times, it was the worst of times. What about you?"

Olivia smiled. "The same. Jack and I are still adjusting to living together, which hasn't been as easy as I'd hoped, but you know most of that." She'd complained often enough during their aerobic workouts on Wednesday nights. "Mom and I are talking now and she's forgiven me. Oh, and before I forget, Will's coming out for the wedding."

Grace paled visibly but didn't comment.

"Now, what's new with you?" Olivia asked.

To her surprise, Grace grabbed a tissue from her purse. "I have something to tell you, but I'll probably cry."

Olivia was aghast. "What is it?"

"Last week I got a letter from Mike Sherman, Dan's cousin in Oregon." She paused a moment to collect herself before continuing. "He wrote after Dan's death and we've talked a couple of times since, but this came out of the blue."

"What did?"

Grace nervously folded the edges of the linen napkin. "Mike really feels bad about this, but he thought it was time I knew that Dan borrowed thirteen thousand dollars from him. Apparently he asked for the loan a year or so before he vanished. Mike didn't want to say anything after Dan disappeared."

"Oh, no—he wants the money back now?"

Grace nodded. "He hated to ask, but he provided the paperwork and sure enough, that's Dan's signature on the promissory note. Mike said it's been over four years and he needs the money. He seems to think I got some life insurance settlement after Dan's body was discovered."

Olivia knew she hadn't. Her opinion of Grace's dead husband had never been high but she considered the fact that he'd burdened Grace with this loan unforgivable. Especially since Dan had to know that Grace wouldn't be able to collect on his life insurance if he committed suicide. Furthermore, the trailer he'd purchased with that money—the trailer he'd killed himself in—was a total loss.

"What are you going to do?"

Grace wadded the tissue in her hand. "What else can I do? I'm refinancing the house and paying him back the money, plus interest. It isn't Mike's fault that Dan chose to end his life."

"Aren't you going to tell him you didn't get any insurance money?"

"No." She shook her head. "It would only make him feel

worse about asking for the money back, and he doesn't deserve that. Frankly I'm grateful he waited as long as he did. If he'd hit me with this any sooner, I don't know how I would've dealt with it."

"What's that going to do to your finances?" Olivia knew things were already tight.

"I'll survive. I've made it through worse times than this."

"I know. Did you tell Sheriff Davis and Roy?"

"Roy said it was another piece of the puzzle falling into place," Grace told her. "He was the one who originally found out about the trailer. We always wondered where Dan got the money…."

Olivia was proud of Grace for taking this latest blow in stride and refusing to let circumstances overwhelm her. She was about to say that when Grace changed the subject.

"On a brighter note," she said with a big smile, "I heard from Cliff."

"You did?" Olivia knew her friend had made a concerted effort to win back the rancher.

Grace almost squirmed in her chair with excitement. "I have to tell you I'd nearly given up hope."

Olivia leaned toward her. "Well, don't keep me in suspense. Tell me what happened!"

"I drove out to his ranch with a batch of chocolate chip cookies ten days ago."

Olivia nodded approvingly. "And?"

"I wanted to weep with frustration when he wasn't home, but I talked to Cal and he was so encouraging. I like him a lot. He said he'd make sure Cliff knew I'd stopped by."

"I like Cal, too." Olivia had only met the trainer once and briefly, but she'd taken an instant liking to him. Although he was quiet, even solemn, she sensed a deep reserve of strength and character.

"Did Cliff call you?" Olivia leaned closer, eager to hear the details.

"No...actually I haven't talked to him yet." But Grace showed no sign of being discouraged. "I received an e-mail."

"What did he say?"

The waitress stepped up to the table, and Olivia realized they'd been so intent on their conversation they hadn't given any thought to food or drink. The young woman took their order for wine spritzers and left.

"Well?" Olivia pressed.

"Cliff thanked me for the cookies. He was very polite and he didn't write anything else, but Olivia, I feel like there's a crack in this wall he's erected between us. He can't ignore me anymore. I won't let him."

"That's great!"

"I'm not fooling myself. I have a long way to go, but that one message cheered me so much I've been walking on air ever since."

"Have you sent him other messages?"

Grace nodded. "Every evening. I mail a card twice a week but Cal told me Cliff's started collecting the mail himself. When I don't send a card, I write an e-mail. He hasn't blocked my name, so I know he's getting those messages, too."

Olivia reached for her menu. For the first time in months, she had the feeling that everything was going to work out between Grace and Cliff Harding.

Thirty-Eight

Maryellen tucked the latest photograph of Katie into a business-size envelope, along with a short note to Jon's parents. She left it unaddressed and slipped the envelope in with the rest of the mail she planned to drop off at the post office Monday morning. She'd fill in the necessary information later rather than risk having Jon find an envelope with his parents' address.

He'd been gone since early morning, and Katie was napping. Maryellen rarely had uninterrupted time these days and she relished these private moments. She was pregnant again, although she hadn't said anything to Jon. All in due time. She wanted the situation to be perfect when she told him.

The front door opened and Maryellen walked out of the bedroom and looked over the upstairs railing. Jon was home earlier than she'd expected. He'd slipped out of the house before dawn for a day trip to the Olympic rain forest.

"Jon." She didn't bother to disguise her delight at having him home. When he'd left, he'd kissed her goodbye and whispered that he didn't know when he'd return.

Now, seeing her upstairs, he smiled, set aside his camera

equipment, and hurried up the stairs, his energy undiminished despite his long day.

Maryellen met him at the top of the staircase and he threw his arms around her waist. "Where's Katie?"

"Asleep."

He wore that special smile of his. The one that told her he'd had a good reason for rushing home. "When did you put her to bed?"

Maryellen gave a coy shrug. "About half an hour ago. What do you have in mind?"

Jon's throaty chuckle sent shivers of excitement down her spine. "First things first. A shower, followed by something to eat and then..." He hesitated, still smiling, and brought her close. "On second thought, I'm not that hungry."

"Oh, honestly," she chided, but she relished his strong sexual appetite.

"Want to take a shower with me?" he whispered.

"Not now. You go, and I'll put together a couple of sandwiches. I wouldn't want you to faint from hunger."

He nuzzled the side of her neck. He held and touched her often. After so many years of living alone and avoiding relationships, Maryellen hadn't been entirely comfortable with his need for frequent physical contact. But the longer they were together, the more accustomed she became to his caresses—and the more she craved them.

"How did your day go?" he asked as he headed into the bedroom, still holding her by the hand.

"Actually it was pretty quiet. Katie and I spent some time outside and then I paid a few bills." For obvious reasons she didn't mention she'd also written a letter. "Did you get the photographs you wanted?"

Jon pulled her into the room with him. "I got several that should work, but the whole time I was trudging through the forest I kept thinking how much more enjoyable it would be if you and Katie were there, too." He released her hand, then sat on the edge of the bed to remove his shoes.

"I've got leftover meat loaf," she said.

Jon looked up at her blankly.

"For your sandwiches."

"Sure, whatever."

Maryellen grinned.

"What's so funny?" he growled, jumping up and catching her around the waist again. He brought her down onto the bed with him and rolled over, trapping her beneath him. He ran his fingers through her hair and his eyes softened as he gazed down at her.

In that moment, she felt his love so strongly she wanted to weep. Pregnancy made her overemotional; she remembered that from before.

Sliding her arms around her husband's neck, Maryellen drew his mouth down to hers. Their kisses were slow and tender. After Katie's birth—when Maryellen realized how much she'd come to love Jon—he'd refused to make love to her. Those months had been agonizing, but now it seemed there was no satisfying him—or her.

"Come into the shower with me," he said between tantalizing kisses.

"It's the middle of the afternoon."

"So?"

"Jon..." Her protests were growing weaker by the moment.

"All right, all right...I'll take my shower." He stood up and walked into the bathroom, shedding clothes as he did. The haze of desire didn't dissipate immediately. Maryellen got slowly off the bed and went downstairs. Times like this reminded her how fortunate she was to be loved by Jon Bowman.

She'd just finished making the meat loaf sandwiches when Jon skipped down the stairs, his shirt unbuttoned and his hair still wet from the shower. She froze when she saw that he was carrying the envelopes she'd left upstairs. Watching him carefully, she hoped he'd set them on the edge of the counter, where they usually put the mail, and leave it at that.

Her heart nearly stopped when the envelopes slipped from his hand and scattered across the floor. They both leaned down to retrieve them.

"I'll get these. Your lunch is ready," she said, hoping to distract him.

It didn't work. "Who's the letter to?" He straightened and held the unaddressed stamped envelope in his hand.

"A friend."

He stared at it for several seconds, frowning.

"Do you want your lunch or not?"

He ignored her question. "What friend?"

"No one important," she said, trying to squelch her panic.

"Maryellen, what friend?" he asked. "You look like a cat with feathers in your mouth. Is there something you're not telling me?"

"What's the big deal? Just someone who stopped by the gallery recently."

He studied her, eyes narrowed. "Do you mind if I take a look?" She knew he probably suspected another man; the truth was even worse.

She pressed her back against the counter, feeling her pulse hammer in her neck. She couldn't answer him.

"Maryellen?"

She turned away. "It's to your parents."

"What?" he exploded.

"Don't be angry," she pleaded, her eyes closed.

He was silent for so long she couldn't bear not knowing his thoughts. Tentatively she turned around, biting her lower lip, afraid her deception was about to destroy her happiness.

"What have you done?"

"I—"

"Is this the first time?"

She shook her head.

He groaned with frustration. "I told you how I felt about my family."

"I know…."

He clenched his fists. "And you decided you knew better? You felt it was your duty to go against my wishes?"

"I—"

"How did you know where to reach them?"

Maryellen took a calming breath. "I found their letters."

"Didn't I ask you to throw them out?"

"Yes—and I did." But until then, he'd kept the letters and that told her he still felt an attachment to his family.

"My father chose to offer me up as a sacrificial lamb. He betrayed me."

"He's so sorry, Jon. If only you'd talk to him, you'd see for yourself."

"Talk to him?" he shot back at her. "*Talk to him!* I spent seven years in hell because of my so-called father. I'll rot before I say one word to him again."

"You don't mean that! You can't have that much hatred in you."

"Obviously you don't know me as well as you think." He whirled around and dashed up the stairs.

Maryellen couldn't leave things as they were. She raced after him. "Please listen," she begged. "Your father isn't well. He's aged and he's frail and—"

Jon sat on the bed and jerked on his shoes. At her words, he grew still. “You’ve seen him?”

This was possibly a worse offense. She clasped her hands behind her and nodded. “They came into the gallery.… I didn’t know who they were but your father wrote me afterward and asked me to act as a mediator between you.”

“What did you tell him?” he demanded.

“I said no—all I did was mail them a letter to let them know about Katie and me and—”

“That’s bad enough.” He stood and brushed past her.

“Where are you going?”

Already halfway down the stairs, he glanced over his shoulder. “It seems I can’t trust you, Maryellen.”

“Can’t we talk? Please don’t do this.”

Jon paused at the foot of the stairs. “There’s nothing to talk about. I need time to think.”

With that, he slammed out the door.

Brokenhearted, Maryellen slumped to the floor on her knees and hid her face in her hands. If Jon couldn’t forgive his parents, it was unlikely he’d forgive her either.

Thirty-Nine

"Peggy," Bob shouted from the patio. "We're going to be late." He wasn't that keen on attending church this morning and would've gladly stayed home had Peggy agreed. However, he knew better than to ask.

His wife hurried out the back door and cast him an exasperated look. "I tried to talk Hannah into coming to worship service with us, but she isn't interested."

As far as Bob was concerned, Hannah was the lucky one. Peggy didn't want to hear it, though, so he attempted to console her. "Until recently, I wasn't interested in church, either, remember?"

Peggy nodded and climbed into the passenger seat. "I don't know what it is with the two of you."

"The *two* of us?" For the most part, Bob avoided Hannah, which wasn't that difficult. She worked odd hours at her dishwashing job at the Pancake Palace. She was rarely home for dinner and frankly Bob preferred it that way. He'd tried to get along with their guest. Two or three times he'd made a genuine effort to talk to her, but Hannah was like a frightened rabbit; she ran for cover the moment Bob approached. He'd given up and settled for hoping that she'd leave soon.

Peggy frowned as she set her Bible in her lap. "Ever since Colonel Samuels phoned, both of you have been edgy and out of sorts."

"That's an exaggeration if I ever heard one," he snapped.

"No, it's not," Peggy insisted. "Hannah's as bad as you—worse, even. She isn't sleeping well. I know because I hear her roaming from room to room at all hours of the night. Of course, you're not much better."

Bob didn't argue; he'd been sleeping fitfully ever since the conversation with his former commanding officer. Bob couldn't explain the reason. It remained as much a mystery to him as his attitude toward Hannah. He'd tried to like the girl, but his negative reaction to her was visceral. Instinctive. Maybe it came from some innate revulsion to cringing, fearful personalities. He hated her clinginess with Peggy and he couldn't seem to change her aversion to him. Well, there was nothing he could do about it.

"Church would be a big help to Hannah." Clearly Peggy hadn't finished worrying about their guest's refusal to attend Sunday morning services.

Bob made a noncommittal grunt. The truth was, he'd had to drag himself out of bed that morning. Just as Peggy asserted, he hadn't been sleeping well. Little wonder. He was afraid that the moment he closed his eyes, the nightmare would return. It often struck without warning. Life would be perfectly agreeable if he could turn in for the night and have simple, pleasant dreams. Unpredictably he'd be thrust back into a Vietnamese jungle, gripped by terror. He hated every aspect of the dream. For years, he'd tried to drown out the noises of that day. The voices. Screaming. Shouting. Crying. Alcohol had only made it worse. If anything, the voices had gotten louder.

Sobriety wasn't helping all that much, either. The voices continued in a low drone that he ignored as much as possible. He'd been fairly successful until Maxwell Russell died in his home. Then the nightmare came back full force.

"Thank you so much," Bob muttered under his breath, angry with his old army buddy.

"Did you say something?" Peggy asked.

Bob shook his head.

Peggy glared at him. "You're certainly in a fine mood this morning."

He didn't bother to answer because she was right. And feeling the way he did, the last place he wanted to be was church.

"Bob," Peggy cried.

"What?"

"You just missed the turnoff."

Damn, she was right. "Let's skip church this morning, okay?"

"Not you, too?" Peggy whined. "First Hannah and now you."

"I don't feel like it today."

"We're almost there. Please, don't be difficult."

Not wanting to get into an argument, Bob sighed and found a place to turn the car around and head back toward Briar Patch Road. Within five minutes, he slipped into an available space in the crowded church parking lot.

Organ music drifted out the open doors. Thankfully they were late enough to avoid all the handshaking and friendly chitchat. In case Peggy hadn't guessed, he wasn't in a sociable mood.

Of course, being late also meant they couldn't get a decent seat at the back of the church. Those who arrived early set claim to the back five pews. He and Peggy ended up sitting in one of the middle rows. That was acceptable, since at least they'd missed the "meet and greet."

Following the music, Dave Flemming stepped up to the pulpit and opened his Bible. Bob had left his at home. Peggy flipped to the book of Matthew, chapter six, the reference listed in the bulletin she'd picked up on the way in. Bob crossed his arms and closed his eyes. He had no intention of listening. He was here to keep the peace at home and for no other reason. For all he cared, the pastor could be talking about the inflated price of dot.com shares.

Then it hit him—one word in particular. *Forgiveness.* He opened his eyes and sat up and started to listen. It was as if Pastor Flemming knew his innermost thoughts and had written the sermon specifically with him in mind. The idea unsettled him.

At the close of the service, the congregation stood and sang together. Normally Bob enjoyed the singing. He had a good baritone and at one time had considered joining the choir. His commitment to the community theater took up most of his free hours, however. It was the theater or the church choir. He'd chosen the theater.

At the end of the song, the service was over and the pews began to empty. Still deep in thought, Bob remained seated.

"I need to talk to Corrie," Peggy announced, then got up and scurried off. Apparently she was afraid he'd argue with her and was gone before he had a chance to tell her to take her time. He had some thinking to do.

Usually Bob resented being left to twiddle his thumbs while Peggy did her socializing, but just now, he was grateful for a few moments of solitude.

He didn't know how long he sat there, alone in the church. Peggy would come and get him when she was ready, he figured, letting his thoughts drift where they would.

"Hello, Bob." Pastor Flemming stepped into the pew and sat down next to him.

Bob knew Dave, liked him well enough to play golf with him every week. They hardly ever talked about God, which suited Bob just fine. To him, a man's faith was a private matter.

"Pastor." Bob smiled in his friend's direction.

"Something on your mind?" the other man asked.

Bob shook his head. The pastor knew some of the story. He'd been the person who'd recommended that Bob contact Roy McAfee in the first place. He trusted Dave. At the time, he'd been desperate, half-afraid he was losing his mind.

"Well, maybe I do need to talk." Bob paused and drew in a deep breath. "What you said about forgiveness kind of hit home, you know?"

Pastor Flemming nodded. "It's in the Lord's Prayer. We recite it so often we tend to forget what it means."

Bob agreed. He'd said the prayer at every AA meeting for years, and had never truly understood the part about forgiveness. "You said this morning that we can only accept forgiveness to the extent that we're able to forgive ourselves." Those were the words that had struck him with such intensity.

The pastor nodded again.

"Some people require a lot of forgiveness," Bob murmured.

"We're all sinners."

"But like I said," Bob continued, "there are sins, and then there are sins. Some of us will never find forgiveness. In certain circumstances, it just isn't possible."

The pastor said, "In such cases, you do what you can and then you forgive yourself."

"That isn't possible, either," Bob said, unable to keep the despair from his voice.

"Remember what else I said, Bob. Your willingness to forgive others is directly related to your willingness to forgive yourself."

That wasn't news Bob welcomed. It had never occurred to him that the two were linked.

He heard a sound at the back of the church and turned around to see that Peggy had appeared. She hesitated when she saw him talking to Pastor Flemming. "You've certainly given me something to think about," Bob mumbled, eager now to escape.

The only way he could figure this out was by himself. He had to stop resisting the memories. Maybe then he could lay them to rest.

Forty

On the last Saturday morning in August, Grace was scheduled to work the animal shelter's booth at the Farmers' Market. On her last stint there, she'd netted Sherlock, who was the remaining kitten in the litter and the only one left without a home. The whole day, she'd had the feeling she'd end up with one of the six kittens that had been placed for adoption. Sure enough, she'd come home with eight-week-old Sherlock.

She always enjoyed the market, especially on days like this—bright and sunny yet not really hot. In the rainy months of winter, she often found it hard to remember how lovely summers could be in the Pacific Northwest.

Today, as usual, the market teemed with activity. The variety of products sold there always impressed her—everything from fresh oysters, plucked only hours earlier from the beach, to knitted afghans.

Grace had her hands full with the animal shelter booth. She'd left Buttercup at home; she was too busy to watch the dog and besides, Sherlock would keep her company. All morning long, Grace answered questions and talked to the children who crowded around, instantly attracted to the kittens. She had ten this Saturday, plus several mature cats, and hoped to arrange adoptions for at least half.

Grace was grateful she was busy, which helped keep her mind off the fact that Will Jefferson was in town. Olivia had phoned shortly after Will's arrival to let her know. He'd tried to call her once, but she had Caller ID, and when she saw Charlotte's name, she let the answering machine pick up. Sure enough, it was Will. Grace feared Charlotte might inadvertently mention that she did volunteer work with the shelter and would be at the market this weekend.

Just when she finally felt she was safe, Grace glanced up and nearly swallowed her tongue. Standing a few feet away from her was Will Jefferson, the man she least wanted to see. Her heart seemed ready to implode. For one crazy moment, all she could do was stare. When her senses returned, she looked sharply away.

Unfortunately, all the children who'd gathered to admire the kittens had drifted off. It was apparently the opportunity Will had been waiting for. He walked toward her, his steps determined and his gaze focused relentlessly on her. He'd always been handsome, and his attractiveness, combined with her schoolgirl fantasies, had blinded her. But Grace wasn't the same woman she'd been a few months ago.

She squared her shoulders, decided there was no avoiding a confrontation, and scooped up a kitten. The heat of embarrassment reddened her face until she realized she had nothing to be embarrassed about. She wasn't entirely blameless, but Will was the one who'd lied.

"Hello, Grace." His greeting was as soft as a caress.

"Hello, Will." It demanded all her strength to keep her voice even and unemotional.

Grace knew his presence would make her uncomfortable

at the wedding unless they cleared the air. She suddenly wondered if Will had sought her out because he wanted to apologize. Like her, he understood that they'd both be at Charlotte and Ben's wedding. They'd have to make peace—even a superficial peace—or the whole event would be too awkward, not just for themselves but their families and friends.

Grace needed to let him know two things: that she was willing to put the matter behind them and that she wanted nothing more to do with him. For Charlotte and Ben's sake, she'd be civil.

"You look wonderful," Will said smoothly.

A sick sensation hit her directly in the stomach. She held the kitten draped over her arm and close to her side, as if for protection. "Olivia told me you were coming for the wedding."

"Yeah, I figured she would." He slid his hands in his pockets and struck a casual pose. "I'll be here for several days." He let that information fall, apparently expecting a response. "I hoped we could get together."

"Get together?" She couldn't have heard him correctly. He couldn't possibly be suggesting they see each other socially.

"Mom and I are going to dinner tonight, but I'm free on Sunday."

"You're asking me to have dinner with you?" The man's audacity was unbelievable. "You can't be serious, Will. You lied to me!"

"You're right, that was unfair, but I've always been fond of you, Grace. I'm here—"

"Where's Georgia?"

He didn't even blink at the mention of his wife. "Home. We each have our own lives."

"I'll bet you do." Grace couldn't disguise her sarcasm. She wondered if Georgia knew she was supposed to have her own life. And how about their cruise? Did they have separate lives there—and separate rooms? Not that any of it mattered.

"I arranged my flight to come in early so you and I could talk. Do you realize what you did? You didn't give me a single chance to explain. You cut me off without listening to a word I had to say."

"Are you or are you not married?"

He sighed heavily. "Married, but this is important, Grace, for both of us."

She shook her head. "I don't have anything to say to you, other than that I don't care to see you or speak to you ever again."

He frowned as if saddened by her lack of understanding. "We both know you don't mean that. You *can't* mean it after everything we've been to each other." He took a step closer. "I've missed you, Grace. These last few months have been hell without you. Don't you feel that, too?"

She was careful not to answer him. "I'm grateful for the lessons you taught me," she said instead.

He nodded impatiently.

"The thing is, I came so close to—"

"You love me, Grace," he interrupted. "You did when you were in high school and you do now."

"I was a teenager then and I'm a woman now. I'm glad to say I occasionally learn from my mistakes."

"We're not a mistake," he said urgently. "Don't you see that what we had was special?"

He was good; she'd give him that. "What we had was a very big mistake. If you arrived early for the wedding because you wanted to see me, then I'm afraid you're in for a major disappointment. If I never see you again, I'll be a happy woman."

He shook his head firmly. "You can't mean that," he said with the same intensity as before.

"I mean every word. Now please...please leave me alone."

He frowned and turned away, but took only a few steps before he turned back. "I'm staying with my mother, so if you change your mind…"

"I'm not going to. Please don't contact me again."

He smiled—a smile obviously calculated to melt her stony heart. "I refuse to believe you're serious. Okay, you have a right to be angry, but I can't divorce Georgia. It would devastate her. But if that's the only way I can have you, then—"

Grace raised her hand to stop him. She'd heard enough, more than enough. "Go. Just go."

He frowned again, like a petulant child, but finally left. All of a sudden Grace started to shake. Her knees felt like they were about to give way and she sank into the folding chair in the animal shelter booth. Gently stroking the kitten on her lap, she closed her eyes and took in several calming breaths.

"Grace."

She opened her eyes to find Cliff standing there. "Are you all right?" he asked. "You look pale."

"I'm fine," she lied. She'd hoped he'd come here today, wished for just this moment, but not immediately after a confrontation with Will.

"No, you're not fine," he said bluntly. "That was Will Jefferson, wasn't it?"

So Cliff had seen her talking to Will. Her first thought was to defend herself, to explain that she wanted nothing more to do with Olivia's brother. Instead, huge tears filled her eyes and trailed down her cheeks.

"You cared about him, didn't you?"

"No," she cried, and knew that was a lie. "Yes…fool that I was. I did care at one time, but not anymore. Oh, Cliff, don't you know? It's you I love. I can't give up on the two of us. I tried to and I'd almost succeeded but then Lisa—"

"You spoke to Lisa?"

Grace winced; she was only making matters worse.

"You and Lisa talked?" he repeated.

Grace nodded, swallowing hard. "She came to see me at the library, and I'm so grateful she did."

"What did she say?"

Grace stared down at the sleeping kitten in her lap. "She said you loved me, too."

He dropped into a crouch so they were at eye-level and tucked his finger beneath her chin. "That was when you started this e-mail campaign, wasn't it?"

She nodded again. She wondered if her barrage of messages had succeeded. This was the first time they'd actually talked face-to-face, and she wanted to throw her arms around his neck. Well, except for the kitten, of course…

Cliff held her gaze for the longest moment before looking away.

"Did it work?" she whispered.

At first she didn't think he was going to answer, but then he gave her a lightning-quick smile. "You're a difficult woman to ignore."

"I am?" Her heart was jumping inside her chest. "Really?"

"Before I knew it, I was hurrying to the mailbox every day and logging on to my computer, hoping there'd be a note from you."

The Internet was part of what had gotten her into this mess. It was only fitting that it should be a means of getting back what she'd lost.

"Are you willing to give me another chance?" she asked, holding her breath for fear of what he might say.

"We can begin slowly."

She bit her lower lip. "Thank you."

Cliff wiped the tears from her cheeks. "How about if we have a cup of coffee and talk once you're finished here?"

Grace nodded, so happy she was afraid she'd start crying again. Maybe they could attend Charlotte's wedding together. She hardly dared hope...

Forty-One

Cecilia knocked lightly on her employer's open door. Mr. Cox glanced up from his paperwork, smiling when he saw her.

"I wanted to remind you that I have a doctor's appointment this afternoon," she said.

Zachary Cox's gaze went to his appointment calendar. "Ah, yes, I see that now. As it happens, Rosie and I are taking the afternoon off ourselves."

Her employer had escaped with his wife for several afternoons this summer. Cecilia suspected they were rediscovering the excitement of being in love, the passion of their early years. "Will Allison be coming in today?"

Mr. Cox nodded absently. "Rosie's teaching her how to knit. Her first project is a blanket for your baby."

Cecilia had proudly shared the news of her pregnancy with Allison a week earlier. "That's so sweet of her."

Mr. Cox smiled again. "You've been very good for my daughter, and this is something she wanted to do for you."

All Cecilia had really done was listen to the girl. She'd been going through a difficult time after her parents' divorce, but she seemed to have made a complete turnaround.

"Leave whenever you need to, Cecilia."

"The ultrasound is scheduled for two-thirty."

"Is your husband going with you?" Zach asked.

Cecilia nodded. "He wouldn't miss it for the world."

"Good. I'll see you in the morning then."

Cecilia returned to her desk, her spirits high. Every day was special. The dreaded morning sickness had slowly disappeared, just as it did the first time.

Now that he'd accepted her pregnancy, Ian was a hundred percent supportive, his attitude one of eager anticipation. She felt more confident than ever in her husband's love.

At two-thirty, Ian was waiting for her at the navy hospital, pacing the hallway outside the technician's office.

"I'm here," she said.

Ian hurried over to her. "How are you feeling?"

"All right. Just as important, how are *you* feeling?"

His grin was so sexy, it was all she could do not to kiss him right then and there. "Excited. We're going to see a picture of our baby."

"I'm excited, too."

He started to open the office door, but Cecilia stopped him. "We should decide now if we want to know the sex of the baby or if we want to wait."

"Do you want to know?" he asked.

"It doesn't matter to me either way."

He agreed. "Me neither." He held open the door for her and they walked into the reception area. Several other expectant mothers, at varying stages of pregnancy, were already waiting.

Cecilia went up to the counter and handed over the necessary paperwork, along with her navy identification. When she'd finished, they sat down next to each other. Ian held her hand and gently rubbed it with his thumb in a soothing, comforting motion. He was nervous, she realized, but then so was she.

It seemed to take forever before her name was called. With a full bladder, she'd found it hard to sit still for that long. But finally it was their turn. Ian entered the inner office with her, after which they were led into the ultrasound room. Once Cecilia was lying on the table, her belly covered with cool gel, she noticed how pale Ian had become. He'd asked to come with her, but now she wondered if this was such a good idea.

"Ian?" Cecilia held out her arm to her husband. His grip was tight as he linked their hands. "Everything's okay."

He nodded. "Of course it is."

The technician, a woman who wore a name tag that identified her as Jody, directed their attention to the monitor. "We should be able to see the baby in just a moment."

As the tiny fetus came into view, Ian rose to his feet to get a better look. "That's our baby?" His voice was filled with surprise and awe.

"That's your baby," Jody said softly, moving the paddle over Cecilia's stomach.

"Is everything all right?" Ian asked. "I mean the baby seems awfully small."

"She'll grow."

"She?" Cecilia repeated.

"I always refer to a fetus as female. Were you hoping for a son?" The question was directed at Ian.

"Either," he answered, staring at the monitor.

"Is this your first child?"

Ian pulled his gaze away from the screen long enough to look at Cecilia. His eyes darkened with pain.

"Our first baby died shortly after she was born," Cecilia explained. "That's the reason Dr. Chalmers ordered the ultrasound. He wants to be sure there aren't any problems with this pregnancy."

Jody patted Cecilia's hand. "So far everything looks perfectly normal."

It had with Allison too, Cecilia recalled, but she'd only had the one ultrasound in the early stages of her pregnancy and there hadn't seemed to be any need for another. Who could have known? Who could have guessed that her baby would be born with a defective heart?

"I'm so sorry about your first baby." Jody's voice was sympathetic.

Cecilia glanced at Ian and saw that just talking about Allison had stirred painful memories. "We're both a little nervous this time around."

"All we want is a healthy baby," Ian added.

"Of course you do." Jody manipulated the paddle a bit more. "Would you like to know the sex of your child?"

"You can tell this soon?" Ian squinted at the screen, as if that would help him decipher what she saw that he didn't.

"A trained eye can."

Ian squeezed Cecilia's hand. "Should we?" he asked.

"You don't want to be surprised?" If it was solely up to her, she'd prefer to wait, but there were definitely advantages to learning the baby's sex in advance.

"I've decided I do want to know," Ian said eagerly.

"All right, all right, tell us," Cecilia said, laughing.

Jody grinned. "It looks to me like you're having another little girl."

Ian let out a deep, heartfelt sigh. "A girl," he repeated. His hand tightened around Cecilia's to the point that it was painful.

"Ian!"

"Sorry," he said when he realized what he'd done. "A girl. We're having a girl."

Cecilia nodded. She was so excited that she could hardly hold back her emotions. After Allison's death, Cecilia had given away all her daughter's clothes, with two exceptions. She'd saved the outfit she'd planned to bring Allison home in, and a favorite baby blanket she'd purchased shortly before the birth. That was it. The two things she'd saved because it was too emotionally difficult to give everything away.

Following the ultrasound, they went to a movie. Ian held her hand all through the show, as if he needed a constant connection with her. They went out to eat afterward, but because they were saving to buy a house, all their budget would allow was a meal at the Pancake Palace.

This was a rare night out and Cecilia chatted lightheartedly during dinner. Only when Ian reached for the bill did she realize how quiet and somber he'd grown over the course of the evening.

"Ian, you're not worried about the baby, are you?"

His denial came far too quickly. "No, the technician said everything was fine. Why should I be worried?"

"I don't know. Why should you?" she pressed, unwilling to drop the subject.

Her husband looked away and when he returned his gaze to her, his eyes were brimming with pain. "It's just like before."

"What is?"

"First, the pregnancy's a surprise, just the way Allison was a surprise."

"But this is a happy surprise."

Ian agreed willingly enough. "I was ecstatic when you told me you were pregnant with Allison."

"You're happy now, too, aren't you?"

He brought her hand to his lips and kissed her knuckles. "It took some adjusting, but I'm pleased about the baby."

"It *is* different this time," Cecilia insisted.

"Is it? Has the morning sickness been different?"

He had a point. "No, that was the same."

"With Allison, the ultrasound didn't show anything abnormal, either."

Again all she could do was agree. "We're married now," she said.

"I married you in my heart the first night we made love. Even before that, I knew I wanted to spend the rest of my life with you."

"Oh, Ian." At times he could be the most romantic man in the world. At others…well, he was a man.

He sighed. "I'm trying not to worry."

"I know, but it really is different with this baby. For one thing, you're home now and you're not scheduled to go back to sea until after my due date."

He sighed, more loudly this time. "No guarantees on that."

"I know, but they won't send you out so soon, especially after you were away for six months. The navy wouldn't be so heartless."

"I want everything to be perfect for you and the baby," he said hoarsely. "I'm trying not to worry, Cecilia, but I can't help it."

"Wait and see. We're going to have a perfectly healthy baby girl."

He closed his eyes. "I pray that you're right."

So did Cecilia, but she had no guarantees to give him either.

Forty-Two

Colonel Stewart Samuels was coming to Cedar Cove sometime in the middle of September. During their telephone conversation, the colonel hadn't been able to give Bob an exact date. Soon, though, he'd be here and as the time crept closer, Bob grew increasingly uneasy.

After the last performance of *Chicago,* Bob removed his makeup and changed clothes. Usually he hung around with the rest of the cast. Tonight, in particular, was a festive occasion, since the wrap party would take place once the set was struck. But the last thing Bob felt was festive, so he made his excuses and left after the show.

In addition to not feeling sociable, he was nervous. Ever since he'd arrived at the theater, Bob had the feeling someone was watching him offstage as well as on.

As he walked into the dark parking lot, an eerie sensation shuddered down his spine. The temptation to whirl around and confront whoever might be following him was nearly overwhelming. He resisted, half hoping that his nemesis would do him the favor of killing him and be done with it.

No such luck.

Since he'd been allowed to live, Bob climbed into his car and started the engine. The headlights shot twin beams across the mostly empty lot. Bob stared out the windshield and, to his disappointment, saw nothing out of the ordinary.

His depression had begun shortly after Pastor Flemming's sermon, but it had been simmering from the time Maxwell Russell had died in Bob's home. Even before the body had been identified, Bob knew this dead man was somehow connected to him. Max Russell had haunted him, reminded him of sins long past. They'd never learned his reasons for coming to Cedar Cove—to the Thyme and Tide. Bob guessed it had something to do with Dan's suicide, but that was only speculation. They'd never know for sure.

Bob pulled out of the parking lot and onto Harbor Street. From town, the road wound along the waterfront. Normally Bob followed it down to Cranberry Point, but as soon as he reached Harbor, a pair of headlights came up behind him.

Bob smiled to himself. So his instincts were right. He'd been watched and whoever was watching had decided to follow him. Surprisingly he experienced no dread or fear; instead he felt a sense of vindication. This proved he'd been right all along.

The car turned off Harbor and onto Cedar Cove Drive, which Bob hadn't expected. Apparently his stalker knew he'd been caught. For reasons he didn't want to analyze, Bob made a sudden decision to follow whoever it was. He found a convenient spot to turn around and speeded after the other vehicle. Bob flicked his high beams on and off and felt a certain satisfaction in letting the follower know he was being followed.

This was all a bit silly, but he stayed behind the car, eager to find out what he could. The vehicle slowed and turned into The Pink Dog tavern. A pink neon French Poodle flashed on the bar's sign. If Cedar Cove had a seedy area, this was it. Workers from the shipyard stopped in for a beer on the way home; they were the Pink Dog's regular clientele. On Saturday nights, the parking lot was nearly full. Bob turned in and watched as the other car claimed one of the few empty parking spaces.

Riveted, Bob sat in his vehicle, staring as a man climbed out of the car and headed for the front door. Bob strained for a better look, but the light was too weak and all he got was a general impression. Tall, with a thick waist, the guy had a beer gut that hung over his belt, faded jeans and a grease-smudged shirt. He didn't so much as glance in Bob's direction. Bob suspected this guy hadn't been tailing him, after all. He looked more interested in a cold beer and a good time than anything to do with Bob.

He waited and then parked facing the front door so he could check out everyone who came and went. Still, Bob didn't know what he should do if he saw the man again—or if he'd even recognize him.

He hadn't been anywhere close to this kind of establishment in years. He knew better. He'd been sober since 1983. For several minutes all he did was stare at the flashing sign. It hypnotized him, that sign, reminding him of days when his best friend in the world was a bottle of beer.

His mouth started to water and the urge for a drink was so strong that he held the steering wheel in a death grip. He could *taste* a beer. He remembered how, on a hot day, there was nothing that satisfied him more.

It felt as if he were in a trance. He was shocked by how powerful the pull was, and he knew he was no more immune to the lure of alcohol now than he'd been the day after his first Alcoholics Anonymous meeting twenty-one years ago.

Bob took out his cell phone. He needed help, and the first

person he thought of calling was Jack. He pushed the speed dial button and waited. Jack had a cell that he kept in his car but constantly forgot to recharge. No answer. With increasing desperation he called the house.

After three rings, Olivia picked up.

"Oh hi, Bob," she said after he'd asked for Jack. "He's on his way home from Bainbridge Island. Did you try his cell?"

"I did. No need to tell him I phoned, I'll catch him later." All Bob wanted was someone to tell him not to go inside that bar. Anyone. He had to *hear* it, because the pull toward that front door grew stronger and more compelling with every breath he drew.

"Of course," Olivia said. After a moment's hesitation, she asked, "Is everything all right?"

"Sure," he lied but realized he must have sounded as desperate as he felt. "On second thought, have him call me, would you?"

"The minute he walks in, I'll let him know. You want him to call your cell phone?"

"Please." Bob didn't bother to say goodbye. He ended the call and put his hand on the door handle. He'd tried. If he walked into the Pink Dog, it was because Jack hadn't answered his phone. He'd been there for Jack countless times over the past fourteen years, but now—when he needed a friend, someone to talk sense into him—Jack was nowhere to be found. Typical. When he needed help, his good friend Jack was unavailable.

As Bob opened the car door, a cool breeze blew inside. He breathed in the scent of the night and closed his eyes, knowing full well that if he walked into that bar, it would be the end. He'd go right back to the hell his life had been twenty-one years ago. Right back to the insanity, the madness that had controlled him.

He placed one foot and then the other on the ground outside the car. He blamed his golfing partner, Pastor Dave Flemming, for this. In his frame of mind, it was easy to cast blame. All this talk about healing and forgiveness. What Dave didn't understand was that some sins couldn't be forgiven. Yeah, he talked about forgiving yourself, but that wasn't an option for Bob, not with what he'd done. Some acts defied forgiveness. A man couldn't slaughter women, children, old people, and ever be the same again. It just wasn't possible. Maybe he should've died that day.

Bob remembered returning from Vietnam. He'd landed in San Francisco, grateful to get home alive. When he was granted leave, he'd been warned against wearing his uniform into town. Returning soldiers were called "baby killers" and had blood thrown at them. Bob defied the order. He would have welcomed the attack. Then the whole world would know what he'd done; he wouldn't have to hide it any longer.

Rocking slightly now, Bob stabbed his fingers through his hair. He wanted a drink. One. He'd stop with one. That was all he needed. After twenty-one years, he knew what he could handle and what he couldn't. One beer would satisfy this need and then he'd turn around and walk out.

Blindly he grabbed the cell phone on the seat next to him. As he stared at it, he knew that if he walked into that tavern he was as good as dead. He might as well blow his brains out the same way Dan Sherman had. Drinking would take longer to actually kill him; that was the only difference.

Death wasn't such a bad thing, he reasoned. People died every day and the people they left behind mourned them, but life continued.

As if in slow motion, Bob hit speed dial for Roy McAfee's home number; fortunately, he'd programmed it in after that other incident. He'd try one last time, reach out. Roy didn't need to know his dilemma, but he could provide human contact, a human voice. Bob gazed up at the heavens, deciding that if his friend didn't pick up, he had his answer. He'd know it was useless and he should just give in and have that beer. Hell, he'd buy the whole tavern a round. But if Roy answered, then God was telling him to get back in his car and drive away. It'd be God's fault if he started drinking again, he thought, hysterical laughter bubbling up in his throat.

The phone rang four times, and Bob swore that each ring lasted ten seconds longer than the one before. When the answering machine clicked on, he bolted upright at the unexpectedness of it.

"You've reached the home of Roy and Corrie McAfee. We aren't available to take your call right now...."

Bob severed the connection and stared down at the phone.

Then he looked up at the night sky again. "That wasn't the deal," he shouted. Roy had answered, all right, but it wasn't really Roy, just his voice on an answering machine. In other words, God had given Bob a half-assed answer.

Bob felt the torture of indecision. He longed to test his strength and prove he was strong enough to have one drink and walk away. But he knew... Everything he'd ever learned in AA told him otherwise. Still, he didn't care. He wanted that drink. Needed that drink. Craved that drink.

The sound of his cell phone ringing jolted him badly. He grabbed it with both hands and fumbled at the keypad.

"Yes," he snapped.

"Where are you?" It was Peggy.

"Why?" he demanded. He didn't want to talk to his wife. Didn't she realize he had a life-altering decision to make?

"Something's wrong. I could feel it. Where are you?"

Bob opened his eyes wide. Could Peggy be the answer to his prayer? He slid back inside the car.

"I thought you'd be home by now," she continued. She sounded troubled. Almost afraid. "This isn't like you."

"I'm all right."

"Are you sure?"

He was now. "I thought there was someone following me again."

"Was there?"

"No…I'm on my way home."

"I'll be waiting."

Bob started the engine and backed out of the space.

He was going home.

Forty-Three

Maryellen stepped out of the shower, hair still wet. It was the afternoon of Charlotte and Ben's wedding. She'd mentioned the ceremony to Jon, but they weren't exactly on good terms. The one time she'd asked, he refused to attend the wedding with her.

He also refused to discuss his parents. He remained civil, but distant and guarded. Every night they slept side by side without touching, without talking. Her beautiful home felt like a prison and Maryellen couldn't bear it.

Being pregnant didn't help. She hadn't told Jon yet. She'd planned to, knowing she should, but as time went on and his attitude didn't change, she realized it was a hopeless situation.

After dressing and blow-drying her hair, she got out an overnight bag and packed as much as it would hold. She added several extra pieces of clothing to Katie's diaper bag, as well. When she was finished, she carried both to the car.

Maryellen was on the verge of tears. She loved Jon and hoped they would be able to resolve their problems, but she'd begun to fear that wasn't possible. Her husband no longer trusted her. He felt she'd betrayed him. He couldn't understand or accept that she'd only been trying to help him reconcile with his family—for his own sake and his daughter's.

With a sleeping Katie over her shoulder, Maryellen gently tapped on the door of the darkroom where Jon was developing film. Whenever he was in the house at the same time as she was, he found a way to avoid her. If she was upstairs, he had some reason to linger downstairs. Meals were a painful experience. They sat across from each other and made polite conversation, but Maryellen simply couldn't connect with him.

"What is it?" Jon called impatiently.

"I'm leaving for Charlotte's wedding now."

"All right."

Maryellen hesitated. "Are you sure you can't come with us?"

"I'm sure."

"Okay." Disappointment settled heavily on her shoulders.

"Give the newlyweds my best."

"I will." Maryellen swallowed painfully. "Listen, Jon, I'm thinking I won't come back after the wedding."

"What?"

"I talked to Mom earlier, and Katie and I are going to spend the night with her."

"Hold on a minute," he said and opened the door.

Maryellen stepped back nervously as Jon's gaze held hers. "You're going to your mother's place for the night?"

She nodded.

"Why?"

Maryellen shrugged. "I need time to think."

"About what?" he challenged.

"I can't live like this," she whispered, breaking eye contact.

He didn't respond.

"I'm sorry, Jon, sorrier than you know." Her voice cracked, and she turned away and left the house.

To her surprise, he followed her to the car. When she'd placed Katie in the car seat, she straightened. Jon stood with his hands in his pockets, staring down at the ground.

"Are you coming back tomorrow?" he asked as she walked around to the driver's seat.

"Do you want me to?"

He didn't answer.

"That says it all, doesn't it?" She climbed in the car, started the engine and drove to the end of the driveway. Her heart was about to break. Hands clenching the steering wheel hard, she lowered her forehead and drew in a deep breath.

The minute Maryellen arrived at her mother's house, Grace knew something was wrong. "You'd better tell me," her mother said as Maryellen carried in her bags.

"We'll discuss everything after the wedding," Maryellen insisted, managing a smile. "It's all right, Mom. Everything's going to be fine."

Her mother looked as if she didn't believe her, and rightly so. Maryellen didn't believe it herself.

The wedding was lovely. Standing beside her mother, Maryellen battled tears. Only five months earlier, she'd stood before Pastor Flemming and vowed to love Jon for the rest of her life. It had only taken her five months to screw up her second marriage. Five months. That had to be some kind of record outside of Hollywood.

The church was nearly full. Charlotte's dearest friends crowded the front pews, wearing red hats and purple boas. Olivia and her family took up two pews. So many people had wanted to share in the couple's happiness. Unfortunately, neither of Ben's sons had been able to come; both he and Charlotte must have been disappointed.

Despite the jubilant mood, Maryellen felt a sense of hopelessness and inner turmoil. The church seemed to get hot and stuffy and the room began to sway. Maryellen sat down, taking several deep breaths, fearing she was about to faint.

"Maryellen?" Grace sat down beside her.

She offered her mother a feeble smile. "I'm pregnant."

Her mother smiled from ear to ear and squeezed her hand.

"Jon doesn't know."

"I think it's time for you to tell him, don't you?"

Maryellen couldn't answer.

The music started then, and Pastor Flemming came to the front of the church. Charlotte and Ben joined him and gazed up at each other with such adoration that Maryellen had to blink back tears.

She heard footsteps behind her and hope leapt into her heart. She turned around, thinking, hoping, desperately wanting the late arrival to be Jon. Instead, Cliff Harding slipped into the pew beside her mother. She watched as they looked tenderly at each other and then Cliff tucked her mother's arm in the crook of his elbow and smiled over at Maryellen and Katie.

Somehow Maryellen made it through the rest of the day. The reception at The Lighthouse was elegant, with vintage wines and the best champagne—neither of which she touched—and a selection of delicious hors d'oeuvres. Several people asked about Jon, and Maryellen invented a convenient excuse. He was busy with a photographic commission and couldn't come; he sent his best wishes. He had, in fact, given the newlyweds a framed photograph of the lighthouse, one that Charlotte had long admired.

Knowing her mother wanted to spend time with Cliff,

Maryellen drove back to the house on Rosewood Lane. Katie was cranky and hungry by then, so Maryellen hurriedly heated her dinner. She was giving Katie a bath when she felt the first painful spasm. The sharpness of it caught her unawares and she nearly doubled over.

Kneeling on the floor in front of the bathtub, she watched as her daughter splashed joyfully, unconscious of the turmoil in Maryellen. No, please God, not the baby. Nothing else happened and she breathed easier.

After a few minutes, Maryellen lifted Katie from the tub. The pain shot through her and she gasped as the blood rushed between her legs. Holding Katie against her, Maryellen sank to the floor.

The front door opened a moment later and Maryellen sagged with relief. "Mom...help...oh, Mom."

Grace was in the bathroom in an instant; Cliff was with her. Her mother's eyes were wide with alarm.

Maryellen was weeping by then. Katie was screaming.

"I've lost the baby...I've lost the baby," she wailed in grief and pain, sobbing openly now.

After that, everything happened so quickly, Maryellen had trouble making sense of it. The next thing she knew, she was at the hospital in Bremerton and a doctor was telling her she'd suffered a miscarriage. As if she hadn't figured that out for herself. Maryellen barely heard a word he said, crying as hard as she was. He asked about her husband, but she shook her head. Jon didn't even know she was pregnant.

It was decided she should spend the night in the hospital and after the D&C, she was wheeled into a private room. A lone figure stood in the shadows. Jon. Apparently her mother had called him. Or perhaps Cliff had; it didn't matter. He was with her.

Maryellen looked at him and fresh tears coursed down her cheeks. She turned her head away.

"Maryellen," he whispered, moving to the bedside. "Why didn't you tell me?"

She had no answer for him.

"I am so sorry." Each word was carefully enunciated.

Deeply depressed, Maryellen could only shake her head. She was sorry, too. Sorry about everything.

Jon sat down beside her and after a moment, reached for her hand and kissed it. She realized then that his eyes were bright with tears.

She started to sob again and stretched out her arms. Jon wrapped her in his embrace and together, with their arms securely around each other, they wept.

Forty-Four

Roy McAfee always checked his answering machine when he arrived at the office. There'd been a number of hang-ups recently. In light of the mysterious postcard he'd received a few weeks back, these hang-ups troubled him. He expected a few occasionally—any business got its share of wrong numbers—but his office had received more disconnected calls than usual in the last six weeks.

Corrie was making coffee after collecting the day's mail on her way into the office. Sitting down, Roy opened the drawer on the left-hand side of his desk and pulled out the cryptic postcard. He still didn't know what to make of it.

He heard Corrie moving around the outer office and realized she was about to deliver his coffee and the mail. Not wanting her to fuss over the postcard, he slipped it back inside his desk drawer.

Sure enough, Corrie entered his office, handing him a fresh mug of coffee. "There wasn't much mail this morning," she said as she placed a stack on the corner of his desk.

Usually she was the one who stopped at the post office.

It was pure coincidence that Roy had collected the mail the day that postcard arrived.

Corrie remained standing on the other side of his desk; she seemed to be waiting for something.

Roy anticipated a comment that didn't come. "Anything else?" he asked.

"Look it over," she said, gesturing to the few pieces of mail.

Roy reached for them and leaned back in his chair while he shuffled through the usual flyers, bills and—he hesitated when he caught sight of the postcard. He stared at the picture of the Space Needle.

"Read it," Corrie said.

Roy turned it over. The message was in the same block lettering as the first one. Only this time it read: THE PAST HAS A WAY OF CATCHING UP WITH THE PRESENT.

"What does it mean?"

Roy stared at the card, as perplexed by this message as he was by the first. "I haven't got a clue."

"There's no signature."

Roy set the card down on his desk. "People who send these kinds of messages generally don't sign their names."

Corrie walked over to the far side of the room and looked out the window. "This isn't the first one, is it?"

At times Roy swore Corrie should be the private investigator. She had real instincts about people, and a reliable sense of what was true and what wasn't.

"Is it?" she demanded, turning to face him.

Roy reluctantly shook his head. Slowly opening the drawer, he brought out the other postcard.

Corrie walked quickly to his desk and picked it up.

He watched her read the short, cryptic message and saw that she was as mystified as he was.

"When did this arrive?"

He couldn't recall exactly. "A few weeks ago."

"Why didn't you say anything?" she cried, throwing down the postcard. "I'm your wife. I have a right to know."

Roy shrugged halfheartedly. "What was the point? Why should you worry because someone's getting their kicks mailing me silly postcards?"

"You're being threatened and you don't feel it's important to let me know?" She raised her voice. "I'm not only your wife, I'm your business partner!"

"Now, Corrie..."

"Don't talk to me as if I'm a child."

"Then stop overreacting. It's just a postcard and if you read it again you'll see it isn't threatening."

Corrie picked up the card they'd received that day and read it aloud. "The past has a way of catching up with the present." She leveled her gaze on Roy. "That sounds ominous to me."

Roy shook his head. "Not necessarily."

"I hope you're taking this seriously." Restless now, Corrie started to pace.

Roy didn't want to upset her any more than she already was—but, in fact, he hadn't taken the threat seriously. Not really. Until this morning. One postcard he could dismiss, but two? The earlier message had been something vague about regrets. Sure he had regrets. Every police officer did. It came with the territory.

"Think!" Corrie insisted. "This must have to do with one of your old cases. So you should review your old cases and narrow it down to someone capable of...this."

Roy shook his head again. "I was on the force for more than twenty years and handled thousands of cases. Do I have regrets about any of them? Damn straight I do, but I always did what I believed to be right."

Corrie refused to let it go. "Could it be someone who was released from prison recently?"

"I don't have a clue." Over time he'd helped put quite a few men behind bars. A whole lot of suspects weren't particularly grateful for his detection skills.

"What about threats? Did anyone threaten you while you were on the force?"

There'd been some; convicted felons often looked for someone else to blame for their bad luck. He was a convenient target, but no one case stood out in his mind.

"Forget it," Roy urged, snatching up a pen, pretending to get to work.

"I can't," Corrie murmured, but she returned to the outer office.

Roy could tell how shaken she was. He wanted to reassure her but didn't know how. He'd wasted time mulling over the first postcard and hadn't come up with anything. If some nutcase wanted to mail him a message on the back of a postcard every few weeks, what could he do about it? Apparently, whoever was doing this derived a bizarre sense of satisfaction from it. In Roy's opinion, his mystery correspondent didn't seem intent on causing him harm.

After a few minutes, he went to check on Corrie, using the excuse of refreshing his coffee. He found her kneeling in front of the filing cabinet, sorting through old police files. He'd always kept a personal notebook about every major case he'd worked, as well as newspaper articles and other information. Corrie, an inveterate organizer, had made files for each year. She had two or three on the floor beside her.

"What are you doing?" he asked as he poured coffee into his mug.

"Checking out our old Cedar Cove cases, plus some of your notes from the Seattle PD."

Roy sipped his coffee and turned to take a look at one of the names. "Parker," he read slowly.

"Harry Parker," Corrie reminded him. "Three years ago. He befriended a neighbor, and was supposedly helping the old man with yardwork and such."

It sounded familiar.

"The old man's daughter, who lived back east, said she suspected Harry of stealing her father blind and asked us to look into it. The woman had good instincts."

"I remember." Roy said. Harry was currently serving time at the men's prison in Shelton for forging checks and theft.

"As I recall, Harry swore you tricked him into a confession."

"I didn't have anything to do with his statement to the sheriff," Roy countered.

"Nevertheless, Harry blamed you."

Roy doubted it was Harry who'd mailed him those two postcards. He suspected this went back to his days in the Seattle Police Department.

"It's none of our Cedar Cove cases," he said.

"What makes you so sure?" his wife demanded.

"I just am. Whoever this is, whatever it's about, it goes way back." The tone of this latest card said as much. Something from his past was about to hit him square between the eyes.

They spent the morning looking through old files and journals, some cases going as far back as twenty years. He ended up with a short list of people to check out, but didn't feel hopeful. This afternoon he planned to make a few phone calls.

Corrie went out to lunch with Peggy Beldon and came back in lighter spirits. While they were at the mall they'd run into a sale of some sort. Roy had stopped counting all the money she'd supposedly saved them by shopping at sales. Interestingly, she found it logical to spend money in order to save it.

"Peggy said something interesting at lunch," Corrie said as she stepped into Roy's office. "Bob thought someone was following him again a little while ago."

This was news to Roy. "He never mentioned it to me."

"That's because after a few blocks, the car went past him. Bob turned around and followed the other car for a short distance, but in retrospect he doesn't think he was being followed, after all."

"I guess that's why he didn't tell me about it."

"Do you remember the night Bob phoned you in a panic because he was convinced he was being followed?" Corrie asked casually.

"Sure. He drove over to the sheriff's office."

"While we were at lunch, I realized something else. Something I'd completely forgotten until Peggy mentioned it."

"What's that?"

Corrie leaned against the doorjamb. "Bob's car was in the repair shop that week."

"That's right," Roy whispered slowly. He was beginning to connect the dots.

"In other words, Bob was driving our car that night and not his own."

Roy nodded. That possibility had never occurred to him and he suddenly felt a little foolish. Once again, Corrie had proved herself a natural detective. "In other words, whoever was following Bob might've been looking for me."

"Do you still think those postcards don't mean anything?" Corrie whispered.

Forty-Five

Grace was meeting Olivia for lunch midweek. So much had happened in both their lives and Grace wanted—no, *needed*—time with her friend. She was dying to talk about Cliff and the way he'd come to sit with her during Charlotte and Ben's wedding. The ceremony lingered in her mind; she'd been moved by its simple beauty and by the love Charlotte and Ben so obviously shared. Tears had blurred Grace's eyes, but she wasn't the only one who'd reacted emotionally. When she'd been able to look up, she saw that several other people were wiping tears from their cheeks. Even Cliff seemed touched by the vows Charlotte and Ben had written, vows that acknowledged love for their dead spouses and love for each other. Currently the newlyweds were off to Victoria, British Columbia, for a short honeymoon.

Naturally Will had been there for both the ceremony and the reception, as had Stan. Grace had avoided them as much as possible, but she was more concerned about Will. However, Cliff seemed to understand how difficult the reception would be for her, and had remained close to her side. Several times Grace had noticed Will heading in her direction, but he stopped when he saw that Cliff was nearby. Grace assumed he'd return to his wife after this, which was just as well.

Grace valued Cliff's protectiveness at the wedding and, even more, the way he'd helped her with Maryellen. His calm presence had kept her focused as they comforted Maryellen and waited for the Aid Car. Afterward he stayed with Katie until Grace could come home.

Maryellen had been released from the hospital the next day. Jon had insisted on taking her and Katie home. Grace sensed that things weren't right between them. Now wasn't the time to pry, though, not when they were grieving over their loss. Still, Grace had every intention of finding out what had gone wrong in her daughter's marriage.

The miscarriage had devastated both Maryellen and Jon, but they were young and there'd be other children. Yet she knew it was difficult to think rationally after such a painful loss, and in her own way Grace grieved for her grandchild.

Grace was looking forward to her visit with Olivia, who'd just had a new grandchild—her third. When Olivia phoned that morning to confirm lunch, she'd jubilantly announced that James and Selina had a baby boy, born early on September eighth. Mother and son were doing fine, and James was one proud papa. They'd named the baby Adam Jordan. Three-year-old Isabella was said to be excited about becoming an older sister.

Grace had good news of her own, most of which had to do with Cliff, of course.

Before he left her on Saturday night, he'd made a point of letting her know he'd be in town on Wednesday and would come to the library. She was pleased and so relieved that they were resuming their relationship and that he was willing to give her another chance.

Just after noon, when Loretta returned from lunch, Grace retrieved her purse and small lunch bag. She decided to wait for Olivia by the totem pole outside the library. They each had a limited lunch break, and Grace didn't want Olivia to waste time looking for her in the library.

They'd already planned to bring their own lunches and eat in the waterfront park. With the refinancing of the house, Grace's tight budget was even tighter. In an indirect way, repaying Dan's loan had been a financial help, however; Grace had gotten a much lower rate of interest and arranged to pay off the house in half the time that'd been left on the original mortgage. She had to keep a close watch on her spending, but she'd manage. The fact was, she'd done a fairly good job of it ever since Dan's disappearance.

Grace loved Cedar Cove's waterfront. She looked out over the marina and across the cove to the Bremerton shipyard. She could see the massive aircraft carrier *George Washington* in the distance and remembered the joy of the wives and families when it finally returned from the Persian Gulf.

"Grace." A man's voice interrupted her musings.

A sense of dread struck her and she turned slowly to discover Will Jefferson. She'd assumed he'd left town by now, assumed she wouldn't see him again, assumed everything had already been said.

"I had to see you one last time before I went home." His eyes pleaded with her.

Grace peered down the hill, hoping to see Olivia. No such luck. She was trapped with Will, and although this was usually a crowded area, there was no one nearby right now.

"I can't believe you no longer care about me," he said in a voice that throbbed with sincerity.

Grace refused to meet his gaze. So far she'd been polite, but that hadn't worked. "Believe it," she said sharply. "You're married. I don't mean to be rude, but I don't want anything more to do with you. I thought I made that clear."

"Okay, fine. I'll divorce Georgia if that's the only way I can have you."

Grace shook her head. She wanted to yell at him to stop harrassing her, to go home to his wife, but the polite little girl she'd been wouldn't let her. Where was Olivia? Grace scanned the street, desperate to find her friend. What could possibly be taking her so long?

"Grace, listen to me." Will sounded hurt and confused. Then, as if overcome with emotion, he gripped her by the shoulders, forcing her to look at him.

"Leave me alone," she cried, jerking herself free.

"I can't! I love you."

Sure he did. Grace might have been a fool once, but she wasn't going to play that role twice, especially with the same man.

"I wanted to talk to you at the wedding, but you stuck to your bodyguard all day long."

Obviously he was referring to Cliff.

"Just hear me out," he said.

"No!" She could hear the desperation in her voice. "The best thing you can do is just go."

"Who is he?" Will demanded. "Is it the guy you were with last Thanksgiving?"

"Cliff is twice the man you'll ever be." Cliff knew the meaning of honor and decency. Even though he wasn't happy in his marriage, he'd stayed for the sake of his daughter because it was more important to him that her world remain secure. Grace could only imagine how difficult that had been.

"I'll prove to you how much of a man I am." Will glanced over at the hotel across the street from Mr. Wok's, the Chinese restaurant, as he placed his hand on her shoulder a second time.

"Leave me alone!" she said, almost shouting. Outraged she slapped his hand off her shoulder.

"At least talk to me. We can spend a quiet afternoon together and discuss this like reasonable adults."

"There's nothing to discuss!" She shook her head vehemently. "Just go. Olivia will be here any minute."

Will heaved a sigh. "I can't leave until you promise to meet me. What about tonight?"

"No!"

"We need to talk," he insisted again.

"I believe the lady said she wasn't interested."

Grace whirled around to find Cliff standing behind her. He'd come into town earlier than she'd expected. He had his checkbook in his hand and she realized he must have stepped out of the bank.

"The bodyguard?" Will asked her in a whisper.

"I would appreciate it if you left," Grace said calmly and clearly although her heart was pounding crazily.

"I believe the lady would prefer it if you left *now,*" Cliff said. He slid his checkbook in his hip pocket, taking a protective step toward Grace.

Will glared at him for a long intense moment. "Frankly this doesn't involve you."

"If it involves Grace, then it involves me," Cliff said coolly.

"I asked you to stay out of this," Will muttered, moving closer to Grace.

Placing himself in front of Grace, Cliff stood shoe to shoe with Will and eye to eye. They scowled at each other, neither willing to back down.

Then, for no apparent reason, Will swung wildly at Cliff.

"Cliff!" Grace cried out a warning. She needn't have worried; Cliff could take care of himself.

He easily sidestepped the punch and delivered one of his own, catching Will in the jaw. The force of the blow sent Will Jefferson staggering backward. He lost his balance, collapsing onto the asphalt. Almost immediately his jaw started to swell, and blood trickled from the corner of his mouth.

Grace brought her hand to her mouth, unsure what to do. Thankfully she saw that Olivia was rushing toward them.

"You saw what happened," Will shouted, pointing at Cliff. "He attacked me!"

"I saw everything," Olivia cried, running the last few steps.

Will's eyes blazed with righteous indignation. "I'm suing you for every cent you own. Olivia, call the sheriff. I want this man arrested on assault charges."

Olivia had her arm around Grace's shoulder. "As I said, Will, I witnessed what happened."

Will stood and brushed himself off. "Stay here so the sheriff can take your statement. I want this...this bully prosecuted."

Olivia frowned at her brother. "You might have a change of heart when I testify that I saw you throw the first punch. From where I was standing, Will, it seemed Cliff was protecting my friend from your unwanted advances."

"I...I—" Will clearly didn't know what to say.

"Go home, Will," Olivia said sadly. "You've behaved atrociously and I'm ashamed of you."

Will stared openmouthed at his sister.

"Let's have our lunch," Olivia said and slipped her arm through Grace's. "Will, I'll talk to you later. I have a few things to say." She smiled at Cliff, but Grace could see that it cost her an effort. "Cliff, would you care to join us?"

"No, thanks." He shrugged carelessly. "I'm heading back to the ranch." His gaze briefly held Grace's before he started toward the parking lot.

"Will I see you later?" Grace called after him.

Cliff turned and shook his head. "Another time perhaps."

Will smiled despite his torn lip. Grace could tell exactly what he was thinking—he might not have her for himself, but he'd done what he could to keep her from Cliff.

Forty-Six

The phone call came when Bob was least prepared to deal with it. He was still shaky; the need for a drink lingered, as intense now as it had been in his first week of sobriety. All that held him together was his love for Peggy, his determination and his AA meetings.

The call let him know Colonel Stewart Samuels was on his way to Cedar Cove and would arrive within the hour. He'd made hotel reservations at the local Holiday Inn Express near the waterfront.

"Are you all right?" Peggy asked when Bob replaced the receiver.

He didn't answer because he couldn't. At first Bob felt numb, but once his blood started flowing again, he felt a deep sense of dread. He wanted this entire mess to vanish, to go away once and for all. This was what he'd feared since leaving Vietnam. Everything he'd struggled to forget, everything he'd hoped would remain forever buried, was about to be exposed. Never had he experienced such vulnerability. The sins of his past were about to tear his life apart. But not only his—Peggy's too.

Two of his fellow soldiers were dead and that left him and Colonel Samuels. It was a distinct possibility that his life was at risk and that the other man could also be a target. He felt almost fatalistic about it; in a way he'd been expecting retribution for those killings in the jungle since the day it all happened.

By the time Bob returned to the States following his stint in Vietnam, he was already drinking heavily. When he married Peggy, he'd managed to keep away from alcohol for a while. But that control was short-lived and within months he'd found solace in having a few beers with his buddies after work. It hadn't taken him long to progress to the hard stuff.

After Vietnam he'd vowed never to speak of that terrible day again. With one exception, he'd kept his word until recent events had made that impossible. He hadn't found it easy dredging up those memories, voicing them. God help him, he'd like to forget Vietnam ever happened.

"Bob." Peggy placed her hand on his arm, breaking into his thoughts.

"I'll be fine," he said hoarsely.

She continued to stare at him doubtfully. He'd never told her how close he'd come to having a drink that night or how her phone call had saved him. Bob didn't consider himself an especially articulate man and certainly not a poetic one, but he thought of Peggy as his harbor, his place of safety.

"Stewart Samuels is on his way," he said as casually as he could. "He'll be here within the hour."

Peggy stiffened.

Bob nodded and realized his wife was as ill-at-ease as he was himself. "When he arrives, I think it'd be best if the two of us talked privately."

Peggy bit her lip. "I'll put on a pot of coffee and make an excuse to leave."

"I'd appreciate it." He brought his arms around her and hugged her close. "I appreciate *you.*" Closing his eyes, Bob breathed in the scent of her hair and the light fragrance of her cologne. Peggy was his life; without her he was nothing. He only hoped she knew how deeply he loved her.

When the white rental car pulled off Cranberry Point and into their driveway, Bob's stomach was twisted into knots. The man who stepped out from behind the wheel bore little resemblance to the officer Bob remembered. Samuels was tall and lean with salt-and-pepper hair cut in a close-cropped military style. Although he wasn't in uniform, he moved in a manner that suggested a soldier's discipline.

Bob walked out the front door to greet him. His heart felt like a sledgehammer pounding against his chest as he moved slowly toward the man he'd once known. The man who'd been his squad leader.

They met halfway and for a long moment stared at each other as if unsure of what to say. Finally Stewart Samuels extended his hand. "Hello, Beldon."

Bob nodded and thrust out his own hand, replying formally. "Colonel Samuels. Welcome to Cedar Cove."

"Thank you."

Neither moved. Samuels broke eye contact first, glancing around at the large two-story house with its brilliant green lawn and flower beds vibrant with color. Peggy's garden was still in bloom, her herbs scenting the air.

"I'm glad you came," Bob said, although that was a patent lie. Samuels was the last person he wanted to see, but it was either face the truth now or regret it for the rest of his life.

Samuels laughed as if he recognized Bob's words for the falsehood they were. "It's time we figured out what's going on here."

Bob agreed as he led the other man into the house. "Past time." He held open the screen door and let Samuels precede him. "Peggy's got coffee on. I thought the two of us should talk privately."

Samuels made no comment. As soon as they reached the kitchen, Bob introduced him to Peggy, who smiled graciously and welcomed him to their home. She poured their coffee and left.

Bob carried their coffee to the oak table in the breakfast nook. He stretched out his arms and cradled his mug with both hands. "The years have been good to you."

Samuels sat across from him, facing the cove. "To you, too."

"Things didn't go so well with Dan," Bob murmured, staring down at his coffee.

Samuels nodded, still gazing out at the water.

"And from what Hannah told us about Max, he didn't fare much better." So much had come to light recently; her life with her father had gradually been revealed, and it was a life that made Bob want to weep with pity. Every day Peggy seemed to have something more to tell him. Hannah continued to avoid Bob, but he now saw that he wasn't the only one. Frightened and shy, the girl kept her distance from most men. He felt equally awkward with her, to a degree he didn't really understand, but he made a greater effort to be tolerant.

"We've both had a lot of years to think about this. Time hasn't made it any easier, has it?"

Bob shrugged. "I tried to forget. The bottle didn't help. Without AA and my wife, I'd be dead by now."

"How long have you been sober?"

"Twenty-one years."

"Good."

"How about you?" Bob asked. Each man had dealt with the tragedy in his own way. Bob had relied on alcohol, Dan had gone deep within himself and Max had drifted for years, never settling in one place or one job.

"Nothing I could say or do has the power to change what happened," Samuels admitted. "I blamed myself. I was the one in charge, the one responsible. I couldn't bring those villagers back from the dead, but I could dedicate my life to my country. I've served the military to the best of my ability."

Bob slowly raised his eyes to study the other man. Looking at him closely he saw haggard features that revealed the torment of the years. His mouth thinned and he swallowed hard.

"I know what you mean," Bob said quietly.

"I'm glad you suggested we talk, but for another reason." Samuels paused long enough to sip his coffee. "After I learned about Max's death, I decided to find out what I could. Two men dead within such a short time made me wonder whether you and I were at risk, too."

Bob considered mentioning his own fears, but remained silent.

"I felt it was important to finally confront the past. I'd spent all these years living with what I'd done. I was up for a Congressional Committee appointment, and I knew that my background would be investigated. What I discovered shocked me and it'll shock you." He gazed out at the cove again. "The massacre was documented in the files of Army Intelligence."

Bob's mouth fell open. "How could it have been? We were alone—no one knew. Someone talked?" Bob refused to believe it. Dan hadn't, and he'd kept his own mouth shut all these years.

"No. A reconnaissance group was there, hidden in the jungle. Snipers had been deployed to the village because of reported Viet Cong activity."

"Just a minute." Bob held up his hand, stopping the other man. His mind was racing, and he actually felt dizzy. This was more than he could take in all at once. "Are you saying someone actually saw everything that happened and reported it?"

Samuels nodded. "A sniper and his lookout. And," he added, "they're both dead. One died later in a helicopter crash, and the other had a heart attack about five years ago."

"The army knew all along what we'd done?"

Again the other man nodded. "As you can imagine, the authorities were eager to bury it as deep as possible, although the army's Criminal Investigation Command had the details." He still hadn't looked at Bob but kept his eyes focused on the water view.

Still Bob didn't fully comprehend everything Samuels was telling him. "The village *was* controlled by Viet Cong?"

Samuels forcefully expelled his breath. "In some ways I think it might've been better if I'd been killed that day. I've never forgotten what I did, or the sight of the women and children I murdered."

"I haven't forgotten, either," Bob added, struggling to retain his composure.

Samuels brushed a hand over his face. "We were doomed the moment we set foot in that village."

The murders of those men, women and children had shaped all four men forever afterward. They could no more go back into the jungle and alter the events of that long-ago afternoon than he could shrug off this load of shame and remorse. Knowing there'd be no official reprisals didn't make any difference to how he felt. Bob sipped his coffee and let it moisten his dry mouth.

"For years I suffered from flashbacks," Samuels confessed. "I was on antidepressants and sleeping pills. I didn't sleep through an entire night for ten years after I got back from Nam." He shrugged. "Often I still don't."

"For me it was nightmares," Bob said.

They were both quiet for several minutes after that, and Bob thought about those other two men, the sniper and his lookout, and what they'd seen. They'd reported it to army intelligence but obviously had never gone to the press. Was that on orders? Or out of loyalty to soldier comrades? He wondered how that experience—and that secret—had affected them. Bob decided he couldn't think about that anymore, not right now.

He broke the silence. "A friend of mine has a couple of questions regarding Russell. I'm hoping you wouldn't mind talking to him."

Samuels's eyes narrowed, and Bob saw his hands clench. "Who is it?"

"A private investigator I hired shortly after Max died. For a while there, I was afraid I might somehow have been involved with his death."

Samuels relaxed his hands. "If I can help, I will," he said simply.

Bob knew Roy was counting on that.

Forty-Seven

"Rachel, phone! Line one," Valerie shouted from the reception desk at Get Nailed.

Smiling apologetically at her client, Rachel reached behind her and grabbed the phone. "This is Rachel."

"Rachel, it's Nate."

Instantly her heart flew into her throat and she blinked wildly, trying to stay calm. "Hi," she said as casually as she could, but her voice was barely more than a whisper. They'd seen each other twice in the last month, at the same time she'd been seeing Bruce. She enjoyed Bruce's company and adored Jolene, but he was more of a friend than a love interest. With Bruce she remained cautious; he seemed to enjoy their dates as much as she did, but there wasn't any deep romance between them and they both knew it.

"Can I see you tonight?" Nate asked urgently.

Rachel frowned. "This isn't a good time for me. Could we talk later?"

"It can't wait. Word just came down that we're shipping out."

The aircraft carrier *George Washington* was leaving the Bremerton shipyard!

"When?"

"Soon. Listen, I know you told me you're seeing this other guy."

"It's not that—"

"I'm involved with someone else, too, but I couldn't leave without at least saying goodbye."

Rachel closed her eyes, not knowing what to say. Before she could decide, her heart answered for her. "All right. When and where?"

He hesitated, and she leapt into the silence.

"Meet me at my place at seven, and we can figure it out then," she said and immediately wanted to kick herself. Was she crazy? This man made her feel weak with longing every time he touched her. Now he was about to leave for what could easily be several months, and she'd just invited him to her home. Even as she spoke, she knew that once Nate was in her front door, neither of them would want to leave.

"Seven. I'll be there," he said, sounding relieved.

"Okay." The line was disconnected.

Rachel's co-workers knew something was up and started questioning her. When she told them Nate was being deployed, it seemed all the girls had advice they wanted to impart.

"Don't do anything stupid," Jane said.

Rachel rolled her eyes. "I'm not going to bed with him, if that's what you think."

"It's exactly what I think," Terri said as she sidled up to Rachel's station. "You're nuts about this guy."

"I don't know what I feel," she insisted, and it was true. Okay, there was a mutual physical attraction, but a relationship needed more than sex. If all she was looking for was physical, she could have it any night of the week. Even in this age of frightening consequences, she knew women who changed sexual partners as often as they changed their shoes. Rachel didn't want casual sex; she wanted an emotional connection and a sense of genuine intimacy.

By the time she finished at the salon, Rachel was totally confused, torn between caution and wild desire. Her last appointment showed up late, so she didn't get home to her small town house until almost six-thirty. The first thing she did was jump in the shower and then change clothes. Her hair was still wet when the doorbell rang. As quickly as she could, she added styling gel to her curls, ran her fingers through them and dashed to the door.

Nate stood there waiting. His eyes widened with appreciation when he saw her. "Hi."

"Hi," she said. "Come on in." Before he could move, she held out a hand, stopping him. "Maybe that's not such a good idea. What do you think?"

Nate grinned. "I'm thinking if I come inside, it could be dangerous." He stared down at his feet and sighed. "To tell you the truth, I don't know if I should be here, but I couldn't stay away."

Rachel had no answer to give him, but she silently rejoiced at his words.

His eyes held hers. "I've got a girlfriend back home. You know that."

She nodded.

"You're seeing that widower guy."

"I am." They'd been honest with each other from the beginning.

He continued to stand there, his eyes directly on hers.

"I'll miss you when you go to sea," she murmured.

"I'll miss you too." He jerked his fingers through his hair in a nervous gesture. "Listen, we could go to dinner if you want. Talk."

"Sure." He seemed as aware of the sexual energy between them as she was. It was best to avoid temptation, she told herself, but she could still enjoy an evening with him—which seemed like a reasonable compromise. "Let me put on a pair of shoes and get my sweater."

"Okay."

He waited by the door as Rachel hurried into her bedroom, got what she needed and returned a moment later. Locking up, she followed him out to his car.

They ate at the Taco Shack and fed each other pickled jalapeños. Nate was the only man she knew who liked food as spicy as she did. They laughed and talked and seemed to have a million things to say to each other. The evening flew by and before Rachel realized it, the restaurant was closing.

"I guess I'd better take you home," Nate said.

She reluctantly agreed. When she'd told him she was going to miss him, she hadn't been flirting; she'd been telling the simple truth. They drove back to her place in silence.

"I'll e-mail you, all right?"

"I don't have a computer," Rachel said. She'd never dated a guy in the navy before, so this was all new to her.

"Oh. That might make it difficult to stay in touch." He was clearly disappointed.

"How long do you think you'll be away?"

"No idea. The navy doesn't let me help with the decision-making."

She smiled at his sense of humor. They arrived at her house, and he pulled alongside the curb but kept the engine running.

They sat for a few minutes, neither speaking. "Rachel, I really enjoyed tonight. Every time I'm with you, I come away wanting to see you again and then I remember…"

She turned and pressed her finger to his lips. "Don't say it."

Nate hugged her, and leaned his forehead against hers.

"I've never wanted to kiss a woman more than I want to kiss you right now. I can't, though, because I know what'll happen next."

Rachel knew it, too.

"But I don't think I can stop myself." Groaning, he closed his eyes, then gently, sweetly, touched his mouth to hers. His arms tightened around her and he sighed. Slowly he withdrew his lips from hers before their brief kiss could develop into anything more. "I'll walk you to your door," he said in a low, husky voice.

"You don't need to. I can see myself in."

"No," he insisted. "My mother would have my head if I didn't."

"Okay." He certainly wasn't making this easy.

He held her hand as they walked to her door, which he unlocked. When he'd finished, he handed her back the keys.

"I'll wait to hear from you," she said.

He nodded.

"Be safe, Nate."

He nodded again, his expression somber.

Rachel lightly touched the side of his face and, unable to resist, brought her lips to his. Like him, she didn't give the kiss a chance to become anything more than a quick farewell. She walked hurriedly inside.

Nate returned to his car and once she'd heard him pull away from the curb, Rachel opened the front door and stood looking down the street. The tears that burned her eyes shocked her a little. She hardly knew Nate Olsen. They'd gone out a grand total of three times, and at the end of every one of these dates, she'd had the impression she wouldn't see him again.

Sniffling, Rachel went into the bathroom and grabbed a tissue. If she was going to fall in love, the least she could do was be smart about it. Oh, no, not her. She had to complicate everything and fall for a sailor who was as good as engaged to another woman.

Sitting in the dark with her bare feet on the coffee table, she continued to bemoan her pathetic love life. The light over her door shone dimly, but it didn't really illuminate the room, despite the uncurtained windows. If she had any sense, she'd get up and turn on the lamp, but in her present frame of mind she preferred to sit in the dark.

Someone knocked on her door, and through her window she could see the shadowy shape of a man. Her breath caught in her throat as she ran to answer it. There, on the other side, stood Nate with his hands shoved in his back pockets.

At first all they did was stare at each other. Then, as if magnetically drawn to him, she stepped closer.

"I don't know what's happening to us," he whispered, "but I couldn't just leave you like this."

Rachel felt the same way.

"For the first time since I joined the navy, I don't want to go to sea."

Rachel didn't want him to leave, either.

"Come with me."

"Where?"

"I don't know. Let's sit on the beach and watch the stars."

She wanted to shriek and sob with joy. "Are you going to kiss me?"

He grinned boyishly. "Probably. Are you going to let me?"

She smiled, too. "I'm thinking about it."

He threw back his head and laughed. "Don't think too long."

Forty-Eight

The alarm buzzed and with a frustrated groan, Ian rolled over and cuddled Cecilia close. Slipping his hand over her waist, he lightly pressed his palm to the ever-so-slight bulge.

"Hmm," Cecilia purred softly as the radio played a Carly Simon tune. "Don't tell me it's time to get up."

He kissed the top of her head. "Afraid so."

She laid her hand over his. "Baby says good morning, too."

"Morning, baby," Ian whispered. The words nearly stalled in his throat. This was the last morning he'd be with Cecilia until after the baby was born. The *George Washington* was being deployed to the South Pacific for the next number of months. Six was what they'd been told, but it could be longer.

Cecilia rolled onto her back and looked up at him with her dark brown eyes. "Everything's going to be okay. Stop worrying."

Ian wasn't sure whether she was trying to convince him or herself.

"I'll be fine. I have friends this time." She rested her head against his bare shoulder.

"Does that mean you won't miss me?" Ian attempted to make a joke out of it, but failed.

"Oh, honey, you know I will."

"Some husbands and wives get into big fights about now. Makes it easier to leave."

Kissing his jaw, she whispered, "I'd rather make love than argue."

"Me, too." He never was much good at arguing with her, anyway. He loved Cecilia beyond reason. And, in spite of his fears, he'd come to believe that if they continued to put off having another child until he felt "ready," it would never happen.

"How much time do we have?" Cecilia whispered as she stroked his upper arms.

He nibbled on her ear. "Enough."

Her smile was slow and sexy as she tucked one silky leg between his. Their lovemaking was hot and urgent. Afterward they held each other for a long time, neither willing to release the other. It meant they had to rush so he could make his quarters, but Ian didn't care.

Cecilia hurriedly dressed to drive him to the shipyard. While he gathered up the remainder of his things, she walked out to the parking area to start the car. Although she'd tried to hide it, Ian had seen the tears in her eyes. She wasn't the only one who felt emotionally shaky; in all the years he'd been with the navy, he'd never dreaded going to sea the way he did now. His attitude must have shown because the minute he slipped into the car, Cecilia offered him an encouraging smile.

"Everything's going to be fine," she assured him again, but he read through her bravado.

Ian desperately wanted to believe her. But he couldn't quite overcome his doubts. Dread almost overwhelmed him as she backed out of the parking area.

"It really is all right, Ian." She gently touched his knee.

"You know this, do you?" He didn't mean to sound so sharp, but every fear caused by the death of their first child was staring him in the face with this second one. The knot in his stomach refused to go away and wouldn't until he knew for a fact that she'd delivered a healthy baby girl.

"I'll send you updates every time I go to the doctor."

"Promise?" Mixed in with his fears was the suspicion that Cecilia would try to protect him from the truth. But he wanted to know every detail of her pregnancy. *Needed* to know.

"I promise," she vowed.

They rode in silence for a short while. All the time Cecilia was driving, Ian worried that when the moment came to leave, he wouldn't be able to do it. His gut told him this deployment was history repeating itself. They'd known Cecilia was pregnant with a girl when he'd left three years ago. She was pregnant again with a girl.

He'd been at sea when Allison was born.

He'd be at sea when their second child was born, too.

Cecilia's ultrasound had looked perfectly normal the first time.

This ultrasound revealed nothing abnormal, either.

Now he was leaving, and the weight on his chest was almost more than he could bear.

Forty-Nine

Maryellen sat on the balcony outside the master bedroom and stared out over the calm waters of Puget Sound. She could see Mount Rainier clearly in the distance. It seemed close enough to touch.

Katie slept peacefully, curled up on Maryellen's lap. The little girl's hand clutched her favorite blanket, her other thumb in her mouth.

Closing her eyes, she breathed in the briny scent of the sea and listened to the muted sounds of late afternoon. It'd been nine days since she'd miscarried her baby. Nine days since she'd slept a whole night, and nine days since her heart was torn to shreds.

Jon had been attentive and thoughtful, anticipating her every need. Yet they lived as polite strangers. He was worried about her, and Maryellen suspected he'd talked to her mother because Grace had been by to visit nearly every day.

At the sound of her husband's footsteps behind her, Maryellen glanced over her shoulder.

"Did I wake you?" he asked.

She shook her head.

"Do you want something to drink?"

She declined with another shake of her head.

Jon sat down in the rocking chair beside the swing. "We haven't talked in a while."

Maryellen cradled her sleeping daughter. "There hasn't been anything to say."

"I'm sorry about the baby." Jon's words were hoarse with emotion. He said it so often, and each time it made her want to weep all over again.

"Do you mind if we don't discuss the miscarriage? There is no baby."

Jon wiped a hand over his face. "I blame myself for this."

"You did nothing, Jon. You have nothing to feel guilty about. These things happen." She repeated what the physician had said, but his words had been of little comfort then and were of less comfort now. However, that was all she had to offer her husband.

"I was angry and stupid."

Maryellen didn't respond.

"You didn't even tell me you were pregnant. You couldn't—because I wouldn't let you."

"Jon, don't. Please don't." She was too depressed to hear him punish himself over this.

"It's because of the pregnancy that you decided to stay with your mother, isn't it?"

Maryellen refused to answer. So many things had gone through her mind the day of Charlotte and Ben's wedding. Jon had been so angry with her and so unforgiving. He'd refused to even talk about it. When she'd left for her mother's, he'd let her go without uttering a single word to stop her. The only reason she was at the house now was that he'd brought her here from the hospital.

Jon got out of the chair and started pacing back and forth. "Maryellen, please just say something."

She looked up at him, puzzled by his outburst. "What do you want me to say?"

"I don't know. Anything. Just don't sit there staring off into the distance. I can't stand to see you like this."

"I'm grieving..."

"For the baby?"

She nodded. "And for us."

Jon leaned against the support column, as if he didn't have the strength to stay upright.

"Less than two weeks ago, you were willing to let Katie and me walk away. Remember?"

Jon didn't answer.

"I know what I did in contacting your parents was wrong," Maryellen whispered, "but I never set out to hurt you. All I wanted to do was help."

"I didn't want your help," he shouted, startling Katie who jumped and began to fuss until she found her thumb again.

With Maryellen's steady hand on her back, Katie quickly returned to sleep. "Let's talk about this another time."

"No." Jon was pacing again, back and forth, like a man possessed. His mouth thinned. "I told you before I don't need my parents, don't want them in my life. You and Katie are the only family I have."

If what he said was true, then he wouldn't have let her drive away that Saturday afternoon.

He held out his hands in silent pleading.

As she continued to watch him, he plowed his fingers through his hair, then straightened and seemed to come to some resolution. "Do you want a divorce?" he asked suddenly.

"No, but I wonder how long our marriage will last."

Her remark obviously shocked him, and Maryellen felt

she had to explain herself. "You so easily cast aside people who love you. If you can cut yourself off from your father and stepmother, then you can do it with Katie and me. In time you probably will."

"That isn't true." He fell to his knees in front of her, clasping her hands and gazing up at her intently. "Look at me, Maryellen. You and Katie are everything to me."

"Until I do something that upsets you."

He stood and put distance between them. "That's not true."

Maryellen didn't have the will to argue. She knew otherwise.

"Do you want me to tell you I'm willing to forget what my father did? Is that what you want me to say?"

"No."

"Then what?"

"I want you to have peace," she whispered.

"Peace?" He repeated the word as if he'd never heard it before. "You want me to *have* peace or you want me to *make* peace with my parents?"

"Both," she said, "but until you find peace within yourself, you won't be able to deal with your parents."

"I was perfectly happy with my life until you came along."

Despite herself, Maryellen grinned. "You only thought you were."

"I don't need them."

"You kept their letters," she said softly.

"I meant to throw them away."

"But you didn't. It must've given you some kind of emotional gratification when they wrote letter after letter, and you never answered."

He narrowed his eyes. "You don't know what you're saying."

She shrugged. "Perhaps not."

"You want me to make peace with them and I can't. I won't. I'm sorry, Maryellen, but even for you I can't do it."

Such a lack of forgiveness was frightening to Maryellen. "I don't expect you to forget what they did, but forgiving is something else," she said.

He shook his head vehemently.

"You must feel a real sense of justification and righteousness knowing how badly they wronged you—and knowing that you're punishing them now."

His eyes blazed, but he held his tongue.

"I don't think I'll ever fully understand the full extent of your pain. Your family betrayed you. They chose your brother over you and you're angry."

"You're damned straight I am."

"You have every right to be. Perhaps they don't deserve your forgiveness, but don't you see what this bitterness has done to you? Don't you understand that until you can let go of this pain, you're incapable of experiencing real joy?"

She could tell he wanted to argue with her, but she didn't give him the opportunity.

"Now you're angry with me," she said, "and I admit it was wrong to go behind your back. But you let me walk away because that sense of righteous indignation was more valuable to you than your love for me."

He opened his mouth to challenge her, but apparently changed his mind. He paced, his steps speeding up, then slowing as he went through some internal argument. "What should I do?"

"Look in your heart. Work on your attitude, your unwillingness to release all this pain."

Jon shook his head, hopelessly this time, as if she was asking the impossible. "You make it sound so easy."

"I know it can't be."

He sighed deeply and his shoulders sagged in defeat. "You're welcome to keep in touch with them if you want."

"What about you?"

His jaw tightened. "I'll wait a while, but I'll try, Maryellen. For you and Katie, I'll try."

In that moment, the cloud of depression that had hung over her since the miscarriage lifted. She held open her arms to Jon and was quickly engulfed in his embrace, with Katie between them.

"I can't ask for more than that," she whispered.

Fifty

Bob had been prepared to dislike Stewart Samuels, but in the days since he'd arrived in Cedar Cove, he'd had ample opportunity to gain a healthy respect for the other man.

Because of a meeting with some old friends from the police academy, Roy had been out of town. As soon as Corrie notified him that Samuels was in Cedar Cove, Roy had altered his travel plans and was due to get back late Monday morning.

By unspoken agreement, Stewart Samuels and Bob didn't discuss Maxwell Russell. For the most part, Hannah had stayed out of sight during Stewart's visits to the house. When Bob asked Peggy about it, his wife was eager to make excuses for her. For some reason, Samuels frightened the girl, but that didn't really surprise Bob. He supposed it was because of Hannah's wariness around men. She preferred her own company and often stayed in her room, where she read or watched television. Peggy was the only one with whom she seemed to feel comfortable.

Roy arrived a little after one on Monday afternoon, and to Bob's surprise Troy Davis, the local sheriff, showed up with him. Stewart Samuels was already at the house when Bob answered the door. He led the two other men into the living room.

"Sit down," Bob instructed everyone when the introductions had been made. Peggy quickly distributed coffee, then sat down next to Bob. He took her hand and they entwined their fingers.

Roy reached inside his pocket, pulling out a small notebook. "I have a couple of questions, if you don't mind?" He looked at the sheriff as if seeking his approval.

"I'll answer them if I can," Samuels assured him, leaning forward slightly.

Roy nodded, his pen poised. "Tell me about the first time you met Russell after his accident."

"We didn't meet. Everything was handled over the phone."

"That can't be," Peggy said and then instantly shrank back as if she wanted to retrieve the words. "I'm sorry. Go on."

Samuels shrugged, obviously a little puzzled at the outburst. "I'm sure I'm right about this, Peggy. Max had the physician contact me to ask for my assistance in getting him into a veterans' facility. He needed extensive plastic surgery. Apparently he had only limited health insurance."

"You never went out to California to see him following the surgery?"

"Never." Samuels was adamant. "I did speak to him a few times, however."

"When was that?" Troy asked.

"I can't recall the exact dates, but it was after he'd undergone surgery, which I understand was successful."

"What did he want to know when he phoned?"

"Actually I was the one who called him," the colonel explained. "The hospital social worker reported on his progress and suggested Max get some counseling. He suffered from post-traumatic stress syndrome. I urged him to sign up for the sessions."

"Did he agree?"

"Yes. The doctor told me later that Max had a number of appointments and they seemed to be going well. I was encouraged the next time I talked to Max himself. I only spoke with his counselor once, but she seemed pleased with his progress."

"Do you know of any reason he'd want to visit Cedar Cove?"

"None, except..." He hesitated and gazed down at his folded hands. "It might've had something to do with the therapy sessions—some desire to reconcile himself to what happened in Nam." Samuels paused. "As I recall, he was tight with Dan Sherman back then."

"Did he mention that he intended to visit Dan?" Roy asked.

"No. Like I said, I only talked to him two or three times."

The sheriff spoke next. "When did you learn he'd been murdered?"

"When Mr. McAfee contacted me," Samuels said, nodding toward Roy. "I've received intermittent communications since then, from Mr. McAfee and from you."

"Peggy," Troy began, turning to her. "You said something earlier."

She shook her head nervously. "I'm sure I misunderstood."

"Misunderstood what?" he pressed.

"Hannah," she said, rubbing her index finger over her cuticles. "We were discussing her father recently, and she told me she saw Colonel Samuels talking to Max shortly before he left California."

"That isn't possible," Samuels told her. "I was in Washington D.C. on assignment nearly all of last year. The only trips I made were to England and Belgium."

"That would be easy enough to verify," Roy said to Davis.

"Let's do it right now," Samuels insisted. "If you have a specific date in mind, I can have my assistant pull up my calendar and we'll go through it online."

Troy Davis accompanied the colonel into the other room, where Bob kept a computer on his desk. Bob had already turned it on, since he'd been using a bookkeeping program earlier. Now, as they waited, Roy sipped his coffee. Bob loosened his hold on Peggy's hand. This wasn't nearly as intimidating or awkward as he'd feared.

"Is Hannah here?" Roy asked.

"She's in her room," Peggy said, "but I'd like to keep her out of this as much as possible. Anytime someone mentions her father, she gets upset."

Roy looked from Peggy to Bob. "We'll need her to verify the facts."

Peggy still seemed uncertain. "She's been through so much already, I hate to drag her into this. As you can imagine, Hannah's easily upset, especially when it involves anything to do with her parents."

"In the long run, this will help her," Roy said.

Peggy turned to Bob. "I agree with Roy," he said. "The only reason she's living with us is because we want to help her. This discussion might put some ghosts to rest for her."

Peggy left and returned to the living room before Troy and Stewart Samuels came back. Hannah resembled a frightened child about to be called to task. She stayed close to Peggy's side, her head bowed. After a brief nod in Bob's direction, Hannah sat on the ottoman beside Peggy. In a gesture of reassurance and comfort, Peggy placed her hand on Hannah's shoulder.

"You never told us that your father was in counseling," Roy said, speaking to Hannah.

"I'm sure I did. Didn't I?" she asked Peggy.

Peggy shrugged. "I'm sorry, I don't recall if you did or not."

Hannah laughed weakly. "What's the big deal? He saw a counselor."

"You said he often carried false identification, too," Bob added.

"We certainly could have used that information earlier," Troy muttered, straightening.

"My father was never able to hold down a job for long," Hannah rushed to explain. Her eyes darted between the sheriff and Roy. "He...he sometimes used a different name in a different town."

"That isn't what you told me before," Troy said. "When I asked you about it, you claimed you couldn't imagine your father doing such a thing."

"I...I was in shock," Hannah whispered, staring at the carpet. "I can't remember everything you asked me. I'd just learned that my father was dead and that he might've been murdered." She buried her face in her hands and Peggy gently patted her back, glaring at the sheriff as if he were purposely intimidating the poor girl.

"Sheriff Davis, is this necessary?" she asked when Hannah started to sob.

"This is a murder investigation, Peggy."

"You think I murdered my own father?" Hannah cried, leaping to her feet. "He was the only person I had in the world! Why would I want him dead?" She gestured wildly at Samuels. "He's the one who's up for some important promotion—he's the one who led those men into that village and killed all those women and children."

Peggy gasped. "How…how did you know?"

"My dad told me all about it while he was in counseling. He was a murderer, and so are Bob and him." She pointed a shaking finger at the colonel. "I think he killed my father, too."

"I was in Europe at the time of your father's death," Stewart Samuels said evenly.

"Sure you were—he was drugged, remember?" she said viciously. "You came to the house and gave him that water bottle and then you left."

"The dates of Colonel Samuels's travel record state otherwise, Hannah," Sheriff Davis said calmly. "If anyone was with your father before he decided to drive to Cedar Cove, it was you."

She shook her head in denial. "I didn't even know he was leaving."

"That's not what you told me," Roy said.

"Then…then there's been some misunderstanding." Hannah began to back away, easing toward the kitchen one small step at a time.

"Stop hounding the girl," Peggy insisted. "Can't you see you're frightening her?"

"I've always found it curious that the drug used to kill Maxwell Russell is commonly seen in date rape situations," Roy said. "It's generally considered a young person's drug."

The room went quiet as everyone stared at Hannah.

"I first noticed the inconsistencies in your answers the afternoon I spoke with you on the phone, Hannah," Roy continued. "I talked it over with the colonel and was able to verify his statements, but not yours. Perhaps you can explain yourself."

"Of course I can," Hannah said.

"You said your father was a good man."

"He was," Hannah cried.

"But he couldn't hold down a job?"

"He tried...."

"He abused your mother?"

"Yes!" the young woman screamed. "Nothing was ever good enough for him. I hated him. I loved him." Her face twisted into a mask of pain and fear. She stood with her hands in tight fists. "He deserved to die. He should've been the one killed in the accident, not Mom."

"Hannah." Peggy was instantly at her side. "You don't know what you're saying."

Shoving Peggy aside, Hannah faced the others. "You're all alike, aren't you?"

"What happened to your mother?" Troy asked.

"She died. My father was the one who was supposed to be killed, not my mother. I paid my friend Davey to put air in the steering column of Dad's car. He'd lose control of the car and it would crash. It was supposed to be so easy, but then Mom decided to go with him.

"I tried to get her to stay home, but she wouldn't listen. Dad wanted her to come along and she refused him nothing." The words were spat out with such anger that her face was contorted. Bob had never witnessed anything like it.

"He suffered, you know. That was good. It made everything better when I saw how badly he'd been burned. Still, it wasn't enough. I could have killed him in the hospital. I wanted to, but when I saw that he was in agony, I thought death was too good for him."

"Hannah," Peggy cried, "don't say any more. You don't mean any of this."

"Yes, I do," she cried. "I mean every single word. My father was a bastard and I hated him for what he did to my mother and me. I could never have friends, bring them to the house. Every time I had a friend we moved. Dad would lose his job again or the neighbors would hear him beating on Mom. He broke my arm when I was six, you know." Her eyes narrowed. "No, you don't know because no one knew. I couldn't tell the doctors what really happened. I was supposed to have fallen down the stairs." She shook her head, her voice rising. "I made him pay for that, too. Davey helped me. He bought me the roofies and told me how to do it. He said I wouldn't get caught!"

"Hannah Russell, you have the right to remain silent," Troy said, standing. He advanced toward her slowly. "Anything you say can and will be used against you in a court of law."

"Shut up," she screamed so loudly it hurt Bob's ears.

"Hannah, please," Peggy pleaded.

"No…not this time," she screeched. "Then Dad started talking to that shrink and he changed. He wanted to start his life over and be happy. I couldn't let him be happy, not after the hell he'd put me through. He deserved to die. I wanted him dead. Dead," she shouted. "Dead and burned and gone forever."

Troy walked over to Hannah with a pair of handcuffs and when she realized she was about to be arrested, she fell to her knees and broke into deep sobs.

Peggy moved to comfort Hannah, but Bob stopped her. Hannah had murdered her own father. All these weeks, they'd been housing the killer and not known it. Peggy turned to Bob, burying her face in his shoulder.

"It's over now," he whispered soothingly.

"Did you know?" she asked, looking up at him.

He shook his head.

Davis led a sobbing Hannah out to his patrol car. The young woman glanced over her shoulder at Peggy as if silently pleading for help. Peggy held her hand over her mouth. This was difficult for her, Bob knew, but she stood silently beside him.

Then Hannah let loose with a string of swearwords that shocked them all. Even from inside they could hear her clearly. The room went completely still after Troy had driven off.

Roy left soon afterward and only Peggy, Bob and Stewart Samuels remained.

"I'm sorry it came to this," Stewart said. "Sorry I didn't confront the past sooner and deal with these issues."

"We each buried that day as deep as we could," Bob said. "Now it's been unearthed…."

"And now maybe the two of us can get on with our lives."

For the first time since he'd returned from Vietnam, Bob felt that was possible. There would always be guilt, but perhaps he could find a way to expiate his sins.

Fifty-One

The aerobics class seemed easier this Wednesday evening, despite the sweat Grace could feel on her brow. Lunging left, then right as the loud music vibrated through the room, she followed the instructor's lead, using every ounce of energy she had.

Perhaps this surplus of vigor was due to her mood. She was still furious with Will Jefferson. She hadn't seen or heard from Cliff in a week. Once again, his faith in her had been shaken, and somehow she doubted she'd hear from him again. Will's express purpose was to destroy any possibility that Grace might find happiness with another man, but she refused to let him succeed. She didn't understand any of it—his willingness to betray his wife, his insistence on a relationship with Grace or his apparent vindictiveness at her rejection. But, dammit, she wasn't letting him ruin her chances with Cliff!

"Good luck, buster," she muttered under her breath and with a burst of energy finished the program. She hadn't come this close only to lose Cliff without a fight. If he didn't call her soon, she'd go back to sending him notes and e-mails.

"What was that you just said?" Olivia gasped as the music ended. Her reddened face glistened with sweat.

"Never mind," Grace whispered. The cool-down exercises started, her least favorite part of the workout. Grace retrieved her mat from the corner of the room, and placed it next to Olivia's. Perhaps it was her age, but it was becoming increasingly difficult to do some of these stretches. Especially the one in which she had to bend one leg and cross it over the other and then turn to the side. She always seemed to be facing in the wrong direction.

"You've been in a bad mood all night," Olivia said when they'd completed the class and walked to the dressing room. "What's gotten into you?"

Grace shrugged.

"Cliff?"

She didn't answer. "Do you have time for coffee?" she asked instead.

"I can't," Olivia said regretfully. "Jack's still at work, and I know if I don't literally drag him out of that office, he'll be there half the night."

"Poor Jack."

"Poor Jack nothing. I feel like a widow! We should still be in our honeymoon phase," Olivia complained. "I wish the management would let him hire an assistant editor."

"They should," Grace agreed.

"You're telling me." Olivia reached for her towel and wiped her face. "I can't apologize enough for my brother. I'm so angry with him."

Grace dismissed her friend's concern. Olivia wasn't responsible for Will's behavior. Neither was Charlotte. The best excuse or explanation they'd come up with was some kind of midlife crisis, but neither she nor Olivia had much sympathy with that.

"What are you doing Saturday?" Olivia asked. "Maybe we can go to brunch or the movies or something?"

"Why don't we go to an afternoon show?" She was working at the animal shelter in the morning, and planning to have dinner with Kelly and Paul that evening.

"You're on," Olivia said as she headed to the showers. "I'll call you later and we can pick a movie."

Grace smiled in agreement.

Still feeling out of sorts, Grace returned to the house. Buttercup, ever faithful, was waiting for her when Grace unlocked the door. She turned on the lights and found Sherlock curled up nose to tail, sleeping on her sofa.

"Hello to you, too," she chided as she brought her exercise gear to the laundry room.

The blinking light on her answering machine caught her attention, and she grabbed a pen and paper, then pushed the Play button. At the sound of Cliff's voice, a huge smile broke across her face. She hadn't heard the whole message before she punched out his number.

Cliff answered on the second ring. His hello was gruff, which was typical.

"Hi," Grace said. "I wondered if I'd hear from you."

"I've been busy."

"I know. Me too. How are you?"

"Okay. You?"

"Better now that I've heard from you." Even over the phone line, Grace felt his smile.

"Lisa called this afternoon. She wanted an update on what's happening between us."

"What did you tell her?" Grace carried the phone into the living room, sat on the sofa and moved Sherlock into her lap. The cat didn't like being disturbed, but settled down quickly enough.

"The truth."

"Which is?" Grace asked, stroking glossy black fur.

"That I can't seem to stop loving you, despite my best efforts."

Grace felt tears prick her eyes. "I can't seem to stop loving you, either."

Cliff exhaled softly. "I know it's a little early, but I was hoping you could join me for Thanksgiving again this year."

"Are you flying out to be with Lisa and her family?"

"No. Since I spent time with her this summer I'll probably just stay here."

"Alone?"

He sighed. "Not if I can help it."

"Would you like to have dinner with me and the girls?" Grace didn't know yet what her daughters' plans were, but it would be easy enough to find out.

"Can I invite Cal, too?"

"Of course." Grace remembered that Cal was one of the bachelors who'd been on the auction block. "Speaking of Cal, has he gone out with Linnette McAfee yet?"

"Nope. I don't think she's too thrilled with her mother setting this up," Cliff said wryly. "And Cal's blaming me, since I encouraged him to participate."

"Is Linnette already living in Cedar Cove?" Grace had been too busy to keep up with the latest regarding the clinic. She knew Linnette had accepted the job of physician's assistant. The lot had been cleared and the structure was going up so fast, it was hard to believe that just a few weeks earlier there'd been absolutely nothing in that location.

"Not yet. I gather she'll be moving here next month to help set things up. According to Charlotte, the clinic should be in full operation by the first of the year."

"That's great. And I guess it means Cal will have his date soon."

"Seems that way," Cliff said. "Frankly I think it'll do him good."

"I think so, too."

"Will I see you before Thanksgiving?" she asked.

"Probably."

"I'll take that as a yes."

"Do you want to come out here Friday afternoon after work?"

"I think that can be arranged," Grace said.

They spoke for a few more minutes and by the time Grace hung up, she felt more hopeful than she had in days.

Buttercup walked over to the sofa to receive her share of attention. Sherlock, still reclining on Grace's lap, lazily opened one eye but didn't object to Buttercup's presence. Grace stroked her dog's head, smiling. She'd worked hard to regain Cliff's trust and was determined never to give him reason to doubt her again. This was one lesson she'd learned and learned well.

Fifty-Two

Corrie McAfee looked up from the playing cards in her hand and sighed as she tried to remember which suit went with which. Giving up, she stared helplessly across the table at Peggy, sending her a silent plea.

The two couples had spent a delightful evening together and after dinner had decided to play pinochle. Corrie hadn't played in years, so her skills were weak, and unfortunately Roy took such games far too seriously. Peggy had been more than willing to be her partner, although Corrie could tell her friend's mind wasn't on the game. For that matter, neither was hers.

"What's your bid?" Roy helped himself to a pretzel as he studied his own hand. Her husband and Bob Beldon had walked away with the first three games and gloried in their triumph a little too much.

"You guys have already won three in a row," Corrie said. "I think Peggy and I could use a break."

"Ah, it's just getting good," Bob protested.

"I'll make some popcorn," Corrie said, hoping the two men would be willing to put the game aside for that long.

"All right, all right," Roy muttered, not concealing his disappointment. He could be so competitive sometimes.

Peggy followed Corrie into the kitchen and leaned against the counter as Corrie set up the hot air popcorn popper. She took a stick of butter from the fridge and cut a generous cube to melt in the microwave. "I can't bear to eat popcorn without real butter," she explained. With the machine making its usual racket, Corrie joined her friend at the counter.

"I still can't believe it..." Peggy let the words fade.

"You're in shock about Hannah, aren't you?"

Peggy nodded. "Not for even a second did I suspect she was capable of murder."

"Have you been to see her at the jail?"

Peggy shook her head. "She's refused all visitors, including me."

That must be hurtful to Peggy, Corrie thought as she dumped the popcorn in a large bowl and poured on the melted butter.

"I talked to Troy Davis earlier in the week and he told me Hannah's decided to take a plea bargain. Once all the legalities have been dealt with, she'll be transferred to the women's prison in Purdy."

"I can only imagine how difficult this must be for you," Corrie said sympathetically. Peggy had grown close to Hannah over the last few weeks. The horror of learning that the young woman was responsible for her parents' deaths had, needless to say, distressed her. At this stage, Peggy couldn't influence the girl's situation at all. The authorities in California had been notified and were in the process of arresting the friend who'd tampered with her father's car and bought her the drug. Extradition papers would be filed against Hannah soon. Unless a deal could be made, she'd stand trial in her home state of California.

"I'm so sorry," Corrie whispered, touching her friend's arm.

"I know. I am, too. She's ruined her entire life." Peggy bowed her head for a moment, then looked up. "What I want to know is when Roy and the sheriff figured it out."

Not sure what to tell her, Corrie shrugged. "I can't answer that. Although we work in the same office, my husband usually keeps his suspicions to himself. Half the time I don't have a clue what's going through that thick head of his. What I *can* tell you is that he and Troy discussed the case now and then and compared notes."

Peggy's expression was pained, as if she was reliving the moment of Hannah's arrest.

"My guess is that Roy and the sheriff went over their ideas together and came to the same conclusion," Corrie said.

"Are you talking about me and my brilliant mind again?" Roy asked as he stepped into the kitchen, Bob directly behind him.

"Obviously we've so outplayed you women that you're ready to admit defeat," Bob said smugly.

"We could always put on a DVD," Roy suggested, scooping up a handful of buttered popcorn. "Nothing goes better with popcorn than a movie."

Bob yawned. "I don't know if we should. It's getting to be the witching hour for me."

"Me, too," Peggy said reluctantly. She turned to Corrie. "Dinner was wonderful. An evening out was just what Bob and I needed to get our minds off this mess."

"It was our pleasure," Roy said. He slipped his arm around Corrie's waist and they accompanied their friends to the front door. When Corrie had retrieved their jackets from the hall closet, Roy politely held Peggy's for her.

"Look," Peggy said when they opened the door. "Someone left you a gift."

A beautifully arranged fruit basket stood on the porch. Filled with apples, oranges, bananas, grapes and a variety of nuts and chocolate, it was wrapped in silvery cellophane and decorated with a large plaid bow.

"Who would send us something like this?" Corrie asked, surprised and pleased, but when she bent to reach for it, Roy stopped her.

"A more important question is who'd drop it off without ringing our doorbell?" His arm restrained her from lifting the basket. "Leave it where it is," he said, frowning.

Corrie stared at her husband. "Do you think it's the same person who mailed us those postcards?" she asked, her voice low.

"I don't know."

"It looks like there's a card with the fruit," Peggy said.

Before Roy could object, Peggy pulled it from the basket. Corrie blinked, half-afraid something might explode in her friend's face. She sighed with relief when nothing happened.

"Maybe it's an early Thanksgiving gift." Peggy handed the card to Roy. "We'd better go."

Bob nodded and after another round of thank-yous and farewells, they headed toward their car.

"Open it," Corrie said even before the Beldons had pulled away from the curb.

"In a minute," Roy muttered. He stepped into the house and Corrie followed him. Roy examined the envelope. It was addressed to the McAfees at 50 Harbor Street, so the fruit had been delivered to the right house. Roy held the small envelope up to a light before he tore it open.

Inside was a single piece of typed paper.

"What does it say?" Corrie asked urgently. She didn't want Roy hiding anything from her. It was only by chance that she'd learned about the postcards.

Roy scanned the letter and gave it to her.

I don't mean you any ill will. I just want you to think about what you did. Don't you have a single regret?

Corrie quickly read the note and looked up at her husband with frightened eyes. "What does this mean?" she asked.

Roy shook his head. "I have no idea. I guess we'll have to wait for the next message."

He placed his arm around Corrie's waist. He didn't have the answer yet, but he would soon. He'd cleared too many cases not to succeed at solving this one.

Whoever was doing this, it was personal. Sending the fruit basket to 50 Harbor Street had breached the sanctity of his home. But he'd find out who'd done this.

His instincts still told him that he and Corrie weren't in physical danger. But there were other dangers, less obvious ones, and Roy knew they could cause just as much harm.

He wasn't prepared to let *anyone* risk the haven he and Corrie had found in Cedar Cove.

* * * * *

Discover what Roy eventually learns about the person who's sending him and Corrie these "messages." You'll want to keep up with your other friends in Cedar Cove, too. How do things go for Grace and Cliff? What about Olivia and Jack? Will Cecilia's baby be all right? And Rachel—will she choose Nate or Bruce?

Watch for 50 Harbor Street *in September of 2005.*